PART ONE

April 2008

CHAPTER ONE

Sylvie

Back then, when life seemed so simple, before she knew what life was capable of throwing at her, Sylvie was a natural worrier. Anxiety followed her around like a small dark cloud, convincing her that something terrible was just about to happen. As a child she worried about her mother's rages, which didn't stop them coming. As a young woman she worried about making enough money as a textile designer, which meant she had to supplement her income by painting houses. As a young mother she worried that Eve would roll onto her front and never wake up, and when Jonathan was late home from work, she worried that something had happened to him.

She wasn't worried, however, the morning he sat on her side of the bed, leaning over to tie his cycling shoes then rolling gently on top of her and kissing her, tiptoeing his fingers up her inner thigh until she gave up all pretence of being asleep and giggled, shoving his hand away.

"Nice arse," she called out, opening one eye as he reached the doorway, causing him to spin and adopt a model pose before blowing her a kiss and clomping down the stairs.

Thirty minutes later she was cutting a piece of toast into slices for Eve, who was meticulously nibbling as far as the crusts then giving each crust a name and personality and dancing it round her small purple melamine plate.

When a police car pulled up outside the house, Sylvie froze. Eve, sensing something, climbed onto her mother's lap, curling up and sucking her thumb. There was no way they could have known, and yet they both knew.

Moments later, the doorbell rang. She knew the police were on the other side. Before she even opened the door she could see their expressions of sympathy, knew they would gently ask her if she knew a Jonathan Haydn. When she said she was his wife, they would look down at the ground for a second, their faces wracked with sadness, wishing they didn't have to tell this young wife and mother that her husband would not be coming home, wishing right now they were anywhere else but here.

For years afterwards she wasn't able to speak of it without her throat closing, or her eyes pricking, but now the words come so easily. My first husband died. Brain aneurysm. Yes. It was a tragedy.

Fourteen years later, she can say the words without feeling a wave of loss wash over her. She can, and does, stop suddenly while walking down a street, or in a store, because she has seen someone who has his walk.

4

Or smell. Or hair. But now she can stop, remember, and keep moving, without being engulfed by loss, and grief, and pain.

She moved to La Jolla, found friends through Eve's kindergarten, and began building a new life in which she was, if not happy, content.

She worked in an art gallery part-time, occasionally exhibiting her own paintings in one of the cafés in town. She had stopped worrying, waiting for the worst to happen, because it had already happened and she had survived.

On her own for three years after Jonathan's death, she had become self-sufficient, a tight unit with Eve. Dating didn't really interest her, despite the kind offers to fix her up; neither did the prospect of merging her life with someone else's. Dating, kissing, making love with someone other than Jonathan would have been a betrayal; it was a step she felt unwilling to take.

When she did take it, it didn't feel like a betrayal. It felt right, as if Jonathan had given her his blessing. Eleven years after meeting Mark, Sylvie does not often indulge in memories of Jonathan. As the years have passed she has, largely out of respect for Mark, allowed them to fade. She was so young when she was with Jonathan, so unaware of the enduring nature of marriage, of the ups and downs, the highs and lows, the work required to keep you in the game.

She had only four years with Jonathan. When he died, they were still in the honeymoon period, never having had a chance to reach the stage where they irritated each other, fought over nothing, simply passed each other in the house barely speaking a word.

Until she met Mark, and for some time afterwards, Sylvie always felt Jonathan was watching over her. She would talk to him in the car, ask him something, then turn on the radio and find her question answered by the lyrics of a song; pick up a book and turn to a random page, to find the words that were exactly what she needed to hear.

There is no such thing as coincidence, she would think, blowing a kiss of thanks to the heavens. This is Jonathan, as loud and clear as he is able to be.

When Mark came along eleven years ago, she knew Jonathan had sent him to her, that it was no coincidence their worlds kept colliding; she knew that this was somehow meant to be.

Even the fact that Mark has always travelled extensively has been a positive. It has allowed her to keep the close bond with Eve, to be present for her in a way that isn't possible when Mark is at home.

This marriage is entirely different from her first. From the beginning this felt less like a fairy tale, more real. She and Mark have never lain in bed whispering fantasies about their lives together, or shared the wonderment of giving birth; they have not had time together without children, lazing in bed all weekend making love, only going out to run to the deli on the corner for paninis and chocolate.

What they do have is what Sylvie now thinks of as grown-up, proper love. She is, still, fiercely attracted to him, respects him enormously; she adores how kind he is, how he takes care of them.

She has watched marriages all around them fall apart in the last couple of years. The words "mid-life crisis" are whispered in knowing tones, as husbands are discovered sleeping with their secretaries, wives having affairs with neighbours, or simply leaving to "find themselves".

Sylvie knew she was safe. Whatever else might come between them, Mark would not have an affair. He was appalled and dismayed each time another couple came undone at the hands of someone else.

"Thank God you, at least, take your marriage vows seriously," Sylvie's friend Angie said. "*He*, on the other hand . . ." she added, narrowing her eyes as she glanced sideways at her husband, "not so sure. But he knows what'll happen to him if he even thinks about it."

They had all laughed, Sylvie with the security of knowing her marriage was sacred. Nothing would ever go wrong.

And yet for the past few months a lot feels as if it's not exactly going wrong, but not going right. Eve will be leaving home to go to college in September, and Sylvie isn't ready. She is starting to feel abandoned, even though rationally, of course, she knew this day was coming; she knows Eve has to leave.

Her job at the bookstore ended in October, and the last six months have been spent attempting to look after her mother, doing the odd bit of painting, although it no longer holds the thrill it once did, and worrying about what on earth she will do when Eve leaves.

She knows her hormones are playing a part, for her periods are erratic, and Mark has started referring to her PMS as OMS, for Ongoing Menstrual Stress, which Sylvie finds either hilarious or infuriating, depending on the day.

She is going through changes; they are all going through changes — significant ones, ones in which they will need to support each other — but Mark seems utterly disconnected. He isn't working out more, hasn't bought himself a new Ferrari or a new haircut, but he is distracted and unsupportive.

As a result they have started squabbling in a way they never have until now.

After years of knowing exactly where she stood, insecurity has pushed its way through the door. Who is she supposed to be if not a mother? If Mark didn't travel all the time she would be fine, because she would have the role of wife to fulfil. It didn't matter before, while she was a full-time mother. But with Eve leaving, and no job, how is she supposed to define herself?

Sylvie needs her husband, but, for some reason, these days he is away more than ever. Sylvie is starting to wonder if her mother's right: is Mark having an affair?

CHAPTER
TWO

Sylvie

Until very recently, Sylvie would always joke that Mark didn't even know how to flirt, let alone conduct a fullblown affair.

Despite his looks, his obvious charisma, and the fact that women flocked to him, he never seemed to be aware of his attraction, which is why Sylvie noticed him in the first place.

Her trolley got away from her in the parking lot of the grocery store. This tall, good-looking, athletic man caught it before it reached the traffic. A laughing thank you followed, when you couldn't not gaze a little at his boy-next-door looks, his gleaming teeth, the dimples that gave him a cuteness and made his looks accessible rather than daunting.

She didn't think about him again until two days later, when she was standing behind him at Starbucks. He turned to see her, and laughed. They chatted briefly, about nothing in particular: What a small world it is! . . . Any more runaway vehicles you need help with?

Once coffee was ordered and collected, they stood awkwardly, before wishing each other a great day and walking off in different directions. This time, he left an impression. Could it mean anything, running into him again? If it did, surely they would have ended up having coffee together, or perhaps him asking for her phone number.

He was not, physically, what she thought she liked, although objectively Sylvie knew he was the type of man that most women would swoon over. She had never liked the big, blond jock-type. She was drawn to thin men, dark, olive-skinned. Intense and funny. Like Jonathan.

Classic good looks had always intimidated her. As pretty as people tell Sylvie she is, she has never felt pretty, nor worthy of the men that all other women seem to want. She has instead been drawn to interesting rather than handsome, flawed rather than perfect. The men she dated in high school were artists and poets and musicians. The Starbucks man, to whom her mind kept coming back, looked like the quintessential football star.

She was struck by his comfort in his skin, and his lack of arrogance. He seemed open and easy, and hadn't attempted to flirt, which she appreciated.

After the Starbucks meeting, she thought of him sporadically throughout the day, each time finding herself smiling. She had never seen him before, and would likely not see him again. She knew nothing about him, other than — now — his name.

Mark.

Ships that pass in the night.

Later that week, as she and Angie were having lunch at Nine-Ten, both chatting animatedly, Sylvie vaguely noticed the three besuited men at the table next to them who were awaiting a fourth to fill the empty chair.

She didn't see the fourth arrive, but she heard him, heard a familiar voice. Faltering, she resolved that she wasn't going to disturb his lunch, but then he looked up and caught her eye, stopping in mid-flow before apologizing to his colleagues and explaining there was someone he had to say hello to.

This time he left with her phone number.

Their first date — Sylvie wasn't entirely sure it was a date — was a hike from the cove to the shore. They talked non-stop, accidentally brushing hands as they walked, and there was an obvious chemistry that made Mark's reticence inexplicable.

He didn't call for a few days after the walk. And just as Sylvie decided she wouldn't hear from him again, he phoned. They met for coffee, and this time he told her the truth.

He was divorced. No children. No serious relationships since. At first he had thrown himself into work as a welcome distraction, which then became a habit, swiftly taking over his life. He was still finding his way when it came to women, and he wasn't at all sure he was ready for dating, let alone a relationship.

He hadn't expected to feel this way.

It explained why he was holding back. Sylvie, who hadn't been looking for anything or anyone either, suggested they become friends.

For five months they were friends, each attempting to ignore growing feelings, neither willing to confess, until Mark showed up at her house one lunchtime, a carton of chicken soup in hand because she was getting over a cold.

He sat on the bed to chat, then, during the heavy silence, he bent his head to kiss her, with a tenderness and sweetness that reminded Sylvie of Jonathan.

That was all that reminded Sylvie of Jonathan.

Mark's body was smooth, and golden, and strong. It was like having a Greek god in her bed. Everything about him was solid and reliable, golden and good. So very different from anything and anyone she had ever experienced before.

When he suggested that Eve should have a sleepover elsewhere on Saturday night, Sylvie arranged it, luxuriating in the entire night with Mark. The next day, he disappeared briefly only to return with a tool box, then he set about putting up all the paintings that had been propped against the wall since Sylvie moved in.

He was too good to be true. Except he wasn't. Everyone loved him. Women wanted to be around him — oh, how they wanted to be around him! — and men wanted to be him. Sylvie, not the jealous type, teased him about the effect he had on women, who did indeed appear to simper when he was with them.

All these years Sylvie had thought she was fine on her own. An independent woman and single mother who not only could do it all, but actually did do it all. She had gone on dates from time to time, but had never allowed herself to fall for anyone. The men she had been out with were all poor facsimiles of Jonathan. None were right. None permanent.

Here, suddenly, was the very opposite of Jonathan, the only similarity being that people reacted to Mark in much the same way as they had to Jonathan, but for different reasons. Jonathan had made people feel special by listening to them, drawing them out. Strangers were surprised at how good he made them feel; they found themselves telling Jonathan their most intimate secrets.

Mark made people feel good with his presence alone. People were drawn to him, vied for his attention; he would stand quietly at the edge of the party and a crowd would always gather round him.

Trite to say it was simply because of his looks, but his looks were impossible to ignore, and admirers were drawn to him, like moths to a flame, with the hope that some of his magic would wear off on them.

Almost a year after they met, Sylvie and Mark, with Eve, Sylvie's mother, Simon and Angie as witnesses, stood before a judge and were married, going home to a luncheon that Angie had prepared for them in the garden. They sat under a white canopy with gardenias at each corner and mock orange blossom spiralling up the pillars.

Eve, then six, danced round the table in a froth of organza and tulle while the grown-ups watched her adoringly. She alternated between Sylvie and Mark, covering both with kisses, climbing on their laps, sitting on one and taking the hand of the other. Simon made an impromptu speech commenting on the fact that Eve was perhaps the happiest person in the garden that day, which brought much laughter.

It was true. They were a family. Meant to be. Eve adored him from the outset, and had been referring to "Papa Mark" long before Sylvie and Mark had discussed marriage, refusing to listen to an embarrassed Sylvie when she tried to suggest another name.

Eve may have been happiest, but Sylvie too was happy. She loved Mark, was content with Mark. She hadn't realized how much she'd missed having a partner until she had one again.

This wasn't the life she'd thought she was going to have, but it was, nevertheless, a wonderful life. She and Jonathan had had plans to travel, to see the world, to live in Thailand, Australia, India; to bring Eve with them, to seek new adventures, to squeeze every last drop out of life.

Her life with Mark includes little travel, and little seeking, on any level. She had loved that Jonathan was a seeker, but loves, now, that Mark is not; he may travel from coast to coast for work, but his lack of adventure makes her think of him as grounded, steady, secure. She knows where she is with him; is grateful for the security, even sameness, at this stage in her life.

In many ways they have a perfect relationship. The amount of time Mark spends travelling hasn't, until recently, worried her. Sylvie kept herself busy. She had a part-time job, until a demanding and unwell mother forced her to give that up.

They had all thought life would be easier once Clothilde, Sylvie's high-maintenance French mother, entered the Assisted Living Facility after the rehab following her car accident, but her mother had never been easy, and moving her from her own home was hardly going to change that.

Clothilde's constant phone calls to Sylvie at work, her requests that Sylvie drop everything to bring her Band-Aids, or a spare key, or . . . anything, became too much of an imposition on Sylvie's colleagues. As much as she loved the bookstore, she had to leave.

Since then, she has wondered if it is boredom that is unsettling her so. That, combined with an impending empty nest and too much time on her hands. Could it be she has inherited her mother's tiresome and restless inclination to create drama where none exists?

When she asked Angie if she thought Mark was having an affair, Angie spat — actually spat out — her coffee. It put Sylvie's mind at rest. Temporarily.

She rarely speaks to Mark at night. The apartment he rents in New York has no land line, and if he has no work events he goes to bed early, and the time difference means that he is asleep by the time she is ready to chat.

Tonight she wants to speak to him, wants to alleviate some of the loneliness that has started descending on these nights when Eve is out with friends. Sylvie has always declined invitations to join other couples for dinner on her own, aware of being a third wheel, yet, with Eve out, the house is unbearably quiet.

When Eve goes off to college in September, leaving Sylvie mostly on her own, Sylvie knows she wants something to change.

CHAPTER
THREE

Sylvie

"I love you, Mom!" Eve puts her arms round her mom, and Sylvie squeezes her hard, grateful for these times when her daughter will still hug her, for there are occasions now when Eve is embarrassed by her, or suddenly makes some hateful comment in preparation for the imminent separation.

Eve steps back, twirling. "How do I look?"

"You look beautiful," Sylvie says, which is true. At seventeen Eve has her mother's petite features and dark hair, her father's olive skin, and, somewhat startlingly, his bright green eyes.

Sylvie imagines all mothers think their daughters beautiful, but Sylvie, schooled by her mother to be nothing if not objective, knows that were she to pass Eve as a stranger on the street, she would still gaze at her prettiness.

Eve turns to the side and looks down, rubbing her hands over her stomach. "Do I look fat?" she asks, frowning. "My stomach is huge. I think this top makes me look really fat."

"Eve!" Sylvie admonishes, staring at her daughter's tiny frame. "You're tiny. You couldn't look fat even if you tried."

"I do!" Eve attempts to grab a love handle, which is in fact merely skin, to demonstrate the weight she needs to lose. "I look enormous. I ate so much chocolate yesterday."

"Evie, I promise you, you're tiny." Sylvie sighs. "I'm worried about you. I'm worried that you keep thinking you look fat when you're so, so thin."

"You don't have to worry," Eve says. "I'd just like to lose ten pounds. Then I'll be perfect."

"If you lose ten pounds you'll look skeletal," Sylvie replies. "Don't lose any more. Please. You've already lost so much weight."

Eve gives her mother an exasperated look. "Mom. I needed to. I was huge before — an elephant."

"Eve, you were never huge. It was baby fat."

"Well, I have ten more pounds of baby fat to lose and then I'll be perfect," Eve says, grabbing her jacket. "Don't be such a worrier." And with that, she's gone.

Sylvie is worried.

Eve, such a chubby, gorgeous baby, grew into a skinny toddler, then, at around ten, like so many young girls at that same age, she went through a plump phase before growing taller and slimmer.

She was an average size until around sixteen, when she announced she was turning vegetarian. This was interesting only because Eve was not a big lover of vegetables, and her version of vegetarianism involved copious amounts of macaroni and cheese, French bread and cookies.

Her weight climbed. Sylvie, saying nothing, attempted to guide Eve to a healthier way of eating without actually referring to her weight, but Clothilde was shockingly vocal each time she saw Eve.

"What is this?" Clothilde would lean forward in her chair, grabbing the excess flesh sitting at the top of Eve's jeans. "All this fat? Eve! You are eating too much. All this American bad food. No boy will like you with . . . this."

Sylvie begged Clothilde to stop saying such things, knowing how much they upset Eve, but Clothilde just pursed her lips. "I don't want a fat granddaughter any more than she wants to be fat, and if you won't tell her, I have to."

"Do you have any idea how upset she is?"

Clothilde merely shrugged. "Good. Perhaps she will stop eating."

It wasn't until Eve had her first major crush that she stopped eating. He had told a friend that Eve had a "pretty face", but was "too big for him".

It changed everything.

At first she announced she was no longer eating carbs. Then no dairy. She seemed to exist on bowls of miso soup and fruit, and Sylvie, deeply concerned, went in to see the school counsellor.

She told Sylvie it was common at this age, that the girls were experimenting with their sexuality, their appeal to boys, that faddy diets were all the rage, and would pass.

Sylvie was not reassured in the slightest. When she brought up the possibility of an eating disorder the counsellor dismissed it — "Everything has to be a 'disorder' these days" — but she offered to see Eve and talk to her about it.

She was hopeless. Sylvie wasn't sure what else she could do without Eve's permission, and so she did nothing, hoping that Eve would turn a corner and, if not put on weight, at least stop losing.

She does, in many ways, seem happier, more confident. She has a busy social life, and perhaps it is just Sylvie worrying too much. Clothilde, delighted with Eve's new tiny frame, gave her a pile of French designer dresses from the sixties that she had never thrown out, which Eve leaped on delightedly, pronouncing them "so *Mad Men*!".

The house is silent, but for the sounds of cicadas outside, as Sylvie stares disconsolately out of the window, desperately missing the nights when all Eve wanted to do was snuggle on the sofa with her mother, sharing a huge bowl of popcorn as they watched a movie.

Now it is just Sylvie. Sighing, she moves to the family room and pushes the sofa to one side with her hip, then moves the armchairs until she is breathless with the exertion, standing back to admire the results.

She goes to the living room and picks up cushions, a throw, some candleholders, returning to the family room to accessorize, wishing Mark were here to see it. Or Eve. Or . . . anyone.

She has already had a glass of wine, and refuses to have another by herself — a self-imposed discipline from which she will not waver — and wanders through the house blankly, thinking of people to call, dismissing them almost as quickly as she thinks of them.

Sitting on the sofa she turns on the television, hoping for a movie, but instead flicks through the channels, resting for only a few seconds on each, always convinced there will be something better, not finding anything she particularly wants to watch.

She spends two or three minutes watching bored housewives rail at each other, knowing that these petty catfights among women are almost always the result of conniving directors.

Sylvie is bored. Not bored enough to have a catfight with one of the neighbours — not yet — but she can understand how your mind focuses on all the wrong things when there aren't enough of the right ones.

It is time for her to do something. She can't sit around doing nothing for the rest of her life; she can't end up like one of these women. She has an idea, one she hasn't shared with Mark. It's 7.45p.m. here, 10.45p.m. there. If not out with colleagues at a work event, he is almost certainly asleep, but she wants to hear his voice, needs him to ease her loneliness, wants to talk to him about this business she has been thinking about.

She moves to the favourites screen on the iPhone and taps his name, settling in for a long chat.

No answer. She sends a text. Nothing. She tries to forget about it, for this is not abnormal, but tonight she wants to talk to him. Determined not to call him again, she reads on the porch for a while, but she has difficulty concentrating — she cannot stop wondering where he is.

Upstairs in bed, she calls again. And again. And again.

She falls asleep, but wakes in the early hours.

She calls again. It is beginning to feel like a compulsion, and even though she attempts to tell herself he must have left his phone in the office, which he so often does, being able to get back to sleep is now out of the question for her.

CHAPTER
FOUR

Sylvie

"Where were you?" Sylvie's voice is a whine. She immediately corrects it, hating herself for sounding needy. For being needy. For being up half the night thinking the worst.

"Honey! I forgot to charge the phone and it ran out of juice. I had no idea you were calling until I left for work this morning. Is everything okay?"

"No. I mean, yes," Sylvie says. "What if it wasn't? What if it was an emergency?"

"But it wasn't. I'm sorry, sweetie. Were you having a bad night?"

Sylvie, curled up in bed like a little girl, says yes in a quiet voice.

"My poor love. Were you feeling lonely?" Mark's voice is so instantly soothing and calming, and Sylvie knows she was being ridiculous, knows her imagined fantasies of the night before — Mark in the arms of another woman — were fuelled by the darkness and have no basis in any kind of reality. "I am so sorry," he says, and Sylvie hears that he is. "I wish I were there with you now."

"I do too," Sylvie says quietly. "I hate the weekends on my own, and this weekend is Angie's party, and I so don't want to go without you."

"You won't have to," Mark says.

"But I do." Sylvie sighs. "She's my closest friend, and even though she knows how I hate going to anything alone, she told me that if I'm not there she'll never forgive me."

"So I'll come with you." The smile in Mark's voice is obvious.

"What!" Sylvie sits up. "You're coming home?"

"I just booked. I'll be home for dinner."

"Mark! Really?"

"I miss you too much."

"Oh Mark! You just made me so happy!"

"Good. I love hearing you say that. It makes me feel loved."

"You are loved! So much! Thank you!"

"Sweetie, I told you I'm going to try to make changes. I get it. Eve's our only child and she's leaving soon, and I know how hard this is for you."

"It's easier when you're around."

"You know, we haven't talked about this for a while, but I think it's time you started thinking about maybe doing something. The part-time job was hard because of your mother, but you need to —"

"— occupy my mind," Sylvie finishes for him. "I agree one hundred per cent. I can't do anything full-time, but I have this idea and I wanted to talk it over with you."

"Something creative?"

Sylvie smiles, remembering back to when she was young, a graduate of Parson's, when all she ever wanted was to be a textile designer. She worked for a well-known designer for a while, until Eve was born and she had an excuse to leave, for she had had enough of doing all the designs, receiving none of the glory.

Since then she has only dabbled in creative things. If she sees a pot she loves, she will buy clay and recreate it herself, or some version of it.

She has hand-blocked sheets of linen, turning them into beautiful curtain panels; she has helped friends design labels, stationery, even gardens.

Creatively, there is little she cannot do, but she has never asked for money for what she does, regarding it as an occasional hobby.

"It has to be creative," Mark continues. "You're the most talented woman I know."

"I'll tell you all about it when I see you," Sylvie says, her anxiety long since forgotten. "I love you."

"I love you too."

As she walks into the bathroom with a smile on her face, she wraps her arms round her body and hugs herself. This is not a man having an affair. This is a man who is, just as she has always thought, overwhelmed with work. But there is no question that this is a man deeply in love with his wife.

CHAPTER
FIVE

Eve

It was not that long ago that Eve was at the centre of her group of girls, giggling and whispering as the boys attempted to show off with ever-more-elaborate spins, dives and jumps into the pool, the girls rating them on a scale of one to ten.

These are the girls Eve has known since kindergarten. They've grown up together, always in and out of each other's houses. They are all Eve's friends, Claudia probably the closest because her mother, Angie, is Eve's mother's closest friend.

The girls still huddle together on a sun lounger, lying on one another's legs and arms, heads leaning on shoulders, intermittently watching the boys while Claudia balances a MacBook on her knees and they crowd their heads together to chat with various people scattered around other homes in La Jolla, pouting and sticking out teenage tongues for photographs.

Except for Eve. Eve, no longer at the centre, sits apart, her jacket pulled tightly round her body, her shoulders wrapped in one towel, her legs in another, her teeth chattering with cold.

She watches and laughs when she is brought into the conversation, but things are different now, and she isn't sure why, nor how to get back there. She doesn't feel like the same person she was before this crazy diet. Before, she was on the inside, but now she feels as if she is always on the outside, watching everyone else being normal, having fun; she wants to join them but it is as if she has forgotten how.

She used to be so carefree; now she carries the weight of the world on her shoulders. The pressure of her senior year, of leaving home; the worry about getting into the right school, about even being allowed to go to the school of her choice.

It all feels too much. She was always desperate to grow up, but now she is on the threshold it is terrifying. Choosing not to eat, controlling her food, makes her feel safe; superior, even. It is something she, and only she, has absolute control over.

It started off innocently. It truly was an attempt to lose weight, to try to get the boy she had always wanted.

AJ was, she had always thought, entirely unobtainable, too good-looking, too popular, which didn't stop him being the subject of her fantasies throughout middle school.

A passing comment to Claudia — he thought Eve was pretty but she was too big for him — set Eve off on her mission to lose weight. AJ was supposed to have noticed, but his family moved to England when she was just eight pounds down, and that was it. The beginning of the change.

There was a brief snapshot in time when she felt she had a good body, proudly showed it off in a striped bikini from Urban Outfitters, not bothering to cover up to go inside and grab a drink, or walk to the other side of the pool.

As a young teenager she felt too self-consciously large to be comfortable, and now, at seventeen, she is still too self-consciously . . . wrong.

Everyone — her mother, her friends, the parents of her friends — is telling her she is too thin, and there is a part of her brain that is able to acknowledge that. For a few seconds. It is fleeting, and quickly replaced with the thought that there are still ten more pounds to go. That she isn't happy yet, and if she loses ten more pounds then she will be perfect, and with perfection comes happiness.

On a low wooden table by the lounger are bowls of chips, guacamole, salsa; a bag of popcorn lies on its side, spilling onto the ground; a plastic container of chocolate-chip cookies, half-empty; soda cans.

Eve stares at the chocolate-chip cookies. They are the ones she used to love. The soft, chewy kind. Buttery, moist, these were the ones her mom would always keep in the pantry, the ones Eve would steal when no one was looking. She can't take her eyes off them, imagines biting into them, feeling the familiar sweetness on her tongue, the sweetness of her childhood. Everything around her fades as she stares at the cookies, wanting to cry.

Her stomach growls. She is so hungry. She has eaten two egg whites today. This is her latest decision. She read somewhere that a singer, whose weight famously went up and down, lost by eating only egg whites. The singer would eat twenty at a time, but Eve feels more in control when she is challenging herself by eating as little as possible. Two egg whites felt like too many. Tomorrow she is planning to have one.

But those cookies are overpowering her resolve. Unable to stop herself, she stands, walks over to the food.

"I'm just going to clean up a bit," she says, knowing they will tease her, for she has always been a control freak.

"Don't!" Claudia says. "You're crazy! Leave it. We'll all do it later."

"You know me," Eve replies with a smile. "Nothing gives me more pleasure than cleaning." Claudia laughs, shaking her head with incomprehension as Eve picks up the spilled popcorn bag and cookies.

No one watches, no one is paying attention as Eve heads inside, her heart pounding, then she stands at the kitchen counter so she can check that nobody comes in, no one can see.

She eats the first cookie, savouring it, closing her eyes, unable to believe she has refrained from sugar, from anything this good, for such a long time. The second, then third, are barely chewed before being swallowed. Eve eats as if she is starving, which of course she is.

Seconds later she stares at the empty container, moving quickly to bury it at the bottom of the trash can, piling newspapers on top of it to hide it. Without thinking, she moves silently into the pantry, pulling down packets of cookies, snack bars, consuming them without thought or taste, gulping them down until her stomach starts to hurt.

She steps back, horrified, racing to the kitchen to find trash bags in which to hide the detritus of this sudden binge. She is filled with shame and self-loathing.

There isn't any question as to what she should do now. The disgust she feels is too much to bear, and there is only one way to get rid of it, and get rid of it she must.

Once the trash bag is filled Eve takes it outside, pushes it to the bottom of the can, then she locks herself in the bathroom, kneeling by the tub. She hasn't ever done this before, but she knows what to do.

She puts her finger in her mouth, reaching for the back of her throat, gagging only slightly. She tries again, panicking, for this food must come out; she doesn't know what she will do if she cannot purge her body of this food.

She tries again, going deeper, scratching the back of her throat, using her other hand to massage her belly as she thinks of the sugar and fat coating her insides, and then, suddenly, her stomach spasms as a wave of chocolate and sugar comes up, followed by another, and another.

Her finger goes down her throat twice more, until she is absolutely sure there is nothing left, then she lays her head on the toilet seat in exhausted relief. Please God, she thinks, don't let me do that again.

The food she ate today was disgusting, but at least it's out of her body. She will never do that again, never eat so much she has to make herself vomit. Tomorrow, as punishment, she will drink lemon water all day. Not even one egg white. Nothing.

Tomorrow she will get right back on track.

CHAPTER
SIX

Sylvie

Sylvie has spent the afternoon making cinnamon cookies, a favourite of both Mark's and Eve's. She bakes when she is happy, and she is hopeful this will tempt Eve to actually eat, for who would not be tempted when they are hit with the smell of cinnamon, vanilla and sugar as they walk through the door?

The text comes in just before four thirty: "I'm going to Jenna's house. I might sleep over."

Sylvie, disappointed, texts back immediately: "Papa's home tonight. You need to be here."

"Why? I'll see him all weekend."

It's true. Sylvie keeps thinking of her as a little girl, picturing them all having a wonderful evening together, Mark and Eve spending hours playing their beloved ping-pong in the garden. But those days are gone. Now Eve would sit there picking at the food, pretending to have eaten earlier. She'd be sulky and difficult because her friends would be doing something else. Mark would challenge her to ping-pong, and Eve would either refuse or play badly, determined not to enter into the spirit of the game, and the evening would doubtless end in a huge fight.

Maybe she and Mark should have a date night tonight, something they haven't done for too long. When he is here they are so often invited to things — neighbourhood barbecues, informal get-togethers — and when he is away Sylvie has a tendency to hibernate in the house.

"Fine," she texts back to Eve. "Do you want me to drop anything off?"

"Yes! Can I have my white lacy top and blue leggings? And my make-up bag? And flat iron? TY!!!"

"OK. Love you," Sylvie types.

"u 2," comes back, as Sylvie reaches out and takes a cookie. Then another. And another.

She knows, of course, that Eve's disinterest in her mother, so recent and so painful, is part of the separation process. She knows it is entirely normal. It is the subject of all the conversations the mothers at school seem to be having nowadays.

Which doesn't make it any less painful.

Sylvie may be many things — wife, cook, friend, confidante, artist, volunteer — but top of the list, the one that is most important to her, is mother.

With Eve going . . . going . . . not quite yet gone, the loneliness is something Sylvie is dreading. She craves conversation. She craves some way to express her creativity. Not company so much as . . . something. An outlet.

And she may have found the perfect thing.

Sylvie is lounging in a bubble bath when she hears Mark's car in the driveway.

She climbs out quickly, whips the plastic cap off her head, pulls on a towelling robe and pads down the hallway to greet him.

Even after all these years she is still excited to see him. Perhaps this is the beauty of a part-time marriage: you never grow bored of each other; being apart so often gives you time to miss each other, to appreciate each other in a way you can't when your life is just pots and pans.

Mark is walking up the stairs as she reaches the top, both of them grinning as Mark sweeps her up to plant a long, soft kiss on her lips.

"I have really missed you," he murmurs, edging their bedroom door open and laying her gently on the bed as her arms snake up round his neck.

"I like it when you miss me so much you come home early," Sylvie purrs. "This is the loveliest surprise ever." She shivers as he swirls his tongue in her ear, his hands already busy moving her robe aside, tracing lightly down her abdomen.

"You smell so good," he whispers, inhaling deeply as his fingers finally reach their goal, smiling as he raises his head to look deep into her eyes. "I love you," he says quietly, gazing at her.

"I love you." She flickers her eyes closed as the sensations start to build, a brief moan escaping her lips, then she opens her eyes and laughs at the intensity of Mark's gaze, the love and commitment she sees there.

Flipping over, she straddles him, sliding her tongue in his mouth, grinding against his hardness as she reaches down to undo his pants. She kisses a path along his chest, his stomach, pulling his zipper down with her teeth, laughing softly as he moans in anticipation, taking him in her mouth and savouring his feel, his taste, his smell, the sounds of pleasure he makes as he gasps.

Afterwards, she curls into Mark's side, wondering how she could ever have questioned his loyalty, his fidelity. Their bodies fit together perfectly, his strong hand tracing up and down her back as he turns his head from time to time to kiss her.

"I don't know what I did to deserve you," Mark says, as he so often does, turning to look at her. "You are the most precious thing ever, and I am the luckiest man in the world."

"No, I am the luckiest girl in the world," Sylvie responds, as she always responds, even though she knows that if what Angie says is true, that in every relationship there is the lover and the loved, with Mark she is the loved.

"So what is this great idea you wanted to talk to me about? It's not . . . Tupperware, is it?"

Sylvie laughs. "No. Nor is it skincare." Over the past year she has fielded at least one invitation a week to attend a house party where mothers she knows from school have transformed themselves into saleswomen, extolling the life-changing benefits of a skincare line, or jewellery, or children's clothes from a catalogue.

She feels guilty if she doesn't buy so she now has a bathroom cabinet filled with vitality pills that she is determined to try one day; jewellery that she never

liked is languishing in a drawer. But she has finally
learned to decline the invitations.

Sylvie does not want to be one of those women.
She has stacks of things she has made over the years,
but she is far too embarrassed to sell them. When she
has received compliments and requests for pots she has
thrown, scarves she has painted, or jewellery she
has beaded, she simply insists on giving them away,
much to Angie's disgust.

Angie has offered to host a sale of Sylvie's things
herself, but Sylvie refuses. She isn't sure what her
resistance is based on, other than perhaps the
ridiculous notion her mother has always lived by, that a
woman's role is to support her husband by looking
after him, not by going out to work. Her part-time job
in a bookstore was fine, Clothilde said. It wasn't a
proper job, just a flight of fancy, a nothing of a job.

Before the accident left her brain-damaged — it was
moderate, but brain damage nevertheless, making her
confused, disorganized, depressed in a way she had not
previously been — Sylvie's mother was the quintessential French-woman. Effortlessly elegant, flirtatious,
charming and coy, she knew how to wrap men round
her little finger.

But there was another side to her, one that only
those closest to her saw. With her family she was sweet
and loving one minute, then violently angry and critical
the next. Sylvie never knew where she stood; she
tiptoed round her, terrified that last hug, that
smothering of kisses was just about to turn into a
rage-filled diatribe.

Clothilde's wrath, her volatility, would snake round corners, slip under closed doors, shriek for Sylvie until she nervously crept downstairs, backing against the wall as her mother ranted and raged over something that had nothing to do with Sylvie.

If she was lucky, her father would be at home, would take her out for ice cream. By the time they returned, Clothilde would invariably be sweet and sunny, wracked with guilt at her behaviour. She would cover Sylvie in kisses and leave her unable to trust anything at all.

Even today, despite all the evidence, she harbours an irrational hope that her mother will change. Even today, despite having a child, a husband, a grown-up life of her own, her mother's volatility still scares her; her mother has more influence on her than Sylvie would ever care to admit.

Sylvie went to art school in spite of Clothilde. She got her first job as a textile designer in spite of Clothilde, and learned to avoid her mother in order to escape the criticism, for she loved her work back then.

Now, as much as she wants to work to alleviate her growing discontent, Sylvie wants to work for the challenge, to have money of her own. Not because Mark denies her, exactly; after all, she has access to their household account. But each time she reaches for the credit card for anything other than a necessity — a hat, some gold wire to make earrings, chocolate leather boots that she doesn't really need, but oh, they are so very lovely — she pauses to think about what Mark will say, and usually ends up leaving them behind.

Mark assures her they are fine financially, but he has a plan to retire in five years, and they have to watch every penny. If they don't absolutely need it, he says, leave it. She has learned to be frugal, and she longs to have money of her own again, to be able to buy those boots without thinking, or those beads, or that top.

Five years and Mark will be home. With her. Not just her husband, but her partner. As hard as it is not having him here, knowing they have a goal to work towards is something she can try to live with.

Sylvie props herself up on an elbow and looks at Mark, curling his chest hair round her fingers. "I've been thinking about candles."

"Candles?"

"It's a bit of a long story, but, yes, I think I'd quite like to make candles."

Mark scoots back to make himself comfortable on the pillows, holding out an arm for Sylvie to nestle in. "We have all the time in the world. Tell me all."

Sylvie will do almost anything she can to avoid visiting her mother, apart from on Wednesday afternoons, when the Assisted Living Facility brings in an arts and crafts teacher to do a project with the residents and their guests.

Clothilde is always there, always participating, always criticizing the teacher, the method, the point. She criticizes loudly and well within everyone's earshot, as Sylvie squirms with discomfort, determining not to come back; but week after week, Sylvie is there.

Once the class is underway and her mother is absorbed, Sylvie finds it almost meditative to lose herself in a creative activity. Whether it's spiralling coil pots out of terracotta clay, beading simple necklaces on a wire, or fashioning papier-mâché vases from newspapers and balloons, Sylvie finds the class not only calming, but inspirational.

However basic the projects may be, the classes are stirring her creativity, and Sylvie goes on to produce items at home she then gives away to friends.

Last week it was candles. Not candle-making, for that would be too difficult and too dangerous for the elderly occupants of the home, but candle-wrapping: taking a pillar candle, measuring and cutting a sheet of beeswax to fit precisely around the outside, then wrapping the wax and securing it with a raffia tie.

It was mindless, and would have been disappointing had Sylvie not engaged the teacher in a fascinating discussion about candle-making. Sylvie learned about the benefits of organic soy wax, which retained the scent of the oils, the importance of using natural wicks so lead wasn't released into the air; she learned about melting temperatures and pouring temperatures, about additives used to harden the wax.

She learned that some waxes hold fragrance far better than others, that most candles require two pours as the first invariably brings bubbles and imperfections up to the surface. She learned that the reason her mother's candles, expensive though they are, invariably end up with a tunnel round the wick, the rest of the candle staying intact, is because she doesn't burn them long enough the first time they are lit in order to create a good melting pool.

At home she went straight to her computer, filled with an urge to make candles herself. Her mother's insistence on new Diptyque candles every couple of weeks was costing her a fortune — imagine if she were able to recreate the scent, or even create something entirely new, that her mother would love, and make them for a fraction of the cost.

Her mother loved fig. That she knew. But fig on its own? Surely she would need something else. Sylvie started looking at other fig candles, noting what other fragrances they used. Amber. Jasmine. Gardenia. Chypre. Chypre? What on earth was chypre? A combination of sensual, earthy base notes, she read. Base notes. Ah. Perfume. That's what she should be researching.

The more she read, the more she began to see it, feel it, and the calmer and more centred she became. It was like coming home to herself. What if she were to produce a line of organic candles at home? What if this could be exactly what she was looking for?

Mark, as pragmatic and practical as he is loving, asks her all the questions she cannot answer.

Costs, margins, sales information, and, finally, whether she has actually tried this before.

"Of course not," Sylvie says with a laugh. "Hello? This is your wife! Do you actually know me? But you know they'll be beautiful."

40

"That's true. Just don't spend a fortune without figuring out the costs involved. I'll help you. I have spreadsheets designed exactly for this. So . . ." His hand is once again moving down her body. "What's the plan for tonight?"

"I have a reservation at George's. I thought we could have a date night."

"Deck or inside?"

"Deck!" She grins. "Told you it's useful having friends in high places."

"If you'd said inside I might have tried to convince you to stay in bed, but," he shrugs, "I can't resist the view. However —" he rolls on top of her — "there's something I just have to do first."

"Not now." Sylvie pushes him away with a smile. "I have to get ready. Promise I'll make it up to you later, though."

Sylvie gets out of bed and walks naked to the bathroom, wiggling her bottom deliberately, grinning over her shoulder at him as she walks, blowing him a kiss as she closes the bathroom door.

CHAPTER
SEVEN

Sylvie

Eleven years and the chemistry between them is just as strong, if not stronger, than it ever was. This, perhaps more than anything else, has been the force that has kept them close. On girls' nights out, when Angie and other friends drink too much, they confess to low libidos, tricks to avoid having sex with their husbands; they refer to making love with much eye-rolling and sighing; everyone laughing as if they all understand, they all feel exactly the same way.

Sylvie doesn't laugh. She doesn't know if these women were once attracted to their husbands, only to have children, work, school runs, cleaning, cooking, dog-walking, driving, life, grind away at that attraction until they woke up one morning to find that attraction had entirely disappeared.

Perhaps they never had it. There were certainly a couple of women she knew who organized business mergers rather than a marriage. Their husbands were never at home; in return they got all the material possessions they wanted. They spoke of their husbands with disdain and disappointment. The fortnightly sex was their payment in kind; a payment that was treated as a necessary but wearying obligation.

Sylvie has never felt that way. Having a husband who is also never at home is where the similarity ends. Not that she doesn't feel disappointment in Mark — she is, after all, only human — but she would never share it with anyone.

Making love is always wonderful. When other women joke about Groupon really needing to do some lifelong deals on Viagra, Sylvie keeps quiet, for she only has to look in a certain way at Mark, now in his late forties, to have him instantly hard.

He, in turn, can stroke her arm in a restaurant and she will catch her breath and cross her legs, immediately feeling the warm rush as she pictures him on top of her, moving inside her.

She had never experienced this before. This sexual heat. Not even with Jonathan. Jonathan was like an old, comfortable, familiar bed. She adored making love with Jonathan, but it wasn't hot in the way it is with Mark. It wasn't . . . sweaty, dirty, uninhibited, wild. It didn't make her try things she never thought she'd try, say things she never thought she'd say.

After particularly steamy sessions, Sylvie often laughs to herself at the dichotomy. So loving and tender, they have the ability to get down and dirty, to experiment with each other, to reveal sides of themselves Sylvie never knew existed.

And if ever she doubts him, if ever she doubts this marriage, and this has started happening only recently, and most often when he is away, he will come back and lick the edge of her ear, or slip a hand under her skirt as she is wiping down the countertops, and all doubts will be forgotten.

They sit now, at George's, a warm breeze playing on their shoulders as a golden sun sets quietly over the Pacific, neither of them talking, both delighting in the extraordinary view, with the overwhelming feeling of being in exactly the right place, at exactly the right time.

It doesn't get any better than this, thinks Sylvie, as contented as a cat, sipping her vodka and lime, her sheer linen tunic threatening to slip off one shoulder as Mark leans forward and plants a kiss at the base of her neck.

She shivers, thinking back to half an hour earlier, the length and strength of her husband, his magical fingers, magical lips, and she is only brought out of her lustful coma by the sound of her husband's chuckling.

"You are unlike any woman I've ever known," he murmurs, when the glow of the sky has muted to pinks and purples, the sun almost gone. "All the guys I know complain their wives never want sex, and here I have a woman who would happily stay in bed with me all day."

"It's true. And not just to sleep . . ." Sylvie reaches over for a plantain chip. "I can't help it. It's you. I was never like this before."

"It isn't me." Mark shakes his head. "It's us. Our chemistry. All these years and it hasn't changed."

Sylvie wants to ask whether it changed with Mark's first wife, but Mark is still uncomfortable talking about her. Not because he harbours any feelings. Not because she was the great love of his life. But Mark sees things in black and white; once they divorced, that was it. Chapter closed. No children, no need to revisit. Done.

He is intensely private. Despite his job in sales, his charm around people, he has a pathological fear of gossip. When he went through his divorce he became the talk of the town, he said, and he couldn't stand it. His ex was the one who left, but she painted him as the one at fault. He learned very quickly that the vast majority of people he considered friends, weren't. Men he had played golf with, metaphorically killed at poker, had over for dinner countless times, disappeared.

It left Mark entirely distrustful of pretty much everyone. Although they have established a community of friends in La Jolla, it has been a slow process; it has taken time. The autumn after they were married, Mark spent the two evenings before Back to School night Googling all the names in the school directory, much to Sylvie's amusement.

"Any potential clients?" she kept asking. "Any sworn enemies from childhood?"

"Ha ha," Mark said. "You may laugh but this is how I get business. You never know who anyone is, and it's always better to be prepared."

In the event, he had a last-minute trip and missed Back to School night altogether.

His distrust of strangers remains, and is compounded by an intense dislike of online social media. That everyone they know runs, as he calls it, "their own private fan club" on Facebook, collecting comments and responses to status updates in lieu of, he says, fan mail, is anathema to him. Before they met, Mark was the victim of identity theft. It messed up his life and very nearly lost him his job. As a consequence he is paranoid about social websites and is insistent about Eve not posting personal information on her profile.

"But, Papa," she used to groan, "it's private. No one sees it except my friends."

"And their friends, and their friends," he said. "I know what can happen, and it's terrible. No photos, no addresses or phone numbers. Trust me."

So Eve has done a great job of convincing her father she has a completely vanilla profile; but she also runs a secret second profile, a secret Twitter, Instagram and Pinterest.

If Mark knew, he'd go nuts, which is why Eve's computer is password-protected, and her friends have been sworn to secrecy or a very painful death.

"I still can't believe you came home early." Sylvie cannot stop smiling, and she reaches out to stroke Mark's arm, his cheek, take his hand. Whatever worries she may have had earlier have gone; she is as loved up tonight as if they were on their first date.

"Where's Eve tonight? What's going on with our girl?"

"She's staying at Jenna's. She's good. I'm still worried about her, though. She wants to lose another ten pounds."

Mark frowns. "I don't like this. Should we be talking to a doctor? Or some kind of food specialist?"

"The counsellor told me it's probably something that passes, but, if it isn't, we can't bring her in without her wanting to come. She refuses to acknowledge she might be overly obsessed."

"God," he exhales. "I hope it does pass. I can't stand the thought of her being at school and us not being able to keep an eye on her."

"I know. That's what terrifies me."

"Which is why I want her to go to USC. This thing she has for going to school on the east coast is just crazy. It's too far from us, particularly with this going on."

"Maybe we should tell her that? If she loses any more weight she'll have to go to school here. Maybe that would make her eat."

"But then she'd expect to go to NYU, and I guarantee it's the wrong school for her, and her being on her own all the way over there just isn't something I'm comfortable with."

"She wouldn't exactly be on her own."

"I mean without a support system."

"But don't your friends at college become that support system? That's how it was for me."

"Maybe, but with these concerns we have I couldn't let her go to school so far away."

"How would we even tell her that?"

"Simple," Mark says, laughing. "It all comes down to a question of finances. We just can't afford it."

"Unless of course my candle business takes off and I become the Martha Stewart of candles."

"True. Then I'd be really stuck. But perhaps you ought to try making a candle before dreaming about world domination," he warns affectionately.

"Don't you worry. I already have the wax and wicks."

Mark leans back, shaking his head in admiration of his wife.

"What?" She grins.

"You just amaze me," he says. "You're so creative, and you're never frightened of doing anything. It's one of the things I love most about you. That you're a . . . doer. You have an idea, and instead of doing what most people do — talking about it but not doing anything — you don't talk about it, you just get on and do it."

"What else do you love about me?" Sylvie teases.

Mark laughs. "I love how relaxed you are, that you so rarely get amped out over anything. You're a free spirit, which I adore. I love that you're comfortable in your skin, that you never try to impress anyone, or worry what other people think of you, or change the way you dress in order to fit in."

Sylvie's eyes widen for a second. "Is there something wrong with the way I dress?"

"Not at all! I love it. It's bohemian, but chic. That's exactly it! You're so unaware of how incredible you are, not in an insecure way, but in this accepting way, where you just live your life. Really live your life. With joy."

Sylvie is quiet for a few seconds. "I don't feel like that these days," she says in a low voice. "I used to feel that joy, but it seems to have gone."

Mark's face falls. "Gone? What are you trying to tell me? Is there something wrong with us?"

"God, no! It's just that I feel . . . untethered." She frowns. "I always knew what my purpose was, but I don't know any more. I don't know what I'm supposed to be doing, and it's unsettling. I can't even put my finger on it, but it's like I'm entering the second part of my life, and I have no idea who I'm supposed to be."

"That's why you want to do the candles?"

"Not necessarily the candles, but something. I just don't know what it is. It's like . . . before I had Eve, I used to know who I was, but I kind of lost myself in marriage and motherhood . . . and now that she's going I have no idea who I am any more."

"You're still someone's wife and mother," Mark says, taking her hand. "As you will always be. I understand how you've lost a part of yourself while raising Eve, but even that isn't lost. It's just been . . . I don't know, dormant. This is the most exciting time for you. You can reinvent yourself, do whatever you want. Go back into textile design, if you want."

Sylvie grimaces.

"I don't mean go to work for some crazy designer who steals all your ideas and gives you none of the credit. I just mean you have time to express your creativity in whatever way you want. You may not know who you are right now, but you'll find out."

Sylvie sighs. "I guess. It just all feels a little overwhelming. It would be easier if you were at home more."

"You've never asked me for that until recently," Mark says. "You've always said you were okay with us having

49

so much time apart. You know I'm trying, but this is new for me too."

"I get it," Sylvie says. "But things were different before. I had Eve. I don't want to be an empty nester with a husband who's never at home."

"I'm working on it." Mark strokes her thumb. "I promise. Don't let's fight. I don't want to spoil a beautiful evening."

Sylvie nods. He's right. Neither does she.

CHAPTER
EIGHT

Sylvie

Eve is huddled in a sweater, despite the warmth outside.

"Aren't you hot?" Sylvie walks into the kitchen, her dark hair flowing over a beaded orange kaftan, and she pauses before opening a closet and reaching down to pull out thick turquoise wrapping paper for Angie's gift.

"I'm freezing!" Eve shivers. "Can we turn the air conditioning off?"

"It is off," Sylvie says. "Evie, I'm really worried about you. I think you're cold because there's nothing to keep you warm."

"What are you talking about?" Eve is almost sneering and Sylvie mentally backs down.

"I just think you might feel better if you ate something. Where's Papa?"

Eve shrugs as she fills the kettle with water and places it on the stove, before pulling a lemon out of the fridge and carefully cutting off a wedge. This is all she's had all day and it is easy. So easy, why not do it another day, or two, she thinks.

"He said he had to run into town."

"What are you going to do for dinner?"

"Oh God, Mom! Why is it always about food?" Eve's voice is a shout.

"It's not, okay?" Sylvie deliberately keeps her voice calm. "I was just worried we didn't have anything."

"So I'll go grab a pizza at Sammy's."

Please do, thinks Sylvie. Please, please let that happen. "Are you doing anything tonight?"

"I might go hang out at the beach. A group of people are going down there. Maybe," she says sarcastically, "we'll make smores!"

"That sounds great." Sylvie doesn't take the bait, busying herself with wrapping the scarf she has painted for Angie. It's not dissimilar to an Alexander McQueen one Angie had been obsessed with a few months ago: a pale grey chiffon that looks almost floral, until you look closely and realize the flowers are in fact intertwined skulls. Sylvie changed the design slightly, adding flowers, and even she is delighted with the result.

The side door slams as Mark walks into the kitchen. "Hey, guys! You look beautiful," he murmurs to Sylvie, then he turns to Eve. "How's it going, kid?" Eve, flicking through a magazine, barely looks up.

"I ran into town to get some wine to bring," Mark said. "Simon's such a wine snob I thought I'd better get something special. And guess what?" he adds, turning to Eve. "Girard was about to close, but I persuaded them to let me in for this . . ." He brandishes a paper bag from behind his back with a grin.

"An almond croissant?" Eve says, the conflict evident in her eyes.

"A Girard almond croissant. Here!" He tosses it onto the table nonchalantly, as if it were no big deal, pretending not to notice when Eve slowly opens the bag and smells.

Sylvie grabs her wrap, trying not to look as Eve takes one slivered almond from the top and places it on her tongue, then suppresses a smile as Eve grabs the whole croissant out of the bag and takes a huge bite.

"Told you!" Mark whispers, referring to Sylvie doubting him when he told her of his plan.

Sylvie bends down to place a kiss on the top of Eve's head. "Slow down!" she says cheerfully. "You don't want to choke!"

A lightness settles around Sylvie as they climb into the car and wind down the valley on the way to Angie's house.

"That was amazing!" Sylvie turns to Mark with a smile. "That's the first thing I've seen her eat in days."

"I have far more up my sleeve . . ." Mark grins. "Chocolate-chip pancakes for breakfast, for starters."

Sylvie laughs. "Remember how she used to love them when she was little? The smiley faces?"

"Damn!" He slaps his thigh. "I thought I was so clever in remembering the strawberries but I forgot the whipped cream. Don't let me forget to pick some up on the way."

They smile at each other, each blissfully unaware that at the precise moment of their smile Eve is on her knees in front of the toilet, three fingers reaching for the back of her throat, retching and gasping until finally, finally, the croissant, barely chewed, has entirely left her body.

The women are chatting away on the sofa, the men standing at the other end of the room admiring the view, an occasional burst of laughter drifting across the space between them.

Angie's house is the diametric opposite of Sylvie's. But despite the concrete and glass, the clean, simple lines, Sylvie, sipping her champagne and listening to the chatter, feels as comfortable there as she does in her own home.

Admittedly, she wouldn't want to live there full-time; she does not understand how Angie's daughter can live there so neatly and tidily, nor their nonchalance at entire walls made of glass, affording neighbours multiple and constant views of their lives, but each time she walks up the glass staircase and into the giant room that serves as kitchen, living room, family room and study, Sylvie is instantly calm.

Angie tells everyone she is hopeless at anything to do with the home, cannot cook to save her life, could not choose a fabric if her life depended on it, but looking round at this room, Sylvie knows that isn't true.

Angie may have paid Lars Bernal, decorator to the stars, to furnish the house, but she also gave him a stack of photographs, torn from magazines, of homes she wanted to emulate, rooms she admired, showing him exactly what sort of design would work for her.

Lars found the low-slung Balinese daybeds, big enough for a dozen people, covered in soft white cushions, but Angie was the one who emailed him pictures she took on vacation at Parrot Cay, with a note telling him these daybeds were exactly what she wanted.

Lars found the huge stone Buddha, who now casts a benevolent eye over the room from his perch in front of the windows, but only after Angie sent him a picture of one similar. Angie found the hand-tinted black and white photographs now above the modern fireplace, itself a simple rectangle in the wall, and guided Lars to replace the gas fire logs with polished river stones.

Obsessed by candles, Angie's current fixation is Bamboo by Nest, the soothing smells of which arise from every corner, creating a haven of peace and tranquillity that slightly offsets the whirlwind that is Angie.

"Okay!" Angie raises a hand, casting an eye over to the coffee table, where the gifts are currently piled. "I know the polite thing to do is to wait to open gifts, but I'm a gift whore. Can I open them now? Please!"

"Would you?" Laura says in mock exasperation. "I didn't want to say anything but frankly I was about to take it home."

"Can I squeal if I love it?" Grinning widely, Angie reaches for a gift as Simon comes over to refill their glasses.

"Uh-oh," he says. "Girl time. I think I'll take the men downstairs to do manly stuff."

"Manly stuff?" Sylvie scoffs. "Are you going hunting, shooting and fishing?"

"We would if we were in Montana," Simon says. "Speaking of which, I thought the four of us were going to go to that Dude Ranch? Whatever happened to that?"

"I'd love to go to a Dude Ranch!" Laura sits up. "I've always wanted to go! Can we come?"

"We should all go!" Angie says. "The problem is finding the right place."

"Right place?" Simon shakes his head in exasperation. "It's a Dude Ranch, my love. Not a Four Seasons. The whole point is to be rustic."

"You can do rustic," Angie says, "and we'll do luxury. I know there's somewhere out there where we'll all be happy."

"We should go to the ranch and let you guys go to a spa," Simon says. "We're not going to find a Four Seasons Dude Ranch. Hey, Mark!" He calls him over. "Dude Ranch. What words come to mind?"

Mark wanders over. "Horses. Cowboys. Long days. Fun nights. Drinking. Great sleep. Good honest work." He grins, leaning down to kiss Sylvie.

"Beans!" Harold calls from the other side of the room.

"Wieners!" adds Rob, and they both crack up.

"Right!" Angie sits forward. "I agree! Horses. Cowboys. Cowboys. Cowboys. Hey, did I mention the cowboys? And chaps . . . mmm. God, I find those things sexy . . ."

"Really?" Simon's face lights up. "I never knew that."

She gives him a withering look. "Not on you, babe. No offence. But the point is, horses and all the good stuff, plus massages, facials, hot tubs, and I'm sorry, but no beans and wieners. There has to be great food, right, Sylvie?" She looks at Sylvie for support, but Sylvie grimaces.

"I'm sorry," she says. "I want to agree with you, but I kind of think a Dude Ranch should be basic. I think it would do us all good to get back to nature and spend all day on a horse. I like the idea of pushing ourselves in that way."

"I knew there was a reason I married you!" Mark nods approvingly. "Low-maintenance," he mutters to Simon out of the corner of his mouth. "It's all about low-maintenance."

Angie lays a beautifully manicured hand on Simon's arm. "Sweetie, I can be low-maintenance. I can do hippy skirts and Birkenstocks. I can even do no make-up and frizzy hair. Would you like that, sweetie? You know how I look first thing in the morning? I can look like that all the time if it would make you happy."

"God, no!" Simon shouts in horror, as everyone laughs.

"Don't say I didn't try," Angie says, turning to Mark with a shrug. "Simon, can you just go and do your manly stuff? We have more important things to take care of," and she reaches for the package closest to her as the men disappear.

"You can always return it . . ." Ginny Meyer, an old friend of Angie's who recently moved back to the area, winces as Angie turns the box in her hands, trying to figure out what it is. "In fact —" she reaches over to try to take it — "it's completely wrong for you. I want to take it back and change it for something you'll really love."

"Don't worry!" Angie laughs. "Whatever you've got I know I'm going to love it. The fact that you and Harold actually live here is gift enough."

"What?" Sylvie exclaims. "Your email had the words 'all gifts welcome' printed at the bottom. I suppose Simon snuck in to write that?"

"He must have done. How awful!" Angie's hand flies up to her mouth in shock. "I would never do anything so rude." She winks, pulling the paper off to reveal a box, which she first lifts then shakes slightly.

"Careful," warns Ginny. "It's fragile."

"Ooh. I love guessing. Is it shoes?"

Ginny smiles. "No, as much as we both love shoes, it's not. It's something else you used to like, and the only clue is you can't wear it."

Angie opens the box, pushing the tissue paper aside to draw out a huge white porcelain mushroom.

Silence descends as everyone stares at the mushroom.

"It's a mushroom!" Angie bursts out.

"A mushroom?" questions Laura.

"No, you don't understand!" Angie is wide-eyed with excitement. "I'm obsessed! I'm seriously totally obsessed with mushrooms! This is amazing! You remembered!"

"As if I could forget!" Ginny laughs. "She came out sailing with us one time —"

"You should see their boat," Angie bursts in. "*Sole Power*. It's beautiful."

"Thank you, but Angie spent the whole time engrossed in some book about mushrooms."

"Well, it's my secret shame. I find that whole underside thing fascinating . . . But, Ginny! I can't believe you remembered!" She stands up and flings her arms round Ginny, who is now flushed with joy.

"I'm putting this with my collection."

"Are you kidding me?" Sylvie's mouth is open. "How do I not know you have a mushroom collection?"

"I told you. It's my secret shame. Secret's out now. Come with me." She beckons them to follow her up the open glass staircase to the master bedroom, where, on a shelf, is, indeed, a collection of mushrooms. They all start laughing, as Angie lovingly places the mushroom in the centre, before turning to take in the view.

"Don't you get freaked out with all that glass?" asks Laura.

Angie shrugs. "Let them watch. I'm a forty-something mother with spider veins and saggy boobs. Enjoy."

"I couldn't do it." Laura shakes her head. "Caroline had the same windows but she's covered the whole thing up with shutters. Gotta tell you, I'd do the same."

The women all turn to her with a chorus of "Who?", "What?", "Why?"

"Caroline!" Laura says. "After the latest . . ."

"What?"

"There's more?"

"No! What happened?"

Laura groans. "I'm not supposed to say anything."

"Oh please!" Angie grabs her and pulls her down to sit on the bed. "You can trust us."

"I know, but we all had that talk about how we wouldn't gossip."

"I wasn't there, but I agree," says Sylvie. "It's bad karma."

"Only if you're telling everyone," insists Angie. "There's a difference between random gossiping and gossiping with your closest friends. Okay, so I know we're not all each other's closest friends, but you three girls are my closest friends, so if we all swear never to repeat, then it's sacred, right?"

Laura leans forward, a flush to her cheeks with the excitement of repeating the titbit she had been so desperate to share.

"So you know Caroline and Bill split up last week?"

"What?" Sylvie is shocked. "I didn't know!" She turns to Angie. "Did you know?" Angie looks guilty. "Why wouldn't you tell me something like that?"

Angie puts her hands on her hips. "Because I was trying to do what we'd agreed to do and not pass on gossip. Furthermore, given how much I can't stand her, I was trying to pray for her and bathe her in healing white light instead of cackling with joy over karma being a beautiful thing."

"Right. So what happened? I thought she had the perfect marriage?"

"So did everyone, until Bill was caught not just having an affair, but . . ." Laura pauses for dramatic effect. "Sexting!"

"What?" they all gasp excitedly. "What does that even mean?"

"Where to start?" Laura sighs. "He's been sleeping with a ton of women, and —" she looks from one to the other — "most of them are pretty . . . let's just say . . . skanky."

"No one we know, then," Angie says. "I swear," she adds, solemnly holding her hand to her heart, looking at each woman, "on Simon's life, I was not one of the skanky hos."

"Don't take this the wrong way, but we're all way too old. He's been picking up all these twenty-something 'dancers', and yes, there are inverted commas round that word."

"Strippers?" Sylvie asks, and Laura nods.

"Nothing's more inelegant than a man's mid-life crisis." Ginny sighs.

"Especially when one of said party girls-slash-strippers is dumped by wealthy married banker boyfriend who she thinks is about to leave his wife and kids for her."

"Hell hath no fury . . ."

"Exactly. So current party girl, who, by the way, looks more like a hooker as far as I'm concerned, and — please! — what kind of man must Bill be to find straw-bleached hair and huge fake tits attractive . . ."

"A normal man," Angie says dejectedly.

"Point taken. Party girl, Tara-Jo, has been tweeting her fury, with all the details of their sexual escapades, and explicit pictures and texts that Bill had 'sexted' her. Gone viral. All over Twitter."

Sylvie's eyes are wide. "Are you serious? That's horrific."

"I know! But these pictures are unbelievable."

"You've seen them?"

Laura grimaces. "I know. I'm a horrible person. But everyone at tennis was talking about it and I couldn't not look. It's like a car crash. You know it's horrible but a part of you can't tear your eyes away."

"What are the pictures?"

"Bill's . . . you know. Huge."

"Erect?"

Laura nods.

Sylvie shakes her head. "You know what? I don't believe it's him. There's no way Bill would do something like that. He's the straightest person we know." She thinks of Bill, big, bluff and hearty. A former baseball star, he's a family man through and through. He coaches Little League. He has three small sons, and an uppity blonde wife with a superiority complex. "No way," Sylvie says. "It's a mistake."

"Mistake this." Laura slides her iPhone over to Sylvie, whose eyes widen as she finds herself looking at a picture that is very definitely of Bill, and very definitely not what he would want his family to see.

Or anyone else for that matter.

"That's horrible." Sylvie places the phone on the bed, screen down. "What a stupid, stupid man. How could he have sent pictures like that to anyone? What's the matter with people? You think it's just kids who don't realize the implications of sending out an explicit photograph. How could a grown man be so stupid? What was he thinking?"

"The little head was clearly doing the thinking." Angie raises an eyebrow.

"Not so little," adds Laura. "I can't believe it's all over Twitter. I swear, if anything like that happened to me I'd never show my face again. Caroline is so humiliated she's talking about moving. Can you imagine? She only found out when she got some anonymous note in her mailbox saying there was something about her husband on Twitter she may not know about."

"Who the hell would do that?"

"Probably this girl. Rough, huh?"

Sylvie shakes her head. "It's worse than rough. It's tragic. I've never liked Caroline, but nobody deserves this."

The others go quiet.

"I know what you mean," murmurs Laura. "She's snotty as hell, but I wouldn't wish this on anyone."

"I agree." Angie sighs. "I never thought I'd say this about her, but my heart is going out to her right now."

"So where's Bill?" Ginny wonders.

"Moved into a hotel. Some of the guys have seen him, but not Rob." She looks at Sylvie. "I bet he'll call Mark. Don't they hang out together?"

"Occasionally," Sylvie says. "Mark travels so much it's hard. I'll ask him, but I don't think he knows anything or he would have told me."

"You know what's truly amazing about all this?" muses Laura. "You think you know people, you think you know a marriage, but none of us ever knows what goes on behind closed doors."

A shout comes from downstairs.

"Angie? What the hell are you all doing in our bedroom?"

"Don't get excited," Angie yells back. "We're coming down now."

Eight people is the perfect number, thinks Sylvie, sitting quietly for a minute as the group talks animatedly across the table.

More guests, and dinner parties become a series of individual conversations, small talk, the reason that Sylvie invariably turns down the invitations when Mark is not around, for small talk is something she has never been good at.

Tonight, the group has bonded, and she does not remember the last time she had so much fun. Mark is at home and they are a couple, doing what regular couples do. Instead of surreptitiously looking at her watch and wondering how they can orchestrate an escape, Sylvie hasn't looked at her watch once; she could stay for hours more.

"I'm telling you . . ." Laura, slightly fuzzy with wine, leans forward to make a pronouncement. "You need to be checking their Facebook and texts. Seriously. I check Abigail's all the time."

Rob shrugs helplessly at his wife's pronouncement, which clearly embarrasses him. "I keep telling her she shouldn't. Abigail would go nuts if she knew."

Laura turns to him defensively. "If our daughter gets into trouble, how are we supposed to find out?"

"Um . . . she tells us?" Rob spells it out slowly.

"Right," she scoffs. "Because all seventeen-year-old girls go straight to their parents when they get into trouble. This way we know."

"But you don't know," Rob argues. "You think you know, and even if you find something out, how are you going to explain it? I just happened to be reading your texts? That'll be successful."

"Our parents didn't know anything we did," Angie says. "At seventeen I was a party girl, and my parents had no idea. I turned out okay, right?" She looks over at Simon, at the other end of the table, for validation, and he grins and blows her a kiss. "You have to let them learn their own lessons. You can't protect them from all that's out there, and nor should you."

"I agree," Mark says. "Our job as parents is to raise them to be good people in the world, and to make the right choices. You can't stop bad stuff from happening, but you have to give them freedom in order to teach them to recognize what the best choice for them would be."

"Mark!" Angie berates him. "You're the dad who won't let Eve post anything on Facebook! How is that giving her freedom?"

"I let her post!" Mark is embarrassed. "I just won't let her post anything personal." The others shout him down.

"Whatever your settings, people have ways of accessing your site," he insists. "You can't even believe how much they can find out about you from a photograph or where you live. Eve is responsible in many ways, but she doesn't understand the risk."

"The risk really isn't that big." Harold shrugs sceptically. "We've all read stories and seen movies, but, honestly, I really don't think abductors are going to show up on the doorstep after targeting your kids on Facebook."

"Really?" Mark says. "Did you see the movie *Trust?*"

"Oh my God!" the women all gasp. "That movie was terrifying!"

"He has a point," Ginny says. "It was so realistic."

They explain the plot to Harold — that a grown man posed as a teenage boy to instigate a relationship with an innocent young girl — but Harold refuses to back down.

"It's a movie," he says. "That's the point. Movies dramatize real life. Facebook has changed the world, and you can't do things the way they were done before. You have to move on and accept the changes."

"I kind of think he's right," Sylvie says, looking at Mark.

"He may be," Mark says. "But I've had the bad stuff happen." He looks round the table. "Years ago my identity was stolen. I didn't just lose money; I nearly lost my entire life."

Everyone sits forward, rapt.

"You have to tell us what happened," Laura says.

"I was sitting with a loan officer discussing a mortgage, and he asked me what I thought of the Escalade. I had no idea what he was talking about. He looked at me like I was an idiot and 'reminded' me I'd just bought a brand-new Escalade."

"You'd remember something like that, right?" Angie laughs.

"You'd think. So it turns out I'd thrown away my expired credit card, and my identity had been stolen by someone dumpster-diving. They had opened a ton of credit cards in my name, all maxed out. It was a nightmare."

"Did you get your money back?"

Mark nods. "Eventually, but it took me almost two years to get my life back. I had no credit rating. It was a disaster. Not to mention I had some guy posing as me."

"Was he caught?" asks Rob.

"Yes. Straight to jail."

"Was he handsome, at least?" Laura asks.

"He was a kid," Mark says. "Twenty-three. His life ruined. But you know what, he almost ruined mine. I was stuck for two years. So . . . that's why I'm paranoid. I have reason to be. I know that people aren't necessarily who they say they are."

"Oh, that we know," Angie says. "Poor Bill." Her hands fly to her lips. "Oops!" She grimaces. "Does it count if we tell our husbands?"

"We already know," says Simon. "We were talking about it in the wine cellar."

Sylvie waits a few minutes before turning to Mark, her voice dropped low so the others don't hear. "You knew and didn't tell me?" She is shocked, and upset. Even when sworn to secrecy, she knows the unspoken part of the deal is that husbands don't count. She trusts him implicitly, and there is nothing she wouldn't tell him; she has presumed that this went both ways.

"Bill swore me to secrecy," Mark says. "This was before everyone found out, after Caroline first got the call. He was trying to stop the worst from happening, and he was desperate. Sylvie, he specifically asked me to promise not to tell you. I tell you everything, but I couldn't tell you this."

"But I'm your wife. Even if you promise, you know spouses don't count. And you know I would never talk about it with anyone."

"I do, but I couldn't go back on a promise. Once I'd said those words to him, I would feel like I was committing a crime by repeating it. Even to you. I'm sorry."

Sylvie nods. "It's okay. I don't like it, but I get it. I just feel kind of stupid, being the last to know. How is he?"

"Desperate. And Caroline's getting ready to move. She doesn't want to face anyone in this town ever again."

Sylvie closes her eyes for a second as she shakes her head, unable to get the unfortunate image of Bill, naked and at full mast, out of her head. "That poor woman," she says. "I can't think of anything worse."

CHAPTER
NINE

Sylvie

The phone buzzes over and over again, but both Mark and Sylvie are deaf to its persistent vibration, until both swim upwards from their deep sleep, Mark registering the phone call first.

He grabs the phone and picks it up, whispering a hello as he crawls out of bed and goes into the bathroom so as not to disturb Sylvie, but it's too late.

She is now awake, heart pounding, squinting at the clock. Who in the hell is calling at 2.36 a.m. on Monday morning, and why is her husband taking the call in the other room?

Sylvie creeps to the bathroom door and listens, then, hearing her husband murmuring softly, a wave of nausea sweeps over her. She can't hear the words, but she hears his laughter. She pushes the door open, catching him mid-sentence.

"Sweetie," he says, holding out the phone. "I didn't mean to wake you. It's your mother."

Sighing, she takes the phone as Mark stands up, kisses her shoulder and heads back to bed, then she sits down on the edge of the bath in the exact same spot.

"Mom? Is everything okay? What's the matter?"

"Nothing's the matter. There are things I need that I can't find. Where is my Hermès blue and orange scarf? My favourite one? I haven't seen it for ages."

"I don't know, Mom. It's probably in storage up in the attic. I'll check. But it's two thirty-seven in the morning. I thought it was an emergency. This will have to wait."

"What time is it?"

"Two thirty-seven. Mom, you can't phone people in the middle of the night."

"You're not people. You're my daughter."

"But I've told you not to phone me late unless it's an emergency."

"I need Band-Aids too. That's an emergency. Oh, and another of those Diptyque candles I like. You know the ones."

Sylvie closes her eyes, inwardly groaning. "Okay, Mom. I'll see you tomorrow. I'm going now."

"Wait! Tomorrow? What about today? I thought you were coming today."

"I can't today. I'm sorry."

"Why? What's more important than visiting your mother who gave up her entire life for you?"

Sylvie's heart sinks. "Mom, I have a doctor's appointment, remember?"

There is no doctor's appointment, but Clothilde, who forgets so much, seems to quieten down when she is faced with her lack of memory.

"In San Diego," she lies. "But I'll be in tomorrow."

"San Diego," Clothilde murmurs. "Pity you never think to bring me into the city with you."

Sylvie says nothing, knowing that her good night's sleep is now over. A disturbance of a minute would be okay, might still enable her to go back to sleep, but a whole conversation? Her body may be exhausted, her eyes fighting to stay open, but she is experienced enough to know that her mind is now alert; there will be no more sleep tonight.

It is the scourge of middle age. She knows Angie and Laura have the same problem and have resorted to Tylenol and Ambien to help them through the nights.

The nights she doesn't sleep, Sylvie gets up, gets things done. She wasted too many nights lying in bed, willing herself to go back to sleep, wild thoughts flying through her head while she refused to push back the covers, refused to set foot on the floor, in case, by some miracle, she fell back to sleep.

Which never happened.

Now, she gets up.

By the time Eve needs to get up for school at 6 a.m., Sylvie will have made breakfast, paid bills, organized files, baked a cake and managed to spend a couple of hours online to research whatever her obsession of the moment is.

It's not so bad, Sylvie thinks, tuning back in to Clothilde.

". . . and where are my pearls, Sylvie? The black ones. I know I had them here and they were in the bathroom, and now they are missing."

"I don't remember you having the pearls there. I think they may be in the safe with the rest of your jewellery. I didn't bring them in."

"Not you. Mark brought them. Or Eve. I don't know . . . someone! But now they are not here."

Sylvie's heart sinks, for this is a regular occurrence, Clothilde deciding some piece of jewellery is missing, making the accusation before anyone has even had a chance to check.

"It's that new nurse. She was admiring my bracelet the other day, and I saw the sly look in her eye."

"Which new nurse? Nancy?" Sylvie almost laughs. "The sweet, quiet one?"

"There's nothing sweet or quiet about her. She's a thief. I'm going to talk to the director this morning."

"Mom, don't. Wait. Let me look for you. They might be here."

"You don't believe me?"

"Of course I do," Sylvie soothes. "But if Mark brought them to you, perhaps he brought them home? Let me just check."

There is a silence, then a harrumph. "Ça va. What time will you come?"

"Around two."

"Maybe this time you'll actually stay? You're never here for longer than about five minutes."

"I'm sorry, Mom," Sylvie forces herself to say. "I will try to stay a bit longer tomorrow. Eve has a softball game in the afternoon, though. I promised her I'd be there because I've missed the last two."

"You can tell her she needs to come to see her *grandmère*. She hasn't been here for weeks."

"No, Mom. She came with me two days ago, remember? You wanted the moisturizer and magazines. Eve did your nails. Remember?"

"That was two days ago?" Clothilde is surprised, although this lapse in spatial awareness, time awareness, happens regularly.

"Yes."

"Still. She doesn't come to see me enough. Here I am, with this terrible life, in this terrible *taudis*, and no one comes to see me. I'm stuck here alone all day, with no family, and no friends. I don't have anyone I can talk to, and no one cares how lonely I am. If you weren't so selfish you'd be here looking after me, making sure I'm not lonely."

Sylvie takes a deep breath. I won't react, she tells herself. I won't take the bait.

"What about all the classes, Mom? There are activities all day that are really interesting. Last week they were doing découpage, remember? We went together but you refused to do it."

"I did?"

"I'll see you tomorrow afternoon. Around two."

"Don't be late." There is an audible click as Clothilde rings off.

Mark is fast asleep when Sylvie peeks round the bedroom door. There is no point climbing back into bed beside him, spending the next three hours thinking about nothing and everything. She drops a light kiss on his cheek then tiptoes softly out of the bedroom and down the stairs.

Downstairs, by the back door, is a large box filled with wax; next to it is a box of essential oils. She may as well see whether she's any good at making these candles after all.

Pouring herself freshly brewed coffee from the cafetière — her mother insisted fresh coffee must be brewed only in a cafetière, refusing even to call it a French press — Sylvie perches on a stool for a few minutes, inhaling the steam from the large cup before taking a tiny, tentative sip.

The kitchen, so ugly when they first saw it, is now charming. Eschewing the cold white on white that seemed to be the current trend, Sylvie had replaced the old melamine cabinets with open shelving resting on pretty carved brackets, all painted a soft dove grey and stacked high with dozens of white plates and dishes.

The countertops are of honed marble, etched, marked, and all the lovelier for it. The patina they so quickly acquired reminds Sylvie of the old patisseries in Paris, where the more aged and stained the marble, the more warmth and charm the patisserie had.

Sylvie laid a soft limestone slab on the kitchen floor, colour-washing the beams above with a pale grey.

Cookbooks fill a floor-to-ceiling hutch on one side, piled haphazardly in varying directions, interspersed with marble pestles and mortars collected by Sylvie over the years.

The oval dining table is in front of the French doors, a painted Swedish bench with faded blue-and-cream-checked cushions pulled up on the window side, four curved French chairs placed around the rest of the table.

It is now a kitchen that is the envy of all her friends. Not because it is perfect, or pristine, or nearly as big as many of their own kitchens, but because it feels like home.

Nothing is perfectly matched, yet everything matches perfectly. Sylvie, born and bred in America, has the sensibilities of her mother, preferring old and interesting over new and perfect, knowing, without even thinking about it, how to mix different styles to come up with something uniquely beautiful.

Picking up the coffee cup, she moves to the table, to a cluster of small ramekins, each filled with essential oils. She dips her head to inhale deeply, a small smile playing on her lips as she closes her eyes and smells again.

She has written down exactly how many drops of each oil she mixed, and in which order. She sniffs the pure Mediterranean fig again. It is sweet and spicy, but, compared to her newly mixed fig, it has no depth, no warmth.

What else does her scent need? She smells again, knowing she is close, but there is something missing. She goes through the bottles she hasn't yet used, pausing at cassis. It is rich and fruity; it might be just what she needs.

She pours half her perfume into another bowl, noting down the quantity in her notebook, before adding three drops of cassis.

Nearly there. Nearly there. Another three drops . . . and it is perfect. She smells the sweetness of fig and orange, the richness of amber, the warmth of sandalwood, the heady scent of tuberose and gardenia, with the cassis bringing them all together.

It is 4.15 a.m. Still plenty of time to get the candles made. Tipping the chips of wax into the metal pot, she waits for them to melt before checking the temperature, adding in the oils, letting the temperature drop to the correct level and then pouring the wax slowly into the waiting glass jars.

Frowning as the wicks bend all the way to the side, she grabs a handful of knives from the kitchen drawer and carefully balances them on the top of each jar to hold the wick perfectly in place in the centre of the candle, and smiles. It may not be the way the professionals do it, but it's doing the job.

Lifting the cookie sheet the containers are balancing on, she walks slowly and smoothly to the back door, trying not to disturb the wax, and sets the tray on the steps.

Back inside, Sylvie examines the contents of the craft closet. Brown paper, raffia, a roll of cellophane. She chuckles, glad she never sorted through this closet, never threw anything away.

Now all she needs is a label. Pouring herself a fresh cup of coffee she sits at the computer and experiments with fonts, sizes, colours until she finally comes up with something she likes.

Candles by Sylvie
MEDITERRANEAN FIG & AMBER

It's not great, but it works. It works even better when she sketches a fig leaf and scans it in, adding it to the label and changing the colours to a warm grey.

"Perfect," she whispers to herself. Elegant and simple. Her mother will approve.

CHAPTER
TEN

Sylvie

Angie flies into Harry's, two shopping bags from Sigi's on her arm, and is unaware of the heads turning to watch this gorgeous redhead who strides through without thinking to look round to see who she knows. She focuses only on smiling at her friend, sitting at the back.

"Oh God!" She dumps the bags on the floor next to Sylvie, planting a kiss on her cheek as she sits down. "Simon's going to kill me. I just spent a fortune."

"Tell him it's your birthday present." Sylvie smiles, for Angie continually vows to stop spending money, but cannot resist popping into Sigi's or Bowers whenever she finds herself passing by with a moment or two to spare. Leaving empty-handed is unthinkable, she explains. It would be "plain rude".

"These are my birthday present," she says, and shows off beautiful sparkly earrings. "He gave them to me the other night after everyone left. Aren't they beautiful?"

"They are. Gorgeous. And speaking of the other night, we had the best time. Thank you so much.

Everything about it was perfect. Honestly, I think I had more fun than I've had in years."

"I know!" Angie grabs a passing waitress and orders a skinny cappuccino, with an extra shot of caffeine. "Wasn't it great? I could barely move the next day, though. Oh my God, I'd forgotten what champagne does to me."

"Right. Because you drink it so rarely," Sylvie laughs, as she pours herself some more tea.

"Not bottles and bottles of it. I tell you, I didn't even mind turning forty, that's how much fun it was."

Sylvie frowns. "I thought you were forty-three?"

"Sssshhh," hisses Angie. "The only people to know that are you and Simon, and if you tell anyone else I may have to kill you." She grins, before lowering her voice. "Speaking of gossip, and I know we shouldn't, but could you believe those pictures of Bill?"

Sylvie sighs. "I can't stop thinking about it. I feel so awful for both of them. Are we sure those pictures mean he's definitely been having affairs? What about that congressman who did the same thing? I don't think he ever did anything other than send the pictures. Maybe that's what Bill did?" she asks doubtfully.

Angie is dismissive. "Where there's smoke . . . In any case, in this instance, unfortunately, Bill has definitely done more than just take pictures. Caroline's discovered all kinds of terrible things. Emails, receipts from Victoria's Secret for underwear she's never seen, and —"

"Victoria's Secret?" Sylvie can't resist a half smile. "Of course she's never seen it. Caroline in Victoria's

Secret? Surely she's much more a designer underwear girl."

"That's the point. She is. The Victoria's Secret stuff is for the mistresses." Angie shakes her head. "Frankly, Simon would be thrilled to have me in Victoria's Secret. The one time I tried a flesh-coloured T-shirt bra he threatened to divorce me unless I burned it immediately."

Sylvie laughs. "I guess Simon thinks Victoria's Secret means black lace?"

"Red, preferably." Angie rolls her eyes. "I do try from time to time. You have to keep things hot to stop them straying, but, honestly, I'm so much more comfortable in the T-shirt bras."

"Wow." Sylvie sits back shaking her head. "Do you really think you have to keep things hot to keep them from being unfaithful?"

"Absolutely!" Angie nods vigorously. "You think it's any coincidence that all these men keep leaving their wives for young women? It's not because they're interested in their brains, or even their hot bodies. It's because those women haven't been ground down by childbirth, and PTAs, and running a family. Those women don't crawl into bed every night hoping their husbands will leave them alone so they can read their magazine in peace and get a decent night's sleep in order to be able to do it all over again the next day. It's biological." She shrugs, sipping her coffee. "Men need sex. It isn't about wanting it, they actually need it, and if you don't give it to them, they'll find someone else who will."

Sylvie wipes imaginary sweat off her forehead. "Well, thank God Mark and I are absolutely fine in that department. Better than fine. I've been known to drag him out of parties because I can't keep my hands off him."

"I don't blame you. If Simon looked like Mark I'd do the same thing," Angie says wistfully.

They both smile, both picturing Simon: portly, receding hairline, brilliant mind and the biggest heart you could ever hope to find.

"Simon is many things, but a sex machine he is not. Mark is just about the best-looking man in town. Maybe in the state," Angie says thoughtfully. "But Simon's all mine, oh lucky girl that I am, and he's a good boy, even if he does need retraining every once in a while. Truth is, I don't know what I'd do without him, and I make damn sure that if he wants red lace and black tassels, I give him red lace and black tassels."

Sylvie bursts out laughing. "Simon would never dare cheat on you. First of all, you're gorgeous and he'd never find anyone like you again, and secondly, you'd cut his penis off."

"I would." Angie nods solemnly. "It's true. I couldn't be forgiving after something like that."

Sylvie frowns. "I'm not sure any of us really know how we'd react until we're there."

"Wow!" Angie looks at her. "That's so . . . magnanimous of you. You'd be able to forgive?"

"I didn't say that. I just think it's impossible to know. Every marriage is different, and it's easy to theorize on how you'd react. Plus, some people have an understanding."

"I don't know. I think that's what people tell themselves when they're frightened of the alternative. How could you possibly allow the man you love to sleep with someone else? Simon's no oil painting, but if I imagine him kissing someone else?" She shudders. "Urgh. It makes me feel nauseous. I may be one hell of a flirt, but I take my marriage vows seriously. Deep down I'm just a good Southern girl, and I can't condone infidelity. Ever. It goes against everything marriage is about."

"I'm not sure I agree," Sylvie says slowly. "Honestly? I'm not sure it's the worst thing that can happen to a marriage."

"What?" Angie barks. "You must be joking! How can a breakdown of trust and publicly humiliating your wife not be the worst thing that can happen?"

Sylvie nods. "I think, in Bill and Caroline's case, the public humiliation is awful. But we're all human; we're all flawed; we all make mistakes. Everyone assumes that if someone's unfaithful it means there's something wrong with the marriage, but I don't know that I believe that's true. Sometimes sex is just sex; it's possible to love someone deeply, and to have sex with someone else. It can be about many things, but it doesn't necessarily mean you don't love your spouse."

"You surprise me." Angie leans back. "I never expected you to say that. Is this the French part of you talking? All men have affairs and all that stuff?"

Sylvie smiles. "I don't know about that. But my parents were married for forty years until my dad died. And —" she takes a deep breath, for this is something she doesn't generally talk about, knowing that her American friends will not, as a rule, understand — "there was infidelity from the beginning."

Angie nods. "Aah. Now I get it. Of course you're going to feel that way if your dad had affairs. At least that explains why Clothilde's such a bitch. She probably had it pent up for years."

Sylvie cannot help another burst of laughter. "It wasn't my father. It was my mother."

Angie's hands fly to her mouth. "I'm so sorry. I should never have said that."

"Don't be. Clothilde is a total bitch. Even I know that. What I've never been able to figure out," Sylvie says sadly, "is why my father stayed. She was so vicious to him, and she'd leave him every summer to go and live with her lover. Can you imagine?"

"He knew?"

"Yup. But he refused to talk about it with me. I have no idea if he put up with it and kept the marriage going to protect me, or because he loved her. I think it was probably a bit of both."

"That's hard," Angie says. "How did you find out?"

"I haven't thought about this for years." Sylvie takes a sip from her cup, casts her mind back all those years.

"My mother was in France for the summer. I was sixteen, and alone in the house while my dad was at work. I loved being alone in the house. I was fascinated by everything of my mother's because it was all so different from everyone else's, and I used to snoop through her stuff, especially her clothes, which were so beautiful. And of course, in the back of her lingerie drawer, cliché of clichés, there was the stack of handwritten envelopes."

Angie's eyes are wide. "Did they smell of perfume?"

"No, Angie. Felipe wasn't a woman."

"Ah yes. Good point."

Sylvie laughs. "It was obviously from someone in France, and I ran downstairs to grab the huge old French dictionary, and spent the next five hours translating the entire collection."

"Did you speak any French? And what did the letters say?"

"Yes, I spoke French but not nearly well enough to read the letters properly. They were from her lover. He lived in an apartment in Neuilly-sur-Seine, and shipped his wife and children off to their home in the hills below Grasse for the summer, where he would visit them on weekends, squiring his elegant mistress, Clothilde, around the hotspots of Paris during the week. He sounded rich. And fun. And exciting. He sounded like everything my dad wasn't, and I just felt . . . sick. I understood why my mother took off, but I wished I didn't. I remember wishing I'd just left well alone. It was information I didn't want to have."

"Did you talk to either of them about it?"

"How could I? I wanted to protect my father, and my mother would have flown into one of her rages. I was terrified of her; I would never have dared confront her."

"Didn't you just hate her?"

"I did, but I hated her before that. And I loved her too." She sighs. "I was so torn with all these different feelings. Mostly, I think, I wanted her to love me. I'm not sure my mother has ever truly been capable of love. She can love on a superficial basis, if you're beautiful, and clever, and a perfect reflection of her, but show any independence, contradict her in any way, and her love swiftly turns to hate."

"Not really hate, surely?" Angie is shocked.

"Oh yes. She has told me she hates me as often as she has told me she loves me. Possibly more. I spent my childhood wanting her to love me, trying so hard just for her to love me."

"God, Sylvie. That's horrible."

"It sounds horrible, but it was what it was. I didn't know any different."

"So . . . what happened to Felipe?"

"This went on every year for the next twenty years. When Felipe died, my mother flew to Paris to pay her respects to his wife and children. Can you imagine? They knew! Apparently it was an open secret. His wife, Odile, had made it quite clear to him that they didn't do divorce in her family; he could do what he wanted as long as he never embarrassed her."

Angie shakes her head. "I knew those French were weird."

"It gets even weirder. After Felipe died, Odile and my mother became best friends! She'd still go to France every summer but she'd stay with Odile in Grasse. There were definitely affairs after that, but no one lasting. Isn't that the most bizarre thing you've ever heard?"

"What about your dad?"

"That's the horrible irony. My father finally dies, giving Clothilde the freedom she's always wanted, and months later she has the car accident and ends up disabled and in a home. Not a huge amount of choice among the men there."

"Well, no wonder she adores Mark," Angie says. "I'm surprised she never made a pass at him."

"Are you kidding? She did! She denied it, but you don't come to the door in a silk negligée when your son-in-law comes to visit, then make sure you bend over far lower than necessary while pouring him coffee."

"Ew. Old people's boobs. Thanks for that."

"My mother wasn't old people. Her boobs were done years ago and they were fantastic. But still, can you believe that? Actually, forget I asked that. Mark ran for the hills, terrified."

They both laugh.

"She still practically climbs on top of him, purring. She's always telling me I have to make more of an effort or he'll leave me for the better-looking woman down the road."

"Which better-looking woman down the road?" Angie perks up. "Me? Because I'll take him!"

"Get your hands off him!" Sylvie playfully slaps her hand. "I think it's the French mentality. She doesn't get that you don't have to dress in silk lingerie and have immaculate hair and full make-up in order to keep your man. In fact, Mark would hate me to look like that. You know my husband: he hates any kind of artifice. She refuses to believe that he can find me beautiful with no make-up and, as she puts it, 'shapeless hippy clothes'."

"I love your clothes!" protests Angie. "And you always look gorgeous."

"Thank you. My mother seems to think that it's not nearly gorgeous enough, and that Mark's about to do a Bill, or at the very least leave me for some hot young woman in a miniskirt and heels."

"You don't think that." Angie is about to laugh, until she notices an expression in Sylvie's eyes. She leans forward, frowning. "Do you?"

Sylvie shrugs. "Not really. But . . . sometimes I wonder what he gets up to when he's not here. Let's face it, it's not as if he wouldn't have the opportunity. Why wouldn't he have a girl in every port? Then I wonder if my mother's right and I should be making more of an effort. Maybe I have competition. Maybe I should be the one buying the red lace underwear."

"He'd think you were having an affair," Angie teases. "Not to mention that Mark loves you and he wouldn't do that to you. Furthermore," she continues, "if he was, I'd have his balls for breakfast. Just so you know. But he isn't. No way in hell."

Sylvie, finally, smiles. "I love you," she says, reaching over to hug Angie. "You always make me feel better."

"I didn't say it to make you feel better," Angie whispers in her ear. "I said it because it's true."

CHAPTER
ELEVEN

Sylvie

The air is completely still, the sunshine warm, as Sylvie kneels in the vegetable garden, pulling out weeds with gloved hands. Happy to listen to the birds as she works, she sits back on her haunches after a while, pulling off the gloves and surveying her work with deep satisfaction.

Years ago she lived near the centre of La Jolla, right on the street, her next-door neighbours almost touching on either side. At that time, she loved being surrounded by people, welcomed the constant movement, the ease of running into town to pick up supplies, pushing Eve in a buggy and bumping into so many friends.

The older she has grown, the more she has become like her father, coming to love the quiet, to appreciate a peaceful life. She had always thought her father loved it for balancing out the whirlwind of her mother, but now she knows it is genetic; it was part of his make-up, just as it is of hers.

She checks her watch. It is far later than she thought and Mark hasn't packed yet. Where is he? She is about to go inside for her phone when she hears the distant hum of his car.

He pulls into the driveway and climbs out of the car, waving and shouting over to her, "I'm late." He moves towards the back door. "Have to run into the shower."

"What happened?" Sylvie yells back. "Where've you been?"

"Got caught up in a conference call. Didn't realize the time." He disappears inside.

While Mark is in the shower, Sylvie gathers his clean clothes from the laundry room, passing Eve's door as she takes them upstairs.

She knocks and opens the door, listening for a second, frowning as she hears what sound like retching noises from the bathroom.

"Eve?" She puts down the basket. "Eve? Are you okay?" She pushes the bathroom door open to find Eve on her knees, vomiting into the toilet bowl. "Oh love!" Sylvie pulls Eve's hair out of her face, rubs her back until her stomach stops heaving, presses a hand to her clammy forehead.

"You're not well," says Sylvie, unable to get a read on her temperature. Eve feels cold and clammy rather than hot. "Do you want me to bring you some tea? Or some crackers, maybe?"

"I'm fine," Eve says. "Dad brought me some ice cream and I just overdid it. I ate the whole thing way too quickly and then felt completely sick. No fever." She gives a wobbly grin. "Don't worry."

"I love you." Sylvie bends down and kisses the top of her daughter's head.

"Brush your teeth," she adds. She slips out of the bedroom and into her own, a niggle of anxiety lodging firmly in her chest.

The doors to the balcony are open, sunlight pouring in. Sylvie can't resist stepping out for a moment and gazing down at the gravel courtyard below, where a small fig tree has replaced the giant one that had been cut down, much to Sylvie's horror, a few weeks before they moved in.

To the side of the house is a pergola, an old grapevine twisting up and over the beams, a clematis scrambling round the vine and covering it with large purple flowers.

Huge terracotta pots, mossy and old, hold large camellias, their glossy dark green leaves showing off the beauty of the white flowers. More pots are grouped together along the driveway, different sizes, all now a greenish-white, thanks to Sylvie sponging them religiously with live yoghurt to encourage the mould, all filled with varying sizes of lavender and santolina plants, boxwood balls.

A weathered bench, faded green cushions piled on either side, is on the balcony, and Sylvie sits down for a moment, closing her eyes in the warmth of the sunlight until she hears Mark shut off the water and walk into the bedroom.

"Hi, love," she says.

She puts her arms round him as he lowers his face to her neck, inhaling her smell.

"Do you really have to go?" Sylvie pulls away with a pout, hating how she sounds like the insecure wife she's always sworn not to be, a wife filled with resentment at being forced to live this fractured life. I won't be that woman, Sylvie vows. Not now, not ever. She forces the pout off her face.

"Hey," Mark whispers, gathering her in his arms, kissing the top of her head and holding her close. "You know it's not for ever."

Sylvie rests her head against his chest, smelling his unique smell — Tom Ford mixed with Mark — feeling the warmth of his skin through her shirt, acknowledging how safe she is in his arms. She wonders where this sadness comes from.

"I know," she murmurs. "I just loved being with you unexpectedly. I'm not ready to say goodbye so soon."

"Lovebug," he says, and holds her at arm's length to look into her eyes. "It's only seven days. There's a possibility I may be able to get back on Wednesday after the pitch. How's that? I don't like leaving either. Trust me, there's nothing I'd love more than to just stay here with you, but there are too many clients I need to visit."

"I know. I'm sure this is . . . oh, pre-menstrual or hormonal or something —"

"Honey," he interrupts, "you're the one who always says we have the perfect relationship, and whoever decided married couples had to live together twenty-four/seven was out of their minds."

"I do think that. At least, I did. I think so much of my acceptance of our independent marriage was also about protecting myself. It allowed me to hold a piece of myself back in case anything ever happened to you."

"Nothing's going to happen to me," he reassures gently.

She dismisses him impatiently. "I know, I know. That's not the point. The point is I wanted it in the beginning, and then I got used to it, but I'm in a different place now, and I want you to be at home more." It is the same conversation they have begun to have quite frequently, and Sylvie knows they will keep going round and round in circles until a change is made.

There is a silence before Mark sighs.

"I want to be at home more too," he says.

"So make it happen."

"It's not as easy as that. Sylvie, why are we having this conversation now when I'm leaving?" The frustration in his voice is clear. "Why are we having this conversation again?"

"Because it doesn't just go away if we don't talk about it," Sylvie snaps. "You're the one with the power to change it, and it doesn't make any sense to me why you don't take on a head of sales to do all the travelling. I'm starting to think you don't want to be at home more."

"Now you're being ridiculous." Mark forces a patient tone. "You know the deal. You know it's only because I have such long-established relationships with the clients and they don't want to see anyone other than me. We've discussed it so many times; it's not something I can change. Not yet. I do hear you, and I want the same thing. I just have to figure out how to transition. Sylvie, I love you more than anything. I will make this happen."

"Are you just saying that to appease me or will you actually do something?" she grumbles, allowing him to pull her close.

He sighs. "Sylvie, I will do something but it just may not happen in the timeframe you want."

"What does that mean? How long will it take? A year? Six months?"

"Within the year," he mumbles into her hair. "I'll figure it out within the year. Now stop being so grumpy and give me a proper kiss goodbye. I promise I'll be back earlier if I can."

CHAPTER
TWELVE

Sylvie

Eve shuffles sleepily downstairs, fleecy pyjama bottoms pooling round her pink fluffy slippers as she blearily sits down on a stool and yawns.

"Morning!" Sylvie smiles. "Sleep well?"

"Yes, but it's too early. It smells good in here. What is it?" Eve bends down, leaning her head on her arms before opening one eye to see a candle sitting in the middle of the counter, the only candle that has no imperfections on the surface, that will not require a second pour.

The only candle that is, by anyone's estimations, perfect.

Eve sits up. "Candles! Mom? Have you been up all night making candles? Because if you say yes, that's a serious problem."

"I won't say yes, then," Sylvie says lightly. "Tea?"

"Mom! I worry about you. You never sleep any more."

Sylvie laughs. "You worry about me? When you're wasting away to nothing?" She silently berates herself as the cloud passes over Eve's face. Damn. Why did she have to say anything? "I'm sorry. I didn't mean that.

But you don't need to worry about me. Apparently it's the curse of middle age. No one else sleeps either."

"O-kay. But they're not making candles and jewellery all night long." Eve stretches over to bring the candle closer, and her eyes widen with surprise. "Mom! You made this? It's perfect!"

Sylvie basks in her daughter's unfiltered praise. She and Eve had always been so close — Eve, the dream child — but these past few months, as the pounds have dropped from Eve's frame, she is often the surly teenager Sylvie never dreamed she would have.

Sylvie never knows what Eve's mood will be, hating how much she lets it affect her own life. When Eve is happy and content, Sylvie feels as if she is bathing in sunlight, but the mere hint of a scowl throws Sylvie into a well of anxiety.

She knows this pattern well. She has lived it for years, although previously Clothilde was the only one to control her moods. Detach with love, she tells herself, repeating the words like a mantra, knowing the only way to retain her sanity is to not let the moods of others affect her own.

Detach with love. Detach with love. Detach with love.

Eve inhales the scent of the candle again. "What's the smell? I love it. It kind of smells like your perfume."

"That's the tuberose. But it's mostly fig. I'm hoping your grandmother will prefer it to the ones she always makes me buy. It will save me a fortune."

Eve shoots her mother a look of disbelief. "Even if she loves it she'd never tell you. Or she'll wait until someone compliments the smell and reluctantly confess you made it, but only after informing them that you clearly inherited her wonderful nose for perfume."

Sylvie bursts out laughing. "Darling daughter, that is exactly what she'll do. How do you know so much?"

Eve shrugs. "I heard you describe her as narcissistic once upon a time. I had no idea what it meant so I looked it up."

Sylvie cocks her head with a smile "And you discovered she's self-obsessed?"

"Um . . . you could say that." She grins.

"She's still your grandmother, though. She still loves you — well, she loves in the only way she knows how to love. You really should go to see her more."

Eve groans. Resting against the table, her long hair flowing over a shoulder, knees pulled up, toes curling over the edge of her chair, she pulls a magazine towards her and starts idly flicking through.

Sylvie cracks two eggs into a bowl, adds a splash of water, then the heavy seasoning she learned from her mother.

Having placed a large knob of butter in the pan, Sylvie waits until the butter is sizzling hot, almost brown, before quickly whisking the eggs in the pan, swirling them with the back of her fork and bringing them together off the heat. A minute later she slides a perfectly folded omelette onto a plate, putting it in front of Eve.

Eve hesitates. Sylvie watches carefully, expecting Eve to say she isn't hungry, but she picks up the fork and takes a bite, groaning with pleasure, and Sylvie is finally able to relax, but she is unable to take her eyes off this almost-woman, so recently a little girl.

Look at her legs, long and lithe. Those feet with long, skinny toes, one calf now resting on the other knee, the ankle moving in a lazy circle as she continues to eat, turning the pages.

"I know you're staring," Eve says eventually. "And yes, I know. You grew me. In your stomach. No, I can't believe it either." And this time she looks over her shoulder, catches her mother's eye, and they both smile, for it is indeed what Sylvie was thinking, always thinks, when she is overcome with a wave of love for her daughter.

Sylvie marvels at her all the time. How did she, who never knew what it was to be comfortable in her skin, produce this beautiful, confident, wise child? Where did she come from? How could they possibly share the same genes? Even though Eve is going through a phase now where she isn't as confident, isn't as sunny, Sylvie recognizes this is not her true nature; since the day she emerged, Eve has always been filled with joy.

Closing the magazine, Eve stands and stretches, ready to go and get dressed for school, before glancing over again at her mother.

"Uh-oh!" Eve backs away slowly, shaking her head, her hands stretched in front of her as if to stop an advancing invasion. "It's coming, isn't it? You're in the middle. It's a big one, right? Do I need to get out of —"

"Yes!" Sylvie exclaims, darting forward to grab Eve, squeezing her tight, covering her head and cheeks with kisses as Eve squirms, giggling. "It's the Wave of Love!

I'm sorry. I can't help it. I just love you sooooooooo much." Eve pretends to try to push her mother away, but both of them know she loves it.

Mark started doing this to Eve when she was little, and Eve, always collapsing in giggles as he scooped her up and covered her in kisses, basked in being truly loved by the only father she would ever know.

When Sylvie finally lets her daughter go, Eve steps back with a frown.

"Mom? What is it? Why are you crying?"

"It's not crying." Sylvie wipes the tears away, still smiling. "I was just thinking how much like your father you are. You're such a good person. I'm happy. I just wish he could see you. I wish he could have known you."

"He knows me," Eve says, matter-of-factly. "I talk to him all the time."

"You do? Still?"

"Of course!" Eve shrugs, as if it were the most natural thing in the world. "Especially at night. We have long conversations."

Sylvie just looks at her until Eve starts to laugh. "Before you ask, no, he doesn't talk back. I'm not certifiable, Mom. He's dead."

Sylvie attempts a smile.

"I'm sorry, Mom. I was trying to be funny. Do you . . . still think about him?"

Taking a deep breath, Sylvie says, "I do, but it's not painful in the way it was. I think about him a lot, and now it feels good. I feel so incredibly lucky to have had him in my life for the short time I did, and of course he gave me you."

"Were you more in love with him than with Papa?" Eve is looking at her with curiosity, as Sylvie blinks. She isn't ready for these questions Eve has started lobbing at her, hasn't prepared the answers, doesn't know the right way to respond.

"Don't say it was different," Eve warns. "Because that's not an answer."

"But it was different," Sylvie insists. "We were so young; so in love. There is something magical about young love, when you still think the world is your oyster and you have your whole life ahead of you."

"So did you love him more?"

"More than what?"

"More than Papa?"

"I loved him differently," Sylvie says. "There isn't another way to explain it." She looks at her watch and squeals. "Eve! You have to get dressed! Oh, and this afternoon you're going to see Grandmère, like it or not."

"No," Eve groans, as Sylvie frogmarches her out of the kitchen. "Please. Anything but that."

"You never know, you might get lucky. She may have another vintage Chanel jacket lying around for you." Sylvie shakes her head with a smile as Eve happily says she'll go.

CHAPTER
THIRTEEN

Eve

Eve waits in line at the checkout, unable to meet anyone's eye, filled with shame at what she is buying, convinced everyone knows what she is planning to do.

She has tried so hard to resist. Has done four days of lemon water, but all she has thought about is food, sugary, crunchy, sweet food, and today, when she was leaving school, she knew she couldn't hold out any longer.

She was supposed to be hanging out with Claudia and a bunch of kids, but she said she had to go to see her grandmother. Instead she went to the 7-Eleven, the place she was least likely to run into anyone she knew, and eagerly filled her basket with junk food, doughnuts, salivating at the thought, barely able to wait to tear off the wrappers, not thinking about anything other than getting the food into her stomach as fast as possible.

It is like this all the time now. She is either fasting, or bingeing before making herself throw up. All she thinks about, all the time, is food. What she has eaten, what she hasn't eaten, what she is going to eat; whether she has been good, or bad; whether this makes her a good person, or a bad one.

She has no time to feel happy, to feel included, to feel truly alive. What once was a drive for success, to get the best grades, to do better at school, has become a drive to lose the most weight, to be as thin as she can be.

She sets herself goals in her head, knowing that the goal will never be quite enough. Each goal she has reached, hasn't felt right.

Eve can't eat in public. She drives out to Marian Bear Park, finds a quiet spot in the corner of the car park where no one can see her, then slinks down in her seat and grabs the first of the grocery bags, pulling out a packet of doughnuts, stuffing them into her mouth.

Something inside her calms down. Even as her outside movements are frantic, tearing at the wrappers, grabbing the food, swallowing without tasting, inside a peace descends as she eats. For those moments she is eating, she feels nothing. Stuffing the food brings her a particular kind of numbness that she has mistakenly likened to peace.

Fast, faster, slower, slow, grinding to a halt as the nausea builds. She sits back, disgusted, ashamed, methodically gathering the empty wrappers, tying them in the plastic bag, climbing out of the car and dropping the bag in a trash can on the way to the public bathroom, where all evidence of the last half-hour will be entirely purged.

She doesn't get straight back in the car today. She sets off down one of the dusty trails, climbing up a small grassy hill, settling down at the top, her arms round her knees.

"Hey, Dad," she whispers, looking up at the sky, the pale puffs of clouds moving across it. Talking to her dad never feels strange. She doesn't remember Jonathan, but she is deeply comforted by knowing she can talk to him, about anything, about things she would never say to anyone else. "Dad, I think I'm in pretty bad shape. I'm not quite sure what I'm doing here, but I can't stop and I can't do anything about it. I keep thinking that at some point it's going to be okay, at some point I'll have to reach a point where I'll be happy, because what's the alternative?" Tears run down her cheeks as she whispers.

"I can't talk to anyone about it," she says. "Only you. But I need you to look after me, okay? I need you to show me what to do." Eve watches the clouds for a few seconds, then raises her head, looking around, waiting to see if something will happen, a branch falling, some kind of sign that her father has heard; but, as always, nothing.

Which doesn't mean he isn't listening. Sighing, she slowly eases herself up with a groan — even sitting on the ground hurts these days, with nothing to protect her joints — and heads back to the safety of chewing gum and the car.

CHAPTER
FOURTEEN

Sylvie

The foyer, with its swirly patterned carpets, whose ugliness is outweighed by their practicality, its huge plastic ficus trees in ceramic pots, and the pastel watercolours of beach scenes hung on the walls in a bid to inject some sunshine, is nothing if not depressing.

Each time Sylvie walks through she feels a cloud of depression descend, lifting only when she enters the atrium, the one room in the home that is walled in glass. Filled with sunlight, it is a room that is truly lovely.

Wherever Clothilde is to be found, Sylvie tries to entice her to the atrium for tea.

She never knows what mood Clothilde will be in, whether she will want to gather friends around her as she charms and disarms, or sit scowling in a dark corner of a depressing lounge, making loud, rude comments about everyone who passes.

Always self-absorbed, before the accident Clothilde was so busy, so social, she was able to reserve her harshest behaviour for her family.

No one is safe from it now. Her friends dropped away, paying only the occasional guilt visit — which gives Clothilde the opportunity to throw thinly disguised barbs about how she has been abandoned, how appalling it is that her so-called friends are so selfish they cannot even come to see her once a week.

As her bitterness has grown, the only person she has to take it out on, other than the nurses, is Sylvie.

As Sylvie turns towards the elevators, she stops. In the corner, their backs towards Sylvie, are two people: a man with thin wisps of white hair, his cane resting against the table, and next to him, entertaining him with her stories as he looks on, Clothilde.

"Mom?" Sylvie bends down and kisses her mother on both cheeks, as her mother stares up at her, almost dazed. "You look beautiful. I'm so happy to find you downstairs."

"I do get out of bed from time to time," Clothilde says. "I have friends to see and things to do. I'm not quite the cabbage you think I am." She rolls her eyes at her friend with a laugh.

"That's not what I think, Mom. I'm glad."

The man stands up awkwardly, wobbling slightly as he reaches his feet. "I'll let you ladies spend some time together," he says.

Sylvie instinctively puts out a hand to help steady him, her mother tutting derisively. "He's fine, Sylvie. Don't patronize him by trying to help."

"I wasn't."

"She wasn't," the man reassures Clothilde, who just sucks her teeth and looks away. "Shall we have tea together today?"

Clothilde then smiles in her most seductive manner. "That would be lovely," she murmurs.

"Charles Fielding," the man says, extending a hand to Sylvie. "A pleasure to meet you. Your mother has told me wonderful things about you."

Sylvie knows this is unlikely, but she merely nods as he leaves them alone.

"You have an admirer!" she teases lightly, sitting in the seat Charles Fielding has just vacated, but her mother scowls.

"Yes. And he's very nice, so don't you start getting any ideas. I saw the way you smiled at him." From anyone else, Sylvie would know this was a joke, but not from her mother.

"Mom! He's old enough to be my grandfather. Not to mention the fact that I'm happily married."

"Still. Being happily married never stopped anyone before." She narrows her eyes at Sylvie. "You stay away from Charles."

Sylvie sighs. "Sure, Mom. He's all yours. Oh! I brought something for you." Sylvie digs into the bag and brings out the candle, now wrapped in brown paper and cellophane, tied with a raffia bow. She proudly hands it to Clothilde, who frowns as she turns it over in her hands.

"What is it? *La confiture?* Jam?"

"No. It's a candle. I thought you might like to try something other than the Diptyque."

Sylvie watches her mother attempt to unwrap the raffia. Any offers of help will be rebuffed, even though she is struggling. Eventually she lifts up the candle and bites through the cellophane, tearing it off with her teeth, then, with the large wad of cellophane still in her teeth, she catches Sylvie's eye and, curling her good hand like a claw, she growls, unexpectedly, like a tiger, before letting the cellophane fall from her mouth, laughing as she sees Sylvie's shocked expression.

"Let the crazy old lady have a little fun!" Clothilde winks before bringing the candle up to her nose, closing her eyes to inhale deeply before letting out a small murmur of pleasure. "*La figue* —" she nods approvingly — "*et tuberose*. And amber! This is nice. I like this."

A warm glow of pleasure floods Sylvie. Even after all these years, after all the therapy that helps her think she has detached from her mother, this joy at having done something right, having done something to please her mother, takes her straight back to childhood. This cord will never be cut.

Her mother is now reading the label. Sylvie sits motionless, itching to tell her mother, but wanting her mother to figure it out, waiting to see her mother's delight when she realizes.

"'By Sylvie'?" her mother asks. "How funny. What a coincidence. Where did you find it?"

"I didn't," bursts out Sylvie. "I made it."

"Made it? What do you mean?"

"I made the candle. As in, I melted the wax, mixed the fragrance, poured it. Remember the candle-wrapping class we did here? I was quizzing the instructor about how to do it. I wanted to make you a scented candle that you would really love. I know you

106

love fig, and your favourite perfume is tuberose, so I came up with this myself." She forces herself to stop, to sit back, for her voice is bubbling with excitement as she waits for her mother's appreciation.

Clothilde gazes at Sylvie, her initial confusion having given way to blankness. She dips her eyes back down to the candle. Saying nothing.

The smile slides off Sylvie's face as she turns her head slightly to stare deliberately out of the window, silently berating herself for trying to do something nice, for being so naive as to think she could do something to make her mother happy.

Picking up the candle Clothilde smells it again.

"It's really very nice," she murmurs. "It smells good and it's pretty. Well done."

Sylvie just stares. Is she hearing what she thinks she's hearing?

"Dreadful name, though." Clothilde inspects the label. "You can do much better. I was always very creative. I'm sure I can come up with something clever. You remember that advertising campaign for the soap? You know that was all me? We were at a dinner for the CEO of . . ."

As she talks, Sylvie drifts off, her mother's compliments reverberating in her head, mixed in with the voice of Sally Field: She likes it, she really, really likes it.

She is brought back to earth with a bump.

"So where is that husband of yours?" Clothilde asks. "He hasn't been to see me for far too long. I'm going to phone him and demand he come to see me."

Sylvie, relieved Clothilde will deal with it directly, says nothing.

"Is he travelling again?"

"Yes. You know how it is. Always on the road."

"Oh yes, I know how it is. A different town, no wife, no children. He's out there having fun. You need to seduce him back home."

"Mom! Are you implying Mark's out partying? With other women? Because that's just ridiculous."

"Ridiculous? For a handsome, young, virile man like Mark? Men can't survive without sex, and if he's not getting it from you, he's getting it from someone else."

"We have a perfectly wonderful sex life, thank you." Sylvie tries to laugh.

"I'm sure you do. But he's not getting it from you enough because he's never with you. How much do you see him? A week a month? Don't be stupid, Sylvie. You need to start making him want to be at home."

"It's not a week a month," Sylvie says furiously, mentally working it out in her head. Surely it's not a week a month. It's always been roughly two weeks a month, half here, half in the New York office or on the road. But, apart from his surprise visit this past weekend, he has been here less of late.

The palpitations start again. Could her mother be right? Could her mother be right?

CHAPTER
FIFTEEN

Sylvie

It has never occurred to Sylvie to check Mark's email. She is not, or has not been, insecure enough to feel she has to delve into her husband's life. There have, of course, been occasions when she has called him and has heard a woman's voice in the background, but, as she well knows, half his colleagues are women. Part of his company's policy is to engender a close team by constant, fun, extra-curricular activities.

Has she, as her mother seems to think, been naive? Should she do the unthinkable and snoop? She is terrified, yet increasingly compelled to do so.

Her brain is firing. First with fear of the possibility being true, then a calmer voice talks her down, telling her how unlikely it is. This is Mark. This isn't Bill. This isn't a man who is flirtatious, a little too tactile with the women in the neighbourhood, a touch too familiar when they've had a glass too many at a party.

Not Mark. Even when so-called friends attempt to flirt with him, shoot him seductive glances, lean in a little too close at a wine-tasting soirée, Sylvie sees him smile then excuse himself, his eyes frantically searching over the heads for his wife to come and rescue him.

They always laugh about it later, Mark unaware that anyone was flirting, insisting women were just being friendly, Sylvie teasing him about his new "girlfriend", able to tease because Mark isn't like that; he has never given her any indication he is interested in anyone but her.

The shrill ring of the phone interrupts her thoughts. Glancing down, she sees it's Angie, and she pulls over to the side of the road to pick up.

"So I just left yoga, and the latest on Caroline and Bill is she's definitely leaving town. House is going on the market tomorrow. Bill told Rob he was having affairs because Caroline hates sex. No surprise there, then."

"True," murmurs Sylvie. "I can't imagine Caroline getting down and dirty with anyone. Least of all Bill. Even though he is rather . . . large."

Angie barks with laughter. "What are you doing? Come over. I've got a million cupcakes left over from the library meeting. If you don't come and stop me, I may have put on three hundred pounds by the end of today."

Sylvie checks her watch. "I have to be home in five minutes. The guy's coming to fix the dishwasher, and I have to make sure Eve goes to visit her grandmother today. Come to me instead. And bring the cupcakes."

Pushing the back door open, Sylvie walks into a quiet kitchen. The only evidence that Eve is at home is a trail of teenage belongings, rather like the breadcrumbs left by Hansel and Gretel, that eventually will surely lead to Eve.

A backpack dumped in the middle of the floor outside the kitchen, a binder in the doorway, a felt hat on the kitchen table. A carton of milk on the kitchen counter, the cookie jar not in its usual place on the shelf.

"Eve?" Sylvie puts her bag down, pausing only to pick up one of the candles to smell it, still amazed that she managed to create this wonderful fragrance. "Are you here?"

She moves through the house, collecting Eve's stuff as she does so, finally finding her in the office, her hand in the cookie jar resting on her lap as she gazes fixedly at the screen. Suddenly Eve bursts out into laughter.

"You jerk!" Eve grins at the screen, realizing at that moment that Sylvie is in the room. "Oh hey, Mom!" She pushes the cookie jar down, attempting to hide it, embarrassed.

"Caught you!" Sylvie says, as Eve blushes.

"Guilty as charged." Eve tries to laugh, although she looks ashamed. "Say hi to my mom," she says to the screen, swivelling it round. "Mom? This is Olivia? She's in New York?"

Sylvie waves at the tiny picture of the pretty teenager, wishing Eve would stop with this upspeak she's noticing in everyone, all their sentences going up at the end as if they are asking a question.

"Hi, Eve's mom!" Olivia waves back. "Wow! You're so pretty! And so young!"

Sylvie shakes her head and laughs. "Your screen must be soft focus, or you've been taking some lessons at charm school."

"She totally has!" Eve drapes an arm round her mother's neck so they are both on screen together. "Isn't she cute?"

She looks at her mother affectionately as Sylvie makes a face at her. "I'm your mother, not a kitten."

Eve pouts. "I know, but you are cute. Isn't she cute?" She looks at Olivia, who nods and gives a thumbs up.

"Okay," Sylvie says as she disengages and turns to Eve. "You want something. What do you want?"

"Well . . ." Eve starts, but then Sylvie remembers what she needs to do.

"You know what? I need to use the computer in here. Can you give me five minutes? Is that okay?"

"Then will you say yes to whatever I'm about to ask you?"

"Then I'll say maybe and I'll definitely think about it. How's that?"

"Good enough." Eve tells Olivia she'll be back soon, and skips out of the room.

Sylvie takes a deep breath as she clicks Outlook open. She is breaking the rules. Snooping means you will find things you don't want to know about, and you won't be able to request an explanation without revealing you have been snooping, which, as everyone knows, is the lowest of the low.

First the Inbox. She scrolls down, looking for women's names, looking for addresses that don't make sense, that could be masking a secret liaison. She finds two addresses that seem ominous, which turn out to be merely from executive assistants at other companies and entirely innocent.

There are numerous mailboxes. Sylvie moves down the list, clicking each one open, finally growing bored with reading sales figures, projections, inventory lists.

There is no evidence whatsoever, but a slight disquiet remains, a fear that her mother may be right, but she has to ignore it, for her mother is not the woman she once was, and her instincts, though once sharp, are not what they were.

Eve appears in the doorway. "Are you done yet?"

Sylvie nods. "Who's Olivia, by the way? She seems nice."

"She is. Really nice. She's a friend of Claudia's from camp. We met on Facebook."

Sylvie gives her a hard look. "Make sure your father doesn't find out. If he knew you were becoming friends with strangers on Facebook he'd go nuts. Is it safe for you to use this computer?"

"Course it is — I like using it because of the big screen. And she's not a stranger, Mom. She's a friend of Claudia's. Anyway, you just met her. Isn't she so nice?"

"She is. She seems adorable. Just make sure —"

"Yes, yes, I know. But can I just tell you? She has this ridiculously awesome apartment in New York, and she's really mature and sensible. And . . . she's going to Columbia." Eve gives her mother a stare.

"And your point?"

113

"That's where I should be going. Columbia. Or NYU. The schools on the east coast attract really great people. I really do want to look at NYU again. Please will you talk to Dad? Please?"

"I'll try again but I can't promise anything," sighs Sylvie. "You know how stubborn he can be."

"When I'm eighteen I can make my own choice," Eve states defiantly.

"You can, but who's going to pay for it?"

"I'll get a job."

"You'll need ten jobs to pay for it. Let me talk to him some more. I know you need to make a decision very soon."

They both turn at the sound of gravel crunching outside, then watch as Angie's vintage blue bug swings up to the house and Angie and Claudia climb out of the car.

Sylvie and Eve go to meet them, Sylvie trying to put those earlier, unsettling thoughts out of her mind.

CHAPTER
SIXTEEN

Sylvie

Angie moans as she licks her fingers, savouring every last dollop of icing she can find.

"Sometimes," she announces, leaning back satisfied, "there's just nothing like a cupcake to make a girl happy."

"Or three to make a girl delirious with joy." Sylvie grins.

"Was it just three?" Angie says. "I'm sure I had three and a half. As yummy as they were, I have a horrible feeling I may suffer later."

Sylvie's smile disappears. "That's something I wanted to talk to you about. I think I heard Eve vomiting the other day."

Angie sits up. "You mean purging? After food?"

Sylvie nods. "I passed the bathroom after she'd just eaten a ton of cookies. I'm pretty sure the noise I heard was of her vomiting it up."

"Was that the only time you've heard it?"

Sylvie shakes her head, explaining about the ice cream that Eve confessed to eating too fast.

"Does she leave the table right after the meal and go to the bathroom?" asks Angie.

Sylvie, having not noticed anything in particular, shakes her head again.

Angie sighs. "She is really thin and she's always bundled up in something. I binged and purged when I was modelling, but it wasn't as serious as it is for some people. As awful as it sounds to say it, I did it to stay thin for the work, not because I had a serious eating disorder."

"But you must have had an eating disorder. It isn't normal to make yourself throw up after eating."

Angie frowns. "I know that's true, but as soon as I stopped modelling, I stopped doing it. It never felt like a problem; I wasn't cold, or . . . furry, my teeth didn't turn black and fall out. Maybe I didn't do it enough. Or I just wasn't very good at it. I'm sorry, honey. I know you're looking to me for answers, but I really think you should take her to see someone."

"Does Claudia know anything?"

"She says Eve always has an excuse as to why she won't eat — she's just eaten, you've got a big meal planned — but she won't admit to having a problem, and Claudia doesn't want to push her."

Sylvie nods. "She freaked out last time I mentioned going to see someone. She's so moody lately I'm scared of doing anything to disturb the peace, even though I know we're probably reaching the point where we'll have no choice."

"Don't wait to reach that point," insists Angie. "You're so much better off intervening now before it's really serious, before she goes away to school. Has she accepted USC yet?"

116

"No. She still has it in her head she's going to NYU. For whatever reason, she's obsessed with New York. I think she thinks it's all *Gossip Girl*."

"That's my daughter's influence, I'm afraid. She's going this weekend and I'm just crossing my fingers they don't get into too much trouble. I spoke to the mother, and the kids are being chaperoned in their apartment during some party." She shrugs. "I just have to hope it's not going to be too wild. When I think New York and partying, I'm remembering Studio 54 and lines of white powder."

"Oh, the good old days," Sylvie says, laughing.

"You got it. And I was truly a kid from nowhere. I had no clue. She's a different child. She's going to be fine."

"Who's going to be fine?" The girls suddenly appear on the porch, their movement through the house silenced by their socked feet.

Angie just nods her head sagely, as the girls roll their eyes then move automatically to the large cake box on the table, like bees to honey.

"We need to ask you something," Eve says, pulling her friend's attention away from the cake box. "Claudia's going to New York this weekend for Olivia's party, and Claudia and Olivia both think I should be there too. Before you say no," she rushes on, "I know what Dad would say but he's not even here this weekend so he wouldn't have to know. And it's much safer for Claudia if we're together, and then I could actually visit NYU as well. Please say I can go. Pleeeeeaaassseeee."

The two girls are almost bouncing with eagerness and Sylvie, feeling somewhat ambushed, looks at Angie for help.

Angie grimaces back. "Are you asking for my opinion?"

Sylvie nods, but Angie shrugs apologetically. "I think it's a good idea. Eve should see NYU. Claudia's already been so she can show her round. Selfishly, I'd be far more comfortable if Claudia was flying with someone else, even though I know that's not exactly relevant."

"Yes!" squeal the girls.

"Hold on," Sylvie warns. "I haven't said yes. I think it's lovely that she's invited you, but I'm not sure how I feel about you being in New York by yourself, with people I don't know."

"You should call Olivia's mom, Mrs Adamson, and talk to her," Claudia offers quickly. "She's really nice and she's planning stuff for the out-of-towners."

Angie frowns at her daughter. "How many out-of-towners are there? I thought this was a small party in the apartment."

"It is! But four girls from camp are going, and some of us aren't from New York, so her mom's taking us to see *Wicked*!"

Sylvie looks at Eve. "You wouldn't feel out of place with all these kids you don't know?"

"I do know them, Mom," says Eve. "We're on iChat and Facebook all the time. They've become really good friends of mine."

"Let me think about it." Sylvie needs time to consider this. "I'll get the details from Angie and I'll think about it. I also have to talk to your father about it."

"No, Mom!" Eve commands softly. "You can't. You know he'll say no, that New York's too dangerous. Please don't tell him. You can't."

Angie is surprised. "Mark thinks New York is dangerous? I thought he spends most of his work time there."

"That's the point," Sylvie says with a sigh. "He says he knows what it's really like. That's why he won't let Eve even consider NYU or Columbia."

"But that's ridiculous," Angie says. "Mark knows better than that."

"I know. It's this thing he has." Sylvie shrugs. "Completely irrational. But he would not be happy about Eve flying to New York —"

"First of all, he's not my dad," Eve interrupts.

This is something she rarely says, rarely thinks about; she uses it only when Mark is saying no to something she really wants. But Mark is the only father she has ever known, and certainly someone she always refers to as "Papa", other than when he is putting his foot down.

"He's my stepdad. I love him, Mom, but even you know how he can be totally illogical some of the time."

"Like the Facebook fear," Angie points out.

"And it isn't his decision to make." Eve is fortified by Angie's agreement. "I'm your daughter therefore you're the only person who gets to decide what I can and cannot do."

Sylvie sighs again. "What about when I say no, you can't buy that leather jacket, and you get Mark to buy it for you? Who gets to decide then? Then it's fine for Mark to step in and overrule me with his decision. It doesn't cut both ways, you know."

"That's different," Eve says. "That's a teenage girl exercising her daddy–daughter rights."

"Oh, he's back to being Daddy now?"

"Depends. Mom, even you have to agree he can be unreasonable."

"Eve, I can't hide this from him, and if he does say no, I can't overrule that. It's too huge. We're a team, a partnership. I can't go behind his back."

"I disagree," Angie interjects, immediately apologizing as Sylvie glares at her. "I'm sorry, but I do. It is your decision. If Mark had a rational explanation, that would be something else entirely, but he doesn't, so in this case you do have the right to overrule him."

"Exactly!" Eve smiles. "You don't have to ask him. He's not even here. Didn't you say he's away until next Wednesday? He doesn't ever have to know."

Sylvie is in a quandary. Having been brought up on such shaky ground, with so many secrets, the single most important requirement she has always had in relationships is honesty.

She has never lied, withheld, kept secrets. Until her mother sowed a seed of doubt in her mind, she has always trusted Mark implicitly. Yet she cannot deny Eve has a point. Mark does have these irrational views; there is also a steely refusal to discuss things he believes absolutely, even when his beliefs have nothing to back them up.

So she understands Eve's frustration, a frustration she sometimes shares.

But while she frequently talks about honesty being the foundation of trust, if she is absolutely truthful, hasn't she sometimes avoided revealing the whole truth?

Sylvie has known about Eve's secret Facebook account for years, but hasn't ever discussed it overtly with her.

Eve often leaves her laptop open, her Facebook home page proudly displayed. Sylvie would have to be blind not to have seen it, Eve stupid not to have realized, but both are complicit in their unspoken agreement to ignore it.

As long as Sylvie's feigned ignorance remains unchallenged, Mark need not know.

She is bemused by Mark's seemingly random bans, finds them tiring and ridiculous; she recognizes her daughter, always popular, will suffer by being banned from this website that has become so essential in the lives of teenagers.

But New York? How could she hide something so big from him? What would that say about their relationship? What, more importantly, would it do to their relationship? And is she prepared to find out?

CHAPTER
SEVENTEEN

Eve

Eve walks up the stairs, anxiety and hope mixing together in her stomach, praying her mother will find a way to say yes, to let her go to the one place she's always wanted to visit, the one place she has never been allowed to go.

Even now she holds out hope she'll be able to go to NYU. She knows it's the place for her; she sees herself striding through the streets of Manhattan, mixing with New York intellectuals, the likes of which she knows she won't find at UCLA.

She lies in bed fantasizing about her future life, refusing to acknowledge the fears that accompany those fantasies: being away from home, from all she knows, from all that is safe.

Her mother has always been her one safe place. Going to New York is something she feels she has to do, something she has to accomplish; it is the place she is supposed to be. And yet even thinking about leaving her mother makes her feel untethered, alone, vulnerable.

What a welcome distraction it has been, to focus on food, rather than on her anxiety. The more she thinks about food — what she's eaten, what she will eat, what she won't eat, what calories she has ingested — the less time there is to think about her vulnerability, her pain, and the better she feels.

Almost . . . high. Or numb. She isn't sure which, but it is infinitely preferable to feeling like a scared little girl, to feeling like her world is about to change, and not having any control over it. This is a feeling she knows she has had before, even though she can't remember the details of her father's death.

"Are you okay?" Claudia turns to her as they throw themselves down on the bed, the laptop in front of them, Claudia already tapping on the keyboard.

"I'm good," Eve nods. "Just nervous. Hopeful. Keeping everything crossed."

A pretty blonde girl appears, waves at them both and gives a big smile.

"I know who you are," she says to Eve. "I've seen millions of pictures of you on Claudia's Facebook."

"Eve, this is Grace," Claudia says. "Yes, this is Eve. I'm trying to get her to come this weekend," she explains to Grace. "We're working on her mom right now."

"Why would your mom not want you to come? What's the big deal?" the girl asks.

"It's not my mom," Eve clarifies. "It's my dad. He thinks New York is filled with rapists and murderers and no one gets out of there alive. And this, by the way, is despite the fact that he works there half the time."

"That's totally freaky," Grace says. "But I get it. My dad has this thing about California. He's convinced that the whole state's going to fall into a fault line and disappear in some ginormous earthquake or tsunami or something. He was there during an earthquake once, and he said it was terrifying and he won't risk his family going there, even though he's also been there a ton. But if your parents are freaked out about New York, you could always stay with me in Connecticut. I'm about forty-five minutes outside New York. Maybe he'd be okay with Connecticut."

Eve shrugs. "I think our safest bet is for him to know nothing."

"I so hope you come out here. By the way, my brother Chris saw some of those pictures and he thinks you're totally hot."

Claudia nudges Eve. "I hate you!" she teases. "Her brother's so hot!"

Eve blushes. "Really?"

"Really. He'd definitely be happy if you came and stayed out in Connecticut. He's going to be around later if you want to iChat with him . . ." She winks.

Eve laughs before groaning. "If my mom says no to this weekend, I think I might kill myself."

"She's not going to say no," Claudia says firmly. "My mom won't let her."

Downstairs, Angie looks at Sylvie. "So. What are you thinking?"

Sylvie sighs deeply. "I can't not tell Mark. I just couldn't be that dishonest."

"What if you asked forgiveness rather than permission?" Angie says. "We have more damned air miles than I know what to do with, so I'll book the flight with miles."

"I can't take your money!" Sylvie, horrified, shakes her head.

"First of all, you're not taking money. It's air miles. Second of all, you're my best friend so, yes, you can. Sylvie, there is no reason why Eve shouldn't go. She and Claudia are the most sensible girls in the grade, and they're best friends. Very soon the pair of them are going to be leaving, then that's it. You want her coming back, and you want her memories of home to be good. We all know this is one of Mark's crazy things, and as long as you tell him when she's en route, there's nothing he can do. So he might get angry. So what? He'll get over it."

"I know you're right," Sylvie sighs again. "It just feels . . . deceitful."

"Sylvie!" Angie berates, growing exasperated. "It isn't deceitful. It's fine. They need to go off and learn what it is to be a little bit independent, for God's sake. We've got girls who have no idea how to raise a little hell. The least we can do is send them away and pray someone forces drugs on them."

"Angie!" Sylvie admonishes, but she's laughing.

"You know I'm right, don't you?"

"No. But I think you might have persuaded me to pretend." Sylvie smiles, instantly feeling better. "I'll call Mark and ask him. If I can reach him, fine. If I can't, then I'll make the decision on my own."

"Good girl," Angie says.

★ ★ ★

Angie is the kind of woman other women ought to hate. At first glance they are inevitably threatened by her looks, her body, her height, but as soon as they meet her they are enveloped in her warm exuberance, her boisterous humour, her loyalty and kindness.

She is a study in contrasts, which is the reason, Simon always says, for the success of their marriage.

"She's like Sybil," he'll sigh, rolling his eyes but casting an affectionate glance at his wife. "You never know which Angie you're going to get."

Sylvie is fascinated by Angie's self-confidence, her comfort in her skin, her ability to set boundaries. At parties Angie is the life and soul, but should anyone make the mistake of overstepping the mark, or flirting just a touch too dangerously with the tall, stunning, redhead, she will politely and firmly shut them down.

She doesn't need to endure an attempted pick-up in order to feel beautiful. She doesn't need a stranger to tell her she's gorgeous in order to feel validated. She has been told those things all her life. They mean nothing.

What matters to Angie are her family, her friends. Loyalty. Trust. Having fun, and knowing when to draw the line. These are precisely the reasons why Sylvie loves her so much.

CHAPTER
EIGHTEEN

Eve

Eve and Claudia, shuffling through JFK, giggling with excitement at their prospective weekend, falter only when they get through customs and step into the Arrivals hall.

It is a multicoloured melting pot. Hordes of people, chattering in every language imaginable, lean over the barriers, in places five deep, waving and shrieking as they spy their long-lost relative. Glum-looking drivers stand dispiritedly holding boards or white pieces of paper on which are scribbled names, half-heartedly attempting to make a connection with every newly arrived passenger.

"Oh shit." Claudia grinds to a halt, the smile sliding off her face. "How are we supposed to find her among all these people? She's not answering her texts. Let's walk out and see if we can find her."

Eve's excitement is replaced with a familiar anxiety. This isn't what was supposed to happen. Of late she hasn't been good at dealing with change, particularly last-minute change. She likes things to be planned, likes to know what is expected, and any untoward circumstances bring up a sense of panic that can be hard to control.

"Are you okay?" Claudia looks at her friend, noting that something appears to be wrong. "What's the matter?"

"I'm okay," Eve lies, although she's not.

"Eve? This is going to be fine." Eve hears Claudia's reassurance, but she can't be reassured, not once she has set down this path.

She loves Claudia. Claudia is her best friend in the world, but Claudia doesn't understand any more what it's like to be Eve. How could Claudia understand when she has never lost anyone close to her, when she doesn't have to worry about her weight, even though she says she does, when her life runs so smoothly, even though she thinks it doesn't?

Eve can feel them drifting apart, and she wants things to be as they were, but they can't be when there are so many secrets Claudia doesn't know: the lies about food, the secret eating, and now the shame of purging — well, the mixed shame and relief, the numbness that comes with getting rid of everything inside.

"I just need to go to the bathroom," Eve says, and Claudia frowns. "My stomach's still a bit upset. I'll be right back. You call and find out what's going on."

She turns to go, rustling in her handbag once she is out of sight, dropping the empty laxative packet into the first empty trash can she passes.

"Oh my God!" Olivia's voice comes ringing down the phone. "I can't believe you're here! When did you get in?"

"About an hour ago," Claudia says. "We can't find your mom. Can you text her and tell her we're here? I'm really worried she left already."

There is a sharp intake of breath. "I'm so sorry. My mom had a last-minute meeting. I thought she was telling your mom you should get a cab."

"Er, no." Claudia attempts a laugh. "As far as I know she just told my mom she'd be picking us up from the airport. What do we do now?"

"Just jump in a cab and come over. You know the address, right? It's on Park but they're renovating the lobby so come to the side on sixty-ninth. I'm so excited! I can't believe you're here! We're going to have so much fun, and guess what?"

"What?"

"Remember Jackson? You thought he was cute when he was here a couple of weeks ago? On iChat? He's coming over later and he can't wait to meet you! He thought you were adorable!"

"Oh my God! He was so hot!" Claudia squeals and Eve laughs. "And what about Eve? Any other cute boys?"

"Just you wait," Olivia says, and laughs. "We are going to have a seriously good time. Get here as quickly as you can!" She rings off, leaving Eve and Claudia looking at each other blankly.

"Cabs?" Claudia asks.

Eve looks round, finally grabbing Claudia's arm and leading her purposefully towards the Taxi sign.

CHAPTER
NINETEEN

Eve

Eve, so outgoing and confident in so many situations, finds herself overawed by the splendour of this world. She has never thought of herself as insecure, has never had the experience of feeling intimidated, but the world from which she comes is small, and familiar, and comfortable.

This — this quiet elegance, with a uniformed doorman holding the door open for them — is as alien to her as another planet.

This mahogany-lined foyer with its glistening crystal chandeliers, vases of heady lilac, crinkly tulips and springy curly willow on every polished table top — this is like nothing Eve has ever experienced.

The opulence of the people who live here astonishes her, the tiny women in fur coats, women whose faces are taut and shiny, their lips large and glossy, the only sign of their advanced age being their stoop and slow, unsteady walk.

The doorman rings Olivia for her approval, as the girls stand wide-eyed before him.

"John!" barks a muffled voice behind them. "John! Get the door!"

Another plastic old lady, her sour expression mostly hidden by huge black sunglasses despite the sun having set hours before, bangs on the glass with her clutch, as three miniature dachshunds scratch at the door.

The doorman drops the phone and runs to hold the door, taking the woman's shopping bags as she sails past without a thank you.

"Take the dogs upstairs," she barks, unbuttoning her coat.

Claudia bends down and holds out a hand for the dogs to sniff.

"Aw. They're so cute!" she coos, looking up at the woman. "How old are they?"

The woman says nothing, just continues unbuttoning her coat as Claudia catches Eve's eye. Did she not hear?

"Um? I asked how old your dogs are?" Claudia tries again.

The woman stops, looks directly at Claudia, appraisingly, and almost opens her mouth as if she is about to say something, then she pulls the leash, saying, "Come!" before disappearing slowly round the corner.

"Did that just happen?" Claudia, beet red, turns to Eve. "Did I say something wrong?"

The doorman makes a face then leans over, dropping his voice to a whisper. "She's one of the meanest people in the building. Don't take it personally. She's horrible to everyone. I'm sorry. Let me get back to phoning Miss Adamson now."

Seconds later they are being shown to the elevator, the doorman drawing two packets of M&Ms out of his pocket and pressing them into their hands with a wink as the elevator doors slide silently closed.

Claudia looks at Eve, her mouth dropping open. "Is this for real?"

Eve shakes her head firmly. "No. It's not. We were joking about it being like *Gossip Girl* but it is! Except it's kind of awful. I have no idea how we got here, but I'm pretty sure I want to get out. Claudia, did you not realize that Olivia must be shockingly rich?"

Claudia looks puzzled, before explaining that you couldn't tell anything about anyone at camp. They all wore uniforms, no jewellery was allowed, and they spent their time going out in canoes and putting on plays.

"But surely you could tell?" Eve asks.

"Eve, we were so young. And it wasn't a rich-kid camp — that was the whole thing. There are other camps that are like country clubs, but you've seen the pictures. This was as basic as it gets. We didn't even have electricity!"

"I guess I just didn't expect you to be this surprised."

"I guess I didn't expect her to be so rich."

"Maybe the apartment's normal?" Eve says doubtfully. "Maybe all the money went into the foyer."

"Right," Claudia says sarcastically and Eve shoves her, just as the elevator whispers to a halt and the doors slide open, not into a corridor, or hallway, but directly into a private foyer.

"Very normal," Eve whispers, taking in the faded Persian rug over rich parquet flooring, the books and orchids anchoring a round walnut table in the centre of the room, brass picture lights illuminating vast abstracts, including, recognizably, some of the greats.

Determined to take it all in her stride, she nonetheless can't help but walk over to a beautiful study of a group of women. Looking closely, she is not surprised to see Picasso's signature in the far right corner, but her respectful appreciation is broken suddenly by a shout of excitement as a blur of white comes barrelling into the foyer.

"Clauds!" Wrapped in white cashmere, blonde hair flying, Olivia flings her arms round Claudia, both of them spinning in circles and jumping up and down.

Other girls follow, two of them doing the same thing, the rest, Eve included, standing back awkwardly as the four girls squeal excitedly, pausing only to talk at the same time. Then everyone stops and laughs, Olivia finally blinking and wiping a tear from her eye.

"You made me cry!" She laughs. "I'm so happy, I'm crying! Girls?" She turns to the girls standing apart. "This is Clauds! I can't believe we're all together again! Oh my God! I'm so rude! Eve! You're even prettier in real life! And you're so skinny! I'm so jealous!" And with no awkwardness whatsoever Olivia gives Eve a big hug, setting all her anxieties to rest.

By the time the introductions have been made all round, Eve thinks she's going to be absolutely fine.

"Where is your mom?" Eve pauses in the doorway of the den as the others squeeze past her, collapsing back on the huge sectional, *The Notebook* playing on the giant flat-screen TV above the fireplace, bowls of

133

popcorn and candy wrappers littering the antique Indian coffee table. "We should go and say hi to her, shouldn't we?"

"We might see her later," Olivia says. "I think she's out. She had some meeting earlier, but I don't know if she got home yet. Don't worry about it. She's cool."

"Eve, right?" A tall blonde girl appears in the doorway: Grace, the girl from the iChat the other night. She is even more gorgeous in the flesh — freckles dusted over her nose in a perfect sprinkle, the perfect touch of sexy huskiness to her voice, athletic bronzed legs that go on for ever — but there is an openness and friendliness to her that is instantly appealing. "I'm so happy you came!" She gives Eve a hug, whispering in her ear, "Now we just have to figure out how to get you together with my brother!"

Eve blushes and grins, knowing she and Grace will be friends.

"I am so glad your mom let you come," Grace says, stepping back.

"As long as my dad doesn't find out, we're good. My mom's cool with pretty much everything."

Grace groans. "Mine is the opposite. She had to phone Olivia's mom last week and set out her expectations. I was so embarrassed."

Olivia barks with laughter. "My mom was convincing, right? Did she do her Betty Crocker impersonation on the phone?" She sighs as Grace nods. "The one thing my mom's really good at is pretending. For years I thought she was actually interested in us, but no! She was just pretending!" The others laugh, but Eve sees a glimmer of pain in her eyes, and keeps quiet.

Hours later, the girls are drinking, getting stoned, texting, with a stream of horror movies playing on the giant TV screen. Grace and Eve are the only two who have quietly abstained, at one point taking themselves into the kitchen to make brownies for the other girls, just to get away from the smoke-filled room.

When they get back, bringing a tray of fresh brownies, the rest of the girls jump up with a loud cheer, digging their fingers into the hot dough.

"How do you guys even know how to do this?" Olivia giggles. "I will love you for ever for this. I can't believe we even had Brownie mix here. My mom's on a constant diet — we're never allowed any of that shit."

"You didn't," Eve says. "We made them from scratch."

"Oh. My. God!" the girls all shriek. "How?"

Eve and Grace look at each other with a disdainful shake of their heads. "New York City girls . . . they're all the same," they say, and then they laugh.

"So what have we missed?" Grace sits on the sofa, relieved that the smoke has cleared somewhat.

"We were just discussing Allegra's blow job technique," says one of the other girls with a smile. "We were going to get a lesson from her."

"No way!" shrieks Allegra, mock-embarrassed.

"Oh come on!" says Olivia. "You can't give six in a night, win the title, and not pass on your techniques. That's just not fair."

"You gave six blow jobs?" Grace is the only one able to verbalize her shock. "To different guys? In one night?"

"It was a dare," Allegra smirks. "I had to. C'mon. I blew it out of the water."

Eve knew that other girls did this, at least she had heard of other girls doing this, but up until now she had thought it was one of those apocryphal myths.

"O-kay," Grace says, covering up a fleeting look of disgust with a shake of her head. "I guess I just don't get it." She turns to Claudia and Eve with a shrug. "I've been with my boyfriend for almost two years. I just don't get why anyone would give multiple blow jobs. I'm not saying it's bad," she says quickly, "it's just, what's in it for you? I mean, yes, I get that you're getting a power kick, but you're not getting pleasure out of it, right? And aren't you worried about getting a reputation?"

Allegra flicks her long blonde hair over to the other shoulder with an insouciant shrug. "It's just a blow job. It doesn't mean anything. It's not like we're doing anything intimate."

"It's. Oral. Sex," Grace persists, speaking slowly. "It is intimate. It should mean something."

"Grace, it's different for you," Olivia quickly intervenes, "because you're in a long-term relationship. The rest of us are just having fun, and this was a dare. She's not a slut or anything."

"Right," says one of the others. "The boys were judging who gave the best blow job. It wasn't just Allegra."

"Did you do it?" Claudia turns to her, but she looks embarrassed and shakes her head.

"None of us did," Olivia says. "It was between Allegra and these two other girls."

"How does that even work?" Claudia asks, enthralled not so much by the blow jobs, but by how sophisticated these girls seem, how grown-up, how cool by comparison with herself and her friends.

"It was, like, one minute each, right?"

Allegra nods, either not knowing or not caring that her behaviour is in any way shocking. "It doesn't even really count. We just went down the line, and at the end they gave their scores. And I won," she says lightly.

"Blow Job Queen?" There is a hint of sarcasm in Grace's voice. She and Eve make eye contact for a split second, registering the incredulous expression on each other's face.

"She was good, I'm telling you. We watched! So now she's giving us lessons." Olivia laughs. "I'm so scared my technique is bad, and that's the one thing guaranteed to turn you into a social outcast. It really doesn't mean anything, though. I know it sounds weird to you, but it's not weird if you live here."

"Plus, our school is really open-minded," Allegra adds. "We're all experimenting."

"Not everyone," Olivia says with a mean smile. "Just you and Mila."

"Oh my God!" shouts Allegra. "You are so not supposed to know about that!" But she's laughing as one of the girls, clearly Mila, purrs and rubs her butt.

"Oh man. Get off! I can't believe you told them!" Allegra pushes Mila's hand away and sits back down, but she's smiling.

"Why not? They're my best friends. Of course I'm going to tell them. Don't worry. I told them it was good."

"She did," Olivia confirms. "She said it was weird, but really good."

Eve, watching her, sees pride combine with relief as Allegra relaxes.

She is repelled and compelled by the dynamic in this room. It is captivating. Or would be, if only she was behind a wall, and not stuck right here, in the middle of it all.

As an anthropological study, there is no doubt in Eve's mind that tonight is priceless. She just wishes it were only tonight, not the entire weekend. With no adult to impose a limit, no one to tell them what they can and can't do, these girls will do anything in order to feel something.

At once older and younger than the girls in this room, Eve does not dole out blow jobs like hugs; she has not, in fact, done anything other than make out with boys, and had a couple feel her up, which didn't do anything for her other than make her worry that perhaps she is a lesbian.

She feels bizarrely unsophisticated in this room of sexually knowledgeable New York teenagers, who talk about sex as if it is nothing, who have everything but seem nothing other than bored.

She is shocked, fascinated, concerned. How can these girls treat themselves like this? How can they degrade themselves by performing oral sex in front of an audience?

Or is she the freak? Is there something wrong with her? She has always been praised for her maturity, her wisdom, but perhaps there's something wrong with her? She doesn't have any inclination to do the things the others are doing, preferring, quite honestly, to go to someone's house, or, better, have a couple of close friends over, and talk. She is happy to be with her parents, occasionally finding them embarrassing, or irritating, or unreasonable, but mostly, until recently, she seemed to be going through adolescence with few pitfalls.

Until she stopped eating; until she started bingeing and purging. She is able, at times, to pretend to be Eve, but most of the time she feels like a shadow of herself. It feels like she is swimming underwater. She can see the people she loves, but she can't quite reach them. She can't quite remember what it is to be happy, and she isn't sure how she got here, nor how she can get back.

Every morning she wakes up and tells herself today is going to be a new normal. She isn't going to throw up today. She is going to eat like a normal person. She isn't going to walk around consumed with shame and hatred. But this resolve lasts, has only ever lasted, an hour or so.

This weekend was supposed to be a good thing. It was supposed to physically remove her from the stresses, be fun, take her mind off leaving home, going to college. Instead she is finding herself with a group of girls she is becoming increasingly uncomfortable with, and right now all she wants to do is go out and find a store that sells ice cream. Lots and lots of ice cream.

"Oh my God! You must think we're all such sluts!" Olivia frowns, drawing in a lungful of smoke, holding it for just a few seconds, before exhaling slowly and passing the pipe on. "It is something weird at our school. Everyone's kind of doing it, and I like how open-minded we all are. I'm much more freaked out about intimacy." She looks at Eve, who smiles and nods, but all she is thinking about is ice cream. Still.

"Me too!" Allegra agrees enthusiastically. "I can, like, do anything with anyone, except kissing. That is way too intimate. I'm only kissing my boyfriend."

"Or girlfriend," teases Olivia. "But yeah. I feel the same. Blow jobs aren't intimate. Kissing is intimate." The girls in the room all nod sagely.

"Oh my God!" Charlotte squeaks. "Can you imagine if it was a kissing competition? Ew!"

"Ew!" they echo, their noses bunched up in disgust. "Kissing Burke Hadley? How gross would that be?" They start giggling, and soon all except Eve and Grace are rolling on the sofa in breathless hysteria, tears rolling down their cheeks as they clutch their stomachs and groan.

Grace, sitting quietly, looks over at Eve and points at the vaporizer. "You didn't have any, did you?" she mouths. Eve shakes her head.

"Want to go for a walk?"

* * *

As soon as the elevator doors are closed, the girls stare at each other open-mouthed.

"Am I on Planet Bizarro or something?" Grace says. "What the fuck? Am I crazy or is there something totally fucked-up with those girls?"

"I thought perhaps there was something wrong with me. That's, like, the freakiest conversation I've ever heard."

"My mom says it's too much money and too little attention. I mean, she doesn't say that about Olivia, because she doesn't really know her, and when she stayed with us over winter break my mom really liked her, but . . . wow. It happens even where I live. The rich kids in my school are doing all this kind of stuff too because they're bored."

"That's what I find so awful," Eve says. "This terrible undercurrent of boredom. Take Allegra. She's totally beautiful, but she has no energy whatsoever. I know she's stoned, and I know I've only just met her, but it feels like she's waiting to be amused by other people because she can't be bothered to make the effort."

Grace laughs. "That's exactly how she comes across. And Charlotte just seems unhappy."

"I feel bad for Olivia. It's like she knows what they're like, and she knows she's not like that, but she's trying to fit in."

"She is. It's amazing to me that someone who has so much feels like she has to prove herself all the time. You know who her dad is, right?" Eve shakes her head as Grace mentions a name that means nothing to her.

"He runs one of the biggest hedge funds in the country. He's worth gazillions, and he's never at home. Olivia says he's been having an affair with his secretary for ever, and her mom doesn't know. He asks Olivia to cover for him all the time. Can you imagine?" She turns to look at Eve with a disdainful expression. "How do you do that to your daughter, never mind your wife?"

"That's horrible," Eve agrees. "Why doesn't Olivia say something?"

"She kind of hates her dad, but she's also scared of betraying him, and she doesn't want to hurt her mom. Also, she's terrified of him leaving. She feels like she doesn't get enough of him as it is. He's always at work, and when he's at home he closes himself in his study or glues himself to his iPad. Her parents pretty much have nothing to do with the kids. Her brother's at Deerfield and Olivia was supposed to go but she refused."

"So when Olivia said her mom had things planned for this weekend and we'd be going to Wicked . . .?"

"I'm sure her mom does have plans, they just don't include the parents. She did get us tickets for Wicked, but we're going alone. No adults." Grace shrugs, before grinning suddenly. "It sucks for Olivia, even though I'm kind of jealous of the amount of freedom she has. My mom's a super-control freak, so I'm kind of blown away by this freedom. My dad's never at home either, so when he is we're all expected to drop everything for family time. I can't even believe he let me come here this weekend."

"You don't live in Manhattan?"

Grace shakes her head. "We're about forty-five minutes away. In Connecticut. New Salem?" Eve nods. She's heard of it. "It's nice. You know, typical suburbia but with bigger houses. There are a ton of girls in my school just like Allegra and Charlotte. Beautiful but insecure. And bored."

"But you're beautiful. And you're totally different from them." Eve is genuinely curious as Grace makes a face. She is, indeed, beautiful, with long limbs and dimples showing off a large and perfect smile. With tousled dirty-blonde hair, she is the picture of the All-American girl.

"Oh my God!" She laughs. "My family's just as crazy, but in a different way. Suburbia sucks too, but it sucks differently. But I do have great brothers, and a great boyfriend, and that definitely helps. Speaking of whom . . ." She grins as her phone buzzes. "There he is!" She stops to read the text. "Landon's game got cancelled. Thank you, God!" As she raises her eyes to the heavens a huge smile spreads on her face.

"What does that mean?" Eve feels her spirits fall. Does that mean Grace is going home to be with her boyfriend? Will Eve be abandoned to these girls with whom she has nothing in common? Picturing the den and the girls lounging on the sofa, recalling the conversations they have already had, the weight of dread settles about her shoulders and is evident on her face.

"I have an idea!" Grace lights up. "Why don't you come back to my house? We could get the train together and you could stay at mine! My parents are out tonight but they won't mind. I know you don't want to go back to that apartment any more than I do. My brothers are at home, which means it can be a little chaotic, but please say yes?"

"Chaotic?" Eve asks, dazed, knowing that she would so very much rather be with Grace than step back inside that room.

Grace laughs. "Just dogs and kids and noise. When my parents go out the boys tend to go a bit wild. Oh please come! I know we don't really know each other, but I can't leave you here with these people. I only came because Naomi, another friend from camp, was supposed to be coming, but she cancelled at the last minute, and then I felt like I was committed. You can get the train back in tomorrow so you still get to hang with the others. Go on," she pleads. "It's only one night and we'll have far more fun together."

Eve is torn. She is desperate to go back with Grace. She may not know her, but knows she likes her. Nothing could be worse than spending more time in that smoke-filled room with those bored girls. Grace's house would be fun. It sounds very much like the sort of family Eve has always wanted: kids, animals, chaos. How different from the quiet of her own family, no siblings, no noise, a mother who studiously avoids anything to do with the PTA.

But wouldn't it be rude? Would Olivia be upset? Even if not, how can she leave Claudia? What might Claudia do in her absence? Isn't it her job to look after her?

Her mind turns over. Eve wasn't even supposed to be here originally. Everyone may joke that Eve is Claudia's guardian angel, but she isn't. It is too much of a responsibility. Claudia is old enough to take care of herself, and it is only for a night. Tomorrow she will come back, go to the theatre, see the sights of New York, do what they had planned.

Grace is still staring at her. "What do you think? Would it be awful for us to go?"

It is a beautiful spring evening. The air is warm, the store windows lit and inviting, and as New Yorkers stride past them, phones clamped to their ear with one hand, leash in the other, their dogs sniffing the sidewalk, no one notices the two young girls standing on the corner, one expectant, the other deep in thought.

A wave of excitement floods Eve. Not sure if this is the right thing to do, she slowly nods, and Grace shrieks and flings her arms round her.

"I'm so happy! We're going to have so much fun."

"You're not going to just leave me and go upstairs with your boyfriend or anything, are you?"

"No! Are you kidding? Landon isn't even allowed upstairs. I'd be grounded for ever. Let me text my brothers that I'm coming home with you . . ." She starts tapping on the screen.

"What do we tell Olivia and the others?"

"The truth." Grace shrugs. "Neither of us drinks or smokes so it's not that much fun for us, and we'll see them tomorrow. Keep it simple."

Eve smiles. Of course. Why twist herself into knots trying to hide that she's not like them? Why not come clean? What was she afraid of: that they may not like her? Might not accept her?

So what?

Back in the elevator, back to the grand foyer, and this time male voices waft through the vast corridors, interspersed with shrieks of laughter from the girls. Eve, so worried about telling them, suddenly feels nothing other than relief that she doesn't have to stay here tonight.

"I know you said her parents aren't around, but you can smell the weed from here," Eve whispers as they grab their bags. "Are they really okay with it?"

"I guess they must be." Grace stops at a glossy demilune table covered in silver photo frames. In each, a tiny blonde-haired woman is smiling widely, her hair perfectly coiffed, skin the colour of caramel, huge diamonds glittering in her ears. In one she is clearly on vacation, sitting on the deck of a yacht, throwing back her head and laughing, the strings of a Missoni bikini just visible under her gauzy tunic; in another she is at the season opening of the New York City Ballet in an off-the-shoulder floor-length mandarin chiffon gown, surrounded by identical women with identical smiles.

"Does that look like the kind of woman who spends much time thinking about her children? Can you ever imagine her pushing her kids at the playground? Or climbing into bed with them for a cuddle? I know it's unfair to judge a book by its cover, but you can tell an awful lot from these pictures."

"Oh God!" Eve says. "We're being so mean. We agree that we like Olivia. We just don't like her friends. We have to stop."

"You're quite right. Bad girls. Let's quickly go in and say goodbye. We have a train to catch."

"Do you think we have to go in and say goodbye?" Eve grimaces at the prospect.

"What are you thinking?"

"Would it be really really awful to text?"

Grace bursts out laughing. "Yes!" she says. "It would be really really awful. Let's do it!" And grabbing Eve's hand she drags her straight back into the elevator and closes the doors before either of them has a chance to change her mind.

CHAPTER
TWENTY

Eve

The train journey passes in a flash, the two of them talking non-stop, passing ear buds back and forth to play each other songs on their playlist, flicking through the gossip magazines they bought at Grand Central, poring over the clothes, fantasizing about their perfect red-carpet dress.

Eve thought about letting her mother know she was going to Grace's, but it is only for a night. She will be back at Olivia's tomorrow. And she has her mobile phone. In these modern times, no one is ever out of touch.

The girls jump off the train and a tall, preppy boy moves towards them on the platform, his face breaking into a smile as he sweeps Grace off the ground into a big hug.

He turns to Eve and extends a hand, introducing himself and adding, "It's good to meet you!"

Eve simply stands, staring, finally remembering to say it is good to meet him too.

So few boys she knows would ever do this. The most she can expect is a "Hey" or a "What's up?" with a simple, wordless nod of acknowledgement being the norm.

Boys her age don't shake hands and say, in strong, confident tones, that it is good to meet her. Boys her age don't take both bags from the girls and carry them to the car, opening the car door for them before climbing in the driver's side.

"Isn't he adorable?" Grace turns to Eve in the back seat, reaching over to stroke the back of Landon's neck as he drives.

"He is," she agrees. "And this is so pretty! Is this Main Street?" They drive past pretty stores, an old cinema, an ice-cream parlour. "It's like something out of a magazine!"

"We're so used to it we don't even see it any more," Landon says with a laugh. "It's good to see it through someone else's eyes."

"Especially when this is your first time here. Welcome to New England!" Grace waves an arm extravagantly, showing off the grand old houses they pass.

Most are set far back off the wide, quiet road, the old stone walls and sweeping driveways leading up to large clapboard houses with elegant wrap-around porches and shiplap barns. Giant maple trees, hundreds of years old, tower majestically over the homes, their soft silvery leaves, lit by strategically placed spotlights on the ground, whispering under a black velvet sky.

Eve is open-mouthed as they drive. It seems each house is bigger and more beautiful than the last, and she has never seen opulence like this.

"Who lives here?" she asks. "This is like a millionaires' town."

"Hedge fund, hedge fund, hedge fund," Landon says, as he gestures at the houses.

"Not all of them." Grace frowns. "You live in a huge home and you're not hedge fund."

"True. And neither are you. But we're the old guard. The ones with the grand houses and leaks in the roof."

"It's true." Grace turns round in her seat again. "Landon's family are proper old money."

"Yes. We're so old, the money has disappeared." Landon laughs, this line being one of his favourites.

"Still," Grace says, "they live in the most beautiful house in the town —"

"But we don't have the money to fix it up," Landon interrupts, not caring in the slightest.

"You do have Sidney, though," adds Grace.

"True. But these days Sidney needs more fixing up than the house does."

"Good point." Grace explains that Sidney lives in one of the cottages on Landon's family estate, and has been the caretaker since his grandparents lived in the house. Now in his early eighties, the only things Sidney can take care of are the dogs.

"Is your house like that too?" Eve asks Grace.

"Nooooo," Landon lets out a whistle with a shake of his head. "It's the opposite."

"It's complicated," Grace says. "My dad is kind of more like Landon's family. If he had his way, our house would be just like Landon's."

"That was before he married the General," Landon adds.

"That's what he calls my mom." Grace grins. "I think she's offended but because she's so impressed with Landon's lineage she pretends to think it's hilarious."

"Your mother wouldn't live in our house if you paid her."

"Yes, she would!" Grace protests. "She'd kill for your house. She'd just do a major renovation first." She puts her hand up to her mouth and says in a stage whisper, with a knowing nod: "New money."

Landon laughs as Grace turns to Eve. "My mom's got this whole perfectionist thing going on. She's all about order and cleanliness and rules."

"Oh my God! The rules!" Landon sighs. "She has them laminated and up on the wall of the mud room so everyone sees them as soon as they walk in."

Eve is intrigued. Rules? There have never been rules as such in her house. Perhaps there have, but they are unspoken. The idea of having something taped up is bizarre to Eve. "What kind of rules?" she asks.

Landon clears his throat. "Rule number one: All shoes must be removed and placed in the correct cubby before entering the house. Coats must be hung. Guests may line their shoes up neatly on the boot rack. Rule number two: Please do not help yourself to food. Ask before taking. Rule number three: After eating, please rinse plates and cups and place in dishwasher. DO NOT LEAVE IN SINK. Please push chair in to table and mop floor with your tongue before exiting . . ."

"Landon!" Grace starts laughing. "It does not say that! But the rest is true. Isn't it so embarrassing? The only good thing is they've been up so long they've just become part of the furniture."

"Now I'm starting to worry," Eve says. "She sounds like she would hate the idea of you bringing a stranger back. Isn't she going to go nuts?"

"No," Grace replies. "She can be pretty uptight, but she also likes all our friends being at our house. That way she feels she can keep an eye on us. We have the basement as our space, and we're pretty much left alone down there. She's much happier knowing we're under her roof."

Eve thinks of her own mother and tries to imagine her with a house full of kids, but she can't picture it. When she was young, she was desperate for siblings, for a large, happy, noisy family. A family much like Grace's. Yet her family also feels as if it is exactly how it was always meant to be.

"I can't imagine my mom with a bunch of kids," muses Eve, "but she wouldn't be a rule person. She gets caught up in these projects, and she doesn't really notice what happens in the house. She likes it to look pretty, but she's all about character rather than perfection. Our house is cosy more than anything."

Grace sighs. "I love cosy. I wish our house was cosy, but cosy and perfect don't exactly go hand in hand."

"Where does it come from, this need for perfection?" Eve leans forward.

"She comes from nothing, and fell in love with my dad, who was from this old, New England family, and I think she always felt really insecure. She says she used to study my grandmother, to try to learn how to dress, how to entertain. Even how to talk."

Landon laughs. "Your mom does have the craziest accent I've ever heard. She's like something out of an old black and white movie. I still want to bow every time I see her."

Grace cracks up. "I keep telling you, it's all fake. She's from Long Island and nobody else I've ever met from Long Island speaks like that. I swear she makes it all up."

"But why would she need to do that?" Eve is confused.

Grace shrugs. "It's just how she is. I guess because she doesn't feel good enough, she tries super-hard to be better than everyone else at everything. She has to have the perfect house, the perfect kids, the perfect life."

"Isn't that really hard for you? Don't you feel under a huge amount of pressure all the time?"

"It is hard," she says quietly, no longer smiling. "I love my mom, but . . . it's hard. Nothing anyone does is ever good enough. Or, rather, anything I do. The boys get away with everything. She's hardest on me because I'm the only girl. And my dad. She's pretty rough on him."

Landon reaches over to take Grace's hand, squeezing it gently, not taking his eyes off the road. Then he slows down to turn carefully between large stone pillars.

Grace abruptly shakes her head, determined to change the direction of the conversation.

"Enough about my crazy family. Here we are. Home Sweet Home."

The car crunches along the gravel driveway, passing two old stone barns on the way, one still a barn and the other the guesthouse, before the house comes into view.

Perfectly symmetrical, it is low-slung, grey, with pretty iron window boxes filled with lilac hyacinths and trailing ivy. Stone greyhounds flank the front steps, with formal gardens of low, perfectly clipped boxwood in front of each wing, topiary myrtles in old iron pots, hydrangeas climbing the walls.

It is as if a small, elegant chateau has been lifted up from France and flown over the Atlantic, dropping down quietly in the leafy splendour of New Salem.

"It's perfect!" Eve whispers, getting out of the car and taking it in. "It's the most perfect house I've ever seen."

"Toldja!" Landon squeezes her shoulder as he passes her to get the bags from the trunk, just as two golden retrievers round the corner of the house, tails wagging furiously as they run over, sniffing excitedly and pushing wet noses into hands for a rub.

Grace bends down, circling her arms round them and resting her head on their backs. "Say hello to Monty and Bruno. My babies." She croons at them, kissing them on their noses before leading Eve round the corner and into the mud room with the infamous rules up on the wall, and then on into the biggest kitchen Eve has ever been in.

"I'm starving," Grace says, and Eve follows her to the fridge, gaping at the four-inch-thick marble countertops, the heavy glass pendant lights, the giant La Cornue range.

A steel bar hangs from the ceiling above the island, holding a cluster of gleaming copper pots, not a mark on them, while a polished concrete slab on antique French iron legs serves as a breakfast table in front of the island.

Grace turns from where she is crouching and rifling through the contents of the fridge, to see Eve, paused by the table, running her hands over the top.

"Poured concrete," she says. "Waxed. Calacatta gold on the exterior countertops. Waterworks faucets. Apparently." She grins. "I think my mom actually hates this whole kitchen but she read it was the latest thing, so we had to have it. She refuses to say she misses our old wood table, even though we keep catching her sneering at the concrete."

Turning back to the fridge she lets out a sigh. "There's nothing to eat. And I'm starving."

"I thought you weren't allowed to take food without asking?" Eve ventures, remembering the rules.

"We're not but we do," Grace says. "She did that when we were all really young and the boys would just eat the entire contents of the fridge. Not that they wouldn't do that now, but she buys food for them and fills the drawers with it . . . The drawers!" Grace stands up and moves to one end of the counter, pulling open what turn out to be refrigerator drawers.

"Yum!" She pulls out an aluminium tray of lasagne, and grabs the phone to text. "I just have to check it's okay." A few seconds later she smiles as her phone vibrates. She takes the lasagne over to the oven, just as footsteps are heard bounding up the basement stairs.

155

He is a male version of Grace. Her long limbs, dirty-blond hair, green eyes. He is, Eve thinks with a start, as he stretches in the doorway, his T-shirt lifting up to reveal a taut, muscled stomach, almost unbearably gorgeous.

"Hey, sis!" he says, then notices Eve. "Oh. Hey. I didn't realize anyone else was here. Hi!" As he walks over Eve wishes she had gone to the bathroom, checked her hair, put some lip gloss on. "I'm Chris, Grace's fantastic older brother. I know who you are! You're the hot girl on Facebook!" He grins as Eve shakes his hand, introducing herself. She is furious that she is blushing and hopes he doesn't notice the hot flush creeping up her face.

"Ignore him," Grace says. "He's the creature from the deep. He only comes up for air when he smells food."

"Speaking of which —" he peers at the oven — "what smells so good?"

"Lasagne. Mom said heat it for thirty minutes. You'll have to wait."

"Okay. Want me to make a salad?" He saunters over to the fridge, pulling out vegetables as Grace gapes and Eve gazes.

"Do you have a fever?" Grace asks. "Seriously. I'm worried. Should I call the doctor? You're definitely not yourself."

"Oh ha ha." Chris grabs a knife and starts chopping cucumber into rough slices.

"You might want to peel it first?" Grace suggests. "It makes showing off so much easier." She slides behind Eve, whispering in her ear, "He's doing this for you!"

156

"You're right," Chris concedes, laying down the knife and walking round to the other side of the island, sitting on the stool next to Eve and turning towards her. "Grace, you ought to make the salad. I'm going to sit here and get to know your friend."

"Let me!" Eve jumps up, embarrassed, wanting to talk to him, but not wanting to blush again, or sound like an idiot, for the power of speech appears to have temporarily left her.

"No," Grace says. "I've got it. You stay there. Or go downstairs — Landon's probably planted himself in front of the baseball, right?" Chris nods. "I'll give you a shout when it's ready."

"Are you sure?" Eve hesitates, but Grace is adamant, so, tucking her hair back behind her ears, she follows Chris down the stairs and into a light-filled room, where almost every conceivable teenage need appears to have been taken care of.

Battered surfboards cover one wall; a couple of huge beanbags are scattered in front of the TV, with the sectional behind; vintage pinball machines are tucked in a corner, with a popcorn machine alongside.

"It hasn't worked for years," Chris shrugs, showing her round. "But it looks great. How are your ping-pong skills?" He walks over to the table and picks up a bat, a challenging look in his eye.

"That's one place you don't want to go," she says with a grin, starting to relax as she walks over to the table and picks up the bat on the other side.

"Oh really?" Chris chuckles. "Do I detect a competitive edge to your voice?"

"When it comes to ping-pong, very much so," Eve says. "In fact, you may find that despite being, as you so clearly are, the consummate athlete, I may be about to wipe the floor with you at ping-pong."

"I like a woman who uses the word consummate in a sentence." Chris winks.

"I didn't mean that kind of consummate," Eve mutters. Don't blush. Don't blush. Don't blush.

He pretends not to have heard. "So, ready?"

Eve nods, picking up a ball and acing it over the net so quickly that Chris barely even has a chance to move.

"O-kay," he smiles. "Now I know what I'm up against. And here I was about to be a gentleman and let you win . . ."

"Bring it on," she teases.

He slams a serve over the net that she shoots back, as fast as lightning, Chris yelping as he manages to return it, after which they rally back and forth, laughing at impossible shots that each of them somehow hits, their game so fast, so accomplished, that Landon tears himself away from the baseball game to come over and watch.

"Where did you learn to get so good at ping-pong?" Landon asks. "I've never seen anyone able to take on this family before. None of us will even bother playing with them any more."

"I gotta tell you," Chris says, as he puts down the bat, "you are the first worthy opponent I've played with in years. You're really good."

"Thank you." Eve is gracious. "My dad taught me. He's ping-pong obsessed."

Landon shakes his head. "Chris doesn't know what that's like at all, do you, Chris?" And he laughs, as Grace's voice comes floating down the stairs, calling them up to eat.

"You truly have no idea how awful it was." Grace and Eve have regaled the boys with stories of the horror of the New York girls, with Grace including, much to Eve's embarrassment, the tale of the Blow Job Queen.

"I knew it," Chris says, slapping the table before looking at Landon. "We're in the wrong town. I'm moving to New York. What's the name of that girl again? What's her address? You said Allegra, right?"

"Yes, and if you want to catch some horrible disease, go right ahead. I'll introduce you," Grace says. "The whole thing was skanky."

"Grace," Chris is now serious, "it's not like that stuff doesn't happen here. You and your friends may not do it, but you know it goes on."

"Of course I know," Grace says. "And we all know who the girls are, but it wasn't so much that they'd done it, as their attitude about it. They all seemed bored. By everything."

"But that's the same out here," Chris points out. "Kids who have everything and nothing at the same time."

Grace sighs. "I know. How did we turn out so well?" Then she catches Chris's eye as they both say at the same time, "Dad!" and laugh.

"Their dad is amazing," Landon explains to Eve.

"It certainly isn't Mom." Grace gathers the plates, helped by Eve, as the boys sit chatting quietly. Eve stacks the plates in the dishwasher, realizing for the first time in months that she is smiling.

For the first time in months, she can breathe.

"Are you having fun?" Grace sees her smile.

"I really am. I guess I haven't been dealing well with all the changes coming up. I've found the whole transition thing kind of stressful. This is the first time I've felt . . . normal."

"You're not sick or anything?" asks Grace tentatively.

"No! Why would you ask that?"

"Just that you're really thin. I didn't want to ask but . . ."

"It's okay. I guess when I'm stressed I don't eat."

"Lucky you. When I'm stressed I dive straight into piles of chocolate." Grace laughs.

"And my stomach just closes up," Eve lies. "I'm getting kind of tired. Would you mind if I went to bed?"

"I'm tired too. Let's go up now. The boys can sleep in the basement."

Eve is the first to wake up. She reaches for her phone, sends a text to her mom saying she's having a great time, then grabs a magazine from Grace's shelves, planning on staying there quietly until Grace wakes up.

It's hard to concentrate knowing that Grace's brother is downstairs, that she's going to be seeing him again very soon, and she puts the magazine down, staring at Grace, willing her to wake up so she can spend more time with Chris.

160

Nothing happens. Eve coughs, then gets up and goes to the en-suite bathroom, ensuring she makes enough noise that Grace can't possibly stay asleep.

Sure enough, when she walks back into the room Grace is stretching, letting out a big yawn. "Hey," she murmurs, smiling at Eve. "Have you been awake long?"

"Hey, you. Not long, but I didn't want to go downstairs until you were awake."

"Good!" Grace says. "My mom has some big fundraiser thing today and we're supposed to stay out of the way. We should get Chris to take us to the diner. They have chocolate-chip pancakes to die for. Let's go and see if the boys are up."

"Should I change?" Eve says uncertainly, gesturing to her plaid pyjama pants and vest.

"I'm not," Grace says. "This is pretty much the uniform out here. Wear my flip-flops and we're good to go. We'll sneak out of the front door so Mom doesn't see us."

Chris is awake, watching sports, when Grace goes to inform him of the plan, and the three of them tiptoe up the stairs. As Eve and Chris lock eyes again, relief washes over her that this isn't something she imagined: he is as hot as she thought, and it does seem like he may be interested in her.

The three of them move quietly through the formal part of the house, Eve pausing only as she passes a table covered with photographs of the family. There's Chris, looking impossibly handsome, tallest in the family group, a huge smile on his face.

161

She hesitates, leaning forward to see better, wishing she could slip the photograph into her bag, before incomprehension, confusion, then shock cross her face.

And as she gasps with horror, Eve's legs give way, sending her plummeting down to the marble floor.

PART TWO

CHAPTER
TWENTY-ONE

Maggie

The ball arcs high in the air, and my left arm points towards the sky triumphantly as satisfaction sets in. I've got it. This is the shot that will win us game, set and match. In slow motion, enjoying every second, my arm sweeps back, and at the perfect moment slices forward, the thump of contact with the racquet exhilarating as I smash the ball over the net at the speed of light.

Kim doesn't stand a chance. Venus Williams wouldn't stand a damn chance. It might well be the greatest shot of my life, and Lara and I grab each other to do a small victory dance as Kim pretends she's totally fine with me, her arch nemesis, finally beating her.

"Great game." Kim forces a twisted smile as she shakes hands over the net. "My ankle still isn't right," she says with a frown, to explain why she didn't crush us. "I'm going back to the bone guy this week. It's really painful. I could hardly run."

"Really?" Lara's voice is pure innocence. "You seemed to be all over the court."

"Are you showering here?" Lara asks as we put our racquets away and pack our stuff.

"Can't. I have the tea at two o'clock at my house and there's a ton of stuff I need to do. You're coming, right?"

"Of course. And I don't believe for a second you've got a ton of stuff to do. You're the most organized person I know."

"It's all an act," I say, although I welcome the compliment. "I still have to make the sandwiches and I can't do those until right before or they'll be soggy."

"You're not using the caterers?" Lara seems surprised.

"For tea? Even I can manage a couple of cakes and some sandwiches." I laugh, dismayed that Lara, that anyone, might question my ability to bake something wonderful.

"Do you need some help?"

I pause for a second. The truth is I could do with some help. I could always do with help, but whenever I let people help me they screw it up somehow. They'll arrange the flowers horribly, set the tables badly, put the chairs out in the wrong positions. I try to delegate because I know it makes people happy to help, but then I end up resenting everyone for not doing as good a job as I would do.

Honestly, it just seems to be easier to do the whole thing on my own.

"I have a couple of wait staff coming so they can do everything," I lie, knowing I'll be frantically running round placing chairs and tables myself, because I've never trusted the wait staff either. "I'll see you later!" I blow her a kiss goodbye and practically skip over to the car park, floating on air at finally putting Kim in her place.

A quick look at the phone — texts from family, nothing important, nothing that can't wait. There is so much I have to do before 2p.m. this afternoon. A deep breath. I can do this. I always do this. I'm known for doing this: pulling off a beautiful event at the last minute.

I check my reflection in the mirror and tuck the frizzy bits of hair back under the baseball cap, before sliding on the ubiquitous large tortoiseshell sunglasses to hide my lack of make-up.

I shouldn't have agreed to play tennis this morning. It's two hours I really need, but how could I turn down the invitation to play Kim after she thrashed me last time? Particularly after I've spent a fortune taking secret lessons in Norwalk three times a week since then.

I swing into an open spot just outside the flower store on Main Street — thank you, God! — and run in to pick up more flowers. Louise is on the phone, but she knows me well enough to know I know exactly what I'm doing, and I walk quickly through the store, scooping up armfuls of tulips, hyacinths, lilacs and some gorgeous lush peonies.

"Anything else?" Louise puts the phone down and wraps the flowers, calling out to Juan in the back to help me take them to the car. "You must be having a party!"

"You know me," I say with a laugh. "There's always something!"

"I don't know how you do it!" She finishes wrapping, and as Juan lifts the flowers she takes the proffered card from my fingers. "All those kids and all that wonderful charity work. Do you ever rest?"

I smile. "You know what they say — no rest for the wicked!"

She doesn't hear me; she is frowning as she looks at the card, then tries sliding it again.

"Is everything okay?"

"I'm sorry, Mrs Hathaway," she apologizes, as if she is embarrassed on my behalf, "but your card is being declined."

I know there is absolutely no reason for my card to be declined, yet I feel instant shame. And it is not the first time this has happened recently. I know it is a snafu with the bank. Mark told me last time that it was because the bank was transferring the funds into a new account with a lower interest rate, but it does not stop my humiliation.

I pull another card from my purse, attempting to explain.

"My husband was supposed to sort it out." We both roll our eyes at the hopelessness of men.

The other card is fine, and I don't realize I've been holding my breath until she hands the card back while the receipt prints out. I make a mental note to phone the damn bank myself.

You'd think, with the amount of business we do with them, they'd make sure we didn't have to have these embarrassments. We smile at each other, with relief, as she wishes me luck with the event, and finally I'm on my way home.

It doesn't matter how many times I drive up this driveway, how many years we have lived here, I still pause at the curve, still find myself unconsciously sighing with pleasure at the beauty of this house.

Sometimes I stop, right here, and turn the engine off, feasting on the elegant symmetry, the French planters nestled between the windows, the huge copper beech that dwarfs the house. I take in the old wooden swing that has borne the weight of all three children over many years; it now hangs disconsolately from one of the majestic branches.

This is the kind of house around which fairy tales are written. It is the kind of house I grew up dreaming about. After school, while both my parents were at work, I would watch hours of television, praying that one of the movies I loved would come on: *The Great Gatsby*, or *High Society*.

At night, I lay in bed dreaming I was Grace Kelly, designing my wardrobe, imagining my handsome prince, visualizing every room of my elegant home.

In the morning, my father would come roaring through the house in his undershirt, and the dreams of the night before would go out of the window. Those were only dreams. How would a girl like me ever have a hope of living a life like that?

As I grew older, I started to realize it was possible. It was unlikely, certainly, but there was nothing I loved more than a challenge, and I was already obsessed with grand lifestyles, the upper classes. I knew everything there was to know about manners, how to behave.

I watched all the movies, read every memoir I could lay my hands on. I could reel off the histories of the Rockefellers, the DuPonts, the Cabots, as if they were cousins.

Do you think I cared that my parents mocked me mercilessly when I practised my accent in the mirror, emulating Katherine Hepburn, the way she moved, the way she spoke? I learned to catch myself every time my Astoria accent slipped through, until there wasn't a trace of it left.

If I changed my accent, my bearing, the things I couldn't change were less important. I was lucky in inheriting my slim, wiry body from my father, but my fair, freckled skin and red curly hair was my mother's family through and through. As my grandmother used to say, I wore the map of Ireland on my face.

Granted, no amount of facial scrubs would give me the porcelain skin of Grace Kelly, but red, curly hair? Long before Nicole Kidman morphed her fiery curls into a sleek blonde mane, I'd already thought of highlights and a flat iron to achieve the same effect.

I'd sit at my parents' table, as groomed and chic as Grace Kelly, my sleek blonde hair tucked in a chignon, a faux Hermès scarf round my neck, attempting to close my ears as my parents screamed across the table at each other.

Is it wrong, I'd wonder, hoping my silence would render me invisible, protect me from their abuse, to want more than this?

Is it possible to reinvent yourself and have the life you're sure you deserve?

This house remains the strongest evidence that it is. My husband, so charming, handsome, successful, is evidence that it is. This gilded, charmed life on Connecticut's Gold Coast, is evidence that it is.

I am grateful, but I will never let my facade slip among the women I have come to call my friends. I am not stupid. I am fully aware of the undercurrent of competitiveness among these women. I'll never let them know where I came from, who I really am, because all that matters is where I am today; who I've turned myself into; the life I've created for myself.

Each time I pull round this corner and glimpse our stone house, the climbing hydrangeas now leafing as they climb up the trellised wall, I take a moment to appreciate how far I have come.

Usually I leave the car in the driveway. Not today. Today I pull into the garage to ensure the house will be picture-perfect for the first guest; there will be no cars to clutter up this example of the quintessential New Salem house.

The pool is open. A little early, but so pretty to see the water rather than the God-awful winter cover, and the planters by the pool have been replanted with huge hydrangeas, already lush and green.

I shake my head with a sigh as I glimpse a flash of orange netting in the middle of the lawn. Despite my rules, despite how many times I tell those boys to clear up after themselves and put their sports equipment away, there are lacrosse sticks and balls all over the yard. I gather them up, put them away, then take the flowers out of the car and put them in the sink in the pool house.

The tea is being held in the pool house. Willow baskets sit on the rented tables, waiting for the flowers; trestle tables are waiting to be covered by the crisp folded linen tablecloths. Printed-out minutes for the meeting, with cute drawings I found, are rolled up in tiny spring baskets, each containing a small sample of a new lilac-scented room spray, donated by a local designer to use as a favour.

I open the French doors, arrange the flowers and use some of the lilac spray, which instantly freshens everything up and makes it smell like spring. Damn wait staff. I should have ordered them far earlier but there's nothing I can do now. I check my watch, take a deep breath, and leave the pool house to them — there's more important stuff to be done at the main house and if I don't get started now, it's all over.

CHAPTER
TWENTY-TWO

Maggie

Thank heavens I made pie crusts yesterday. Pulling the covered tart pan out of the fridge, I open a can of pear halves — and yes, I know it sounds so terribly déclassé, but even Jacques Pepin advises canned pears — slice them thinly and set them aside, then I pull out eggs, almonds, flour, vanilla and sugar, mix them all together and pour them into the crust.

An hour later, a perfect pear and almond tart sits on a crystal cake plate. Alongside sits a plate of buttermilk scones, still hot from the oven, with strawberry jelly in a bowl in the middle. Rows of tiny triangular sandwiches line up on platters: cucumber, smoked salmon, cream cheese and watercress. And finally, the one thing I didn't make although I shall pretend I did: a plate of delicate ice-cream-coloured petit fours.

Last year the tea was at Kim's, and frankly, although I don't want to be bitchy, it was somewhat ostentatious. Some might even say vulgar. She had a band in the garden, for heaven's sake. The food was delicious, but there was so much of it! And the flowers were so big you couldn't see anyone sitting opposite you; plus, seating charts for a tea is a little . . . too too.

What I've learned, after all these years of studying how to do things correctly, is that less is always more. The truly rich don't wear thick make-up with huge diamonds dripping in their ears; they don't drive Aston Martins and overwhelm you with enormous flowers and endless food on silver platters.

The truly rich keep it simple. Less is more. Pretty spring flowers in wicker baskets. Home-made food. Tea served in pretty porcelain teapots on small tables round the pool.

It will be the personification of understated elegance. I will, in short, show Kim, mistress of the thirty-thousand-square-foot stone mansion, how it should be done.

It's going beautifully, and I couldn't be happier. The sun is shining down as the women chatter excitedly, complimenting one another on their pastel-coloured dresses and wide-brimmed sun-hats, their gold and diamond jewellery glinting in the sun as they turn their heads to see who else has arrived.

In a break from the traditional white wine, I've decided to serve champagne, but I've placed a spoonful of pomegranate seeds in each glass, and the seeds bubble around as in a hand-held sophisticated lava lamp, bringing a sparkle to the very event itself.

Lara nudges me as Kim walks in, carefully tiptoeing across the grass in her strappy high heels so she doesn't sink in, a simple cream sheath dress showing off her Bikram yoga-d body perfectly, a huge feathered fascinator exploding from the side of her head. A Chanel bag is over one shoulder; under the other arm is a Havapoo, or Peekapoo, or Maltipeke. I never can tell one from the other.

"I hope it's okay to bring dogs?" Kim air kisses both of us then puts the dog down. "Although she's not really a dog. She thinks she's my baby! I have to take her to the groomers after so it saves me going home."

"Of course!" I lie, watching as the dog chooses just that moment to squat and pee. Great.

Kim makes a big show of pulling down her sunglasses and peering over the top of them, looking round at everything.

"Look what a beautiful job you've done!" Kim gushes, and I am about to thank her, genuinely thrilled at her genuine compliment, when she ruins it by continuing: "It's so . . . country! How cute! You must have done those sweet flowers yourself!"

I am speechless. Lara reaches a hand behind my back and gently pokes me, as I try to maintain the falsest smile I've ever had to fake, not knowing what to say next. What I want to say, in my best Astoria accent, is, "Fuck you, bitch. Bring it on." But of course I wouldn't do that.

Lara to the rescue. "She's the most talented woman I know!" she enthuses. "Wait till you taste the food. The almond tart is ridiculous! And she made everything herself! I hate her."

"I'm impressed." Kim turns as someone walks past with a plate of petit fours. "You made those yourself?"

Shit. Trust Kim to point out the only things I didn't make. I'm not giving her the satisfaction, though. No way. I nod.

"That's so weird," she says, reaching out for one. "They look exactly like the ones I always get from Great Cakes." Kim takes a bite. "And they taste exactly the same! But exactly! How on earth do you make those?"

"With great difficulty," I lie, hoping my face isn't as red as it feels. "It took me days to get them right. I'm so glad they look professional!"

"I'm telling you," Lara jumps in, "she should have her own TV show. Oh Maggie," she adds, "you're needed in the pool house." And thankfully she drags me away.

"Am I going crazy or is she the biggest bitch ever?" We're huddled behind the pool house with Heather, the newest addition to the group, who is still trying to discover the lay of the land, and is reluctant to cast an opinion, no matter how hard we push her.

"She seems pretty nice to me," Heather says tentatively. "But I don't really know her."

"You really don't." I shake my head. "I suppose you should be grateful she's being nice to you. She's a bitch with me. Always has been, and I honestly don't see her being that bad with anyone else."

Lara drains her glass. "She's threatened by you. She was the Queen Bee in Richmond, or Charlotte, or wherever the hell she lived before, and she moved here expecting to be the same. Why else do you think they built the biggest and ugliest house in town? She's desperate to be what she can never be. She doesn't realize that however much money she has, however much she gives to charity, however many events she goes to, it can never buy her class. You're old money, Maggie. You were born with class. And the jealousy is killing her."

I shrug as if to say, I guess you're right, but I don't look her in the eye. A snapshot of my parents flashes into my mind. My father in a stained vest, mother in apron and house slippers; permanent sounds of shouting and television. Oh, if only you knew . . .

If only you knew.

It is traditional for last year's chair to introduce this year's, and I will confess to a hint of dread as Kim chinks her glass with a spoon until silence descends on the gathered women.

To polite applause she announces the money raised thus far before encouraging everyone to sell more tickets and make this the best year ever, although I know she doesn't mean it; I know she wants last year to remain the best year ever.

"Finally I want to introduce and thank this year's chair, someone you all know: Maggie. I'm sure you all know that Maggie made all this delicious food herself, which makes me so jealous." She laughs. "I had to pay a small fortune to Cinnamon Catering!" Everyone laughs, for Cinnamon Catering is indeed a small fortune.

"Next time I'm paying Maggie!" Kim jokes. The crowd laugh again, a little more nervously this time, the guests turning to gauge my reaction, but I refuse to react right now. I'm saving this to discuss with Lara later. Did she really just publicly declare that she thinks of me as her damned staff?

I grit my teeth as I run my familiar mantra through my head. What would Jackie do? What would Grace do? What would Katharine, Babe, Brooke do? They would be gracious and polite. They wouldn't react.

"But seriously, the pool house is adorable, and everything's so pretty. You've done a wonderful job." I continue to smile through the condescension, finally stepping up to say the requisite few words of my own.

I am about to take a deep breath to speak, when I pause. Did I just hear a shout from the house? I start again, but there it is. Definitely a shout. I stop, as the door of the main house opens and Grace tears across the lawn towards me, Chris following fast behind her.

She is sobbing out loud, distraught, and my blood runs cold as I run to her, knowing that something is terribly, terribly wrong.

Chris catches her and grabs her arm, trying to pull her back, but she shakes him off and screams at him.

"I have to tell her!"

My heart pounds so loudly, it is all I can do not to scream: What? Who? An accident? Visions of skewed limbs on highways flash through my mind as nausea rises.

"Grace," I manage, my own voice on the verge of hysteria, no longer bothered that everyone I ever cared about impressing is now standing in my garden watching me in astonished, mesmerized silence. "What is it? What's happened?"

178

"It's Dad," she sobs, collapsing on her knees on the grass. "He has another family."

No accident. No one is dead. I have no idea what she is talking about. I have no idea what those words mean. I blink.

"Mom!" she cries, her voice that of a little girl, filled with pain. "Those times he's in California on business? He isn't. He's with his other wife. And daughter. I met her. She was here."

"Grace, you've made a mistake," I say slowly, for this is not happening. This cannot be happening. My daughter is clearly having some kind of a nervous breakdown, or trying to humiliate me in front of everyone I know.

"Grace," I continue, my voice now steely, "I have no idea what is happening to you, but get inside now." I will not let this happen. Someone, anyone, get my daughter out of here. "We will deal later with whatever game you're playing."

"It's not a game," she shrieks, her eyes filled with pain, and I have to give her credit, because if there were Oscars for amateur acting she'd deserve one. "Eve. My friend. She was here. She recognized him. He's her father."

I stand there, blinking. I have no idea what she's talking about.

"This is clearly a mistake," I say, and attempt a gracious laugh as I look round the gathered circle of fascinated, shocked women. "Will you please excuse me while I try to find out what's going on?" And as I begin to walk across the grass, I find my legs are shaking, and everything suddenly seems just a little bit numb.

CHAPTER
TWENTY-THREE

Sylvie

Of late Eve has become secretive, locking her bedroom door, demanding privacy. Sylvie hasn't ventured into Eve's bedroom for a while, but while Eve is in New York for the weekend, and must surely be having a good time or Sylvie would have heard from her, Sylvie can use the time to sort out her room.

Perhaps she can find out why her daughter is changing so drastically before her eyes; but that isn't a conscious thought, at least not one she will recognize.

Thank God she doesn't have what so many of the other mothers of teenage girls have. When they report finding bowls filled with mould under the bed, Sylvie breathes a sigh of relief. Eve is organized and tidy, even does her own laundry. She can't bear mess of any kind.

Her room smells permanently of lavender thanks to an organic room spray that she keeps both next to her bed and in the bathroom, but which she uses somewhat obsessively.

In the old days Sylvie and Eve would go through her closet together, deciding what should stay, what should go, what could be gifted to friends. While risky to do this without Eve, Sylvie is fairly certain she can pull out the clothes Eve no longer wears.

But as soon as she opens the closet door, she finds herself unable to move, sadness sweeping over her. Here are all the beautiful clothes Eve can no longer wear. The cute white pants, the embroidered skirt, the lilac dress she wore to prom, all of which are now huge on her.

Eve was able to wear most of them until recently, cinching the waists in tighter and tighter, until even she had to concede the impossibility of the situation. Lately she has been living in leggings and layers of clothing to keep her warm.

Sylvie reaches for a pair of Toms that are almost worn through, pulling out the shoe boxes they're resting on. They should be empty, but something is in there. She opens the first one to find it stuffed with empty food wrappers. All the shoe boxes are filled with empty food wrappers. Oreos. Twixes. Empty cake boxes pulled apart and flattened. Cheetos. Doritos. Nutella. Chip bags. Family packs of chocolate.

Enough food to satisfy a family of many for a very long time.

It is exactly what Sylvie has been dreading. Eve cannot be as painfully thin as she is unless she is throwing up all this food she is eating.

The evidence can no longer be ignored. Eve is bulimic. Anorexic. Both, maybe. Either way, this is a fully fledged eating disorder. They can't wait for Eve to grow out of it; they can't bury their heads in the sand any longer.

Eve may not agree, but she no longer has a choice. Sylvie gets her mobile and pulls up a number she programmed in a few weeks previously. UCSD's Eating Disorders Treatment Center.

"Hello," she says. "My name's Sylvie Hathaway. I think my daughter has an eating disorder and I'd like to make an appointment to bring her in. Yes, Tuesday would be great."

Making the appointment doesn't make her feel better. She sorts out the rest of Eve's closet, terrified of what else she may find, relieved there is nothing. All the while, her mind is whirring, and she feels wracked with intense emotion: sadness for her beautiful daughter; anger at the awful illness; guilt that she's let it develop so far; fear for what lies ahead. But being overwrought will not help Eve and she recognizes she needs to do something to calm herself down.

Yoga. Remembering how much it calmed her down on vacation, Sylvie Googles Prana Yoga Center, for she has heard good things about it. There is a class in thirty minutes and somewhere in the coat closet downstairs is a yoga mat.

Prana is offering a one-week thirty-dollar Intro Special, which is perfect. This is exactly what she needs.

Sylvie tries not to worry about Eve as she drives over to Prana. She breathes in deeply through her nose, jumping sharply as her mobile snaps her back to reality. She pulls over to the side hoping it's Mark, who seems to have gone AWOL. She hasn't managed to speak to him for a couple of days and is starting to feel uneasy about it.

It is not Mark. It is Clothilde. Hiccuping.

"Hi, Mom. Are you okay? Do you have the hiccups?"

"Obviously I do. Where are you?"

"On my way to a yoga class. Do you need something?"

"I feel sick." Sylvie is dismayed to hear Clothilde slurring ever so slightly. She isn't supposed to have alcohol, but various caregivers have been persuaded to sneak her in a bottle of good wine.

"Have you been drinking, Mom?"

Clothilde doesn't answer. "They're ignoring me," she says.

"Okay, Mom. I'll come over after my class."

The phone goes dead and Sylvie shakes her head. No goodbye, no thank you, no appreciation. But there never is, she tells herself. It's not Clothilde's fault. She is the way she is. The problem lies with Sylvie expecting anything different.

At least, she realizes, parking the car close to the yoga place, Clothilde's call managed to take her mind off a daughter with an eating disorder and a husband who seems to have disappeared.

The calming energy washes over Sylvie as she turns to look at the women walking in; exchanging smiles with each other, they are lithe and toned, exuding serenity.

"I'm sorry." The long-haired girl behind the desk hands back her credit card with a sympathetic grimace. "It's denied."

Sylvie frowns. "Would you try it again?"

She does, with the same result.

Mark cut up the other credit card the last time he was at home. He was consolidating, said they would no longer use the Visa, but the Amex should be fine. She checks the card, suddenly wondering if she somehow gave the girl the Visa by mistake, but there is no mistake.

"My husband must have forgotten to pay." She cannot hide her dismay. This is not the first time this has happened. As busy as Mark is, paying bills is crucial. Sylvie has offered to take on this responsibility, to ease Mark's pressures, but he won't hear of it.

Sylvie hands over thirty dollars in cash, noting that she is down to forty-three dollars. Lately she has tried to carry cash, for precisely this reason: if Mark is late paying a bill, she doesn't want to have to get caught short.

With ten minutes to go until the class starts, Sylvie sets up her mat, before quickly texting Mark.

Again.

> Where are you? Am getting
> worried. And PAY AMEX
> BILL. Got denied again. I love
> you but call me! Xxx

Driving over to her mother's, still in her yoga gear, no make-up, which her mother will hate, Sylvie does feel much better.

The undercurrent of anxiety over her husband's whereabouts is still there, and her fear for Eve, but she thinks of the yoga teacher telling them to focus on their breath, on the present, on the current moment.

Perhaps she is finally on her way to becoming a yogi after all. She hates all the sun salutations, but the end, the Shavasana, lying on her back and focusing on her breath, relaxing her entire body? She could have stayed there all day.

As she drives she finds herself appreciating everything around her in a way she certainly didn't as she drove out to the class. Look how beautiful the trees are, the bright blue sky with just a few puffy clouds lazily floating along. How lucky is she to live here, to have this life, to have Eve, to be married to a man she adores?

This state of calm is not something she has experienced often of late, and she's determined to enjoy it for as long as she can, because, God knows, it's going to be over as soon as she arrives at Clothilde's.

The home is a bustle of activity. The director is in the lobby as Sylvie walks in and waves her over as she moves to the elevator.

"She's already on her way," the director explains breathlessly.

Sylvie looks at her blankly. "What?"

"The ambulance left a few minutes ago."

Sinking. "What are you talking about?"

"You didn't get our messages? Oh Mrs Hathaway. I'm so sorry. It's your mother. She appears to have had a stroke. They're rushing her over to Scripps —"

Sylvie has already turned and is running back to her car, too ashamed, too guilty to look that woman in the eye. She knew something was wrong, but her goddamned yoga class was more important.

She knew something was wrong, but she put herself first.

She is just as self-centred, as self-absorbed, as selfish as her mother always said.

CHAPTER
TWENTY-FOUR

Maggie

As I enter the kitchen, still shaky, I turn to look out of the window to see everyone who matters in this town standing outside in small clusters, whispering about me. Instantly I realize that unless I want to find myself a social outcast, I had better get myself back out there quickly and repair the damage my daughter has done.

I have no idea why she said what she said. It must have something to do with the teenage emotional hell that I keep reading about, and that I have always prided myself on not having yet experienced.

I consider calling Mark, who had to leave early this morning for the airport, but dismiss the thought. There will be time to deal with all of it later. Now I need to call on every ounce of grace I can find, and smooth this over as best I can.

I take a deep breath, picture Jackie Kennedy and glide outside, ignoring the descending hush, a smile on my face.

"I have no idea what my daughter's talking about," I say, my voice a tinkle of nonchalant laughter. "Teenagers!" I roll my eyes. "Such drama! Some television show, I'm sure. More champagne, anyone?"

No one can accuse me of not being the consummate hostess.

There is not, as I had hoped, a babble of conversation, a sigh of relief. Instead I see glances of sympathy as women come to say goodbye, gathering me in their arms, many of them women I barely know.

They hug me close and whisper things like, "You're going to be fine," and "You're so strong," and each time I pull back and reassure them, saying, "Grace has been under so much stress. She's a straight-A student, but I think it's been hard."

I perform beautifully.

Kim comes up and embraces me so tightly I have a mouthful of feathers. It's only when I start to cough that she releases me.

"Poor Grace," she says. "I do hope it's not the beginning of a nervous breakdown. What a terrible shame for the tea this year."

I could stop her, contradict her, but suddenly I am terribly tired, and being away from everyone is the only thing that starts to make sense.

Grace can't stop crying, and I want to comfort her, but I can't. We have been over and over this, and each time her story doesn't change — this girl, Eve, picked up a photograph of Mark and turned white, saying Mark was her father.

Mark is not here to fill in the missing links. None of which make any sense. But this no longer feels like teen drama; it feels like something that could be real;

something that could be so terrifying that my mind is refusing to even fully contemplate it.

Thank heavens Lara is here. She is the one who manages to comfort Grace, and then slips a glass filled with whiskey into my hand, whispering that she "couldn't find any brandy".

"Doesn't matter. I hate both." I drain the glass, grimacing as I set it down. "Thanks."

"Grace," Lara says gently, "why don't you tell us again?"

And she does.

When she has finished, I am calm. What proof does this girl have? It doesn't make sense. What makes sense is that she saw Grace's life, her home, her lifestyle, and she was jealous. I have no idea why she made up this terrible lie, but it is so clearly a lie.

"It's not true," I say confidently. "You said she was overwhelmed by this house? It sounds like some fantasy this poor girl cooked up when she saw how we live. I hate to say it, and I don't mean this condescendingly, but it sounds like she was jealous and was looking to hurt you."

"I was there, Mom!" Grace bursts out. "She wasn't lying. She was as shocked as I was. She wasn't making it up, Mom. I believe her."

"That's your choice, Grace. But I don't, I'm afraid." I am suddenly furious that Grace believed some hick from California. That she ruined my reputation because of some ridiculous jealous child. I start to shake with rage. "Good God, Grace. You realize that you interrupted my tea, and exposed this ridiculous lie to all the women in town? That, Grace, is unforgivable." I am more furious by the minute. "You embarrassed me in front of all the women I know because of a fantasy some girl cooked up? I don't even know what to say. I am sick at what you did."

"What I did?" Grace shouts. "All you care about is your image. You think this is so unrealistic? You think this couldn't happen to your perfect life? So where is he when he's not here? How come days go by when none of us can get hold of him? And all you care about is how you look in front of the stupid women in this stupid town. You make *me* sick!"

"Grace Elizabeth Rose! Don't you dare speak to me like that! You are grounded!"

"You can't do anything," she screams as she storms out, pausing only to shout over her shoulder, "And you're the one who's going to look stupid, not me."

I try to laugh it off to Lara with an "Oh, teenagers!" mumble, but Lara just looks at me with more sympathy than I am comfortable with right now.

My voice comes out in a whisper. "Do you think it might be true?" I can't even conceive of the full horror of that.

She shakes her head. "Absolutely not. Mark? No way. I think you're right. This girl was clearly jealous and wanted to try to hit Grace where it would hurt," she says. "Honestly, Maggie? There's no way Mark would do that. How could he, anyway? It's not like you don't know where he is." She laughs, but I look away, thinking of all the times I call his number and there's no reply.

All the times he's travelling and I never give it a second thought. So he has an office in California. Everyone here has a husband who travels, or has an office elsewhere, or stays in the city Monday to Thursday. We know some of the husbands are sleeping with other women on their away days, but we're pretty sure we know who those husbands are.

Not Mark. Mark isn't one of those. Mark isn't one of the husbands who drinks too much at the Christmas parties and flirts with my friends. He hasn't ever been caught drunkenly making out with someone's wife in the backyard.

When Mark's in California he's working. Having early nights.

Except, what if he isn't? But if he isn't, what does that mean? I look round, at this beautiful life I have created, we've created, and I look back at Lara for validation.

"You're sure Mark isn't doing anything?"

"Why don't you call him?" she says. "I think this is something between the two of you, and you need him to reassure you, not me."

I groan. "I can't believe this happened today. In front of everyone."

"They'll get over it," she lies. "We always think everyone's talking about us but frankly we're all too busy."

I give her a stony-faced look and she shrugs. "Okay, okay. So everyone will be talking about it, but so what?

Who cares what anyone else thinks? Those of us with teenage girls are well aware of the histrionics and drama — you'll be able to pass this off easily."

There is a long pause. "Not if it's true." My heart leaps into my mouth at the thought.

"No. Not if it's true. But it's not. Go on, call him."

"I'll call when you've gone," I say, for I do not want Lara, even Lara, to know that I might not be able to get hold of Mark.

I do not want Lara, even Lara, to know that despite her soothing words of wisdom, despite my own explanations, as reasonable as they sound to my own ears, I am terrified, utterly terrified, that Grace may be right.

CHAPTER
TWENTY-FIVE

Sylvie

Bare-faced, eyes closed, tiny in her vulnerability, Clothilde lies hooked up to an assortment of wires, monitors, IVs, as Sylvie sits in a chair pulled up close to the side of the bed and stares at the blankets, her mother's hand resting in her own.

The doctors have talked to her in hushed voices. Explained that Clothilde has had a massive stroke, suspecting her high cholesterol led to a blood clot in her heart travelling up to her brain.

They tell her it's a waiting game. They can do CT scans when the oedema, the swelling, subsides. If the swelling subsides.

They can make no predictions until that happens, leaving Sylvie sitting quietly in the ICU, holding her mother's hand, wishing she had turned up earlier. She has been reassured it wouldn't have made a difference — Clothilde was having the stroke when she called Sylvie; even if Sylvie had gone straight there, the journey would have taken twenty minutes, and the outcome would have been the same.

But what if Sylvie had called the home? Insisted they check on her? Clothilde had played wolf so many times, complaining about this and that, insisting Sylvie called the director, that Sylvie had stopped taking any notice.

Who could blame her, for not calling the home? Other than Sylvie, herself, of course.

Clothilde doesn't look like Clothilde, lying here. She looks like a shrunken facsimile of herself. In a hospital gown, without her omnipresent make-up, there is nothing scary about her, no indication of the sheer force of her personality.

A nurse comes in, fiddles with the IV, and smooths back the hair on Clothilde's forehead in a gesture so loving it makes Sylvie, awkwardly holding her mother's hand, feel ashamed.

"You're her daughter?" the nurse asks, and Sylvie, with a sudden lump in her throat, nods.

Sylvie's eyes well up as the nurse lays a hand on her shoulder. "It's all going to be okay," she says. "It's all part of God's plan."

"Do you think she can hear?" Sylvie asks.

"If there are things you want to tell her, now's the time," she smiles. "They always say hearing's the last sense to go, so, yes, I think she can hear."

She pads quietly out of the room as Sylvie drags the chair closer to the head of the bed, thinking of all the things she should be saying to her mother.

She should be telling her stories, reminding her of happy memories, recalling all the wonderful times they shared together. She should talk about her childhood, remind her of France.

She should tell her she loves her.

But the words won't come out.

⋆   ⋆   ⋆

Hours later there is no change in Clothilde's condition, the oedema neither going down, nor up. She is stable, whatever that means. Sylvie could spend the night in an uncomfortable cot, but it's better, the kind nurse said, for her to go home and get a good night's sleep. They would call if anything changed. Anything at all.

Sylvie takes the elevator down, climbs into her car, and leans her head on the steering wheel, almost dizzy with emotional exhaustion.

Her phone has three voicemails, none of them from Mark. The director of the home, increasingly frantic, informing her that Clothilde is going to hospital.

First the proof that Eve has an eating disorder, then Clothilde having a stroke. She stares at her phone, at her numerous unanswered texts to Mark, and her head fills with a childhood memory of her mother's sharp, superstitious voice.

"Bad things always happen in threes."

Someone is at the house. She sees a pickup truck and a towing truck in the driveway. The garage door is open, the lights are on. Sylvie, never frightened, feels a wave of fear, followed by anger. Who the hell are they and what the hell are they doing in her garage?

She screeches up and slams the door, striding over to them. "Who are you and what are you doing in my home?"

"Are you married to Mark Hathaway?" one says, checking a clipboard before proffering a piece of paper. She nods cautiously.

"We're here from the Debt Collection Agency."

195

Sylvie hesitates, less righteous now. There has been some mistake. There has to be.

"What Debt Collection Agency? I don't know what you're talking about."

"We've been instructed by a number of credit agencies to collect on your debts."

"What debts? We don't have any debts. What are you doing?" Sylvie takes the paper and frantically calls out to two of the men, now rolling Mark's Harley-Davidson out of the garage. "You can't take that. I'm going to call the police."

"Ma'am? You may want to read that paper. We also need to collect the Porsche and the Range Rover."

Sylvie doesn't even glance at the paper, just snorts with undisguised laughter.

"Porsche? Range Rover? Are you out of your mind? This is clearly a mistake. See?" She slows down her speech as if talking to a child. "See my car? Does that look like a Porsche or a Range Rover to you? No? That's because it's a very old Volvo station wagon. I think maybe you have the wrong address. Or the wrong Hathaway. Or something. We don't have a Porsche, have never had a Porsche. I wish we could afford a Porsche, but this is all we have."

The men look at one another, confused. They are used to excuses, but this woman's reaction is genuine. This is not a house, nor a woman, that has a Porsche and Range Rover hiding anywhere.

One speaks up. "What does your husband drive?"

"He doesn't," she explains with a smile. "He's hardly ever here and when he is he drives the Volvo. Please.

196

Put the Harley back. I won't even report you. It's fine. Let's just forget about it."

He examines his papers. "His other address is Ponus Ridge Road, New Salem, Connecticut?"

"No!" She laughs. "He stays in an apartment in New York City. I'm telling you, this is a mistake."

The foreman flicks through a sheaf of papers before finding what he's looking for.

"Mark Anthony Hathaway. Born fourteenth of July, nineteen sixty-four."

Sylvie, now confused, nods.

"CEO of Hath Office Solutions Inc.?"

Sylvie nods again.

"Two registered addresses. One in La Jolla, one in Connecticut. And you would be his wife, Margaret Alice Hathaway? Married twenty-seventh of September, nineteen eighty-six?"

"I'm so sorry," Sylvie says, and she starts to laugh. "There's obviously been a mix-up at the office. You have the right Mark Hathaway, but the wrong wife. I've never heard of Margaret whoever, and he doesn't live in Connecticut. He has an office in New York and a rental apartment in Manhattan. You need to check your paperwork. I'll have to ask you to leave."

The foreman frowns, flicks through his papers, frowns again.

"I'm not getting it," he murmurs to himself, turning the pages back. "He's definitely married to Margaret Alice in New Salem. I just can't figure out who you are."

CHAPTER
TWENTY-SIX

Sylvie

It's a mistake, Sylvie tells herself. A terrible mistake. She tells herself this even as she sits in front of the computer, even as she feels slightly numb, even though a tiny voice is telling her that it's not a mistake, that something is very, very wrong.

She hesitates over the keys. There is nothing Google will not be able to solve, and perhaps — a faint dash of hope filters in — perhaps there will be some sort of explanation.

It takes Google less than five seconds to bring up Margaret Alice Hathaway, seconds more to discover she does indeed live in Connecticut, is known as Maggie, and has a husband called Mark.

It isn't proof, she tells the voice. There must be thousands of Mark Hathaways. Sylvie moves the cursor to images, and her screen fills with small photographs of Margaret Alice Hathaway. Numerous pictures of this preppy blonde in a group of identikit women, smiling at some benefit or other.

Sylvie doesn't find the proof until page five. Just when she is about to believe that it has been a mistake, there is Mark. With Maggie. And their children. At a picnic at their sailing club.

Sylvie gasps, as if a dagger has gone straight to her heart. This time there is no mistake.

More Googling brings up more information. Their children; their home; their lives.

Sylvie's fingers fly over the keyboard as her silent tears drip down, and when she has gone through all the information she can find, she gets up to walk out of the room, only to discover her legs can't support her. Slowly, her back to the wall, she sinks down to the floor, where she curls up, her entire body heaving with sobs.

The phone rings as Sylvie lies tucked up in the foetal position, too exhausted, too shocked to move.

She lets it ring, not moving until the phone clicks to the machine only to start ringing again as soon as the first call has ended.

Her entire body feels like lead as she moves to the phone. But she snatches it up when she sees it's Eve.

"Eve!" She tries to sound normal, upbeat; as if her world hasn't just fallen apart.

"Hi, Mom." Her expression is flat, dull.

"Where have you been? I tried phoning you for hours yesterday. Is everything okay? I've been so worried."

There is a long pause.

"Eve? What is it?" Sylvie can hear panic in her voice; she forces it down. Does she know? Of course not, how could she know? "Do you need me to come out and get you?"

"No. I'm with Claudia."

"Just tell me, are you okay? Do we need to talk when you get home?"

"Yes." Eve's voice is small. Sylvie is terrified, but she knows her daughter, knows not to push.

"I love you," she says.

"I love you too."

After Eve's phone call, Sylvie sits at the desk for a while, looking at the pictures, trying to make sense of it. She calls Mark, over and over, but his phone is switched off, and she realizes she has no way of getting hold of him. He has designed his life in such a way that he can disappear, has always disappeared, and only now does so much make sense.

Later, she moves to the kitchen and pours herself a large vodka. At the kitchen table she sits sipping her drink, a reel of her life with Mark going through her mind, trying to pinpoint how he got away with it, how she could have been so stupid.

Her head fills with the sound of the deep narrative tones of Harry Nilsson from a childhood musical, saying something about seeing what you want to see and hearing what you want to hear. It is so obvious, now, to see how he got away with it. She just doesn't know why. If this woman was already his wife, as she clearly was, why did Mark marry Sylvie? Why not just have an affair? Why not be honest, at least with her?

Angie zooms up to the house and lets herself in, coffees in hand, to find Sylvie still at the kitchen table, a half-empty bottle of vodka in front of her.

"It's a bit early in the day, isn't it?" Angie frowns. "I know it's five o'clock somewhere, but it's barely lunch —" She takes one look at her friend's face and sits down, laying a hand on her arm. "What is it? What's happened?"

Sylvie looks up at her, then bursts into tears. As Angie takes her in her arms and strokes Sylvie's back, her heart is in her mouth at the thought of what might have happened.

It is Angie's turn to drink the vodka.

"I can't believe it," she keeps saying, looking at Sylvie and shaking her head. "I just can't believe it." She knocks back a full glass of vodka in one gulp and reaches for the bottle to top them both up. "If you hadn't found the pictures I wouldn't have believed it. I can't. I mean, this is Mark. Mark! How can this be true?"

"I don't know." Sylvie shrugs. "But I know that it is. And the worst thing of all is there's a part of me that isn't surprised. There's a part of me that . . . knew."

Angie's mouth falls open in shock. "You knew?"

"I didn't know he had another wife —" she is slurring now, her voice impatient — "but I couldn't shake this feeling that something was up, something wasn't fitting into place, but I couldn't face it. Every time I started to think it was odd when he didn't call for a few days, or that maybe he was having an affair, I'd just push it deep down. I can't believe I've been so unbelievably stupid."

"If you've been stupid, we've all been stupid." Angie takes her hand. "Mark is the last person in the world I would expect this from. He's charming and funny and —"

"Don't," whispers Sylvie, a lump rising in her throat. "I can't bear it."

"I'm sorry." Angie has tears in her own eyes. "I just can't believe it."

"I know. I can't believe it either. I keep thinking it must be a mistake. And that this should happen now, of all times! I honestly don't know that I have the strength to go through this. I've got my marriage being a sham, my daughter being ill and my mother on her deathbed."

Angie falters. "I didn't realize it was that bad. Is she really on her deathbed? I thought she was going to recover."

"She's not going either way right now. I want to feel upset. My mother is lying in a medically induced coma, possibly on her deathbed, and I feel nothing. If I'm really and truly honest, I'm hoping she won't recover." Sylvie looks at her friend, stricken. "How disgusting does that make me? What kind of a person must I be?"

As Sylvie silently weeps, Angie puts her arms round her. "You're a little girl who was abused," she whispers. "Your mother has treated you disgustingly your entire life, but it's not your fault. It's not your fault."

Sylvie says nothing, just lays her head against Angie's shoulder and allows herself to be rocked, allows the tears to fall freely.

Later, when they have bypassed tipsy and gone straight to drunk, when Angie has decided to sleep over to make sure her friend is okay, they sit by the computer, scrolling through the pictures.

"Look at those kids!" Angie shouts. "Christ, Sylvie. They all look exactly like Mark. Fucker. She looks awful." Angie peers closely at his wife. "Stepford Wife on steroids, no? Weird that he should be married to someone so completely different to you. She's just so . . . blonde! And perky! And . . . pink. And green! I hate her," she growls, and Sylvie starts to laugh.

The laughter grows until Sylvie tips over the edge to sobs, then Angie, who has always been able to hold her liquor far better than her friend, helps her into bed and tucks the duvet round her so tightly, so comfortingly, that for a minute Sylvie feels safe, and warm, and loved.

CHAPTER
TWENTY-SEVEN

Sylvie

It is the middle of the night and the phone is ringing. It is not Clothilde, she registers, pulling herself out of her deep, hungover sleep. Who, then, is calling at this hour?

Mark!

"Hello? Hello? Hello?" Sylvie's tone is urgent, but there is no response until she asks quietly, her voice almost a whisper, "Mark? Is that you?"

"It's not Mark," the caller says.

Instantly, instinctively, Sylvie knows exactly who it is.

"Is this . . . are you Maggie?" Sylvie asks tentatively. There is a long silence. "You're Mark's wife?"

"As are you, I understand," says Maggie.

"I didn't know," Sylvie offers eventually. "I just found out myself."

"I realize that," Maggie says. "It's just all a bit . . . overwhelming. I don't really know what to believe any more. Have you seen him?" she asks, quieter now.

"I haven't," Sylvie says. "I thought perhaps he was with you."

Maggie laughs wryly. "And I with you. He's definitely not here, and he's not answering his phone.

No one at his office is picking up. It seems he's disappeared."

Sylvie blanches. "I'm having the same experience. And worse. I've had debt collectors here."

Maggie snaps to attention. "Debt collectors? What do you mean? They showed up and took things from your house?" The fear is evident in her voice.

"Apparently they are not legally entitled to enter without your permission, but of course they intimidate you to the point where they do whatever they want. They loaded Mark's Harley onto the truck, but didn't get into the actual house."

There is a short pause. "I'm sorry, what did you just say?"

"They took Mark's Harley-Davidson."

"Mark has a . . . Harley-Davidson? Oh God. Buck, our fourteen-year-old, will die!" At this Maggie starts to laugh. It is at first a giggle, then a full-throated chuckle, before hysterical laughter leads to a round of sobbing.

Sylvie says nothing. She sits quietly, knowing the Mark she has known, and loved, is a very different Mark to the one married to the woman on the other end of the phone.

Hiccups, then sniffs; the sound of Kleenex being pulled out of a box, loud snorts.

"I'm so sorry," Maggie apologizes hoarsely. "I don't know what came over me. I'm scared. And angry. And sad. And I have no idea what to do. I can't believe this betrayal. I'm furious, but then I keep hoping he's going to show up and tell me everything's fine."

"He's very good at explaining his way out of things," Sylvie murmurs in agreement. "There were times when he'd disappear for days, no calls, no texts. I'd be there worried sick, but he'd come back and say —"

"He was at a sales conference? Away with no mobile phone service? Broken phone?"

"Of course he said the same things to you. It makes sense now. But at the time he made the implausible sound plausible, even though there was a part of me that always sensed there was something wrong."

"Isn't it ironic how much we have in common?" Maggie says. "Perhaps I shouldn't say this to you, but I have been furious with you."

"Of course, you would be. But I didn't know," Sylvie says. "I would never have got involved with him had I known."

There is a silence. Then, "I don't even know what to believe any more. I just know this is the worst thing that has ever happened to me."

Sylvie is silent. She doesn't need to say anything. It may not be the worst thing that has ever happened to her, but it's pretty damned close.

"Oh God!" Maggie starts to weep. "What if he's left us with nothing? What if I have to work? How do I support a family myself? Our children?" Sylvie hears Maggie's voice rising to a panicked whine. "I don't even know where the finances are."

As Maggie's hysteria builds, the calmer Sylvie becomes, fighting her irritation at how spoiled Maggie sounds.

"Maggie, I have no idea what your situation is, but my advice to you is to start figuring it out. You'll have to sift through every piece of paper you can find. I'll have to do the same. You need to go to every bank you know you have accounts with, and talk to all the credit card companies so you have an accurate picture. You may be fine." She doubts this, but doesn't want to bring Maggie back to the edge of hysteria. "As for working, most people do that. I've worked most of my life and, even though Mark didn't want me to have a full-time job, hard work doesn't scare me, and it shouldn't scare you. As mothers we do what we have to do to look after our children. I may not be able to have the life I have had for the last eleven years —"

There is a sharp intake of breath. "Eleven years? That's how long you've been married?"

Sylvie pauses. "You didn't know?"

"I . . . I didn't realize." Her voice sinks. "How do you hide something like that for eleven years? How did he get away with it?"

"Because we let him," Sylvie offers simply. "I wanted to believe him, so I turned a deaf ear even when his excuses were so implausible they had to be lies."

"And I was too self-obsessed to notice." Maggie's voice is a whisper, and Sylvie, unexpectedly, feels a pang of sympathy at what the other woman must be going through.

CHAPTER
TWENTY-EIGHT

Sylvie

Sylvie has driven her own car to the airport to meet Eve, despite Angie's insistence that it is crazy for the two of them to drive separately.

"Something is wrong with Eve," Sylvie explained. "I feel that she knows . . ." She sighed. "That's crazy. She can't know. But I sense something. I need to drive her home alone."

Now Sylvie stands next to Angie at the airport, vaguely aware that around her there is a sea of people whose lives are continuing unchanged, whereas, knowing that everything in her life is a fraud, she is only pretending to be normal and is as uncomfortable in her skin as she has ever been.

"You're okay," Angie keeps saying. "You're okay."

But Sylvie doesn't know if this is true. She must be okay for Eve; she must be strong, must somehow find the words that Eve will be able to hear, but how can she knowingly cause her daughter — already in such a fragile state — yet more pain?

Claudia is first out, with Eve, so painfully thin, seemingly more so, although this may be because Sylvie hasn't seen for her a few days, lagging behind.

The girls are subdued, quiet, and Eve's eyes are swollen. The two mothers meet eyes across the heads of their daughters as they hug them, Eve not wanting to let go. As Sylvie holds her, she feels Eve's tiny, frail body shudder with a silent sob that Eve must have been holding in, and Sylvie waves to Angie that they should leave.

Everyone in the airport recedes and Angie and Claudia quietly walk away, while Sylvie rocks her daughter, her own face wet with tears.

"Let's go to the car," she says finally. "We can talk then."

By the time they have reached the car, Eve has clammed up. She has pushed the emotion away and sits staring blankly out of the window.

"Were the girls unpleasant?" Sylvie asks, trying to reach her.

"No."

"Did something happen with a boy?"

"No."

"Eve, what happened? I can't help you unless you tell me."

Eve turns to look at her mother, her face stricken. "I can't tell you," she whispers.

Sylvie pulls off at the next exit and parks, then turns to her daughter. "Eve, whatever has happened, whatever you might have done, I love you and I won't judge you. You have my word that I won't be mad, but something is wrong, and you need to tell me."

209

Sylvie watches the confusion flit across Eve's face, and waits silently until Eve opens her mouth again.

"It's Dad," she says eventually. "I found something out . . ."

"He has a family in Connecticut," Sylvie says dully, knowing that Eve knows.

"How . . . You knew?"

Sylvie shakes her head. "I found out yesterday. How did you find out?"

Eve starts to tell her the story, haltingly at first, then in a rush of words, ending with her sense of horror as she walked through the house and noticed the photographs, saw her father with another family, her explosion at Grace and running out, wanting to be anywhere but there, wanting to do anything to stop the pain.

"There is some pain that can't be stopped." Sylvie holds Eve's birdlike hand, stroking her fingers, feeling every bone and joint through the skin. "And you and I need help with this."

"What has he said? How has he explained it?" Eve is less interested in help, more interested in an explanation, but Sylvie gently brings her back.

"I haven't spoken to him. His phone is switched off. But, Eve, I need to talk to someone about this." She is lying. The thought of sitting with a therapist and exposing her shame is horrifying, but this is the only way to have Eve agree to see someone.

Looking at her now, seeing just how frail and sick she looks, Sylvie knows that this is likely to push Eve over the edge, and that isn't a chance she can afford to take.

"And you need to talk to someone too."

Eve's eyes harden, and as she pulls her hand away Sylvie notices, suddenly, her protruding collarbones, the sharp planes of her shoulders, the hollow pockets round her eyes.

How could she not have realized Eve had got this bad before, her condition compounded by her doubtless eating next to nothing in New York?

"Is this about the food?" Eve says, wary now. "Because I'm not sick. If this is a trick to get me to see a therapist, it won't work. I've told you a million times, I'm just not hungry. Especially not now."

"I know," Sylvie replies, careful to acknowledge Eve. "That's what concerns me. You've been through a tremendous amount, more than any teenager should have to go through, and you don't have to go through this on your own."

"I'm fine," Eve mutters. "I'm coping."

"Coping isn't the same as living," Sylvie says. "Trust me. I know." She watches as Eve, struggling to be strong, to prove to her mother that she's fine, suddenly sags, her face crumpling as she bursts into tears.

CHAPTER
TWENTY-NINE

Maggie

Shock doesn't hit all at once, I have learned. You discover something so awful, so life-changing, the only way you can cope is to jump straight into denial.

It hits you, you stop believing it, start to explain it, then it hits you again. You start to justify, look for reasons why; you look round at everything you have built, everything you love, everything that defines you, and you realize that nothing, nothing, is what it seems.

That's when you throw up, or faint, or sit on the floor, numb with shock, with your arms hugging your knees, tucked in a dark corner for hours and hours.

At some point I go into Grace's room. I am being a terrible mother. I should be there for Grace but I haven't got it in me. I walk in to find Grace curled up on her bed, Chris sitting next to her, one hand resting on her back, as he reads her *A Little Princess*, her favourite book when she was small.

I start walking over, thinking I should be the one to comfort her, but hesitate when she opens her eyes and narrows them as she looks at me.

"Where is he?" she spits, her expression cold.

"Who?"

"Your husband," she says.

"I don't know." I have no idea why she seems so angry with me. "I've left messages. I don't understand what's going on. I'm trying to find out. Maybe there's an explanation."

"Yes. I already know what it is." Her voice is flat. "You drove him to it."

I gasp.

"You know you did," she continues, hatred spewing from her. "You're so mean to him all the time, always shouting at him, at all of us, always wanting everything to be perfect. No wonder he went looking for another woman. You know how Eve described her mom? Laid-back. Laid-back!"

As her words rise to a scream they pierce my heart like a knife.

"She said her mom was easy-going. He couldn't wait to get away from you because you're such a fucking control freak, and now you've ruined all our lives."

"Grace, stop!" Chris implores. "We don't know anything yet."

"Yes, we do," she says, turning on him. "We know that we spend our lives walking on broken glass in case we do anything to upset her, but Dad found a way out. I don't blame him. I wish I could find another mom."

I back out of the room then. I don't want her to see the tears running down my cheeks. I don't want her to see me curl myself up on the floor of the bathroom, with the door locked, groaning with pain as I rock back and forth, wondering just how much pain a person is able to withstand.

213

★ ★ ★

Later, I sit numbly at the kitchen table as Lara stirs tea bags into hot water, then carries the mugs over to the table and gently slides one in front of me, adding the honey I would usually add myself, for I seem to be incapable of doing anything.

"Do I call the police?" I raise my eyes to hers. "A lawyer? I don't know what to do. She said she's going to call the police."

"She? Oh. The other wife."

"Her name is Sylvie." I stir the honey and watch it dissolve as the liquid moves in lazy circles in the mug. "She seems much stronger than me."

I haven't stopped thinking about my phone call with her yesterday. Before I spoke to her I had imagined her as some seductive, omnipotent, evil bitch. I hadn't expected her to be another woman in pain. I hadn't expected to hear the humanity in her voice.

She didn't ask about my life with Mark, but I told her anyway. Perhaps I shouldn't have done, but I needed her to hear. Whether she knew about me or not, I needed her to hear, needed perhaps to validate myself, my life, my children's lives.

I have three children, I told her. Chris Hathaway, Grace Hathaway and Buck Hathaway. I have been married to Mark Hathaway for twenty-two years.

He is a natural athlete, was a hockey player at college, but now prefers tennis or golf. He hates lace-up shoes unless they're sneakers, won't eat fish unless it's salmon, and his favourite movie of the last few years is *Old School*. He loves the Rolling Stones.

My husband. My love.

My voice had completely broken by the time I finished speaking. There was more to say, so much more. I wanted to tell her what a wonderful father he is; how he looks when he's moving inside me; how irritated I get when he comes up behind me, grabbing my butt, and how he always thinks it's funny.

I wanted to tell her how he proposed. At his dad's sailing club in Kennebunkport, after a drunken evening with his dad, who was trying to keep a low profile, which was hard given how well known his dad was. Mark and I sneaked outside to the deck for a cigarette and Mark produced his grandmother's ring, proving he had planned this in advance, taking my breath away as he solemnly, drunkenly, fell onto one knee.

I wanted to tell her what a great husband he is. How he does all the shopping, ferries the kids around to everything when he's home, can fix pretty much anything in the house.

I wanted to tell her how sick it made me feel to describe a man who sounds perfect, who is anything but.

But I couldn't tell her of my disgust that I was describing a man I hadn't noticed in years. I hadn't seen him because I was too busy climbing the social ladder to care about Mark.

And I couldn't tell her that mostly I feel sick because, in remembering the good, I'm reminded of

215

what I have always known to be true. It's what Grace screamed at me today.

I don't deserve him. I never did.

I am not good enough.

CHAPTER
THIRTY

Maggie

The doorbell rings. I ignore it, muting the television just in case Kelly Ripa's voice drifts out of the window to the driveway, letting the intruders know I'm home.

This morning the reality hit me all over again: the shame, the fear. And I was right back to square one, to wanting to stay in bed and hide for the rest of my life.

The doorbell forces me up, to furtively peer through the shutters. A black Range Rover in the driveway, a blonde in tennis whites climbing back in and driving off, doubtless having left something on the doorstep.

I can't get out of bed. I haven't heard from Mark. I've left countless messages, from the relatively sane "let's talk about this" kind of message, to the late-night sobbing "how could you do this to your children, how could you do this to me?" kind of message.

I go into the bathroom and my eye falls on Mark's shaving kit, tucked in the corner, and as grief crumples my face again I hold onto the counter for support. I can't believe this. I can't believe this is actually happening to me.

I'm not sure which is worse: losing Mark, or losing my life.

I'm not sure it matters any more.

There is a smell in the bathroom, and it takes me a little while to realize it's me. Days of lying in bed, not showering, not brushing my teeth, leads to me wrinkling my nose in disgust as I pull my nightgown over my head. Then I pause to examine myself in the mirror. Am I really so flawed, so awful, so inadequate that my husband needed to find someone else?

I turn to the side, cupping the pot belly I can't get rid of, no matter how hard I work out, how many juicing, aka cleansing, aka starvation diets I do. Other than that, my body is honed at the gym, sculpted at Pilates, my hair cut, highlighted and blown out regularly.

Botox keeps the frown lines at bay, Perlane gives me back the cheekbones I never had. I like to think I look young for my age, rather than someone who has had work done, but all the girls I know have the same treatments I do, and think the same thing, and I look at them and know exactly what fillers they've used. And where.

My face doesn't look so good today. Not eating for just a few days has given me a gaunt, wild-eyed look. My hair is stringy and greasy, a big zit forming just below my hairline.

I step back and cup my breasts, holding them up, defying gravity. Is it this that Mark wanted? Is it that I am not particularly interested in sex? Of course I used to be, when we first met. Before we were married we were wild, but somehow I became less and less interested once I had walked down the aisle.

Then came Chris, then the others. Neither Mark nor I had the energy to pretend, wanting nothing more than to fall asleep to the dulcet sounds of the television set.

Mark was always exhausted from travelling. Isn't this what happens to all married couples after a while? No one in this town is having sex. Not with their husbands, at any rate.

I have friends who have indulged in discreet dalliances, but if I'm not going to have sex with Mark, I'm certainly not going to have sex with anyone else, and not, as others I'm not going to mention have done, with the trainer or the landscaper or — heaven forbid — the contractor. Why on earth would I risk all this to end up right back where I started?

When was the last time Mark and I made love? A month ago? Two? The night of Grace's play, I think.

Oh God. Was it really January? Months ago! Mark instigated it, as always. It was quick, and nice, as always. We ended with a peck, then I rolled over to sleep and Mark went downstairs to work. As always.

I wonder how often he and Sylvie made love. I wonder if he was as disinterested in her as he was in me. Did he use the same moves? Was she better than me? More active? Did she do things to him I would not do?

I won't think about this now. I can't. It is all I can do to deal with the enormity of the impending change: what it means for me; what it means for the children.

They are creeping around the house as if they are frightened of me.

Except Grace, who is hardly ever here. She is staying with various friends, something I would normally disallow on school nights, but I haven't got the energy for her hatred, her disdain, her pain.

I've turned on the shower and crawled back into bed to wait for the water to heat up, when my bedroom door opens. Startled, I grab the covers and pull them up, terrified one of the Range Rover ladies has infiltrated the house, will see me like this, will report the godawful mess I'm in.

It's Grace. I sink back, relieved, before wondering why she isn't at school.

"What time is it? Why are you home?"

"I don't know. I don't feel well."

I attempt to sit up, to appear as in control as I did before my world fell apart, and I peer at her closely. There is something strange about her. Something off.

"Grace? Have you been . . . drinking?"

"God, no!" she spits. "Are you crazy?"

"I'm sorry. You just look . . . odd."

"I told you. I don't feel well."

"Maybe have a little rest for an hour or so then I'll take you into school? I know life is really hard right now, but this is your final year and it's important. Please don't screw it up because of this."

She gives me a withering look. "You're not exactly the best person to be giving me that advice," she says.

"I know, but you've got your whole life ahead of you and I don't want you to ruin it."

"It's already ruined," Grace says, the pain apparent in her eyes.

"Oh sweetie," I say, and pat the bed, longing to put my arms round her and make it better. "This is horrible. I wish I could make it better but I can't. We just have to support one another and do the best we can."

Grace doesn't make a move from the doorway. "Support one another?" she snaps a sarcastic bark. "You haven't been out of bed in six days. You missed my chorus recital and horse show. Thank God people have been dropping off food because you're nowhere to be seen. Jesus, Mom. This isn't all about you. We've lost our father, and right now we have no one who's there for us."

"I'm trying," I say, but my voice cracks. "I'm trying to be there for you. I want you to talk to me about it. I want to help you . . . I just . . . don't know what to do." I start crying for real.

"But you don't want to help!" Grace shouts. "You just lie in bed all day doing nothing. I wouldn't want to talk to you about it anyway because it's all your fault! Dad wouldn't have left us if you weren't so controlling. I understand why he's gone. I hate living here with you. The only thing that ever made it bearable was Dad being here. I hate you," she yells. "You've ruined my life!" And she turns to leave, slamming the door behind her.

How do I reach her? How do I help her? How do I help any of my kids when I know what they're saying is true? When I can't even get out of bed to look after them? Not only was I a terrible wife, I'm also a terrible mother. She's right.

I lie, numb, staring at the ceiling, listening to the shower in the bathroom run and run, and I honestly have no idea what to do or how to handle this life on my own.

Or whether I want to handle this life at all.

I'll admit it. I lie in bed thinking about suicide. I can't see the point any more; I don't care about anything any more. I could do pills. Or slash my wrists. Part of me knows I would never do it, but there is another part that needs to try this on. How would the children be? Would they even care? And Mark. What sweet revenge would that be for him to have to carry that for the rest of his life.

I am brought out of my sick, twisted thoughts and back to my senses by Buck. Lovely, sweet Buck, so young yet so perceptive, so loving, so good.

I hear him knocking gently on the bedroom door and calling hello five minutes after Grace has gone, then he comes in with a cup of coffee and a plate of cookies.

"I thought you might like this, Mom." He leans forward, kissing my cheek, and I gaze at him with tenderness.

"I'm sorry," I whisper, as my eyes brim over. "I'm sorry I'm being so pathetic. I just haven't been feeling well."

"It's okay," he says. "It will be okay with Grace too. She's just hurting. You know what a daddy's girl she is, and she can't deal with him just disappearing."

"How about you?"

Buck shrugs and looks away. I know he's in pain, but he won't tell me. Not yet.

"I'm okay. If I stay busy it keeps my mind off it a bit. You should do that, Mom. You should really get up and get busy. I swear it works. Not permanently, but for a bit. Until someone reminds you."

"You're right." I sit up and sip the coffee, although my stomach can't handle the cookies.

"Busy. I need to get busy." I smile, before mulling over the last part of his sentence. "Buck, when you say until someone reminds you, have people said anything to you at school?"

He shifts uncomfortably and gives a small shrug.

"What are they saying?"

"Not much. Just they heard my dad has another wife and life in California. A couple of people asked if it was true my dad was a con man."

I groan. No wonder Grace is staying at home. Kids can be so cruel. They have no idea of the impact of their words. Everyone talks about bullying, feels they are cognizant of the dangers, yet all it takes is one unconscious comment, one observation that trips off the tongue, and a child's self-esteem is destroyed for years.

There was a case of Facebook bullying at school last year. At the time even the kids admitted that their dad had been right about Facebook. He has always insisted the children stay away from social media sites — he is paranoid about the lack of privacy, terrified of the damage that can be done to people's lives by thoughtless, careless words published online.

"Is that what people think?" I ask. "That he's a con man?"

"Just a few. They said we'd have to sell this house and end up with nothing."

"What?" I am now spitting with anger. "Who said this? I want to know who's saying these things."

"I don't even know their names," Buck lies. "Just kids in another homeroom." He looks up at me, a hint of fear in his eyes. "Is it true?"

"No!" I state firmly. "We know Dad has disappeared, and we know he has other people he cares about on the other coast, but none of the other stuff is true. We're not selling the house, and he is absolutely not a con man. And he loves you, Buck. Even if he leaves me, he's not leaving you. I promise."

Buck clearly doesn't believe me. I don't believe me. I don't know what to believe, but I want to protect these children as best I can, and however much Mark has betrayed us, he is still their father and they need him.

"You want me to make my lasagne tonight?" I ask, and Buck grins and nods his head vigorously.

"Tell you what. Get Chris to drive into town and pick up ground beef and mozzarella, and I'll cook. I'll even get out of bed and eat with you." I ruffle his hair before pulling him close for a hug. "I love you, Buck."

"I love you too," he mumbles, getting up and turning just as he reaches the bedroom door. "And Mom? Could you maybe shower before coming down for dinner?"

★ ★ ★

I have just stepped out of the shower when the phone rings. I wait for one of the children to get it, but when I peer at the number I see "unknown", which means it could be Mark.

I snatch it up, instantly breathless, my heart sinking as I hear Kim's fake-concerned voice.

"Maggie! I didn't think you'd pick up! Everyone's been calling you for days. We were so worried."

"I'm fine," I say. "Thank you for your concern, though."

"But are you really fine?" Her voice is like honey, so slippery and oozy you'd never know what a bitch she is. "I just wanted to let you know you're in all of our thoughts. Is there anything I can do, Maggie? Anything at all?"

"You could find my husband," comes out of my mouth, and I mentally curse myself. I didn't mean to say those words out loud, and certainly not to Kim. "I'm kidding," I cover up quickly. "We're just figuring it all out."

"So it is true?" she says. "He does have this wife and child? Linda was a divorce lawyer and she says he's definitely going to jail. You poor thing. This must be so awful. And I heard the money's all gone. Oh Maggie. You must be in hell. I just cannot even imagine what you must be going through. Honestly, if I had to sell this house I think I might kill myself. Especially after you've put so much work into it. Where are you going to move to?"

"Kim," I say firmly, "I don't know where you're getting your information, but that's certainly not true.

Our finances are perfectly fine, and, as far as the house is concerned, we're not going anywhere."

"Really? But I heard —"

"I really don't care what you heard. It's not true. I have to go now. Thanks for all your concern." This last bit was dripping with sarcasm, and she can't have missed me slamming down the phone while I gnashed my teeth in fury.

When you are on top in this town, the world is your oyster. I have only ever been on top. I have been the one feeling more grateful, blessed, lucky than those poor souls who have gone through changes in life circumstances that make the rest of us shudder with horror.

The woman who lives in a huge house, until her husband leaves her for the brighter, shinier, younger model then pays for killer lawyers and accountants who make the beleaguered wife look insane, and claim poverty until the divorce is finalized, when husband and shiny second wife build a bigger, better, more impressive home, while the first wife, now ground down by divorce, squeezes into a rental apartment above someone's garage.

The first wife, once one of us, has a "closet sale". Scores of women lucky enough to have held on to their wealthy husbands claw frantically through piles of Chanel, cashmere, Hermès, sifting through diamonds and pearls, paying whatever the poor former wife is asking, refusing to feel guilt at benefiting from someone else's misery.

226

I would go to the sales too, but never with any sense of relish. The thrill that others seem to feel at the downfall of a friend is not something I can share. I am always aware that my status is built on fragile foundations, and the fear of losing what I've created stops me from feeling anything but relief that it's not happening to me.

There, but for the grace of God . . .

It could be us. Any of us. Each time we see the first wife, now working in a clothes store, or getting her real estate licence, it reminds us of the fragility of our own marriages.

After the obligatory "Hi, how are you?" and "You look fantastic!" and "You've lost so much weight it must be the Divorce Diet!" we try to get away as quickly as possible, away from the reminder that this could be us if we're not careful.

Which is why we are Pilate-d, yoga-d, highlighted, tanned, waxed, Perlaned, Juvédermed. We take it for granted that we are all top tier, and we plan on staying there, on keeping our husband's attention, on making sure we don't become like her.

Yet here I am. Alone. Betrayed. Humiliated. And the subject of everyone's attention. The object of their Schadenfreude. Oh how they delight in talking about other people's misery, attempting to hide their joy with sympathetic expressions, murmurs of concern, casseroles left on the doorstep, as if being left is an illness, an affliction.

Which of course it is.

I want to know what people are saying. I want to tell them none of it is true; but I don't know what's true and what's not. I only know that bad rumours are like multiple games of Chinese whispers: one salacious rumour will only produce more, until the end result bears no resemblance to the truth.

I can't march into town. I can't even drive through. The prospect of seeing sympathy in people's eyes fills me with horror. And shame. I cannot, I shall not, be an object of pity.

I cannot, I shall not, take their phone calls. Welcome their visits. Not until I have somehow managed to get over the humiliation, the devastation of everyone knowing what I have always tried to hide, the shame that is the reason why Mark has left.

That I am not enough.

Later, I get angry. It fuels me, gives me the energy to get dressed, go downstairs. Anger sees me pulling dishes out of cupboards, layering pasta and tomato sauce, furiously grating Parmesan cheese over the top. Buck and Chris move quietly round me, laying the table without being asked, feeding the dogs without complaint.

Buck even goes outside to gather up his lacrosse stuff. I watch him out of the window and see him go into the pool house. Everything has been removed, all evidence of the day everything changed.

I pour a glass of wine and follow him outside, walking slowly to the edge of the lawn, then I turn and look back over the pool, to the terrace and house.

Whatever the rumours are, whatever ends up being true, I will not lose this house. I could not be happy anywhere else.

Even if I have to take on the most expensive lawyers in the business, I will not end up in some garage apartment on someone else's property, having to take Buck out of private school, even, heaven forbid, working.

I will not go back to where I started. I heard what Sylvie said, about gathering information, finding out where we stood, but I haven't been ready. I'm almost there, though.

Am I scared of what I might find? No. I am terrified.

The boys sit at the table as I spoon lasagne onto plates and pass them over to outstretched hands, with warnings to be careful, plates are hot.

"Where's your sister?" I look from one to the other, but they both shrug.

"Go tell her it's dinner."

Chris looks at Buck to do it; Buck stares straight back at Chris.

"It's your turn," Buck says. "I fed the dogs. And I picked up stuff in the yard."

"Yeah, because it's your stuff," Chris says. "I laid the table. And got the mail."

"Jesus!" I shout, banging the spoon on the table, which makes them both jump. "Stop fighting. Just go tell her."

"I'm glad I'm going away next week," Chris mumbles as he pushes back his chair belligerently.

"You know what?" I turn on him. "Me too." He stomps upstairs to get Grace, and I instantly regret snapping at him.

"I'm sorry," I say as soon as he walks into the kitchen. "I didn't mean it. I just can't deal with the fighting right now."

"'K," he mutters, and I sigh.

"Did you tell Grace?"

"Yeah. She says she's not hungry."

I walk to the foot of the stairs and yell her name, which is something I never do. I have a no-yelling policy. There's something so déclassé about screaming through the house; it makes me think of my parents. I have even indoctrinated the children, much to their disgust, to actually walk from room to room with the phone if there is a call for someone who is in another part of the house.

Yet here I am, breaking all the rules.

"What?" she yells back.

"Get down here!"

I wonder how long it will take. A week ago she would never have dared speak to me like this. A week ago she was respectful and polite. I feel as if my daughter has been swapped in the middle of the night for this sullen, rude, furious child who I am finding it increasingly difficult to like.

"What?" She lingers on the landing looking at me with disdain.

I temper my voice. "It's dinner time."

"I'm not hungry."

230

"I don't care." I grit my teeth. "We are all sitting together as a family, and you are joining us. You don't have to eat anything."

"We're not sitting together as a family," spits Grace. "Just in case you hadn't noticed, Dad is missing. Thanks to you. So I won't be joining you."

"You damn well will," I say, speaking slowly.

"I damn well won't," she replies, before pushing past me, slamming her shoulder into mine, then running out of the back door and disappearing up the driveway.

I stand there shocked to my core.

I have no experience of this. I have no idea what to do. So I close the door, walk into the kitchen, ignoring the open mouths of both Chris and Buck, and pick up my fork.

"You may start," I say, and I force down a mouthful to try to bring a little normality to what is rapidly becoming a life I do not recognize at all.

CHAPTER
THIRTY-ONE

Grace

Landon's mom is trying to treat me as if everything is normal, but she's being extra careful, and I know she's trying to be a mom to me right now, in the way my own mom isn't.

She hasn't asked me anything, hasn't brought it up, but is suddenly treating me as if I'm another family member. Sure, Landon and I have been together for ages, and I've always got on really well with his family, but I've rarely been included on their regular weekend outings to, say, Cedar Point, and now I'm invited sailing as if I've been a permanent member of the crew.

Not to mention that Mrs Carver has offered me use of the guest room whenever I feel like it. She even replaced the white quilt with a blue and white one that used to be her daughter's because it makes it warmer, and she's filled the shower with fresh shampoos and conditioners. The brands I use.

I'm staying here tonight because I can't face being at home. Everyone in the house is asleep, including Landon. He has made jokes about tiptoeing across the landing, but I warned him not to. The last thing I need is for his mother to kick me out, and I will not go home. I refuse to go home.

I climb under the covers and prop the pillows behind my back, pulling Landon's old teddy bear onto my knees, making him sit there, then open his arms to give me a hug.

He's squashy, and scratchy. Bits of him are still furry, but most of the fur has been loved off. I rest him on my shoulder like a baby, and pat him on the back as tears well up in my eyes.

I should be at home. I shouldn't be here, in this unfamiliar room that is becoming more familiar by the night. I want to be there for my brothers, Buck in particular, but every time I see my mother, I feel this wave of fury, and it's all I can do not to explode.

I blame her. I do. And I hate her for it. For seventeen years I have lived with her, watched how she treated Dad, how she took him for granted, barked orders at all of us, put all of us down, and how, eventually, she drove him into the arms of someone else.

I wanted to hate Eve, but I couldn't. I wanted to hate her mother, but I couldn't even do that. Everything Eve had said about her mom, before we'd figured things out, sounded amazing. She sounded like the mother I wish I'd had. She was, it seems, the wife my dad wanted too.

But how could he do that to us? How could he just walk away from us? I understand that he's not answering Mom's calls. I understand why he'd want to get as far away from her as possible, but to not answer

233

my calls? To ignore me? I have never been through anything so painful in my life.

My father, the man I have spent my entire life worshipping, has disappeared. As I grew up, the only thing I was ever sure of was that I was a daddy's girl; that my father loved me; that no matter what happened, my daddy would be there for me. How wrong I was.

Which leaves only my mother, whose love I have doubted as far back as I remember. My mother, who is quite the most self-absorbed and selfish woman I have ever come across, who has never really cared about us, never put aside her own concerns to think about our needs. And now she doesn't even care enough to keep pretending to be a good mother any more. She doesn't care about putting on a show.

She just stays in bed.

So I don't feel like I've lost one parent. I feel like I've lost both.

And we three are left, like orphans, to fend for ourselves. Chris is back in New York, the drama too much for him, but I am seventeen so I am still at home, and Buck? Buck is barely a teenager. Buck needs his mother. I know, in her absence, I should be the one there to take care of him, but I can't stand it any more, can't stand being around her, knowing she is the one to blame for all of it.

I always knew my mother never loved me. I never knew, until a few days ago, that my father never loved me either. I sit, teddy on my shoulder, tears silently rolling down my cheeks until the entire house is quiet. I watch the clock until it is after midnight.

The Carvers go to bed early. They like cocktails before dinner, large ones, then wine with the meal. They encourage us to join them, rules and laws be damned. This means they sleep early and heavily, and I know where all the liquor is kept.

When I am absolutely sure everyone is asleep, I tiptoe down the hallway and listen outside everyone's door. Huge snores from both Mr and Mrs Carver, lighter ones from Landon.

I make my way downstairs, using my iPhone as a flashlight. In the pantry is three-quarters of a bottle of red wine they opened earlier tonight. I know they won't notice if it's missing. Landon's always joking that they have no idea what's in the cellar. I fold it into my robe and go back upstairs, softly shutting the door and sitting back down on the bed.

I never used to like wine. Nor vodka. Nor, in fact, any alcohol in particular. I am finding that the more you drink, the more you develop a taste for it. The Carvers have delicious red wines. Granted, you are not supposed to swig it from the bottle, but I am still able to appreciate it, and I will say one thing: it definitely helps take my mind off all the shit in my life.

CHAPTER
THIRTY-TWO

Maggie

At four in the morning I am staring at the full moon, not even trying to get back to sleep. The computer is next to me on the bed, open to tab upon tab of men leading secret lives.

I am stunned at how similar their stories are.

And stunned at how stupid I have been.

There are, apparently, eight key deceptions used by spouses leading a double life, all of which I have spent years explaining away.

1. *Change in sexual appetite.* Of course Mark had a change in sexual appetite. So did I. Who has the time and energy with children and the craziness of our lives? Surely this is the same for all the married couples we know? How was I to know this was a sign?

2. *Hidden money or financial records.* It has never been officially hidden, but I have no interest in any of that. Mark takes care of the money. He always has. He's a hugely successful businessman who was able to buy the company he worked for, and build it into

something that enabled us to live the life we always dreamed of. When I see a bank statement, my vision starts to blur. I'm sure I could have been more involved if I'd wanted to be, but I didn't. That was Mark's job. I was busy raising the children — was I really expected to keep an eye on that too?

3. *Regular clandestine contact with an ex-spouse or ex-girlfriend/boyfriend.* There are no ex-spouses or girlfriends, and, my God, I hope there are no ex-boyfriends. That would be one betrayal too many. There's no clandestine contact with anyone, because there isn't anyone. Although, I suppose, clandestine would mean I wouldn't know about it. But as charming and handsome and loved as Mark is, he didn't bring old friends to our relationship. He always said he was making a fresh start with me. I never questioned it. Maybe I should have.

4. *Hidden or inaccessible pagers, mobile phones or e-mail accounts.* He has one mobile phone, one email account, and no pager. That I know about.

5. *Frequent travel.* Of course. His clients were on both coasts. I didn't like it, hated how many events I had to attend unaccompanied, but I understood. It all made sense. Then.

6. *Exclusion from the usual "couples' events".* When Mark is here, he comes to "couples' events". Admittedly, he doesn't like large

crowds of people he doesn't know, but neither do I. He is exceptionally private, and careful about our social circle. We have built a circle of people we trust. No. A circle of people Mark trusts. The truth is, I never understood it. I'm beginning to understand it now.

7. *Deceptive body language.* What does that mean? Does it mean he shiftily looked away when I asked him where he'd been the last few days? He didn't, and I never asked. It never occurred to me to question him. Sometimes, obviously, I expressed my discontent at constantly having to go to events by myself, but so many husbands here are away that there was always someone else on her own, usually a group, so we'd meet first for a cocktail. It was fun. More fun usually than going with Mark.

8. *Mysterious use of cash for "incidentals" or poorly explained expenses.* Why would he get cash from me when he is the one working to provide for us? Wait . . . We were supposed to be taking the kids to Aspen for a winter break and he cancelled at the last minute. He didn't say he wouldn't be able to come but that we should still go; the whole thing was just cancelled. The hotel had made a mistake and double-booked, and there was no other availability. The kids were devastated. I'll admit, it sounded odd. No other availability? In Aspen?

Now that I think about it, when I told Mark

that I'd just find another hotel he went nuts and said that the kids had been too spoiled, that there would be no Aspen this year, end of story.

He apologized later, explained that he'd been under tremendous stress, but went on to say that he was so worried the kids had been brought up with an enormous amount of privilege and he wanted them to have a time out; he wanted them not to fly somewhere glamorous for a vacation, but to learn to amuse themselves at home.

It sounded plausible at the time.

The money.

Why aren't the credit cards working?

Sylvie seems as concerned as I am. Mark is worth millions. This doesn't make sense. Money doesn't just disappear. If Mark has disappeared, and no one could deny that now, he must have taken the money with him.

But why would he have left us with no working credit cards? I don't write cheques, but I need to find out what's in the accounts. He wouldn't have emptied out our accounts. We're his family: his wife, children. Whatever else he may have done, I know he will not have left us stranded.

Debt collectors are another issue entirely. That's a business issue. I'm sure he has the real money, the big money, somewhere.

Find Mark, and we'll sort this whole mess out.

★ ★ ★

Today I am strong enough to start digging. Today I need some answers. This morning I will be going to his office. I am certain he won't be there, and his employees are refusing to pick up my calls, but someone will know where he is, and I will not leave until they tell me.

I will sit in their office all night if I have to. All week. After that, I'm going to the bank.

CHAPTER
THIRTY-THREE

Maggie

Usually when I go into the city, it's with the girls for a shopping trip. Sometimes we go to the theatre, more often we're hitting Bergdorfs or Barney's, leaving someone's SUV in a garage for the day, pumped up with adrenalin at spending money, leaving our suburban lives, pretending to be big city chicks.

We stride confidently into stores, trying on everything, tossing expensive designer clothes next to cash registers as casually as we would buy magazines.

We giggle and trip our way up Madison Avenue, arms laden down with clothes that must be worn immediately, the rest shipped straight to Connecticut in order to avoid the tax.

I pass those same stores today expecting to feel a pang, but I don't. Just as I feel no pang knowing I will not be returning to Theory to collect the pretty items so carefully wrapped, waiting in a bag on the floor behind the counter.

I do not need them. I never did. Clothes and jewellery were of interest to me only as a passport out of my working-class life, a life of shouting, and poverty, and nothing to look forward to.

Those accoutrements became more interesting when I married Mark, when I saw how effective they were as currency among the young families with whom we socialized.

My sense of insecurity was so rampant, my fear of rejection so strong, I believed that however perfect my accent, however highlighted and blown-out my hair, however impeccable my manners, I would never be truly accepted unless I became more them than them.

I grew up thinking class was the determining factor, but when I moved to Connecticut I quickly realized it was money. Nobody cared about old money. The fact that Mark came from an old moneyed Mayflower family was relevant only to the old guard. To the new, it was relevant only if he had the money to go with it.

I put pressure on him, I'll admit. My competitive nature came out. I saw the power these girls wielded simply because they had the most expensive jewellery, or the biggest house, and I wanted to feel powerful too.

I pushed Mark to buy the company. When he finally said he had found investors, had raised the money to do so, I was thrilled. The *Gazette* listed him, some years later, as the millionaire CEO of Hath Office Solutions, and the only thing that would have made me happier would have been a "b" instead of an "m".

I pause outside Gucci, think of the bags I may need to sell if my worst fears come true. Not that the bags matter. Not that any of the possessions matter. They may have given me power, but in a world that is so superficial, so meaningless and narcissistic, it is no power at all.

Oh how ashamed I am.

I keep walking, idly wondering what I will do if Mark is there. The thought of him, so handsome, devastating in his navy suit, lighting up the room with his smile, is like a dagger in my heart, and I cannot help a sob coming out.

I do not want to cry again. I do not want my mascara to run down my face when I have spent so much time attempting to look like I am strong, unbreakable; like I am the kind of woman who will no longer be played.

And yet I cannot help but know that if he apologizes, looks deep in my eyes and asks my forgiveness, explains this was something that got out of hand but he cannot, will not, leave me and the children, I may not be able to resist.

If he swore blind that he would never see Sylvie again, never be unfaithful again, wanted to go back to how it was in those first, early years of marriage, would I believe him? Would I want to try again?

Bastard.

I grind my teeth as the anger rises, imagining myself slapping his face, storming out, taking the children and making sure he never sees them again, taking the house, all his money, and ensuring he spends the rest of his life paying for what he did to me.

I catch sight of myself in the tinted windows of the stores I stride past. I feel terrible, but I look fabulous. High patent heels, short skirt, swingy coat, Prada bag slung over my shoulder. I am the image of city chic — you would never know I live my life in suburban splendour. I look, in short, like the trophy wife the other trophy wives aspire to be.

How could Mark even think of being with anyone else?

More to the point, why do I already know the answer to that particular question?

I march up to the security guard at the desk, photo ID already in hand, and give him the name of the company. He frowns.

"Tenth floor?" I remind him. "Hath Office Solutions? Mark Hathaway?"

The other guard leans over. "Oh yeah! They moved."

I stare at him. "What? When?"

"About a year ago? Yeah. It was just over a year ago."

"But . . . that's impossible," I sputter. How would Mark not tell me something as big as moving his company? Why would he not tell me? I stare at the guard, attempting to quieten the questions in my head, before realizing he is saying something.

"I'm sorry, what?"

"You want a forwarding address?"

I am so grateful I could throw my arms round him in a giant hug. I settle for the best smile I can muster given the circumstances, which unexpectedly lights up the guard's face in return.

"You have a nice day," he says as I leave, and I know it's going to be a lot better than it was looking five minutes ago.

244

★　★　★

I have never felt unsafe in New York, but I have always stayed in neighbourhoods I know well. Striding down Madison Avenue, 57th Street, hitting restaurants on the Upper East Side, I am confident, safe, I belong.

This is not a neighbourhood I have ever been to before. I step gingerly over the legs of a homeless man who is leaning against an overflowing garbage can, his hand outstretched, and I avert my eyes, only to see a line of grimy people shuffling through a doorway marked "Free Methodone".

Slipping my left hand in my pocket I work off the diamond rings, instantly feeling better with bare fingers, then I pull my jacket a little tighter and look back down at the piece of paper in my hand.

I stop outside a dingy building, sandwiched between a mobile phone store and the kind of convenience store you only go into if you're a tourist, a drug addict, or desperate.

Even as my brain computes that the information on the piece of paper must be wrong, I am kicking a cigarette butt aside and pushing open the door to study the black board on the wall that lists the companies in those white plastic letters that can be pulled out and rearranged in seconds.

In other words, temporary.

There it is. Second Floor. Number 203. Hath Office Solutions. I'm not nearly as confident as I step into the elevator, all well-rehearsed speeches having flown from my mind, and I'm pretty certain I have a look of horror on my face. The corridor is dingy; there are several light bulbs missing, and the carpet saw better days about thirty years ago.

I knock on suite 203, moving my ear close to the door, pausing but hearing nothing. I knock louder, before grasping the handle and taking a deep breath as I prepare to confront, if not my husband, the people who know where he is.

CHAPTER
THIRTY-FOUR

Maggie

The door is not locked. It opens smoothly, but there is no one inside.

No one has been here for months.

There are desks and phones and dozens of boxes, all covered in a thick layer of dust. Even without the dust this is the kind of grimy hellhole that would drive a person insane.

It doesn't make sense. Nothing makes sense. Why would Mark have moved offices? Why would he ever have moved to an office like this? There must be a mistake. Or at least an explanation.

I wander to the window, taking in the cracks in the wall, the yellow, damp patch on the ceiling, and I know I'm about to throw up. I grab the wastebasket and retch, but nothing comes up other than painful, sharp bile.

I prise open a box, to find it stuffed haphazardly with papers. Order forms. All genuine. All Mark's company. Huge orders. So it isn't all lies.

Then I pull out a letter informing Mark of impending legal action for non-fulfilment of a paid order. I reread it before placing it back in the box, stacking the boxes together, and taking them all downstairs, where I pile them into a cab and take them back to my car.

They know me well at the bank. Not because of financial dealings, but because we attend all their social events, and when Ray, the manager, had a baby, we sent a basket of personalized bibs.

Ray is on the phone when I pop my head round the door. His face lights up when he sees me, and he gestures for me to sit down while he attempts to extricate himself from his conversation. I exhale as I sit. Surely if there were a problem he would have phoned me. He has known me for years. If there were no money, Ray would not have kept quiet.

"How are you, Mrs Hathaway!" He puts down the phone. "It's good to see you!"

"Busy, busy, busy," I reply, as I always do. "How's Janie? And the kids?"

"They're grrrreat," he says, rolling his Rs, as he always does.

"Nina must be in fourth grade now?"

"Fifth!" he exclaims proudly, turning round a photo frame on his desk for me to see how big they are.

"Oh Ray, they're adorable!" My eyes mist slightly as I remember when mine were that young. "I can't believe how quickly it goes."

"I know!" He smiles, before leaning forward and shuffling some papers. "I'm glad you came in, Mrs Hathaway. I've been leaving messages for your husband. We really need to get hold of him."

I stare at him. Do I tell him Mark's left me? What if he then refuses to give me information about our finances? But it's a joint account. Surely I'm entitled to know how much money is in there.

"Is everything okay?" I ask first.

"I'm sure it's fine." He pulls a file from a cabinet behind his desk, flicks through it, then frowns. He goes back to the beginning and reads through it again, this time more carefully.

He clears his throat, then stands up, the file in his hands. "Mrs Hathaway, would you mind waiting here a minute? I just need to speak to my assistant manager."

I watch through the blinds, but I can't hear anything. The assistant manager is explaining something; Ray listens, says something, then they both look at the file.

Ray comes back, his brow creased. "We really do need Mr Hathaway to come in," he says, attempting to disguise, with little success, the slight panic in his voice. "I know he travels a lot, but he needs to at least phone us today. It's actually rather urgent."

I can't not tell him. "Ray, I don't know where he is. He's left me."

His expression changes to shock as he stumbles over his words. "I'm . . . I'm so sorry."

"Here's the thing, Ray. I presume he's left me. He seems to have another family in California. All I can tell you is that he's disappeared. None of my credit cards are working, and I'm down to about a hundred and twenty-six dollars, which is nothing with two children at home to feed, and I have no idea what to do."

I burst into tears.

★ ★ ★

There is no money in any of the accounts.

The various accounts, and there are many, that Mark has opened over the years — based on his good standing, long relationship and, at some point, large amounts of money — are all overdrawn.

The total overdraft amount is $764,483.33.

"I don't understand." I am staring numbly at the papers in front of me. "How can the bank let someone reach an overdraft of this magnitude? This is three-quarters of a million dollars. Why . . . how does this happen?"

Ray looks worried. "I don't understand either. I'm going to have to start an internal investigation. I authorized an overdraft facility last year when there was a significant amount of money in the accounts. But it was for two hundred thousand. I'm not sure how . . ." He sighs, and I realize suddenly that his job is on the line too. He may not know how this happened, but he's the manager here, and therefore responsible.

"Ray?" I set the papers down on the table. "How do these things happen? How do accounts empty? How are overdrafts allowed to grow to this size? Are you telling me there's no money whatsoever? Nothing? Everything's gone?"

He shuffles repeatedly, delaying the inevitable, but the expression on his face says it all, and when I stand to leave my legs are wobbly, and I forget to say goodbye. Or thank you. Or tell him to send my best to Janie. It's all I can do to get to the door.

CHAPTER
THIRTY-FIVE

Maggie

You would think I would be completely numb, but, as I head to the car, my brain goes into overdrive, frantically trying to find a way out of this mess.

This is, after all, what I am good at. I did not run all these committees because I have pretty clothes. Although that helps. I am, as my children relentlessly complain, controlling, organized, super-efficient. I am resourceful and determined.

Look at the life I have been able to build out of nothing.

The life I now need to save.

With no access to credit cards or money in the account, I need cash, and fast. The fridge is empty, I have three mouths to feed, and in my purse, right now, is $126.32.

I make a mental inventory of what I can sell. We have valuable paintings, furniture, jewellery, clothes. So much stuff. I shudder at the prospect of hosting a closet sale, becoming one of the women I have pitied. There must be another way, and right now, with under two hundred dollars to my name, I need to find it.

I pull into the car park of the grocery store. I know we have pasta at home, and if I buy a can of tomatoes and cheese, a lettuce, I can at least throw together an inexpensive dinner for the kids tonight.

As a shard of sunlight glints red off a stone, a memory sparks. Four years ago, Mark gave me an antique ruby necklace for our anniversary. It is beautiful, and one of a kind, but it is so ornate, the gold chain so heavy, I have never done more than admire it in the closet.

I didn't tell Mark. When he asked why I never wore it, it was easy enough to tell him I wore it all the time and if he were at home more he'd realize that.

The night he gave it to me we were having dinner. The Griggs were with us, and Lizzy spent the whole evening drooling over the necklace. On the way out we ran into Kim, and of course she noticed the necklace immediately.

She swooped like a vulture, scooping it up to examine the diamonds and ruby, knowing it was real, knowing it must have cost a fortune.

I saw how she coveted it and I enjoyed her disappointment when Mark told her it was from an antique dealer in New York, was one of a kind.

Lara told me Kim was obsessed with my necklace for months. She trawled the Internet repeatedly trying to find another, or one similar. She was planning to go to the dealers in New York to see if they could find her one, and had even asked Lara to get her a photograph.

I wore it once, provocatively, for the Ladies Tea at the tennis club. Even I recognized it was a little over the top, but how could I not, when Kim was going to be there? She made a beeline for me, pointing out the necklace to all her girls, who had heard all about it.

"If you ever get sick of it," she said, "I'll buy it from you. I'm serious."

"I doubt I will," I said, and laughed, "but I'll keep it in mind."

I was sick of it already, but I would never have sold it to Kim.

The thought of having to phone her is horrifying, but it's the lowest-hanging fruit. How much is the necklace worth? I vaguely remember it being valued at eight thousand dollars.

Eight thousand dollars is a fortune. To think Mark could spend that amount on a gift without even thinking . . . If I'm careful, that could last a while, at least until I manage to sell some other stuff, find a job, figure out what to do next.

I pause by the canned goods and whip out the phone, scrolling to Kim's number, shuddering in anticipation of the mock sympathy in her voice.

"Maggie!" She picks up almost before the phone has even rung. "I've been so worried about you. I'm so glad you called. I wanted to know how everything is. Have you heard from Mark?"

"Everything's fine." I keep my voice as light and breezy as possible. "I'm actually phoning for a different reason. I was going through some stuff today and realized I really have to get rid of the things I don't wear or use. I was about to take some of the jewellery to Sotheby's, when I remembered you quite liked one of my necklaces, so I just thought I'd let you know in case you were int —"

She actually gasps. I hear it. "The antique ruby necklace?"

"Yes."

"I love that necklace. I'll take it. Seriously. How much do you want for it?"

My mind starts whirring. I had thought the full eight thousand, but what if she loves it so much she'd pay more? That would be wrong . . . but I'm destitute . . . and God knows she can afford it . . . and the price of gold has gone up . . . really I should have it valued . . . but I haven't got time . . . but but but but . . .

"Maggie? Are you there? Hello?"

"I'm sorry. You dropped out. What did you say?"

"How much do you want for the necklace?"

"I don't know," I falter, embarrassed now. "It was valued at eight thousand?"

"Eight thousand?" She has the audacity to laugh. "In today's economy? Wow. I think that's a little steep," she says.

"Really?" Two can play at that game. "Do you have any idea what's happened to the price of gold?"

"I know gold is expensive," she says condescendingly, "but this is an antique, and antiques aren't holding their prices."

"Not according to Sotheby's," I lie.

"I'll give you four," she says.

"Kim, I just told you it's valued at eight. I have the paperwork. I would take eight."

"I'll give you four and a half," she says.

254

I'm so tempted, but then I remember her face when she saw the necklace, her obsession with finding one just like it, her competitiveness with me — and I know I can pull this off.

"I'm so sorry, Kim," I say, and I am proud of myself for sounding authentically apologetic. "I wanted to offer it to you first, but Sotheby's are willing to put eight as their reserve."

She snorts contemptuously. "Well, good luck with that!"

"Thank you!" I sound almost stupidly perky. "Betteridge have some pretty estate jewellery. You might find something similar in there. Good luck!" I end the call, smiling to myself as I count the seconds.

. . . eight . . . nine . . . ten . . . eleven . . . twelve

The phone rings. "I'll take it." No charm to her voice this time. "Can I bring a cheque over in about half an hour?"

A cheque would be swallowed up.

"It will have to be cash," I say.

There is a silence as she waits for an explanation, which I won't be giving.

"Fine," she huffs eventually. "Make it an hour."

I slide the phone into my back pocket and turn the corner to find two women I know huddled together, whispering. They break apart as they see me, plastering false smiles on their faces as they embrace me.

I do the same false smile, the same "Hi, how are you", and no one mentions the tea, or my collapsing, or the fact that my husband has disappeared; but they

255

have definitely, but definitely, overheard the conversation I have just had with Kim, and will doubtless be spreading it all over town within minutes.

I know this is true because when I reach the car I realize I forgot the cheese and I have to go back inside, and as I walk down aisle seven I hear one of those women, Kristy, in aisle six, already on her phone, relaying my conversation, my obvious desperate need for money, with a relish that makes my heart pound and leaves me shaking and breathless.

So I turn the corner of that aisle and stand still as Kristy reaches up to the top shelf for a box of pasta, oblivious to anyone around her, anyone who might hear her private phone conversation, until she turns and sees me, when, to her credit, she widens her eyes in horror, stops talking mid-sentence, and turns a greyish shade of spray tan.

As I walk out she runs up and grabs my arm. "I'm so sorry," she says. "Maggie, I don't know what to say. I'm so sorry."

I turn slowly, sick to my stomach, knowing that there is nothing I can do about the Kristys of the world; knowing this town is full of Kristys; knowing this kind of personal disaster is what fuels them, and nothing I will say can change it, although perhaps this might make her think twice.

"Kristy, I'm going through the worst thing I have ever been through in my life. I truly and sincerely hope nothing like this ever happens to you, but, if it does, I hope the people you once thought of as friends treat you better than you have just treated me today. I hope,

256

for your sake, they don't have loud, public conversations on their phones, relishing in gossip and other people's misery." Kristy is standing there with tears trickling down her cheeks as I continue. "There are a couple of sayings I have always loved. The first is: people show you who they are not by what they say, but by what they do. And, the other is: when people show you who they are, believe them. So thank you, Kristy. Thank you for showing me who you are."

I turn then and get in the car. At the end of the road I glance in the rear-view mirror, to see Kristy still standing there, not moving a muscle.

"What are you doing?" Grace is in the doorway of Mark's office, emanating waves of her constant hostility towards me. I am grateful she is spending so much time at Landon's, grateful not to have the additional worry of Grace's mood.

I try not to react to her, not to withdraw, but to recognize that as hard as this is for me, it is so much harder for Grace.

But I can't make it better. There is nothing I can tell her to bring her father back. When she screams at me that it's my fault, I know she's probably right, and there is nothing I can say.

"Sorting out stuff." I barely look up from the boxes, the piles of papers I have been going through until I am exhausted from the process.

As organized as I am, Mark has always been in charge of the household, and God how I wish that hadn't been the case. How I wish I had thought to take charge earlier, but of course he wouldn't have allowed that to happen, for how could he otherwise have woven this vast web of lies?

And it is vast.

Despite my resourcefulness, each time I open a new envelope, a new box, my chest tightens at what I might find.

Unpaid bills. Threats of bailiffs. Letters with threats to sue from companies who have paid him in full then never received anything. Papers that were served. None of it makes sense. How could he have got away with it for so long? And why? Why did he let it get to this?

I still don't believe, can't believe, that the money's gone. Far more likely, surely, that he has removed money from our accounts and has it elsewhere.

For all I know, he's in Bermuda by now. Or Brazil. He has surely disappeared with millions, for he is worth millions, I am certain. I remember reading an article about the company when he was sales director. The money is somewhere. It has to be.

When I find Mark, I'll find the money.

I look up at Grace. "I'm trying to figure out what's going on. It seems Daddy's finances are a bit of a mess."

"What does that mean?"

I know I shouldn't tell her, shouldn't show her, but I'm sick of being blamed for this, of Grace walking round shooting me devil looks when her father remains the angel who can do no wrong.

I hand her a letter in which a client is threatening to sue Mark.

258

Grace reads it with a frown. "So? I still don't understand."

"I'm not sure," I say. "I think Daddy was in some financial trouble. That might explain why he's disappeared."

Fear glints in her eye. "Financial trouble? Are we in financial trouble? Do we have to sell the house?"

As gently as I can I tell her I don't know what's going to happen with the house, but I can't help casting a glance at the pile of house-related papers, including a repossession notice.

"We can't sell the house," Grace says, her voice starting to rise.

"Hopefully we won't have to, honey," I soothe. "We'll figure it out."

"But not if we sell the house. This is my home. This is the only home I know. You can't sell this house."

"Grace, I don't want to sell the house either. I love this house just as much as you do, and it's my home too. I have no idea what the future holds, but I promise you we're all going to be okay."

"No!" Her voice breaks. "We're not. How do you know that? If Daddy doesn't come home we're not going to be okay." She looks round wild-eyed, noticing a stack of things in the corner. "What are those?"

I have stacked three Matisse lithographs that Mark was given by his father, and that I'm pretty sure are worth some money. An antique clock and walnut writing box.

"Those are some things I'm thinking of selling," I explain.

Grace squats down and looks at the prints as I brace myself. "You can't sell these," she says through gritted teeth. "These are Daddy's. They're from Grandpa Jack, and someday they are for us. This one's mine —" she points to one — "and I don't grant you permission to sell them. None of them. All of this is for us."

"You don't have a choice," I say wearily, no longer caring. "If you want to eat, live, do all the things you like to do, we need to get some money, and quickly. Your father has disappeared and left us with nothing. Do you understand? Your father, who can do no wrong, has left all of us with nothing but a huge goddamned mess. Whatever I can sell to make some money, I'm going to damn well sell."

Grace grabs her print and runs out of the room. I think about going after her, but realize I haven't got the energy. She comes back once more to stand in the doorway and glare at me. "I hate you," she hisses. "You are a selfish bitch, which is why he left. And I'll never forgive you."

Once upon a time I would have jumped up and reprimanded her immediately. She would have lost the car, the phone, the privileges. She would have been grounded for a month. I would have terrified her with fire and brimstone into an apology.

Today I don't care. Today I'm too busy trying to figure out what in the hell to do next.

CHAPTER
THIRTY-SIX

Grace

I haven't been able to face anyone since this happened.
I've been skipping school by pretending to be sick,
thereby avoiding pretty much everyone I know.

Mid-summer will be harder. I'm in tennis programmes,
horse programmes and sailing programmes. Right now
I'm planning on keeping away from everything,
although my guess is none of it has been paid for
anyway, so I may well end up on my own all the time,
which will be a lucky escape.

Tonight is the first night I've agreed to go out. Poor
Landon. He can't stay at home any more, not when all
his buddies are out partying, and Jamie is eighteen, so
this is a big deal. There's no way I can say no.

Anyone who's anyone is going to be there tonight.
Which is everyone. Normally I wouldn't care — being
seen in the right places doesn't mean anything to me,
and so although I am perfectly happy to go to these
things it's because I want to spend the evening hanging
with the guys, not because I want to be seen. But
tonight I know everyone's going to be talking about me,
and I haven't figured out how to handle it.

I wouldn't describe myself as one of the "populars", but I know that's how others see me. I see myself as someone who gets on with pretty much everyone, but who stays away from the mean-girl stuff.

Honestly? Life's just too short. And when you have a serious boyfriend, things are different. You don't have time for the silly, bitchy stuff. Not that I ever did.

I've never spent time around the girls who whisper about the other girls, nor have I ever been a girl others have whispered about. Until now. I know it's not me, it's nothing I've done, but that's not how this town works. You are your family and your family is you.

So, yes. I'm nervous. I have this vision of walking in and having everyone's eyes turn to me while a silence descends on the room, groups of people pointing and whispering, "That's the one whose father has another family."

I have to go out sometime. And this is Landon's best friend. There's no way we can miss it. I'll just make sure I look the best I've ever looked — I'll out-Blake Lively Blake Lively herself, and I'll have them all whispering. This time for the right reasons.

Landon bought me a dress a few days ago. It was on sale, a flouncy peach chiffon with delicate spaghetti straps, perhaps the most gorgeous dress I've ever seen. I hated that he bought it for me, that he had to buy it for me, even though his face was so filled with grown-up pride as he counted out the dollar bills and handed them over.

I tip my head upside down and blow it with cool air to get the windswept look, leaving some Velcro rollers on the ends while I dust some glow on my cheekbones.

A lash of mascara, a sweep of clear gloss, thin gold hoops in my ears, then I slip on the dress, finish drying the hair-wrapped rollers and untwist them, spraying the loose curls into place.

I've looked such a wreck for what feels like so long that I'd forgotten I ever looked like this. I'd forgotten I could ever look like this.

The peach dress sets off the tan I have unwittingly acquired this spring, the sun bringing out natural highlights in my hair. My cheekbones shimmer, my face looks healthy, and happy.

I reach to the back of the nightstand and pull out a half-bottle of vodka, listening to make sure there are no footsteps, no forthcoming knocks on my bedroom door, before I take a large swig.

I look so good you would never know how crappy I feel inside. Abandoned by my dad, my mother a mess, my whole world is coming apart and nobody but Chris and Buck and Landon seems to care.

Honestly, without Landon I don't know what I'd do. Without Landon and a couple of sips of vodka each night, just to take the edge off things.

CHAPTER
THIRTY-SEVEN

Maggie

Lara is a good friend, but she doesn't understand. She cannot understand.

As compassionate as she may be, I see her own fear reflected back at me. Not one of these girls is thinking of how best to help me; they're thanking the Lord this isn't happening to them.

The only person who understands in any way, shape or form, is Sylvie.

Sylvie is the only other person who knows that the police are looking for Mark. She told me last week that she was going to contact them and register him as a missing person. But since then we've both had visits from the police in connection with the charge of bigamy, and we've been told that there are warrants out for his arrest in connection with fraud, embezzlement and larceny.

How ironic that the woman I should be hating most in the world has become my only solace. Who better than her to understand what I am going through? Who better than her to dwell alongside me in my well of self-pity?

I try not to phone her often — I am aware that she does not seem to call me, or rely on me to hold her up — but when things are looking dark, when I don't think anyone else will understand, I find myself picking up the phone and dialling California, knowing that something about Sylvie will always soothe me.

She doesn't let me dwell in my pitying place too long. She scoffs when I whine, is horrified by the fact that I care what anyone in this town thinks. When I confessed my reluctance to hold a closet sale, to publicly out myself as a subject of pity, she was stunned.

"Are these your friends?" she asked. "These women? Do you trust them? Do you feel safe with them? Do you love them and feel loved by them?"

I had to think. Heather. Casey. Kim. Even Lara. The women from tennis. The committees. The charities. The women who walk through the revolving door of cocktail parties that passes as a social life. Are they truly my friends? Could I answer yes to any of the questions Sylvie just asked?

I honestly don't know.

What I do know is that I am not as strong as Sylvie. I know that she is holding up better than me.

Even the kids are holding up better than me. Chris is away at school; Grace spends her time with Landon; Buck has eschewed hanging with his lacrosse pals recently, to hang with his mom instead.

I want him to be with friends, but I don't push him away the way I used to, when I was too busy to have children hanging off me with their endless needs and wants. I need him now, my sweet fourteen-year-old, this man-child who hides his pain from me by constantly checking I'm okay.

I don't want to be that mother the kids have to look after. I don't want them to have that responsibility, yet there is something so comforting in having a child, this child, here.

As the baby, Buck has always had a soft spot in my heart. Untrue to say he is a favourite — they are all my favourites at different times, Chris as my firstborn, Grace as my only girl — but Buck was unexpected, a delightful surprise when we had decided we were done. The minute I gazed into his eyes I saw sweetness reflected back at me.

These past few days he has hung out with me on the sofa in the family room. We make big bowls of popcorn and watch TV shows, movies. Right now we are in the middle of *Sherlock Holmes*, episode three of the British version, when the doorbell rings.

I groan as I set the popcorn down. "Are you expecting anyone?"

He shakes his head.

"Will you get the door, Buck?" I look at him pleadingly. "I don't want to see anyone."

"Aw, Mom," he grumbles, but he's already shifting.

I pause the movie as I wait for him, but stand up when I hear men's low voices at the door. I go into the hallway to see Buck looking terrified, two uniformed policemen standing in front of him.

"Mrs Margaret Hathaway?" The older one with a kindly face looks at me, and I nod, grasping onto the hall table for support as my legs feel a little wobbly. "Wife of Mark Hathaway?"

"What's happened?" I whisper.

"Everything's fine," he says calmly. "I'm Sergeant Scarper. Can we go somewhere private to talk?" He casts a quick glance at Buck.

I lead them into the kitchen, where they refuse my offers of a seat, a glass of water, coffee.

"Mrs Hathaway, your husband, Mark, has been arrested by the California State Police Department."

I gasp, even though I have been expecting this.

"He was apprehended on the beach in Santa Monica and brought in for being drunk and disorderly. They then discovered he had a Missing Persons Report filed in California, and —" he exchanges a glance with his partner — "a number of outstanding warrants in both California and New York for fraud, embezzlement, grand larceny, and . . ." He clears his throat and averts his eyes.

I know where he's going, know how hard this must be for him, and I cannot believe I'm going to hear this out loud, that Grace was right and it hasn't all been a terrible mistake.

"And it seems he has now confessed to being legally married . . ." The poor man is embarrassed; he doesn't know that I know. ". . . to, um, two women at the same time. The California State Department has confirmed the legality of the marriage in California. Do you have a copy of your marriage licence?"

My legs are not my own as I walk out of the room to get the marriage licence, only to see Buck standing just outside, stricken.

He has heard everything.

PART THREE

CHAPTER
THIRTY-EIGHT

Sylvie

Sylvie and Eve are back at the UCSD's Eating Disorders Treatment Center for their first consultation with Dr Lawson. He is sympathetic and kind. Old enough to be unthreatening, he has twinkling eyes and a shiny, bald pate. He is, fortunately, nothing like Eve's father, neither number one nor number two.

They were referred to Dr Lawson following their initial appointment and Sylvie has already had a lengthy telephone conversation with him. Today she was relieved when he asked if he might have some time alone with Eve.

That was an hour ago. Sylvie is starting to lose patience, sitting in the waiting room, flicking through out-of-date *People* magazines, sighing heavily as she looks at her watch repeatedly, as if that will make the appointment end sooner.

What are they doing in there? Why is it taking so long? Should she demand to be let in? She is Eve's mother, after all.

"Mrs Hathaway?"

She looks up to see Dr Lawson in the doorway.

"Eve's just getting some blood work done," he says. "Would you come into my office? Please," he gestures to a chair, "have a seat."

And he begins to explain.

"Eve is, as you suspected, suffering from anorexia nervosa, but more lately, it seems, she has been bingeing and purging in a way that suggests bulimia nervosa. We will know much more about the state of her health when the blood work comes back, but there are certain markers that indicate she is in need of immediate inpatient treatment."

Sylvie forces herself to stay calm. "What kind of markers?"

"You will have noticed that her body is covered in a downy hair, and her hair is thin and stringy. Her last menstruation was five months ago. Mrs Hathaway? Mrs Hathaway?" The doctor leans forward, knowing what her unresponsive gaze means, having seen this so many times before. "This isn't your fault."

Sylvie looks back at him, and like every mother who has ever sat in this chair before her, she does not believe him.

"The girls I treat are very clever at hiding these disorders, masters of deception, in fact. They'll tell all the lies in the book, making all of them sound just plausible enough that you begin to distrust the evidence you can see with your own eyes. You wouldn't have known Eve hasn't menstruated for months, nor that she has fainted twice in the last month. I'm telling you this not to make you feel guilty, but to ensure you know that, for someone with anorexia, this is normal.

They will do everything they can to blind the people they love to enable them to continue controlling their food."

Sylvie wipes away a tear. "Is this about control? I keep reading it is but I don't understand what that means."

He nods. "This is the age when teenage girls start to feel overwhelmed. They're getting ready to leave home, and however excited or mature they may seem on the outside, the truth is that many feel utterly out of control, which is when they start to control the one thing they feel they can. Add more complications to that — moving house, divorce, loss — and these things can spiral quickly."

"She told you about her father?"

"She told me about both her fathers."

Sylvie swallows but says nothing.

"That must be very hard for both of you. Part of Eve's treatment will involve significant therapy, both individual and group, and these are some of the issues we'll get to the bottom of. But, Mrs Hathaway, I'm also concerned about you. To have discovered this betrayal, at the same time as your mother is seriously ill, is going to be very hard, psychologically, for you to deal with on your own. I hope you don't mind me asking, but is there someone you are considering seeing as well?"

Sylvie is used to pushing down her feelings. She is used to pushing pain and fear and loneliness aside, focusing on projects to take her mind off however bad things

273

might be, distracting herself until the emotion has subsided enough for her to carry on with life.

Mark's disappearance has been like that. She has busied herself making candles, shipping them off in boxes to whoever Angie tells her to, insisting she is fine, refusing to give in to the fear.

The regular phone calls from Mark's other wife have helped. They have cast Sylvie as unofficial therapist rather than evil other woman; the strong one; the one who can help heal.

It is a role Sylvie was born to fulfil — hasn't she, after all, spent her life trying to heal her mother? When Maggie breaks down in tears on the phone, Sylvie is the one able to talk her through, to point out that life will get better, that there is a life beyond Mark, beyond his betrayal.

Sylvie is the one able to help her husband's other wife, and in doing so she has found she is able to help herself.

Staring at Dr Lawson, she is about to smile, to reassure him she is fine, for she is the caretaker. Why would she need to see a therapist?

His eyes are full of compassion as he looks at her. "Mrs Hathaway?" he repeats. "Who is taking care of you?"

Sylvie starts to cry.

CHAPTER
THIRTY-NINE

Sylvie

Sylvie hugs Eve goodbye and walks out of the room with a smile and wave, as if she is perfectly fine, waiting until she is safely in the elevator before collapsing against the wall, emotionally drained.

Eve has been begging and pleading for Sylvie to get her out of here. She is crying, screaming, wailing, hiccuping; promising to eat, swearing on everything she has that she means it; that this time will be different. The regimen they have agreed with Dr Lawson involves prescribed eating during the day, with intravenous feedings at night to ensure Eve gets the nutrition she needs, and Eve is terrified.

They are aiming, he said, for a weight gain of two to three pounds per week, which is when Eve started to lose it.

Sylvie cannot stand to leave her alone, but it is time for Eve's first therapy, and Sylvie has to go now anyway, to visit Clothilde.

Sylvie strides through the foyer of the clinic, digging in her purse for the car keys, not noticing a couple sitting on chairs by the door. The woman nudges the man, who jumps up and whips out a camera, taking Sylvie's picture.

Startled, Sylvie is about to ask what on earth is going on when the woman approaches, holding out a tiny black tape recorder.

"Ms Hathaway? We're from the *Star*. We understand your daughter has just been admitted to this rehab clinic. Is this collateral damage from her finding out about your husband?"

"What?" Sylvie's voice is like stone. "How did you find out I was here?"

"Is it true, then?"

"I'm not answering anything until you tell me how you knew I was here." They must have found out from an employee here at the clinic, an admissions nurse . . . someone. How could they have been so indiscreet?

"Facebook," the woman admits. "Some of your daughter's friends have been posting about it."

"Oh shit." Sylvie closes her eyes for a second then turns on her heel and walks out through the door, blanking the two reporters as if they had never existed at all.

She can't go to Clothilde. Not until she finds out what's on Facebook and gets it taken down immediately. Turning into her driveway, she sees a slew of vans with antennae on top and scores of people milling around her house.

Reporters.

Shit.

She reverses quickly, driving straight to Angie's. Her friend opens the door before Sylvie has even parked the car.

"Where've you been? I've been calling you all morning." Her usual smile is missing, her face deadly serious.

"Where do you think I've been?" Sylvie snaps. "I've been admitting Eve into rehab and planning to go and see my mother, but I can't. The press have got hold of the story."

"I know."

"What do you mean, you know?"

"Because it's all over the fucking television news."

"Oh Jesus. Is it bad?"

"It's worse for the other one. She's being portrayed as a snooty social-climbing bitch. 'Superior' and 'cold' are words I remember."

"She doesn't sound superior. She sounds devastated."

"Sylvie, you haven't watched any of this stuff yet, have you? Well, you should see his house." Angie shakes her head. "It's insane! It's fucking huge! What the — ? Who the hell is this man? This other Mark is all Porsches and diamonds, and she's all Chanel and this crazy moneyed lifestyle. This isn't the man we know at all."

Sylvie sits down. "Do you think he still has money?"

"I don't know. He's certainly been spending it. Not on you, though. God! When I think of what a hard time he gave you over that jacket you wanted last year. What was it? Two hundred dollars? Three hundred?"

Sylvie shrugs. "Something like that."

"And she's swanning around in sable bloody coats. I could kill him."

Sylvie leans back and closes her eyes, resting her head on the cushion. "I'm just so tired. I have no idea what to tackle first: Eve and her anorexia, my mom with a stroke, or, the pièce de résistance, my sham marriage and lying, cheating husband. I keep bracing myself for what's next."

"Nothing's next." Angie sits next to her. "Don't you know? Bad things always come in threes. That's it. Those are your three. Now it's nothing but good all the way."

"That's hardly likely given that the press are camping on my doorstep. I can't even go home. And presumably they're looking to expose everything in my private life. Angie, I don't know how I'm going to survive this."

"Don't be overdramatic," Angie tuts. "That's my job. You're going to be fine because you're a survivor. And thankfully, unlike the other one, who has clearly spent her life trying to hide her humble beginnings, you have no secrets. What are they going to find out about you? That you're an obsessive gardener? That you make great candles and have been known to stay up all night doing so? Big fucking deal."

"What if they start asking people in town about me? What if they're already interviewing mothers at school?" Sylvie shivers in horror.

"What are they going to say? That they don't know you well but you seem lovely? The only person who knows you really well is me, and I'm certainly not going to say anything —" She is interrupted by the ring of the doorbell. "Be right back."

Downstairs Angie opens the door to find a lone reporter, notebook in hand, on her doorstep.

The reporter opens her mouth to speak, but Angie, with her most charming smile on her face, gets there first.

"Take your notebook and pen," she says, "and shove them up your arse. And yes, you can quote me on that."

Upstairs, Sylvie is on the phone, scribbling notes on a pad. She finally says goodbye and turns back to Angie, as white as a sheet.

"Who was that?" Angie sits next to her.

"The bank." She is numb. "They're foreclosing on the house. The mortgage hasn't been paid in months."

"I can't believe it! Oh God. What did you tell them?"

"I . . ." Sylvie opens her mouth to speak, but can't find the words. "I couldn't say anything. I feel too sick."

"How much is owed?"

"I don't know. I didn't ask."

"First mistake. What's your monthly mortgage?"

"I have no idea."

"God, Sylvie. Promise me you'll never get into this situation again?"

"If I ever get into this situation again I'm killing myself."

"I mean with the finances. I just mean that you have to have an understanding of where you are financially."

"But Mark handled —"

"No. He mishandled."

"But it was his money."

Angie barks with laughter. "Because he stole it?" She lets out a heavy sigh. "I know, I know. You didn't know he stole it, you thought he earned it, but, even so, you are his wi— You thought you were his wife. It's a partnership. Do you think of your house as Mark's house?"

Sylvie shakes her head.

"Exactly. It's your home. Both of you. It's the same with money, and as a partner you need to know where you stand. I'm the worst person in the whole world with figures, but I force myself to go through the credit card statements, and I know exactly what's coming in and going out. How else do you think I know I can afford to splurge on designer handbags?"

"Angie?" Sylvie, who has nodded in agreement even as she zoned out, brings her attention back to her friend. "Where in the hell am I going to live? How am I going to pay for anything?"

"We're not going to let you live on the streets." Angie covers Sylvie's hand with her own. "Worst case, you'll come and stay here until we figure it out. We will figure it out, I promise. Get the financial information together and we'll talk to Simon. For all you know there's a ton of money in a hidden account. You need to look through everything you can get your hands on and access his accounts. We're all assuming there's nothing there, but how do you know? Isn't it far more likely that he has a secret account?"

Sylvie's shoulders drop as she sighs. "Three weeks ago I would have said Mark was the last person in the

280

world to keep any kind of secret, financial or otherwise. The worst part is how stupid I feel. How stupid I must be that I didn't realize my husband had a whole other family. All those times I couldn't get hold of him, or he'd disappear, and even though I'd have this feeling something was up, I let myself believe his excuses were real. That's the worst thing. I'm so ashamed I can't stand it. This was my husband. The man I knew better than anyone else in the world. What the hell does it say about me and my judgement? How am I ever supposed to trust anyone ever again?" She groans. "How can I have been so stupid?"

"If you were stupid, we were all stupid," Angie murmurs. "Every single one of us. Simon's a financial genius, and he didn't doubt Mark for a second. The day we found out, he was so shaken up he sat at the kitchen table for the entire day without moving and went through almost an entire bottle of vodka. No one knew. No one even suspected."

"I just don't understand why. Why did he do it? What kind of man looks you in the eye knowing he's lying? Knowing he's going to hurt you?"

"You could ask him," Angie offers.

"No." Sylvie shakes her head vigorously. "I won't do that. He's ruined our lives, and right now I don't even want to look at him."

"He hasn't tried to contact you?"

"No."

"When he does you must ask him about the money," Angie advises. "Even if you have to pretend, find out

281

where the money is. He must have something. You have to find out. Promise? Please?"

Reluctantly Sylvie nods.

"As to why he did it, God only knows," Angie says sadly. "Simon said he saw a show recently about love frauds, men who do what Mark did; they were described as sociopaths and narcissists. Except they all stole money from the women they were involved with, which isn't the case here. Maybe he really was in love with two women. Maybe he couldn't make a choice. Or wanted to leave his first wife but couldn't leave his kids."

"But why marry me, then? Why not just have me as his partner?" Sylvie bursts out. "Why break the law?"

"Given his recent arrest, staying the right side of the law doesn't seem to be of huge importance to Mark, does it?" Angie raises an eyebrow.

"I wish I understood," Sylvie says, pressing her fingertips around her eyes as a headache starts to form. "God only knows how Eve's going to deal with this. This is the last thing she needs right now. I don't even know where to start in dealing with that."

"You don't have to," Angie says, leaning forward. "That's what the therapists are there for. Truly, she's in the best possible place. There's nowhere safer for her to work out her stuff than where she is."

Sylvie stands up and extends her hands to the ceiling in a big stretch, knowing Angie is right, even if she doesn't quite believe it herself.

"You're going?" Angie asks. "Are you ready to deal with the press?"

"No. You're coming with me. You can deal with them."

Angie grins. "That's my girl. Nothing I like better than a good fight. And if I curse like a mad woman they'll never air it. Would it be sick to say I'm looking forward to this?"

"Yes. Entirely."

"I won't say it, then," she grumbles, and the two women walk down the stairs.

CHAPTER
FORTY

Maggie

"Mom? Who are all those people in our yard?" Buck is walking past the window, crunching on an apple as he calls through to the kitchen.

"Landscapers?" I call back hopefully, because the landscapers had to be fired, and the grass is at a level that may never have been seen before in New Salem. Buck offered to cut it himself, but of course I haven't owned a lawnmower my entire adult life, and now a lawnmower is the last thing we can afford.

"Do landscapers drive *News 12* trucks?" I hear Buck say, before he groans under his breath and adds, "Shit. This isn't good."

I gasp when I join him at the window, seeing the NBC and CBS news trucks outside, the crowds of people standing around my front yard, reporters speaking into camera and gesturing towards the house, crews setting up, even having the temerity to eat their bagels and rest their paper coffee cups on my goddamn lawn.

"That's her!" someone shouts from outside. The crowd turns as if one, breaking into a run towards the

284

house as I dart back from the window and lean against the wall, breathing hard.

Safely in the kitchen, my heart pounding, I phone the police station.

"They are trespassing on private property. Please come and get them out of here immediately." I'm angry and scared and panicking, and just then the doorbell starts ringing.

"Just ignore it," I hiss urgently to Buck, who, well-brought-up boy that he is, was almost certainly just about to answer the door and politely tell them his mother is not willing to talk.

The phone rings. Lara. I snatch it up.

"Are you okay?" Lara's voice bursts down the phone. "This is just awful! Oh Maggie. I am so sorry."

"Lara, why is the press here? What's going on?"

There is an awkward silence before Lara speaks. "Oh Maggie. You're all over the news."

"What news?"

"Everything?" Lara says timidly. "It's been a couple of days now. I guess because Mark got arrested it was on the local police blotter, but it's gone national."

"What does that mean, 'gone national'?"

Lara hesitates, but how can she not tell me? "It's the big story on all the morning shows today. The *Today Show* are running a piece on bigamists, and *Good Morning America* have a piece coming on in about ten minutes, all about you and Mark and his life of cons."

"Do they actually have pictures of me?" I am aware that my voice is a whisper.

"I don't know where they got them from. Tons. And they're speaking to people who know you, although none of your real fr— Oh my God! Is this live?" She stops. "They're reporting from outside your house right now?"

"Oh yes. Just when you think it can't get any worse, it does." I hear a noise in the basement and tell Lara I have to go, then I head downstairs and find Buck glued to the TV, the entire screen of which is currently occupied by a picture of our house, and a reporter speaking live to camera.

"His wife, Maggie, is described as a pillar of the community," the reporter says, sweeping her hand to take in the house as the camera pans, "and, up until recently, queen of the ladies who lunch out here on Connecticut's Gold Coast. But it's a far cry from where she grew up, in a humble blue-collar home . . ."

I don't hear anything else, for a picture of my childhood home suddenly flashes on screen, more derelict and disgusting than it was then, the chain-link fence in the front, a snarling dog leaping and barking at the camera.

I am not proud of myself for what happens next. Shame and rage combine into a force that is too overpowering for me to control, and before I even think about it, with fury pulsing through my body like a red vein of anger, I'm running up the basement stairs to the front door and flinging it open, marching down the steps and straight to the reporter who is still speaking, live, to camera.

"How dare you!" I shout. "How dare you trespass on my property and embarrass my children. Get off my property now."

The reporter is unfazed. "Mrs Hathaway, did you know your husband was embezzling money?"

"Get the hell out!" I demand, searching for the police to help, but there are none to be seen.

"Can you at least tell us how you found out your husband has another wife and daughter?" the reporter continues, in her smooth, professional, modulated tones.

"Get the fuck out!" Oh sweet Jesus. Did I have to curse live on air? Did I have to curse while standing in my greying bathrobe, my not-too-clean bra clearly visible, my hair, unbrushed and tangled, framing my fury as I advance on the reporter, ready to kill if anyone takes a step closer.

She backs down, and I take a deep breath, knowing my dignity will never be restored after this; knowing that all round town women are glued to their televisions, mobile phones in hand as they call everyone they know, eyes wide with the thrill of horror at my public humiliation and downfall.

Me. The woman I used to think they all aspired to be.

CHAPTER
FORTY-ONE

Sylvie

Sylvie sits on a bench overlooking the ocean, sipping from a bottle of water, berating herself for feeling so nervous. This is Mark, for God's sake. The man she lived with and loved all these years.

The man who lied to her all these years.

She hasn't spoken to him on the phone, and wouldn't let him come to the house, as his attorney had suggested, after she borrowed money from Simon to bail him out. She isn't even sure why she put up bail, only that with Eve being so fragile she couldn't bear for her daughter to think of Mark in prison.

They are meeting at Torrey Pines — the State Reserve. While beautiful, it holds no romantic memories for either of them, is neutral enough to remove the possibility of running into anyone they know.

Not that running into people is a problem for Sylvie. She holds her head high, refusing to be seen as a victim in this. She is still Sylvie: mother, daughter, friend, artist.

She can't describe herself as wife. Not any more.

The women from school have rallied round, inviting her out with them, sending letters and emails expressing their dismay and support for her. Sylvie rarely accepts these kind invitations, but knows they are genuine.

Keeping busy is the distraction she needs. During the day she paints houses, at night she makes candles. Whatever she can do to get by. Too much quiet time and she finds herself dwelling on the past, the movie of her life with Mark running through her head, rewinding and replaying, as she tries to figure out why.

She hears him before she sees him, the butterflies in her stomach instantly waking up. She stands and turns, quickly rearranging her features to hide her shock at his appearance.

Mark, always so debonair, handsome, so very much the Californian boy next door, looks terrible: so thin his pants are hanging off him; his face gaunt; deep shadows under his eyes. Always immaculately dressed, his polo shirt is stained and worn.

If you didn't know better you might mistake him for a homeless man.

He stops in front of her and drinks her in.

"You look wonderful." The tears in his eyes seem genuine.

"You look terrible." Sylvie cannot help it. They both smile, and for a moment she forgets what he has done, sees only the man she has loved, sees the possibility in that smile — before she dislodges the thought with a shake of her head.

"Oh Sylvie," he says, reaching for her hand, but she takes a step backwards, noting the dismay in his eyes. "I'm sorry." He backs away himself, unable to meet her eyes. "I didn't mean to make you uncomfortable."

"It's fine," she says. "Shall we . . . walk?"

The path is narrow, a sandy trail along the cliffs by the water. They walk in silence, Sylvie hyper-conscious of not touching Mark, moving off the path and into the grass to avoid their arms brushing by mistake as they move.

Eventually Mark says, "I'd like to try to explain —"

"Oh, I don't think you can," Sylvie stops him. "I didn't contact you for an explanation. I contacted you because Eve has been very ill and I thought you ought to know." Sylvie continues walking, turning only when Mark grabs her arm and pulls her round to face him, his expression stricken.

"Eve? What's the matter? What is it?"

There is no doubt. Dr Lawson was right. Whatever he might have done, Mark is Eve's father and he loves her. It is clear on his face. He truly loves her, and there is no question in Sylvie's mind about what she must do.

Not for herself, but for her daughter. To help her daughter heal.

She explains, then forces herself to keep her hands by her side as Mark, knowing his own part in this, begins to weep.

When the weeping stops, she asks quietly, "Where are you living?" But she knows the likely answer.

"I'm in a shelter," he mumbles. "It's not great. I had a few nights on the street, though, so this is the Four

Seasons by comparison." He attempts a laugh, but how can Sylvie laugh at how far he has fallen?

"You can stay in the guest room." She turns to him, registering his widening eyes. "No —" she steps back, away from his hands as they reach out to her — "this isn't anything other than a kindness. I'm not sure why I'm doing this, but Eve needs your presence."

What have I done?

All the way home her emotions tumble from one extreme to the other. Pain, love, hurt, disgust, betrayal, pity. If she had a choice, she would never see him again. She has endured so much pain in her life already and she has learned that the only way to deal with extreme pain is by removing herself from it, moving on.

Her love for her daughter won't let her do that.

This isn't about her any more. This is about Eve. She hasn't even told Dr Lawson she is doing this, and will wait for the right time to tell him, but she is sure it is necessary.

Mark shows up that night, contrite, his possessions in one faded bag.

"I know you can't forgive me," he says as soon as he steps over the threshold, in a clearly well-rehearsed speech, "but, Sylvie, I never meant to cause anyone harm. I fell in love wi—"

"Stop!" she says sharply. "I don't want to hear it. You can stay in the guest room, but I am not interested in being your friend, let alone anything else. I am not interested in an explanation. I would be much happier if you spent your time away from the house when I am home, and I do not want you discussing this with anyone other than your attorney. I need to talk to Eve's doctor about the possibility of you coming to see her."

Mark, overcome with relief at not having to return to the men's hostel while he awaits the trial, closes his eyes briefly and nods, all traces of confidence, even arrogance, long since gone.

CHAPTER
FORTY-TWO

Sylvie

Angie whirls round, fire flashing from her eyes. "Are you out of your fucking mind?"

"No. Yes. I don't know." Sylvie frowns. "I hate it, Angie. I can't stand seeing him, yet there's a part of me that feels like it's right that he's in the house; it's where he belongs."

"He's lucky he even has a fucking house!" Angie scowls. "If it weren't for us lending you money that house would have been in foreclosure. God, Sylvie, I knew you were a saint but this is pushing it." She leans forward, her voice suddenly low. "Don't you dare let him back. Don't you dare let him charm himself back."

Sylvie laughs wearily. "As bizarre as this sounds, I know that won't happen. I'm not doing this for me. I'm doing it for Eve. He is her dad, and she needs both of us right now."

Angie pauses. "Is that what your therapist said?"

She nods.

"And how about Eve's doctors?"

"Haven't brought it up yet. That's next on the list."

"But why in your house?" Angie demands. "That's what doesn't make any sense. He's committed the ultimate betrayal, yet the consequence is that he gets to live in your wonderful house with you doubtless waiting on him hand and foot."

"First, I'm hardly waiting on him. I've told him to stay out of the way when I'm around."

"And he's respecting that?" Angie is doubtful. "No cosy dinners for two on the terrace?"

Sylvie thinks of how it has been the past few days, the two of them in the same house, circling each other carefully, both anxious to stay out of the other's way. As she walked past the guest-room door this morning, it opened, revealing Mark wrapped in a towel on his way to the bathroom. She stopped and stared, unable to tear her eyes away from his thin, pale frame, a shadow of the man he used to be.

"I look like hell," he offered softly. "I know. I understand they have great workouts in prison," he attempted to joke. "They say it's all you have to fill your days."

It was the first time he had mentioned prison, and Sylvie, in an instinctive response, automatically wanted to comfort him, tell him it's going to be okay.

But that's not her job now. And even if it was, she couldn't possibly tell him it's going to be okay when it very probably isn't.

Her job now is to push away all remaining vestiges of the love she used to have for her husband.

"No!" Sylvie answers Angie vehemently. "I cook a meal, put some on a plate for him and leave it outside his room. I've told him I'm not interested in socializing."

Angie shakes her head slowly. "I don't know, Sylvie. The whole thing is weird. Why would you let him back home? He can still attend daily therapy living somewhere else."

"You want to know the truth?" Sylvie bursts out. "I feel sorry for him. He looks terrible. He's so thin and gaunt; he looks like he's been living on the streets."

"Good," huffs Angie. "Serves him right."

"Angie," Sylvie urges, "he's facing ten years in jail. His life is over. I feel sick every time I look at him, but not as sick as he must be feeling inside. I don't know why he did what he did because I am too busy running to visit Eve and my mother in their goddamned hospitals . . ." Her voice breaks with a sob. "And when I get home there is no one there for me, and even though I will never forgive him, there is some measure of comfort in having another body in the house. There is some measure of comfort in knowing that I am not entirely alone."

"I'm sorry." Angie feels terrible. "I can't even imagine what you must be going through and I can't judge. I didn't mean to. Just swear to me you won't be sweet-talked into bed by him?"

"Cross my heart and hope to die," Sylvie says, without a smile, as Angie walks over to give her a hug.

It is Eve's first time out of rehab. A day pass, designed to slowly integrate her from inpatient to outpatient, when she will continue the therapy and twelve-step meetings, starting each day at her mother's house with a phone call to her sponsor.

"Great, Mom," Eve mutters as she sinks into the passenger seat, buckling herself in. "My first day out of prison and you're taking me to another hospital."

Sylvie is about to jump on the defensive but then she looks over to see that Eve is smiling.

"I'm kidding, Mom. I know I have to see Grand-mère. How is she?"

A deep sigh from Sylvie. "She's not good. The swelling in the brain hasn't gone down since the stroke, and she's not conscious."

"Is she going to die?" Her face shows curiosity rather than fear.

Sylvie shoots her a look. "Yes. Well, we're all going to die, but in Grand-mère's case it's sooner rather than later."

Eve stares out of the window wordlessly. When she turns back, Sylvie is shocked to see tears have welled up.

"Evie, sweetie? I'm so sorry. I didn't want to cause you any more pain, but you need to see her. You need to say your goodbyes, just in case."

"I don't even like her," Eve bursts out in a sob. "She's evil. I have no idea why I'm crying."

Sylvie knows. She reaches over and takes her hand.

"Loss is hard," she says quietly. "Especially when you're young. You've already been through so much. I wish this wasn't happening now, but we have to assume there's a lesson in it for us. There has to be, otherwise what would be the point? But I think there's more here. I think this loss is bringing up the loss of your father."

296

Eve is sobbing openly now. "I don't even remember my father," she says. "How can it be?"

"You may not think you remember, but it's there, and this is your first loss since your dad. It has to trigger your subconscious. We'll talk to Sonya about it tomorrow, okay? Or do you want to call her when I take you back?"

"I'll wait until tomorrow," Eve says, and Sylvie makes a mental note to call the therapist as soon as she is on her own.

Sylvie, always attuned to energy, knows something is wrong as soon as she walks into the house. Mark is not in his room, but at the kitchen counter, nursing what looks like a large Scotch.

"What's the matter?" Sylvie asks immediately. "What's happened?"

"I'm so sorry," he starts. "It's my fault. I picked up the phone without thinking."

"And?"

He sighs. "It was Maggie. She went ballistic. I tried to explain that I was just staying here, that there was nothing between us, but she refused to believe it. She's on the warpath."

"Warpath? What does that mean? Warpath?"

"She said she was going to sell her story to the press, and that we'd both be sorry."

"What?" Sylvie stands still. "What goddamned story? The press already know everything there is to know. Don't they? Mark? Is there more you haven't been telling me? What the hell else is there?"

"Nothing more. She thinks we're together. She thinks we're hiding the money and we planned this —"

The shrill ring of the phone interrupts him.

"Don't answer it," he groans. "It's probably her."

Sylvie ignores him, snatching up the phone.

"Mrs Hathaway?"

"Yes?"

"This is Dr Rothenberg from Scripps General Hospital. I'm so very sorry, but I have bad news. Your mother has had another stroke."

"What? But I've just seen her . . . I thought she was stable."

"I'm very sorry."

"How is she . . . is she . . .?" Sylvie, feeling strangely empty, can't say the word.

"I'm afraid your mother has passed away. We did everything we could. I'm so sorry for your loss," he says awkwardly. "It may be of some comfort to know she is at peace now."

I doubt that, Sylvie thinks. She's probably demanding to be at the front of the line at the pearly gates. But she merely thanks him and puts down the phone, gazing blankly at the tiles behind the stove, feeling something, but not sure what that something might be.

Now it's Mark's turn to ask what is wrong, all thoughts of Maggie having been forgotten.

Sylvie turns to him, her face expressionless. "My mother has died."

"Oh Sylvie." Mark extends his arms to her in a gesture of sympathy, but Sylvie shakes her head and

298

moves away from him, explaining she just needs to be on her own.

She steps outside into the garden, breathing in the lavender as she makes her way to the mossy old bench in the cutting garden. She curls up on the cushion with her knees to her chest, laying her head on her hands as she stares up into the velvety sky.

Which is when it comes to her.

This doesn't feel like grief.

This is relief.

CHAPTER
FORTY-THREE

Sylvie

Sylvie can feel Maggie's eyes burn into her, but she refuses to turn and acknowledge her, feeling only sadness that when they had almost formed a friendship, Maggie allowed a false set of assumptions to swallow her up in hatred.

The courtroom is deathly quiet save for the scratchy scribbling of the illustrator, her coloured chalks perfectly capturing the grim determination on Sylvie's face; the distraught near-hysteria on Maggie's.

At least the truth will come out today, here, in a court of law. Maggie may not have believed Sylvie, may have convinced herself Sylvie and Mark were in this together, but today she will know she is wrong.

Sylvie looks over at Mark, who gives her a small smile, which, were you to notice it, you might see as a smile of encouragement. Were you Maggie, you might see it as confirmation of collusion and love.

Maggie notices the smile, for she cannot take her eyes off either of them, desperately searching for evidence to support her belief, and she feels an almost-uncontainable rage flood her body. She does not know Mark's smile is a smile of shame. Of apology. Of

300

acknowledgement that he has fucked up everything in his life he has ever cared about.

He thought that moving back in would open the door a crack, allow him to find his way back to Sylvie's heart, but he was wrong. No matter what he tried, he hit a blank wall, until Sylvie eventually had to ask him to leave, the humiliation being too much for both of them to bear.

Coolly Sylvie looks at the lawyer, confirming her name, address, various technicalities, and eventually her legal status as married. The lawyer then asks if she recognizes her husband in this courtroom.

"I do."

"And can you point him out to us?"

Raising a hand she points quite clearly. As the lawyer continues to question her, drawing out the details of when and how she found out that Mark was also married to Maggie, Sylvie is aware that Maggie's expression has morphed from one of fury to one of distress.

Maggie, on the stand yesterday, sits motionless, the picture of the wronged wife. Sylvie, portrayed in the press as The Other Wife, glances over at her from time to time, seeing how she is biting her lip, wiping tears from her eyes, playing the sympathy card with everything she has.

The court case is oddly dull. Far less dramatic than anything on television, it is also less painful and less theatrical, apart from the sobs and sniffles and noisy nose-blowing coming from Maggie.

"And how did you inform your daughter about the existence of Mrs Margaret Hathaway?"

"My daughter had found out," Sylvie says softly. "She and Mark's daughter had met and befriended each other. She went back to the family home in Connecticut." Sylvie looks over at Eve. She is sitting next to Angie, who holds Eve's hand tightly and gives Sylvie an almost imperceptible nod.

Sylvie brings her attention back to the lawyer.

"I'm sorry," she says. "Can you repeat the question?"

"Did she inform you she was aware of another wife?"

"Yes, she told me after I picked her up from her trip to New York. And Connecticut."

At this, Mark turns to look at Eve, and Eve looks at him. Merely looks. No judgement in her eyes, no pain, just looks at him as if he is a stranger, holding his gaze until he finally breaks it and turns back. Watching them, Sylvie feels a wave of anxiety.

Eve can't keep hiding her emotions, can't use food, or anything else, to numb herself to her fears. Looking at Eve, in this courtroom, Sylvie knows it was a mistake to let her come.

Damn. Why didn't she trust her instincts and refuse to let Eve be here? And what is the fallout from this likely to be?

"I can't believe that bastard turned to stare at Eve," Angie hisses as they walk down the corridor during the adjournment for lunch. Eve walks behind, texting, her attention glued to her iPhone, while Angie steers Sylvie through the crowds.

"This way." She turns down a narrow corridor. "The press are swarming at the front so I got us sandwiches in an office down here. You were great! I was so proud of you." She lowers her voice to a whisper as she adds, "But I wanted to kill that bastard when he turned and stared at Eve. Did you see? What the hell was that about?"

"I saw," Sylvie says. "I don't know. I don't know anything about him. I looked at him today and felt I was looking at a stranger."

"I had the same feeling. I always adored Mark, but I feel nothing other than hatred when I look at him now."

They stop by the women's bathroom and Angie says, "I've got to pee. Damn middle age. I have a bladder the size of a pea these days. You coming in?"

As they both go inside, a flush is heard in one of the stalls, then the door opens and Maggie, straightening her shirt, walks out, stopping in horror as she realizes who has just walked into the bathroom.

"Great." Angie sighs. "I can hold it. Come on." And she starts to pull Sylvie out.

"No, it's okay." Sylvie puts out a hand to stop her friend, then takes a deep breath before turning to Maggie, who is standing at the sink.

"Maggie, I am sorry. I'm sorry for everyone involved. This is a horrible mess. I know you blame me, but I hope you believe what you heard in the courtroom today. I never knew. I never would have got involved had I known about you. And nor did I take him back afterwards. I felt sorry for him and offered him a roof. That was all."

"It doesn't matter," Maggie says bitterly. "None of it matters. My life is ruined, and whether you knew about me or not, it wouldn't have happened if he hadn't met you. How can I not blame you? You may not want to admit it, but it's all your fault, like it or not."

Angie steps forward. "Are you out of your fucking mind? You think Mark did this because Sylvie has some kind of hold over him? Do you not understand that the man you were married to is a liar, a cheat and a thief? Not to mention a complete fraud. Have you not been following the news? This isn't just bigamy, lady. This is grand larceny and fraud. If it hadn't been her, it would have been someone else, because he operates on lies. Blaming my friend is crazy. Blaming anyone other than him is crazy."

"Who the hell are you?" Maggie, in full New Salem superior mode, manages to look down at Angie, despite being several inches shorter.

"I'm her sister," Angie lies confidently. "And my best advice to you, sister, would be to get over the blame and get on with your life."

"I'm not your sister," Maggie sneers. "Get on with my life? How am I supposed to get on with my life when I have three children, a house that I am being evicted from any day now, and no goddamned money?" Her voice rises, her patrician accent disappearing as her Astoria roots creep in. "How am I supposed to get on with my life when my friends have all deserted me and I can't walk down the street without everyone whispering and laughing? How am I supposed to carry on when I have nothing? Nothing!"

"Try doing what the rest of us do." Angie gives a withering shake of her head, ignoring Sylvie's hand on her arm as she tries to stop her. "Try working for a living. Get off the fucking pity pot and get a job. Stop blaming everyone and start figuring out how you're going to live."

"You have no idea!" sobs Maggie. "You have no idea what it's like to be me . . ."

"You're right," Angie says. "Thank God."

Sylvie finally pulls Angie out of the bathroom, but turns back to say, "I wish you luck. Maybe think about starting again somewhere. Somewhere they don't know you. Build a life somewhere else . . ."

"And get a damned therapist," Angie yells over her shoulder as the door shuts behind them. "Do you think there's any chance that drinks vending machine has vodka in it?"

CHAPTER
FORTY-FOUR

Sylvie

"And how do you find the defendant?"
The judge asks the question three times.
"Guilty."
"Guilty."
"Guilty."

Sylvie waits alone in the cell. Her back is straight as she sits in an uncomfortable steel chair pulled tightly into the table, an identical chair the only other piece of furniture in the room.

She is dreading seeing Mark. No longer angry, she feels, mostly, disgust. There is little he can say that will change her mind, but his lawyer played the sympathy card well: how could she deny a man going into prison for ten years the wish to see her one last time.

The door opens and he is brought in. He holds his hands out for them to unlock the handcuffs, before he sits at the table, his lawyer standing in the corner as chaperone.

"Thank you for coming to see me," he says. "How are you?"

"I'm okay." Sylvie, feeling awkward, doesn't know how she is supposed to be with him.

He closes his eyes for a second. "I want to try to explain."

"Really, Mark. I'm sorry for everything you're going through, but I don't care —"

"But I do," he interrupts. "That's the point. No matter what you believe, I still love you, and I needed you to hear that."

"Why?" She laughs bitterly. "So I'll wait for you to get out of jail?"

"No. Because I needed you to know that this was real."

Sylvie stares at him in amazement. "Are you out of your mind? How could this possibly be real when you had another wife and other children? When everything was a lie? There's something wrong with you, Mark."

"I never wanted to hurt anyone. If you really want to know the truth, I never loved Maggie. I married her because it seemed like the right thing to do at the time, and my parents wanted me to, and I didn't know how to say no. By the time I realized I'd made a mistake, I didn't know how to get out, and I couldn't leave the children. I wouldn't leave the children. I never expected to meet someone else. I never expected to fall head over heels in love with someone in the way I did with you."

Sylvie glares at him, not softening in the slightest. "So you decided to have an affair, and then marry me, for Christ's sake! Why marry me? Why do any of it?"

"Because I was terrified of losing you. I loved you — love you," he corrects himself, "and I love Eve. I'm terrified for her. I'm terrified of what she looks like, how thin she is. Sylvie, I can see all her bones, and she's blank. It's like —"

"Please don't," Sylvie says. "I am with her doctors all the time. Please don't talk about Eve when you don't know."

"I'm sorry. It's just . . . I couldn't imagine life without you, without both of you, and I knew I couldn't ever tell you the truth. The only way I could see of keeping you both was to make a commitment."

"To commit bigamy."

"I never thought of it like that," Mark insists, his eyes filling up. "And you are so different from Maggie. Life was always so simple with you. I felt more alive with you than with anyone else."

"Which is why you robbed Peter to pay Paul?" Sylvie's voice is flat.

He shakes his head. "I didn't intend for that to happen. I thought I could do it once to dig myself out of a hole, then use the next order to set things right. I never thought, never intended —"

"Stop," Sylvie says gently. "Enough."

He looks at her and reaches out a hand just as the door opens and the guard signals that they are done.

"I love you," he says, pleading with her to take his hand. "I'm sorry. Please believe me."

Sylvie looks at his hand, then ever so briefly brushes it with her own before standing up.

"I know," she says. "And I do."

CHAPTER
FORTY-FIVE

Maggie

When we were selling our first home, I delighted in getting the house ready for potential buyers. I bought armfuls of fresh flowers before every viewing, ensured cinnamon dough was on hand to bake in the oven, filled the house with irresistible smells of lit fires and scented candles.

Just as back then, the realtor phones to let me know when she will be showing the house, but I'm no longer the owner. The bank has repossessed my beautiful home, and the phone calls from the realtor are merely a signal for me to leave; there is no incentive for me to beautify the house, for none of the proceeds of the sale will be mine.

Not that I could beautify it now, I think, looking out of the window as sadness threatens to drown me. The gravel driveway is covered in weeds, the boxwood hedges shaggy with new pale-green leaves sprouting off in all directions. The apple trees have dropped their fruit; what hasn't been eaten by deer has rotted and soured on the ground.

Inside, there is an air of emptiness, of a home unloved. Dust covers the surfaces of what little furniture is left, unless I'm able to emerge from my depression enough to notice and sweep a hand along a table top.

To think that once upon a time I would have been mortified that the realtor has to show up half an hour early, armed with fabric spray, beeswax, scented candles, room fresheners. She has to move furniture to cover the stains, polish the pieces that remain.

I don't bother doing any of these things for her. I no longer have the energy to care.

As more and more possessions are sold, faded marks appear on carpets throughout the house, and there are large squares on the walls where pictures once hung.

It is hard to believe this was ever a house filled with family love and laughter. In fact, I'm not sure it ever was.

But it's not potential house buyers who are coming today. Today is the day of my closet sale. The day I become one of the women I used to pity. I am mortified.

At the bottom of the stairs I take a deep breath and pause, listening to the women bustling around the living room. My eyes automatically go to the wall facing the stairs, where the huge antique gilt mirror used to hang.

It was the mirror in which I always gave myself one last check, making sure my make-up was perfect, my hair frizz-free; ensuring I looked the part.

That the mirror has been sold is irrelevant now. I no longer glance approvingly at myself in darkened store windows; I resent even having to see my two-inch roots and wrinkled forehead in the bathroom mirror.

The mirror sold for four thousand dollars, two of which, thank God, I got in cash. The blank holes around the house are the only reason I still have electricity and oil. At some point, everything will be reclaimed by the bank, or the police, or the creditors, but until that point I have a family to feed.

"There you are!" An older woman with short grey hair, neat and precise, walks into the hallway holding a crocodile purse. "We're just getting everything set up, but we think there's a mistake on the price."

I bend down to peer at the price tag.

"It says fifteen thousand dollars," the woman says, and laughs.

"No, that's right." I see the incomprehension in the woman's eyes. "I know it's a crazy price but it's the bag everyone around here wants. It will probably be the first thing to sell."

"Oh goodness!" The woman shakes her head. "I had no idea anyone ever spent this much money on a purse! Goodness! This looks like it's going to be the best sale we've ever done. Are you sure you don't want to stay? Most of our estate sales have the owners present. They love seeing how much their old things are going for."

I look at her as if she's crazy, then give a mere shrug of my shoulders. "Not me, I'm afraid."

"I understand. It can be painful, parting with things you're still emotionally attached to." Her eyes soften in sympathy, as I just nod. It's less that I'm emotionally attached, more that I'm horrified at the prospect of seeing the vultures gleefully picking over what's left of my beautiful things.

I told Lara I'd be away, as if I was nipping over to Nantucket for a couple of days. Ha. I wish. I have no idea where I'm going, but I need country. Trees. Fields. Nature. Maybe a beach, or lake. Somewhere where I don't have to think about what's happening inside my home.

The house that used to be my home.

Yesterday, when I spoke to Lara, she asked how the organization of the sale was coming along. What could I say? That it made me feel sick?

"I bet Kim will be the first one there," I said bitterly.

"Probably!" Lara laughed. "I just want you to know that I'm not going, okay? I know you're selling these things because you have to, and it wouldn't be right. I need you to know that."

"You're a good friend," I said. "I hate the thought of everyone picking over my things. I knew you wouldn't be going, but thank you for saying that to me. It means a lot."

The estate sale woman — what is her name? Oh yes! Evelyn — is still standing there. "Are you off anywhere n— Oh dear!" She turns at the sound of a car and frowns. "I told the press they couldn't come in."

"The press are here?"

"All of them." Evelyn sighs. "I'm not sure we're going to be able to keep them out. Oh, but that's not press. That's a local."

"How do you know?" I step away from the window so I can't be seen, nor photographed with a long-lens camera.

"Black Range Rover," Evelyn murmurs, peering outside.

"Oh yes. Definitely local."

"Someone you know?"

"Could be one of a hundred."

"We said no early birds. I do hate it when they ignore what we state quite clearly in the ad."

Whoever it is, I don't want them to see me, not face to face. I don't want them to witness my shame.

I thought I had friends here; I believed I had earned loyalty and respect from the women I saw almost every day, be it at school, a committee meeting, a charity event. Those same women are now appearing on television, giving their opinions and comments about my marriage, telling stories about Mark, about us. Women more interested in their fifteen minutes of fame than in protecting a woman who has hosted them in her house numerous times.

Grabbing my bag, I practically run to the safety of the kitchen, but just before I close the door I hear a familiar voice from the hallway.

"I'm so sorry I had to come early. I have an appointment in the city but I wanted to stop by. This is just too good to miss." My heart is in my mouth as I listen, shocked. I would know this voice anywhere.

It is Evelyn's turn to charm. "There are certainly some beautiful things here. The purses are on this side, and there's wonderful jewellery over there. This is truly one of the best sales we've ever done."

"I'm sure. Nothing but the best for Maggie Hathaway. Oh well, one woman's loss is my gain," she says with a laugh.

The estate sale woman has the grace not to join in. "I'm Evelyn. Let me know if you need any help."

"Thank you, Evelyn. I'll take that Birkin, for starters." There is a pause during which I imagine her turning the Birkin over in her hands. "Fifteen thousand? I know it's crocodile, but look at that scratch! And that one? That's far too much."

"Oh," Evelyn says nervously. "Gosh. I hadn't noticed those. I see what you mean."

"I'll give you five," the woman says confidently. "Five thousand dollars. Cash."

"I'm going to have to check with the owner . . ."

"Five thousand? For a used purse with scratches? No one's going to offer you more, I promise you."

"You have a point." Evelyn sounds doubtful, but I know that in her opinion five thousand dollars for a purse is still obscene. "It is rather badly scratched."

"Good. I'd like to look at those necklaces too. And the earrings. Those purses are interesting but priced much too high. Trust me, I know what these are selling for in consignment stores and it's a lot lower than that. Can I just start a pile over here? I'm Kim, by the way."

"Nice to meet you, Kim."

In the kitchen I am shaking at this final betrayal.

How could Lara do this to me?

I resist the urge to burst through and let her know I know. I've done enough damage to myself already. I just need to get out.

I race to the car, put my foot down hard and accelerate out of the driveway, scattering the clamouring reporters and cameramen. No one can keep them out of the house, but who cares any more? There is nothing they can say or do that could make my life worse. There is nothing people I don't know can do, anyway; but there are still things my "friends" can do to hurt me. Clearly.

I drive on the interstate, in shock. I've lost my husband, my life, and the respect of everyone I know. Even the few I thought were friends have proved to be more interested in profiting. I am well aware that in the newspapers and on the blogs I have been publicly declared a fraud, my humble beginnings doubtless the subject of much mirth along the scrubbed wooden tables in Le Pain Quotidien.

I have lost everything, but in doing so I can't help but start to wonder what that "everything" meant.

Mark was described by all who knew him as "the perfect husband". I may have been blind to his betrayal, his other marriage, but that aside, what kind of a husband was he really? Hardly ever home — and, when he was, he would frequently step outside to take a "conference call"; would disappear into his office for hours, closing the door so as not to "disturb anyone". Then there were the times he would go missing for days, be totally out of reach.

It is beginning to dawn on me that this wasn't a marriage. This was an arrangement.

An arrangement that didn't make me happy; an arrangement that was so unreal, I'm questioning not just my marriage, but everything connected with it.

The furniture, the clothes, the stuff — already mostly gone, and none of it missed.

The friends who have all disappeared, the parties to which I'm definitely no longer invited, the committees I will never be asked to chair again — does any of it matter? Did any of it ever matter?

The only things that matter are the children. They are the only good that has come out of this marriage. And I will never forgive Mark for what he has done to them.

I keep driving, these thoughts whirring through my head, no idea where I'm going, aware only that the further away I drive from New Salem, the calmer I become.

I exit on a whim, take roads because I like the look of them, noticing the leaves hanging over the roads, the bright green of the grass, the farms dotted around, cows grazing peacefully in the meadows.

Guilford. Old Saybrook. Old Lyme . . . I follow a sign to Ashlawn Farm, curious as to what I might find, delighting in coming across a coffee roaster and café. I settle into an old wooden chair on the porch of a charming farmhouse, sipping delicious coffee as I look out over the fields, not realizing for a while that there is a smile on my face.

A few others join me on the porch. We smile hello, make small talk, and it is only when I am left alone again that I realize, providing I can convince Chris and Grace and Buck of this, that I have found the place to start the next part of my journey. Left up to me, I would never set foot in New Salem again.

316

At the ripe old age of forty-four, I find myself starting again with absolutely nothing, and the only thing of which I'm certain is that this is the place in which to do it — a town that has finally managed to fill me with peace.

PART FOUR

June 2011

CHAPTER
FORTY-SIX

Maggie

There is a trick to opening the passenger door of the big old Wagoneer I bought soon after I moved here, but I haven't quite managed to master it yet. The ad described the jeep as metallic cinnamon, but it's very clearly orange, and having a fancy name for it doesn't make it more valuable. Neither does the sticking door.

It opens perfectly from the inside, but not from the outside, unless, the previous owner explained, you pull up, twist slightly to the left, and quickly pull out. Or something like that. I don't remember, those early days being such a haze. On beautiful days like this, I'm happy to keep the window open and just fling my purse through the window to the passenger seat.

The purse itself is somewhat incongruous, although I'm probably the only person for miles who would know that the tan leather tote, now bashed and worn, ever-present on my shoulder, is Hermes, one of the few relics of my former life. It was a bag I tried to sell, along with everything else, but it sat in the consignment store for months, until they phoned for me to collect it.

Most of our stuff had been sold before the creditors came to collect. When they arrived to take an inventory, seizing everything of value in an attempt to recover some of the money Mark owed, they were — thank the Lord — unaware of the antiques and clothes scattered around various homes and consignment stores in Fairfield County.

I was terrified they would demand the cash from the sales, so when we moved up here I just piled the kids into a rented car and left town without saying goodbye to anyone. One day I was there, and the next gone. Who would have even missed me?

Up here, in Old Lyme, it is a very different kind of life. A simpler life. A country life. A life that celebrates warmth and honesty and human connection. A life that would never think to worship at the altar of money or success.

The Wagoneer was parked on a front lawn, with a note in the front window advertising it for sale. Its bright colour and wood trim filled me with nostalgia every time we walked past. It made me think of *The Brady Bunch* and David Cassidy, of being a child and expecting that everything in the future would be happy, fun, filled with perfect people who handled all painful situations with laughter and, of course, the help of an always-smiling Alice.

"Let's just ask," I said, finding myself walking up to the front door one day while Grace groaned, the idea of the car horrifying her, the idea of this whole new life so far away from everything she knew — combined with the betrayal that she was having to deal with every minute of every day — horrifying her.

The elderly owner didn't stop talking so it was an hour later that Chris drove the car down the driveway as Buck and Landon, who had remained at Grace's side those first few months, whooped and cheered. Even Grace forced a smile.

"That's what I'm talkin' about!" Chris high-fived Landon while I shook hands with the owner, and they both fought to drive it home, declaring it the coolest car ever, and announcing that they would now out-retro even the most trendy, retro kids.

"It's the colour," Chris stated definitively. "Orange! Man, that is the colour! That's what makes it so cool!"

"It's not orange," I insisted. "It's metallic cinnamon."

Later that night, Chris was still on a high, which had been amusing until around seven, and was latterly wearing distinctly thin.

"Chris," I said with a sigh, as the fact of owning a huge, orange, painfully old car brought the reality of my life into stark and rather depressing relief. "Can you please stop talking like a hipster and start talking properly?"

"Sorry," Chris mumbled, the reality of his life sinking in at the same time.

Soon afterwards the kids all went upstairs to their bedrooms in our tiny, rented house.

Now I can't believe how life has changed for all of us. Chris, working for a publisher in New York, no longer talks like a hipster; Grace is managing to pay her way through NYU by working; Buck is happy, settled with new friends at his new school. And I have come to love the Wagonneer. I've named it, or her, Paula, after Paula Deen, because the car is big, loud and makes people happy. Not the residents, who are used to the car, but the tourists who flock to the village during the summer and who have been known to stop me on the way out of the grocery store in order to take a photograph.

Throwing the purse through the window, I walk round the car and get in, vaguely aware that I really need to bring it to the gas station to use the vacuum on the interior — the floors are a diary of Buck's pre-school, post-school, pre-game, post-game, permanent snacking. Crumbs, wrappers, empty To-Go cups have somehow found their way to the floor of the rear seat, where they roll around, the last drops of whatever milkshake or Frappuccino or smoothie he had now forming a shiny patch on the rubber mat, sticky to the touch.

To think this used to be my idea of hell. It's about as far away as you can get from my Range Rover of old, the black showing every speck of dirt on the outside, the matt black carpets cleaned whenever I wanted. Which was often.

If my friends could see me now . . .

But they don't see me now. And they weren't friends, however much they continued to pretend. For a while they attempted to get in touch with me — emails and phone calls from Lara, or Heather — but my continued lack of response eventually sent them away.

At the traffic lights, I look over at the phone on the passenger seat. I'm pretty detached from the phone these days; there's nothing so urgent it can't wait. I'm not exactly deluged with calls from A-type committee members insisting I sort out a problem. Thankfully I'm no longer the recipient of gossip — friends calling to do a post-mortem on the party we all went to the night before, lamenting, in horrified whispers, the job the decorators did with the host's living room, and for so much money.

I look at the screen and frown. There is a missed 203 call. New Salem? It isn't a number I recognize, but nevertheless it is still unsettling, an unwelcome reminder of a past I'm trying so very hard to put behind me.

Swinging off the road, I pull the car slowly past the grand old mansion and along the worn gravel driveway to the carriage house at the back. I gather the mail on the stoop of the porch, just as the phone rings. Presuming it's Buck, I answer without looking, flicking through the mail distractedly, realizing in that split second before pressing the answer button that this is a 203 number. It's too late.

"Maggie? Maggie? Is that you? Is this still your number?"

"Yes," I say, putting the mail down on the small iron-work table, found at the dump and resprayed by Chris to a steel grey. "Who is this?"

I once read that you should train yourself to always smile when talking on the phone — it makes your voice sound more welcoming — and it was, for me, a habit that became entirely unconscious, a habit that was broken in one second on the day I found out my husband had another family.

I no longer bother to smile when picking up the phone, unless it is genuine and I am feeling particularly happy about something. I no longer care about social graces, or what people think about me, or needing to make a good impression. None of those things matter. Not when your whole world has been turned upside down.

"Maggie!" The voice at the other end of the phone gurgles with laughter. It is familiar, but I can't quite place it. "It's Lara!"

I say nothing. What, after all, am I expected to say? Lara the Liar is how I have thought of her these past years. Lara who secretly bought all my most precious things, bullying the estate sales woman into accepting far less for everything than she ever should have done, hiding them until I was safely out of the way.

Lara, who pretended to be my friend while publicly berating the "two-faced" women who "swooped in like vultures".

I never told Lara I knew. I saw her when I had to — mostly when she dropped in unannounced after I stopped picking up the phone to her or calling her back — but she knew something was wrong, and if she didn't know for certain, she must have figured it out when I left without saying goodbye.

Yet Lara continued to call for a good couple of months after I left, until the message, couched in my unresponsive silence, could presumably no longer be ignored.

"How are you, Lara?"

"It is so good to hear you, Maggie!" Lara says, her voice attempting to envelop me in warmth, in the way it used to. "We have missed you!"

I pause. "Thank you." How can I say I miss them too? My memories of my old life have been so tainted that it has been hard to remember the good times we had, when life seemed, in some way, simple.

"I cannot believe you're still on the same number and I got you! Everyone talks about you all the time — wonderful things — and we've all been worried about you, especially when no one could get hold of you. Is it true you're living in the country somewhere? Essex?"

I lower myself onto a chair, looking round at the trees. "Close. Old Lyme," I say. "I guess it is country."

"Well, here's the thing. The girls and I were talking just the other day about how we need a break, a great girls' weekend somewhere, and of course we got to remembering our old girls' weekends with you, and Casey and I thought, let's come and see you! A girls' weekend! Wouldn't that be fun? It will be just like old times."

This is the very last thing I want to do. I remember, so clearly, hearing Lara's voice in my house, introducing herself as Kim so that I wouldn't know of her betrayal. How can I pretend that never happened; how can I forgive and forget? And what would we possibly have in common now?

"Maggie? Are you there?"

"Sorry. Yes. Bad connection."

"There's something else," Lara says quickly, her voice now serious. "I wanted to say this in person, but if I don't say it now I won't get to see you in person and I won't be able to tell you. Maggie, you were a good friend to me and I treated you horribly."

I wait. Silently.

"I've been carrying this around for so long and I kept trying to call to tell you, to apologize, but you wouldn't return my calls, and then these awful people just moved into your old house, and it got me thinking about all the good times we had there, and I knew I had to call. I bought your things, Maggie. Not Kim. It was me. I bought your purses, and your jewellery, and I talked the woman into accepting much less than they were worth, and I never told you."

"Why? Why would you do such a thing?"

Lara takes a deep breath. "I'm so ashamed. No one ever knew this, but Steve had been unemployed for almost a year. He'd given me this crazy budget, and I hadn't been able to buy anything, and I just went a bit nuts when I knew all your beautiful things were going to be sold. If it helps," she adds miserably, "I haven't worn anything, or used any of the bags. I couldn't. Every time I even look at them I'm filled with shame. And then you didn't return my calls, and I thought you knew, and I tried to just let it go, but I couldn't. And I miss you, Maggie. And I am so, so sorry I did that."

It sounds genuine, but what am I supposed to do? I can't just roll over and say "Fine, let's go back to being best friends, because an apology two years after the event is better than no apology at all".

"I'm giving it all back to you," Lara says. "I'm never going to use it and I realize I can't keep it. These things are yours."

I look down at my sensible black clogs, the only shoes I can bear to wear for my waitressing job, then turn to take in my tiny rented carriage house. A bark of laughter escapes me, for what would I do with the crocodile hand-bags and sparkling jewels here? I'd have to go through the hassle of selling them again, knowing prospective buyers up here are few and far between.

"I don't want them," I say finally. "I don't need them any more. I'm glad you told me, and it's . . . well, it's thoughtful of you to get in touch and offer them to me, but no, thank you. No."

"Then I have to give you the proper money for them," Lara says. "I don't remember the exact amount, but I know roughly. Let me at least do that. I owe you that."

How I'd love to be in a position to say no, but I can't. An injection of cash could buy Buck the new lacrosse pads he's been longing for, not to mention college. An injection of cash could go into a rainy-day fund, not to be used until and unless the kids really need it.

"That would be great," I say. "I appreciate your honesty. Thank you. Lara, can I ask you something? How is my old house?"

"Oh Maggie!" Lara groans. "These awful people have moved in and they've torn out all your gorgeous plantings and put in a tennis court. And the hedges have gone in the front, and they've built this huge stone wall with a fence on top so no one can see anything, and it's not a pretty stacked wall, but one of those ugly ones we hate!"

I smile as I listen to Lara. Being human means none of us is infallible and we screw up. But we're entitled to forgiveness. It becomes clear to me that there are many sides to the same coin. I suddenly understand that I have demonized everything associated with my old life, including the people I once called friends. And yet here is Lara, sounding like Lara. Hearing her voice brings back the good memories, the times she supported me, the fun we had.

"It's good to hear from you," I say. This time I mean it. I realize that the shame, anger and humiliation that led to me cutting off the limb of my former life don't need to drive me today, so as we say goodbye we promise to stay in touch, Lara saying she'll come up and stay at the Bee and Thistle, and I make the appropriate excited noises, even though she and I both know it will never happen.

As I stand up I notice a parcel on the floor beside the back door; it is covered with a clean checked dishcloth. Picking it up, I pull a corner of the foil wrapping aside, and steam wafts out from a freshly made rhubarb and apple pie.

I manage to use my elbow to open the door, then set the pie on the counter, before turning and tripping over Buck's backpack in the middle of the kitchen floor.

Beggars can't be choosers. This became my mantra whenever Buck complained about the house being small or dark, or that he was missing our basement and the swimming pool in the summer.

The truth is, I love this house. The fact that it isn't mine, but rented from the older couple in the main house, affords me a freedom I didn't expect. When the pilot light in the boiler goes out, or the window won't open, or the pipes start clunking and groaning, I don't have to make phone calls and dole out hard-earned money, I just walk across the yard, through the pathway between the trees, to bang on the back door of Mr and Mrs Wellesley's home.

They call me the daughter they never had, and in turn they are, without any question in my mind, the parents I always wanted.

Mrs Wellesley — or Mrs W, as she insists on being called — leaves home-made pies, jams, vegetables picked from their garden, on my front porch.

Monty and Bruno, the golden retrievers that were Mark's, that Buck refused to allow me to put up for adoption, are allowed to romp round the property freely, both of them usually lying down next to Mrs W as she gardens.

"They're my new best friends," Mrs W will say proudly, patting both dogs on the head. "I honestly don't know what I did before they moved in. I know they're only dogs, but they're such good company!"

I assume the Wellesleys don't know my story. I may have been in every newspaper for a while, but that was when we were still living in New Salem. No one here has ever said anything, or given me that look, curiosity mixed with sympathy, that tells me all I need to know.

I was all over the papers as the "perfect" Connecticut Trophy Wife. Highlights by Warren Tricome, make-up by Laura Mercier, heart pendant from Temple St Clair. Swathed in cashmere and pearls. More Stepford than Stepford.

Not any more. I catch sight of myself in the glass door of the microwave and tuck a strand of strawberry-blonde hair, streaked with grey, behind my ear.

It hasn't been cut in ages, and I'm growing to quite like it long and wavy. Natural. I don't bother with make-up any more either. I have no idea how Patty manages perfect make-up at work. Any cosmetics I've tried slide off my face within half an hour.

The Botox, Perlane and facials I used to have every three months are completely unaffordable now, even if I wanted them. The frown line in the middle of my forehead is clearly visible, but everyone here thinks I'm in my thirties.

I realize the irony of that. I can now see that when I was really in my thirties, when I was trying to be the perfect housewife, mother, volunteer that I was convinced I needed to be in order to fit in, when I was trying to attain perfection through all the exterior accoutrements, I managed, unwittingly, to age myself ten years.

These days my skin, unhidden by layers of foundation, powder and illuminating minerals, glows with good health. Early nights and fresh air, little alcohol, save the odd glass of Prosecco with Mrs W, have definitely brought a sparkle back to my eyes.

Years of yoga, Pilates, the bar method, zumba, anything to try to beat the curse of too much rich food and too much alcohol, have given way to walking for pleasure, and being on my feet all day for work. My legs have never been so toned.

I still can't believe how different this life is, nor why I felt so insecure before. It hasn't been easy adjusting to the new circumstances, but I'm grateful I'm no longer driven by the need to impress. Who would I need to compete with here? The other waitresses, Patty and Barb? Mrs W? We're all equal. The Wellesleys may live in a grand and beautiful old house, but I know for a fact they don't see me as lesser because I rent their carriage house.

Patty, who has worked every day of her adult life, is a single mother of four kids, and is the woman who inspires me most of all. Whatever lemons life has thrown at her, she's used to make sparkling sweet lemonade that is filled with zest and joy.

The old Maggie judged first, asked questions later, judging precisely because she knew, deep down, she wasn't good enough. It took losing everything to realize that I'm more or less okay. Exactly as I am.

"Helloooo?" Mrs W's voice floats in from the porch.

"In the kitchen!" I say. "Come in! Tea?"

Mrs W strides in, keeping on her gardening clogs, and I remember the ridiculous rules I imposed during all those years in New Salem, terrified of anyone coming to the house and finding it less than perfect. What's the worst that can happen? Mrs W trails in some mud? So what?

"I wiped my feet!" Mrs W smiles, wisps of grey hair escaping her pony tail, which is mostly hidden by the large straw hat. "I wanted to check you got the pie before the critters did."

"I did! And you're wonderful! I love rhubarb, and Buck, as you know, will be thrilled."

"That's what I meant to tell you!" Her eyes light up. "Mr W's taken him down to the boatyard to start getting the boat ready. Buck said practice wasn't until later and he'd done his homework. They'll be back by five. Is that all right with you?"

All right? It's better than all right. It's perfect. My kids spent their whole lives waiting for Mark to be a father. When he was at home, if he wasn't running outside for "conference calls" — or calls to his other family, as I know now they were — he could be great, but he was gone so much that the kids missed out on the little things that bond a parent and child together.

Not that I was much better. Instead of spending time with them when they were small and needy I handed them off to nannies. Or babysitters. Or anyone I could pay to amuse them, while I organized bake sales, meetings, charity galas.

It is a wonder they have turned out as well as they have. Chris, so funny, down-to-earth, easy-going. Grace, so confident and beautiful, although these past few years have taken their toll. I'm not in touch with her. I try, but she hasn't forgiven me. She continues to blame me for Mark's infidelities, his betrayal, and she refuses to answer my emails and calls.

Grace moved up here with us but was back in New Salem, living at Landon's, within the week. She started school, ended things with Landon soon afterwards, and seemed to be out of control.

I'd find photographs of her on Facebook, looking out of it, bottle of vodka in hand, kissing some random boy.

I was horrified. And upset. And concerned. I phoned Grace, and I'll admit that I didn't handle it well. I was still trying to come to terms with everything myself, still in that awful space of being terrified of life on my own, and I didn't say anything right.

I'm ashamed of it now. I demanded to know why she was drinking, told her what happened to girls who were easy. Grace became angry and belligerent, and we both ended up screaming terrible things at each other.

It happened another couple of times too, before eventually leading to what I think of as the Cold War. I have apologized. Many, many times. I've tried to explain, but my words fall on deaf ears.

"She's just being a teenager," Patty said, when, in despair, I turned to her and Barb for advice, support, a friendly ear during a break at work.

"You should have seen me at the same age," Patty went on. "I was a regular hellraiser. Don't you worry about the partying. If she didn't do it when she was younger, she's just getting it out of her system now. It's all part of the process, honey. It's how they separate from us. Apart from Mikey," she mused, referring to her youngest son, who was living back at home with Patty after his divorce a year and a half previously. "I damn well wish he'd separate from me. He turned round yesterday and said wasn't this great, us living together. Why would we ever want to change?" She shuddered with horror.

"Did you point out you might want to change because you were sick of doing his piles of laundry every day and having to clean up after his mess, and lend him money when he conveniently forgets to go to the bank?" Barb asked.

"Damn right I did. Little squirt hugged me, planted a big kiss on my forehead and told me he knew I was joking. Lord help me," she muttered as she hurried into the kitchen to fetch the order for table eleven. "What did I do to deserve this?"

Grace had always been so good; she had risen above the drinking, the drugs, the sexual experimentation talked of in hushed whispers by the mothers of her classmates. Grace had always been the perfect child. The one in the steady relationship with the boy from the right family; the girl no one had to worry about.

With luck, and God's mercy, Patty may be right. I've learned to let go, because there's nothing I can do about it until Grace comes round. And she will come round. Surely.

Grace wanted to be in the courtroom during the trial but I refused to allow it. She said she needed to see him, but I knew it was only going to cause her more pain.

And how could I subject her to the photographers, the journalists, the stares? Mark's lawyer had the temerity to suggest we all show up, his supportive family, so that he could portray us as having somehow forgiven Mark, allowing the jury members to humanize him.

I didn't want to humanize him. I wanted to kill him. At the very least, I wanted him to suffer.

I saw immediately that not letting Grace attend was a mistake. That was when she stopped speaking to me entirely. That first Christmas Grace went to Tulum in Mexico with her room-mate's family. The boys and I spent Christmas with Mr and Mrs W, themselves on their own because their daughter was living in London and their "free-spirited" son was living in Thailand. Or perhaps it was Vietnam. They weren't entirely sure, but they were sure that the boys and I were part of their family.

I put the kettle on the stove as Mrs W sits down at the kitchen table and pulls off her gardening gloves, staring down at her knobbly, arthritic fingers as she slowly stretches them out, sighing with the pleasure of it. I am filled with love for Mrs W, and I lean down spontaneously to kiss her on the cheek. She looks up at me, beaming with pleasure.

"Now what did I do to deserve that?" she asks.

"Nothing. You're just you. And you're wonderful."

Mrs W straightens up, clearing her throat, but I see the glistening in her eye. I have no idea why Mrs W's children both moved so very far away, but I do know how much they are missed.

"I thought perhaps you and Buck would like to come for dinner on Saturday. Nothing fancy, but Mr W's been out foraging fiddleheads, and we're planning to cook them up. How about it?"

"That would be lovely. I'll check Buck has no other plans, but I'm definitely free."

Mrs W suppresses a frown, and I know exactly what's going through her head. She and Mr W have long been concerned that, other than work, or to ferry Buck around — although he is now old enough to borrow Mr W's old pick-up truck, therefore no longer needs a ride from me — I have no life.

They'd never dare come out and say it, but now they've given Buck the keys to the kingdom they're always hinting that I should do more, go out more, have a life of my own.

It was a little while back that Mr W showed up at the carriage house before school, wondering if Buck was interested in using his old pick-up truck, a 1958 Hunter Green Ford F100. He kept it in a garage up the street, and no one had driven it for years. It probably wasn't very cool, but it was serviceable, and it seemed a shame to let it just sit when Buck was now driving and really old enough not to be pestering me crazy for rides everywhere.

Buck, who had no idea what a 1958 Ford F100 was, almost fell over when Mr W slid the garage doors open to reveal the coolest old truck he had ever seen, a truck that truly is the envy of all his friends.

Buck has friends. Many of them. But I do not, and I'm okay with that. It is hard moving to a new town in your forties, with children who are too old to allow friendships to form with the mothers at mommy and me playgroups, or outside the classroom door in pre-school.

338

I don't need friends. Look what happened last time. I am friendly with the other waitresses at work, and there is the crowd I have coffee with at Ashlawn Farm, and that is enough.

Mrs W is looking round the kitchen and her gaze falls on the bottle of wine on the counter. "Oooh," she says, her eyes lighting up. "How about a little drinkie? It's five o'clock somewhere."

CHAPTER
FORTY-SEVEN

Sylvie

Blinking her eyes open, Sylvie tries to ascertain from the sliver of sunlight on top of the curtains whether or not it is a nice day, but eventually she jumps out of bed and throws the curtains open, smiling briefly at the sight of a clear blue sky and a low sun that promises to grow bright and warm.

Her joy doesn't last long. By the time she has reached the bedroom door, ready to check on Eve just down the hallway, it has been replaced by the ice-cold fear that lodges itself in her heart at exactly this time, every day, just after she wakes up.

Sylvie silently opens Eve's door, and it is only when she peers over the mound of duvets and sees her daughter sleeping peacefully and breathing regularly that she can face the new day.

Sylvie bought this house shortly after Mark's trial, torn between staying in a house she really loved, although she was apprehensive that memories of Mark would leap out from every corner, and starting again.

Angie found the house. She had been driving past, saw the For Sale sign and screeched into the driveway, charming the owner into giving her a viewing there and then. It was the perfect house for Sylvie, she realized, before picking up Sylvie and bringing her back to see for herself.

Sylvie hadn't even been sure she would move. It was clear she needed more room for her growing business, but she could have added on to the old house, could have renovated to bring the house up to date in her current style.

The memories of Mark hadn't lingered in the old house in the way one might have expected. Perhaps because Sylvie had decorated it herself, it had always felt like hers. Even the bedroom held no trace of Mark, particularly since Sylvie had instantly removed the giant television screen he had insisted upon.

But the house Angie took her to that day worked its charm. It was just like the old one, only brighter, lighter, with more room and incredible views.

"This is the house for Figless Manor," Angie had said as they stood on the balcony outside the master bedroom, gazing towards the mountains in the distance. Sylvie turned to look at her, a question in her eyes.

"Oh, I didn't tell you? Figless Manor's your new line. Simon came up with the name. Isn't it fabulous? Remember how you used to call your house Figless Manor when you first moved in? When the old owners removed the fig tree? I was telling someone the story, and Simon suddenly said it was the perfect name for a line of jellies and jams, and he's right."

"Angie, I don't make jellies and ja—"

"Not yet, but why not?"

Sylvie lit up, flinging her arms round Angie. "You're right! Why not?" she enthused. "You're a genius."

"Simon's the genius, but I'm not far behind. But imagine living here! It's perfect. You can have your studio here, your workshop — hell, even a commercial kitchen. It's just right for you."

"Let me think about it," Sylvie said, knowing there was little to think about. She waited three days to be sure, spending her time pouring candles, for at that time she was still doing them at home, then went to the grocery store to buy food for dinner that night, and stopped at Angie's on the way home.

Angie didn't stop talking from the moment she opened the door. Her doctor had prescribed her Ambien, as an antidote, it seemed, to the Adderall he didn't know she was taking. This was not only enabling her to do all the things she wanted to do in a day, but had also seen her lose twelve pounds.

"So I woke up this morning having had this weird dream that Simon and I had had crazy monkey sex for hours last night." She leaned over the table as Sylvie started to smile. "Which is weird in itself because I don't have those dreams. And I certainly don't have crazy monkey sex. If we do anything it's a quickie. My God! Who has the time for anything else? But this was . . . hot! Like, seriously hot! I'm not going to go into detail, but we did things I never would do."

"You're so funny!" Sylvie smiled, appreciating Angie's lack of boundaries, even as she knew she would never make the same confession.

"But wait! So this morning I'm lying in bed thinking about this dream, and I don't remember the whole thing, just bits of it, and then Simon rolls over, and he's all super lovey-dovey, and he looks at me and says, 'Wow. What got into you last night? You were amazing!'"

Sylvie's mouth dropped open. "What? It was real?"

"I know! Except I can't remember. Well, I can remember, but like you remember a dream. Not like it actually happened. But Simon has completely fallen in love with me all over again. So when he went to work, I Googled Ambien and uninhibited, because let me tell you this was seriously uninhibited . . . okay, okay . . . I won't go into detail. But, Sylvie, this is a whole thing. Ambien sex. It's like this whole thing out there where people have this crazy totally uninhibited sex, and don't remember anything."

When Sylvie stopped laughing, she shook her head. "Only you."

"Only me what?"

"Only you could take an Ambien and have crazy sex and not remember it. Other people take Ambien and eat the contents of their fridge every night."

"I'd kill myself," Angie announced seriously. "Or Simon would divorce me. But I was always terrified of Ambien because I thought I'd be the eater. And it turns out I'm the crazy nymphomaniac! Who knew! I'm telling you, if you ever think there is a problem in your marriage, just take an Amb— Oh SHIT! Oh Sylvie. I'm such an ass. Forget I said that, okay? I can't believe I just said that."

"No, it's okay," Sylvie said. "Really. This is me. And you're you. I forgive you."

"I'm such an idiot — I'll blame the Ambien." Then Angie sat forward, her face serious. "So, Simon spoke to you about the financials, right? You know you can absolutely afford it, plus you get to write off a ton of stuff. You're doing it, right?"

Sylvie nodded. "How could I say no?" she said, laughing as Angie squealed and threw her arms round her.

Sylvie pauses by the mahogany table in the hallway. Taking centre stage, commanding in a large silver frame, is a black and white photograph of Eve, taken before she got ill, when she was so beautiful it is almost heartbreaking to compare it to how she is now.

Sylvie had hoped a new home might mean a fresh beginning, might give Eve the ability to move on, to start a different kind of life, start eating again, but Eve is declining fast, and Sylvie still struggles to accept her inability to help, her powerlessness over Eve's decisions not to get better.

She still makes meals for her, despite the knowledge that Eve will only drink a clear chicken broth, if anything at all. She is, she says, still going to Overeaters Anonymous meetings, still talking to her sponsor, but Sylvie can see it isn't helping.

Watching her daughter disappear before her eyes is, without question, the hardest thing Sylvie has ever been through. Harder than the grief over Jonathan, the betrayal of Mark. Eve is her flesh and blood; Eve is all she has; if Eve doesn't . . . if anything happens to Eve, if she makes herself disappear permanently, Sylvie knows she won't be able to go on.

She won't want to go on.

Eve spends much of her time at home in her bedroom. She comes downstairs to make tea — drinking copious amounts to try to stay warm, even in mid-summer — or curl up in front of a movie. She is always swathed in layers of clothes and has withdrawn so completely from life that Sylvie considers it a small miracle each time she leaves the house.

Sylvie had hoped this summer would see her get better, but although she is still in therapy, it is not as intensive, and Sylvie is terrified Eve has regressed. She booked a trip to Mexico, just the two of them, but Eve, who has no energy any more, refused to go.

She sleeps, reads, watches reality television shows on Bravo. She glides round the house like a tiny ghoul-like bird, her eyes once again sunken, her hair lifeless and dull, her teeth almost too big for her face.

Sylvie joins Eve to watch the reality shows in a bid to regain some kind of a connection with her disappearing daughter. It has worked, to a point. They are able to find common ground, a meeting point, in their shared disgust at some of the antics, in their amazement at what women will do for, if not fortune, then fame at least.

The connection is shallower than any connection Sylvie has had with her daughter, ever. She is so terrified of upsetting Eve, of causing a fight, of Eve losing even more weight, that she treads lightly; she no

345

longer talks about the great elephant in the room; she tiptoes as carefully as if she is walking on glass.

These pointless shows, however, allow them to have a semblance of a relationship. Better to be able to bond over this, than to feel, as she has been feeling these past few months, as if they are merely ships that pass in the night.

Life has been almost overwhelmingly terrifying for months. Once a week, Eve weighs herself, with Sylvie watching. It is the only time Sylvie allows Eve to have knowledge of her fears, and each week, as Eve's weight stays the same, Sylvie is flooded with relief.

She has only managed to retain some sanity, has only been able to put her fears for Eve aside temporarily, by throwing herself into work. Shortly after Mark was arrested, she and Angie drove throughout the state giving candles to people to sample, getting them into stores on consignment. This was funded by Angie and Simon, who believed in the business more than she believed in it herself.

A couple of months later she was approached by the homeware buyer of one of the large chain retailers, who had stumbled across the candle while on vacation in Malibu, and once they took her, everyone wanted her.

Simon brokered every deal, Angie coming to each meeting as her marketing manager, seducing clients with her long red hair. The candles led to accessories — a manufacturer with factories in China was able to produce her designs in what seemed like a matter of days — and then to the lines of jellies and jams, and within two years Figless Manor was recognized as one of the greatest success stories in the home arena, an area that no one since Martha had been able to tackle.

As the woman behind the company, not least a woman who first found fame as the unknowing wife of famed Boy-Next-Door Bigamist Mark Hathaway, Sylvie found herself at the centre of a media storm. She was portrayed as the woman who bounced back from nothing to create a home empire; the woman who, when her home life collapsed, put her energies into helping others build the perfect home.

And now she has the perfect home herself. Limestone floors and old bleached beams. Ancient vines scrambling over pergolas. French doors and bookcases, a light-filled arched gallery linking one side of the house to the other, the arches leading into the Great Room, greater due to its enormous stone fireplace, and views of nothing but mountains and trees.

But she would give it all up in a heartbeat to have her daughter healthy and well again.

CHAPTER
FORTY-EIGHT

Maggie

"Are you here for the evening? Shall I make dinner?" I have no idea if there even is anything for dinner. I'm pretty sure the fridge is empty, but maybe I can cobble something together from leftovers and rice. My teenage boy doesn't much care how it tastes, as long as there's enough of it.

"Why don't we go out?" Buck says. "I thought maybe we could go to River Tavern?"

Oh my sweet, naive boy. There is nothing I'd love more than to go to my favourite restaurant in the area with my grown-up boy, but it isn't in my budget, and he knows that. Birthdays only. I look at him, so earnest, so lovely, and I wonder if I could make it work, just this once; if I should just throw caution to the wind and go.

"My treat," he says, impatiently pulling a wad of cash out of his back pocket. "I didn't want to tell you until I finished my trial and got offered the job properly, but I'm helping down at the boatyard. And this is my first pay! So I want to take my mom out for dinner because you need a break."

CHAPTER
FORTY-NINE

Maggie

used to feel beautiful, but only when I'd had my hair blown out, my make-up expertly applied, when my clothes were the best of the best. These days I put hardly any thought into my appearance. If it's comfortable, I'll wear it.

Fleeces for warmth, jeans, worn-in clogs that were supposed to be just for work but have become so comfortable they're the shoes I wear all the time.

But tonight, for only the third or fourth time since I moved here, I make an effort — how could I not? I can't afford the Keratin treatments that used to give me silky straight glossy locks, but as I stare at myself in the bathroom mirror I impulsively grab Buck's gel and scrunch it into my hair, watching as lovely loose curls replace the frizz.

I pull what little make-up I own out of the drawer and gently dab concealer under my eyes to hide the shadows, and around my nose to hide the tiny spider veins that have recently appeared.

A pink blush, swept lightly across the apples of my cheeks, a golden shimmery powder illuminating my

N

"Oh Buck!" My eyes fill with tears as Buck p
arm round me. "That's . . . so lovely. But you
spend your money on me. You have to save it."

"I plan to. But I also planned to do this with th
payment. Go get showered and dressed and we'l
made a reservation for seven thirty."

I gaze at my son, so handsome and prou
seventeen so mature. How did he become so grow
So responsible? I beam at him, before sud
catching sight of my reflection in the window. M
is a mess, there are shadows under my eyes, my li
dry. How can I possibly go to the best restaurant i
area looking like this?

"You'll scrub up fine," Buck says, seeing wha
looking at, knowing what I'm thinking. "Think o
as your practice run, because I know you're goin
have to start dressing up soon for your girls' night
with your friends at work. And yes, I know y
happy in jeans, but c'mon, Mom. I know you still
nice clothes. You have an hour."

I shake my head with a smile. I can't argue with
but as I'm halfway up the stairs I stop, turning to
"Buck? Isn't this job going to interfere with sp
How are you going to manage schoolwork and —"

"Mom!" he interrupts, so much like a man th
almost want to cry. "I'm handling it. Remember yo
not going to interfere any more?"

"Right. Right," I mutter. "Sorry." And I go upst
to shower, still not knowing whether to laugh or cr

cheekbones, a dab of mascara, and Blistex to soften my lips.

I should make an effort more often. Even with the barest amount of make-up and my hair still wet, my face is transformed. I like what I see.

In the corner of my room, hidden behind a folding screen, is a coat rack with most of my clothes on it. At the back, hidden behind the sweatshirts, the fleeces, the heavy sweaters, are a handful of clothes, in plastic suit covers, that I had all but forgotten about.

The clothes from my former life, the ones that were too good to give to Goodwill, but not good enough to be accepted by the consignment clothes store a couple of towns beyond New Salem.

"Not quite designer enough," said the snooty girl as she flicked through them idly, looking not at the blouses but at the labels, a sneer almost visible on her face as she handed them back to me. She didn't thank me for coming in, nor say goodbye, merely turned her head, snapping gum in a decidedly irritating way, and grew busy doing something else in a manner that was altogether too superior, I thought, for a twenty-something working in a consignment dress store.

I meant to take them to another, less-judgemental consignment store, but life had been so busy back then, all my energies going into trying to support my kids, trying to find a new place to live, that I never got round to it.

So here they are! These blouses I tried to get rid of, that were not good enough for the girl in the consignment store, but that are more than good enough, probably too good, in fact, for my new life.

The olive-green chiffon top with the long sash that wrapped round and tied in a large bow. Bought at a small boutique on Nantucket one summer, it was beautiful, if not by anyone I had ever heard of. I hold it up, remembering how much it suited me. What was I thinking in trying to get rid of it?

A baby-blue silk tunic, embroidered with silver thread and tiny silver sequins. I remember wearing this all summer one year, in our rented house on the Vineyard. It is still as lovely as I had thought back then.

An ivory silk T, with long chiffon sleeves, cut on the bias with an asymmetrical hem. I had always loved it, but had never worn it. It was far too edgy for the conservative girls of New Salem.

There are a few more. A black evening vest that was Armani, but the label had fallen off, hence the consignment girl's disdain; a navy-and-cream-patterned blouse, with large floaty sleeves; a hot-pink kaftan that, again, I never wore, but always loved.

I feel a surge of happiness that I kept these beautiful clothes I had almost forgotten about. I will wear them all, but not in the way I once did, teamed with strappy Manolo Blahnik sandals, and large, glittering diamonds.

I'll wear them to suit who I am now. With jeans, and boots. Maybe even clogs.

I pick up the ivory silk T then return to the bathroom and tip my head upside down to blow-dry the curls. I crunch the stiff dried gel until it is soft, tipping my head back with a shake and letting the soft curls flow in a waterfall down my back.

I am ashamed to admit it is a few seconds before I can tear myself away from the mirror.

I look nothing like the glossy, overly made-up, highlighted, straight-haired, bejewelled and intimidating trophy wife.

Nor do I look anything like the Maggie who burst out of her house to confront the reporter on live television: dowdy, weary, colourless. A woman who didn't care what she looked like, had gone through something so painful, it was clear for all to see. A woman who recognized her life had stopped, and didn't seem to care whether it started again or not.

The woman looking back at me in the mirror is fresh, natural, approachable. She is soft and pretty. She is a woman you would want to talk to. You would want to be friends with her.

I would want to be friends with her.

Not because she wields power, but because she is real.

CHAPTER
FIFTY

Maggie

Buck holds the door of the River Tavern open for me to go first, and I pause for a second, a swell of pride washing over me as I look at my handsome, grown-up boy. He has dressed up, in a button-down shirt and chinos, and his hair is swept off his face in the way he knows I like it, rather than in the Bieber-esque sweep that he, and all his friends, have been doing of late.

The restaurant is warm and bright. It is like walking into sunshine. Every table is taken and there are delicious smells. A handful of people stand chatting at the bar in the front room, while the buzz of happy conversation fills the entire place. We're greeted by a smiling girl, who seems particularly enthralled by Buck, before being led to a table in the back, against the wall of windows.

"Mom, you look amazing," Buck says, as the girl, reluctantly, leaves. "I haven't seen you like this in such a long time."

"Like what? Dressed up? I don't usually have the occasion to," I reply, as the waiter hands me the drinks menu, but I'm thrilled. "I wanted to look nice for my first grown-up mother-son date."

Buck smiles before shaking his head. "It's not just dressed up. You seem . . . happy. I haven't seen you happy since . . . well . . . Honestly? I don't know that you've ever looked this happy." He grins. "You seem younger, which is really weird. Maybe it's the curly hair. It's just a totally different vibe and the whole thing suits you."

"Wow! That's a lot to dissect. Meanwhile, when did my teenage son become so perceptive?" I reach over to squeeze his hand for he is right that tonight I feel happy.

I am happy to be exactly where I am, with my son, in this restaurant. I am happy to look round the room at my fellow diners, none of whom I know, and yet feel the kinship of our shared humanity. I am happy to sit, finally comfortable in my skin, and be truly part of, and in, the world again.

I realize that over time, without really noticing it, I stopped looking to run away. I stopped wading through life wondering how everyone could seem so normal when everything in my world was upside down. These days I don't find myself watching a movie, or reading a book, and spacing out for a few minutes as I acknowledge that absolute happiness exists, but for other people. Not for me.

I no longer feel as if I'm behind a glass wall, able to see, but not to join in. Able to speak, but only the basics, for my voice had gone, drowned in a sea of shame. I'm no longer hiding away, declining all invitations to girls' nights out with Patty and Barb, venturing out only across the garden to Mr and Mrs

Wellesley, and only because they nurture me like a daughter, have only ever provided a place of safety, and comfort, and love.

I'm not counting the hours until I can go to bed, wanting a few hours' respite from the numbness, fighting the wish that I could stay in bed for days; perhaps for the rest of my life.

I am here. Present. Happy.

Sitting in the River Tavern, across from my handsome son, who is currently having a long conversation with the waiter about the giant molcajete on the counter, peppering him with questions about how the guacamole is made; how come the avocado doesn't get stuck in the holes.

Yes, I really am happy.

Our meals have been eaten with gusto, Buck making me laugh all evening with stories of school, his friends, their girlfriends. I still can't believe how lucky I am with Buck, with this child who tells me everything, who trusts me enough to talk to me honestly. Every now and then I remind myself not to count my blessings yet. Once upon a time I thought I could have said the same thing of Grace.

Grace. A cloud descends whenever I think about Grace. I keep writing to her, but she hasn't responded. I'm kept in the loop by Buck, and occasionally by Chris, although he is busy with his life in New York, too busy to do more than text every now and then.

I don't blame him. I don't blame Grace. I just wish things were different. You reap what you sow.

How can I blame my children for not wanting to be with me, when I didn't want to be with them? I hate admitting this, and I have only been able to see it since my world fell apart, but throughout their childhoods I had no idea how to be with them, how to be present, how to be a mother.

How could I have known? I was raised by wolves myself, both parents out working all day, leaving me entirely to my own devices. I had a key and would come home from school every day to a silent house. I'd make myself a snack, do my homework, clean the kitchen and do laundry.

When my mother got home from her cleaning job she was exhausted herself; too tired to be interested in me.

How could I have known how to parent when I wasn't parented myself?

"Am I a better mother now?" I ask, smiling at Buck, who is moaning with pleasure at the date pudding we are supposed to be sharing, which is currently in the middle of the table, three-quarters of it gone, while my spoon lies untouched in front of me.

"Than when? Before? New Salem?"

I nod.

"Mom! How can you even ask? You know you are, but it's an unfair comparison. Life was so different; you had so much more stuff going on. And the three of us kids were at home — well, until Chris went to school. But it was different."

"It was, but Grace thinks I was a nightmare. Controlling and critical. I'm only able to see now how true that was, but I'm not like that any more, am I?" I want to be sure I've changed as much as I think I have.

"No, Mom," he says, shaking his head. "You're not. Don't take this the wrong way, but it took a while until you seemed like a mom again. I mean, you were home all the time, and you were there for me in a way you never were back then, but it was almost like you were only half there. You just seemed so . . . sad. The Dad stuff, and Grace, and then we hardly ever hear from Chris. It felt a bit like I was the only one who had you back in some way, but I lost you too."

"I'm sorry." There is a lump in my throat and I blink back tears. "I did lose myself, and I know it's been hard, but none of it meant I didn't love you. Any of you. I am back, though. Really back. I wish Grace would give me another chance. Have you . . ." I look down at the tablecloth. "Have you heard from her recently?"

"No. She hasn't been on Facebook so we haven't chatted in a while. Chris saw her a couple of weekends ago, I think. He posted something about going out in New York and taking his sister to the Spice Market."

I force my face to retain its pleasant demeanour, as false as that feels given the pain of knowing so little about two of my children's lives. I know hardly anything about Chris's work, his friends, what he does in the evenings, whether he's finally learned to do his own washing. I have no idea how he's coping. I know even less about Grace.

"So how was Grace? Did Chris say anything about her?"

358

To my dismay, Buck shakes his head. Of course they didn't talk about it. Chris has other things going on, and Buck is seventeen. Why would they be interested in discussing Grace?

But I can't stop myself asking another question: "Do you know if she said anything about me?"

"I don't know, Mom. I'm sorry. Want me to find out?"

"No. I'm sorry. It's okay. She'll get in touch when she's ready." I blink the pain away and force myself to leave the memories, the regrets, and come back to the present. "How did you turn out so well? Unless I'm wrong." I raise an eyebrow. "You're not dealing drugs or anything when I'm not around?"

Buck laughs. "And risk coach kicking me off the team? Are you kidding? Maybe it's because I'm the youngest. Maybe I'm too dumb to be angry about it." I watch his face grow serious. "Of course I was hurt, and I didn't understand, but . . ." He shrugs. "I guess I never thought that Dad did it because he didn't love me. Who knows why he did it. Maybe he just wanted to try a different kind of life, and got in too deep before he could stop it, but I never felt that he did it because I wasn't good enough. I think that's the crucial difference between Grace and me. I think she thinks it's her fault."

"She doesn't," I say quietly. "She thinks it's my fault."

"Yours. Hers. It doesn't really matter. The fact is that blaming doesn't get you anywhere. It keeps you stuck. Blaming stops you from moving on with your life." As he reaches for another spoonful of pudding, his words strike to the core of my being.

Kissing him goodnight after thanking him for the most wonderful treat I have had in years, I pad upstairs to my tiny bedroom under the eaves. The walls are papered in an English floral-print wallpaper, and there are pretty striped curtains and window seats with large, tasselled cushions.

Mrs W had decorated the carriage house for when her son and daughter would come and stay, expecting it to be filled with grandchildren, friends. This bedroom was for the daughter she rarely sees, her dreams, expectations and love embroidered into every cushion, sewn into every square of the blue and white quilt.

The bedside lamps cast a warm glow as I climb into bed, propping the pillows up behind me as I reach for the computer and set it on my lap. As I stare at the screen, Buck's words still echo in my head.

"Blaming doesn't get you anywhere . . . blaming stops you from moving on with your life."

It is, finally, as clear as day. That is why I haven't been able to move on. I was too busy blaming.

I blamed Mark — for the shame, the lies, the deception, the financial mess, the stealing.

I blamed Sylvie. Others may have thought she was as much a victim as me, but I knew that had it not been for her, had Mark never met her, I might still have a faithful husband. I might still have the life I thought I always wanted.

360

But most of all, I blamed myself. How could I have been so stupid; how could I not have questioned his obvious lies; how could I have been so accepting?

I believed because I wanted to believe. I went against every instinct that told me something was amiss, and chose to ignore all the signs because I didn't want anything in my life to change.

A weight I have carried on my shoulders for over two years finally leaves me.

It is time to let it all go.

CHAPTER
FIFTY-ONE

Sylvie

The iPhone vibrates and Sylvie takes it out of her pocket. It is a text reminding her that the team from *Sunday Times Style* will be here at nine to shoot the house. Her assistant is picking up breakfast for everyone, does she want anything? And the hair and make-up emailed last night to say Sylvie had cancelled them. Should they be rebooked?

She texts back that she has breakfast here, and no, she doesn't want the hair and make-up people back.

When the media started becoming interested in her, they sent hair and make-up people to make her look beautiful, arriving with tool kits and bags filled with cosmetics. They accentuated her eyes, contoured her cheekbones, twirled and curled her hair so she looked like a painted doll, but, as she said to Angie afterwards, she looked nothing like her. She looked, in fact, entirely fake.

"The whole point of Figless Manor, of the woman behind Figless Manor, is that it is about comfort, warmth, accessibility. How can I talk about people letting go of this concept of perfection when I'm sitting on my terrace looking like a mannequin?" she asked.

Now she insists she does it herself. She applies more make-up than she would ever usually wear, and makes a little more effort with her hair, gathering it back in a loose chignon, using the curling tongs to add a couple of soft, feathery wisps to frame her face, but she still looks like Sylvie.

She checks her watch. Another half-hour until her assistant gets here, closely followed by the photographer and his team of stylists. This quiet time in the morning, with no one in the house save sleeping Eve, and Alfie, a large black and white cat who showed up on the doorstep one day and hasn't left, is the time she treasures most of all. Switching her once-again vibrating phone to off, she plans to sit down, in peace, with her coffee — but first she goes into the laundry room.

She quickly tips the dirty clothes from the basket into the washer, sighing as coins fall out of a pocket. Damn. She always forgets to check pockets. The clothes come out, and it isn't a coin at the bottom of the machine, but two small black discs.

Sylvie picks them up and frowns at them, feeling in Eve's pockets for more. Three more. She moves them in her hand, feeling the smoothness, their surprising heaviness, before she suddenly realizes what they are.

Weights.

She stares at the discs in her hand. This is the reason it has been fine. Eve has been weighting her clothes.

Sylvie turns the phone on again and speed dials Dr Lawson. He isn't in yet but she leaves a message explaining what's been happening, and as she talks she feels her anger rising. She shouldn't be angry, she knows that getting angry is the worst thing in the world, but she's so tired of this, of these tricks, of Eve just refusing to get better.

She marches into Eve's room and shakes her awake.

"What?" Eve stirs, bleary-eyed, propping herself up. "What's the matter? Is something wrong?"

"Yes, something's wrong," Sylvie says, opening her hand. Showing her the weights. "I know your little secret. I know you've been weighting your clothes. I'm sick of this, Eve, do you hear me? I'm sick of this stupid illness and you not eating. When are you going to get over this? When are you going to just grow up and take responsibility and get better?"

"It's not my fault," Eve says. "I want to get better. I'm trying. I hate what's happened to me."

"So why don't you just eat?" Sylvie shrieks, now at breaking point. "Why don't you just sit down at the table and eat a goddamned meal?" And she throws the weights over the bed before walking out of the bedroom and slamming the door.

CHAPTER
FIFTY-TWO

Buck

"Take it easy, Hathaway!" I distantly hear coach yell as I slam my opponent into the wall at the side of the rink, growling in rage as I push him back again.

I have no idea how I'm able to play lacrosse and hockey with such fury, such passion, because take me out of the rink, off the field, and I'm the most mellow dude you'll ever meet.

But here at Norwich Ice Rink, let's just say I have something of a reputation during the games. Not when I'm practising, but when I'm put in an organized competitive situation a whole other side of me comes out. Maybe it allows me to tap into a rage that's so deep I barely register its existence, although no psychologist would be surprised after what my family has been through.

I let the guy go and follow the coach's directions, catching the eye of a group of girls who've started following our team. The other boys have known most of them for ever, and apparently I'm the "fresh meat" that's bringing them to the games.

They're cute, but I'm not really interested in any of them.

For months after my dad disappeared, my mom kept talking about needing to take me to see someone; how important it was for me to talk about it, share my feelings. It took ages for me to get her to understand that I didn't have anything to talk about.

I never felt the way Grace did, that my dad did this because he didn't love me, or that I was to blame. People fuck up; he had fucked up, but it didn't have anything to do with me. It did force me to grow up, though. I may be seventeen, but I feel twenty. Maybe twenty-five. When I look at this group of girls, cute and giggly, following my every loop and slash round the rink, despite knowing we are the same age, I feel old enough to be their father.

The girl at the River Tavern on the other hand? The one who showed us to the table the other night? Who must be around twenty or twenty-one? Now she is definitely worth revisiting.

We win the game, but I decline the offer of celebratory ice cream. I've got a job at the boatyard to get back to, and I wave a general goodbye in the direction of the girls, walking off to the truck.

I throw my bag in the back, then I feel a hand on my arm. I turn. It's one of the girls. The prettiest, in fact. If I were to be interested, which I'm not, this would be the one.

"Hi," she says, and smiles. Seductively.

"Hi." I pause, hand on the door handle. "Rachel, right?"

Her face lights up. "How did you know?"

"I've seen you around."

"And you're Buck."

"Buck Hathaway." I extend my arm to shake hands, the way I've always been taught, which seems to throw her a bit. She looks down, giggles, then shakes my hand.

"This is the coolest truck in the whole world," she says, looking over it. "I see you driving round and I could just die of jealousy. I'm driving a smashed-up Honda, and I dream of an old F100."

I'm impressed she even knows what this is, and no, she didn't check the tailgate.

She scuffs a flip-flop in the gravel and looks up at me, biting her lip in a way that is designed to be part cute, part suggestive. "So I just came out to see if you were interested in hanging out with a bunch of us tonight?"

"Hanging out?"

"My place. Around eight. My parents are going out. You should come. Do you have your phone? I can text you my addresss."

I get out my phone and give her the number for her to send the text, thanking her for the invitation.

"I'm not sure I can make it, though," I say, forcing an expression of regret onto my face. "My mom asked me to do some stuff for her. But I'll try to get out of it, okay? I'll do my best."

"I'll be much more fun than your mom," she pouts. "Promise." And with that she turns and walks back to the rink, deliberately swinging her butt in a way that is just the tiniest bit tempting.

But here's the thing. She still isn't my type. And she definitely isn't much more fun than my mom. There was a time when that would have been true, but my mom has become the coolest mom I could ever have wished for, and far more a friend than a mom, although there are still certain things I would never, ever tell her.

So while she knows my dad writes me long letters from jail, I would never tell her that I write back to him. I didn't write back at first, but Chris was gone, and I missed him. I wanted Dad to know about me getting onto the varsity team, and the truck, and what was going on; but telling him anything personal took a little while. Trusting him at all took a little while.

I'm careful not to talk about mom. He doesn't ask, and I don't tell. Nor do I ask anything about his other life. We started when Dad sent me a book, *A Separate Peace* by John Knowles. He asked me to read it and let him know what I thought, and that evolved into this book thing we share, like an unofficial mail-only book club.

We've been taking turns choosing books to read, then writing to each other about them. Dad always chooses something like *The Catcher in the Rye*, or *Lord of the Flies*, and he was worried about my choices, but he thought Gary Paulsen's *Hatchet* was great.

I also wouldn't tell Mom about Grace's partying. I'm on Facebook with her a few times a week, and half the time I can hardly understand what she's saying because she's slurring. She swears she's not drunk, only tired, but I'm not twelve any more.

I got mad at her a few months ago, and she refused to speak to me for three weeks, until I apologized. I told her I was wrong, and I haven't brought it up since.

I can't talk about Grace's drinking with Mom, as Grace still doesn't speak to her, and it would only make things so very much worse. Chris is convinced it's nothing serious, just the usual partying at college, and maybe he's right. Maybe it is. The last couple of times she's come up on Facebook wanting to chat I've ignored it because seeing her drunk just makes me mad. I'd rather talk to her during the day.

When I get home from the boatyard, I kiss Mom, grab half a sandwich from the fridge and the carton of milk, and take them upstairs without Mom seeing. The computer clicks and whirrs as I swig, then I log in, boxes immediately popping up all over my screen of people wanting to chat.

Grace. I ignore her.

"C'mon, little bro," she writes. "I know you're there. I just saw you go online. Wanna video chat? I haven't spoken to you for ages. I want to say hi."

I know she's probably drunk. I know it's going to make me mad. But it's my sister. And I love her. And right now I'm all she has.

CHAPTER
FIFTY-THREE

Sylvie

Sylvie lets herself into the house, leaning against the door for a few seconds, exhausted, trying to regain some equilibrium.

She calls out for Eve, knowing she is at home, given the presence of her jeep in the driveway. The house echoes, which means nothing other than that Eve is in her room, but as always Sylvie rushes upstairs and knocks on the door, waiting for the anxiety in her chest to lighten as Eve tells her she is there, breathing, alive.

This afternoon she went to see Dr Lawson. He was, after all, in charge of Eve, and although Eve is no longer in intensive outpatient therapy, she continues to talk to him from time to time.

Dr Lawson was concerned to hear about the weights, more concerned when he looked through the records and discovered that Eve hasn't been checking in, hasn't turned up to her last two therapy appointments, has been, in fact, absent without leave.

"Why didn't you call me?" Sylvie struggled to keep her voice calm. "How could you let this happen without telling me?"

He was contrite. "I don't know how this happened. I need to talk to my staff and try to find out, but right now my primary duty is to see Eve. You need to get her in here, today. I can clear my afternoon, but this kind of relapse requires immediate intervention. The sooner she gets here the greater our chances."

Sylvie's heart jumped into her throat. "What do you mean, the greater our chances?"

He didn't say anything. He didn't have to. Sylvie already knew this disease kills. But she'd hidden her head in the sand, refusing to face the possibility that this meant life or death for Eve.

As she knocks again, louder, on Eve's door she knows she can't hide any more.

No reply.

She pushes open the door. Eve is not in her room. Neither is her laptop. Nor her suitcase.

On the bed is a piece of paper.

Mom,

I love you, but I can't stand this. I need to be on my own for a while so I've gone away. Don't worry, and don't try to find me. I'll be in touch soon.

Evie xx

Sylvie sinks down onto the bed as a howl of pain escapes her lips.

CHAPTER
FIFTY-FOUR

Maggie

The feeling of being happy has softened, without disappearing. I don't remember the last time I felt this way: more than happy . . . alive. I've come back to life. I have no idea how, or why — I didn't even know this was something I wanted, but these past few mornings I've woken up with this crazy excitement about all that life has to offer.

Even my tips are bigger at work. Patty and Barb keep teasing me about my secret boyfriend being the cause of this newfound giddiness, but — sadly — I have no way to explain it other than a seismic shift in the core of my being.

I swing a U-turn by the grocery store, remembering that Mrs W dropped off a vast bowl of peas, picked this morning, ready to be shelled, and although I have never been a particularly keen cook, I have a sudden impulse to make a pea soup.

At the grocery store I fill my basket with remembered ingredients: shallots, bacon, butter, chicken stock; sour cream and chives to garnish. I pause by the bread to grab a couple of loaves of fresh soda bread.

"Maggie?" I turn as George walks up to the checkout, a large smile on his face. I put down the basket and give him a big hug.

George is one of the crowd I meet at Ashlawn Farm. I haven't seen him for a while, and it is only now, stepping back and looking at his familiar creased face, that I realize how I have missed him.

"Ethel away again?" I look down at his basket: one can of Campbell's soup, one frozen dinner, a pack of frozen spinach and a huge tub of caramel crunch ice cream.

"Sssh. Don't tell her about the ice cream. She'd kill me."

"That frozen stuff's more likely to kill you," I say. "You need some fresh home-cooked food. Why don't you come back to my house? I was planning on making a pea soup. You can keep me company while I cook, and take some home — there's more than I know what to do with."

"I can't disturb you," George says, in a very unconvincing way.

"You're not disturbing me. Maybe you can have a look at the car — a red light has just started flashing on the dashboard."

"Well, why didn't you say so!" George's face lights up. "I'll be happy to do that for you! Shall I follow you home?"

I'm clearing away the soup bowls and George, having sorted the car with a top-up of oil, is sitting happily at the kitchen table with the local paper in front of him, apparently in no rush to leave.

"Ethel seems to be travelling a lot these days," I say carefully, placing a plate of cheese and crackers in front of him. "It must be quite hard for you to be on your own so much."

"Oh no." George pops a cracker into his mouth. "Not when you hear her complain. It's peaceful when she's gone, but don't tell her I said that."

"So that's two secrets so far . . ." I grin. "No mention of ice cream or complaining. Is that the key to a happy marriage, then?"

"Happy?" George barks with laughter, which soon dissolves into a coughing fit. "Sorry. Cracker got stuck. I'm not sure Ethel and I could ever be described as having a happy marriage."

I slide into the chair opposite him. "Really? But weren't you in love with her when you married her?"

"In love? Pshaw. All you young people talk about being in love, but real life isn't like that. We were right for each other, certainly. Our families knew each other, and the time was right, and I think each looked at the other and knew we had found a good fit."

"You never wanted . . . more?"

"Oh, I had more." George smiles wistfully as my mouth drops open.

"You had an . . . affair?" I'm shocked.

"Of course not!" George says, affronted. "But I did have a great love, and it was everything it is supposed to be, but great love and great marriages do not always go hand in hand."

"What do you mean?" I lean in, fascinated. "Why couldn't you marry her?"

"Her family had their own plans for her, and we were from very different worlds. We always knew she would be marrying one of her own, and we just had this very brief time together when everything in my world seemed brighter, and better, and more beautiful because she was in it."

"Oh George," I say with a sigh, reaching over the table to stroke his hand. "That's so sad, that you couldn't be together."

"It's not sad, it's life . . . We both accepted what had to be."

As George is about to leave, the door handle turns and Mrs W, clutching a bottle of Prosecco, stands in the doorway.

"We've got the most wonderful news! . . . Oh!" She stops dead in her tracks when she sees George.

"Come in!" I'm thrilled to see her. "Come and sit down. What's the news? This is my friend George Pawley."

"Oh I know George," Mrs W says.

"Hello, Leona." George, straightening his shoulders, sounding crisper, pulls a chair out for Mrs W. "Please sit down."

Mrs W lowers herself into a chair, looking up at George once she is seated, their faces softening as they gaze at each other.

I notice how their eyes have lit up, both of them smiling. Can Mrs W have been the great love he was just talking about? They're certainly both giving that impression. I look from one to the other, realizing that of course George knew where she lived, hence his reluctance to leave. He must have been hoping to see Mrs W before going home.

"Would you like a glass of Prosecco?" I ask Mrs W when George has left, but she shakes her head.

"I came to tell you that we have a lovely surprise. Cole is home."

"Cole, your son?"

"There isn't any other," she says, and her face is beaming. "I wanted to ask you to join us for dinner. Bring the rest of the pea soup. We'll eat around eight?"

CHAPTER
FIFTY-FIVE

Maggie

I have so few pretty clothes left, but tonight I want to look, if not pretty, then at least decent, and wear something better than the jeans and sweatshirts that have become my daily uniform.

I have one pair of black leggings that are ratty at the hem, but if I turn them up the loose threads are barely noticeable. Ballet flats, and a loose, thin, fringed sweater bought back in February, when North Cove Outfitters was having their closing-down sale, and yet to be worn.

I'm curious to meet Cole. I know little about him, other than that he is enormously loved, and enormously missed. There are pictures dotted around the house, of a young handsome man, hair in a buzz cut, smiling widely at the camera. Or of him as a little boy, the expression on his face impish and naughty as he looks over at his sister.

He was born the same year as me, I remember that. He has never been married, and despite his parents talking about previous girlfriends, I have often wondered if he is gay, and, given his parents' waspish, old Yankee sensibilities, reluctant to tell them.

Whoever he is, I want him to like me. I want to make a good impression, so I have done my hair carefully, and added lip gloss and mascara for this special occasion.

"Hey, Mom —" Buck pauses on the path as we walk through the garden, waiting for me to catch up — "what if you and their son fall in love and get married? Wouldn't that be cool! Then they'd be my grandparents for real!"

"Don't be silly," I shush him. "And can you just keep your voice down? Never mind the fact that marriage isn't something that needs to be part of any conversation, I don't ever want to get married again. And even if I did, this is not the man for me."

"How do you know?" Buck grins. "You've never even met him."

"I just know. Trust me."

We continue up the path, Buck softly singing "Love is in the Air", as I keep my mouth shut. Anything I say at this point will only encourage him, and I'd be lying if I said I wasn't a tiny bit curious.

There are voices coming from the living room in the front, but I go through the back door, as I always do, and into the kitchen, where I set down the soup and bread. Elsa is there, the "woman that does", and has done, for Mrs W for almost forty years. She is tiny and round, her eyes are always twinkling, and a smile is always fixed on her face as she bustles about.

She gives me a big hug, ruffling Buck's hair as he goes straight to the tray of hors d'oeuvres and sticks a

378

finger into the artichoke dip, sucking it clean with a loud sound of approval.

"Buck!" I'm horrified.

"What? Elsa always lets me have a taste, don't you, Elsa?"

"*Si*. He's a growing boy, missus. He needs his food."

"No wonder you're over here all the time. Please tell me he's not eating you out of house and home?"

"I love it," Elsa says. "All the children are grown up and gone now. I love having this boy around." She looks over at Buck with love in her eyes, and once again I am filled with gratitude at landing in this place, with these people who have become my family, a family so very much more functional, and loving, than my own.

I leave Buck in the kitchen with Elsa and walk down the hallway into the foyer, then into the living room, I look round me, loving this house. It has an old-world elegance that is rarely found any more. The walls of the living room are panelled and painted, hung with oil paintings of Wellesley ancestors, which are lit by ancient brass picture lights; there are groupings of mohair sofas, damask hard-backed chairs, ottomans with the books now removed, waiting for trays of hors d'oeuvres.

The chintz curtains are held back with heavy corded tassels. The rugs are Persian, and threadbare. No one ran in to replace them with a plush new version at the first sign of a stray thread. It is the very fact of their age, and disrepair, that makes them beautiful.

Some might describe the room as old-fashioned, or dated, but few could argue about it being formal without being intimidating.

It is the look I always wanted, the look I tried to have in the "formal living room" in the New Salem house. Of course, now I realize I could never have achieved that look, for this is a room that has been put together over many years, with love, and care. No interior designer chose those paintings, nor embroidered the cushions. The furniture is ancient, glowing with beeswax that is rubbed into a shine by a conscientious Elsa.

Standing by the sideboard, placing the crystal decanter back on the polished surface, is a man who must be Cole. He is taller than I imagined, and bearded, not at all how he looks in the photographs, most of which were taken at least a decade ago, it seems.

There are deep creases round his eyes when he smiles, which he does when he comes over to introduce himself, and I am instantly struck by how handsome he is. I wasn't prepared for this, which is ridiculous really, given how good-looking he is in the photographs.

Perhaps I hadn't thought that he would . . . strike me. It is more than just looking at him and finding him handsome. It is almost as if there is something in his face, his being, that resonates with me.

And I didn't anticipate that. I find myself looking over at the photos of the clean-shaven, short-haired man in the photographs on the table next to us. He follows my gaze.

"I'm Cole. An older, hairier version of the me over there."

I blink as I look up at him, eventually recovering to respond in kind, to introduce myself, to laugh in a way that I hope could be described as "prettily" when he tells me he has heard so much about me.

"You're not what I expected." He gazes at me and my heart does a tiny flip. "It's funny. I remember getting hold of a newspaper when I was in Cape Town, and reading about you. When Ma told me your name, and about you moving here, I put two and two together, but you sounded nothing like the description in the paper."

I freeze. My face goes red hot as I stare at him, my eyes widening with shock. He is talking as if it is nothing, as if everyone knows. But no one here knows. A wave of nausea washes over me as I stammer, trying to figure out what to say next.

"I've said something to upset you," he says, his face falling. "I'm so sorry. I should never have brought it up. It was insensitive."

"No, no," I murmur, moving to the sofa, desperately hoping the flush will fade, desperately trying to think of how to move through this.

"Maggie?" Mrs W says quietly, moving to sit next to me, laying a finger softly under my chin to turn my head so I'm looking directly into her eyes. "Maggie, dear. Did you think we didn't know? Of course we knew. We Googled your name as soon as you applied to lease the carriage house, but we don't care a whit about what happened in your past. Not least because none of it was your fault. We just wanted to look after you," she continues, smiling, "and now you're part of our family. You're all part of our family." She places a hand on my knee and gives it a reassuring squeeze.

"We like a bit of scandal in the family," Mr W adds heartily from across the room. "It spices things up."

"And your story has nothing on some of the Wellesley scandals," Mrs W says. "We have a cousin long-suspected of murdering the gamekeeper, who was murdered himself after he got involved with the mob."

"What about Althea?" Mr W says. "She was sent to live in Bermuda so she wouldn't have to testify in the case about the missing —" He lowers his voice to a whisper to say the family name, a name instantly recognizable in every household in the country. "She was the only witness and Aunt Evelyn flew her out so she couldn't be subpoenaed."

"Did she know what happened?" My curiosity is piqued, my flush faded, and I would love to know.

"Oh yes," Mrs W says, before being shushed by her husband.

"Let's just say he won't be turning up at the Martha's Vineyard compound any time soon," Cole says. "And no, Althea didn't do it. I really am sorry," he says again, turning to me. "I didn't mean to embarrass you. As you can see, no one here gives a damn."

I exhale with relief. "You've made me feel much better," I say, and then, to my horror, I burst into tears.

Now this is embarrassing. I have no idea why I'm crying, but as I gratefully take the cotton handkerchief Mr W draws from his pocket and quietly hands over, I realize I've spent my whole life not feeling accepted, terrified that if people knew the real me, my real family, they'd want nothing to do with me.

When Mark betrayed me my worst fears were realized as my hidden shame was revealed and the house of cards I'd spent years constructing came crashing down around me. I hadn't, as I so stupidly thought, finally been accepted by the kind of people that matter, the hedge funders, their trophy wives. I was dropped like a dirty shirt, proving what I knew to be true all along.

I wasn't good enough.

Despite all the changes I've made in the last few years — moving here, working, leaving my old life behind — the weight of my past, the weight of that huge secret, has been hanging round my neck like a huge, heavy stone.

I may have found the real me, I thought, but what if they discover who the old me was. What if they realize the waitress at the restaurant is not just "Maggie", but the woman from the famous bigamy case.

Here, today, in this wonderful room, with these wonderful people who have looked after me so well, I know, beyond a shadow of a doubt, that for the first time in my life I am truly accepted. They have known all along, and have not judged me for it.

They don't think the real Maggie isn't good enough, nor do they judge who I was, who they might have presumed me to be after I was described so horribly in the newspapers.

"How about a drink?" Mr W, clearing his throat, uncomfortable with this display of emotion, stands up and moves to the sideboard. "Brandy, I think," he says, but Cole and I catch eyes and start to laugh.

"Maggie's not overwrought, Dad!" Cole says. "Brandy's a little much, no?"

"I know!" Mrs W says. "How about a glass of Prosecco?"

During the roast beef, Cole announces he'd like to go for a walk after dinner.

"I missed the beach," Cole says. "Can we go down to the beach? There's nothing as beautiful as the beach at night."

"Missed the beach?" Mr W laughs. "We've had postcards from Thailand, Fiji, Bora Bora. You've had plenty of beach!"

"It isn't the same as the beach in Old Lyme," Cole replies. "There's only so much white sand and turquoise water a man can take."

"That's a hard life," I tease, trying to catch Buck's eye, gesturing he should help clear the table.

"What?" Buck asks, frowning at me then looking down at his plate, confused. "Is there something wrong?"

"No, honey. I was trying, very subtly, to get you to help clear the dishes."

Buck jumps up, embarrassed, and reaches for Mrs W's plate.

"It's all right, dear." Mrs W waves him to sit down, and Buck, unsure what to do, looks to me for direction. "Elsa will do it," she continues.

"I know Elsa could do it," I say, "but I'm raising him to be somebody's husband. Think how his wife will thank me for all the training I'm doing now."

"You're quite right," Mrs W says. "Young people have to be taught. You're doing a lovely job, Maggie. Buck is just a delightful young man. You have trained him well — isn't that right, Wells?" she asks her husband. "Children and dogs. Much the same, at least according to that man we like . . . What is his name? Small. Mexican. Come on. Who am I thinking of?"

"I have absolutely no idea." Mr W stares at her, bemused.

"Oh yes, you do, Wells. We watch him all the time. You do that thing he says. You know: tssst!" She makes a hissing noise that causes both dogs, lying by Mr W's feet, to look up. "See? Tssst!" She does it again, looking at the dogs. "Dog . . . whisperer! The Dog Whisperer! Now what's his name? Oh Lord. My memory is so bad these days." She looks helplessly at her husband.

"Cesar Millan?" Buck offers.

"That's the one!" she shouts triumphantly. "He's always talking about the pack leader, and it's just the same with children. They need to know who their pack leader is, who to respect."

"Does that make me pack leader?" I grimace. "I'm not sure I like the sound of that."

"It does, and it's good. The pups need to know who's in charge. What's that other thing he says? That it's never the dogs who are crazy or bad, but their owners. Once the owners change their energy, the dogs are fine. Calm, assertive energy. All the problems stem from the dogs not knowing where they stand, and not being able to trust the person who ought to be pack leader."

"Just so you know . . ." Buck sits back down at the table, leaning in to Mrs W conspiratorially, lowering his voice to a whisper, "I only let her think she's the pack leader. It keeps everybody happy." And he winks as we all start to laugh.

I stand on a rock as the wind picks up; it messes with my hair until eventually I just unclip it and let it blow back, free form.

The others have begged off. Wimps. Buck was invited to hang out with friends; Mr and Mrs W declared that after such a huge meal the only thing they'd be good for was bed.

Which left just Cole and me. Something tells me they might have all done this on purpose.

I breathe in, closing my eyes, almost tasting the salt and sea, and fling my arms out to the side as I tip my head back. Admittedly, I may be a little tipsy from all the wine at dinner.

"This is wonderful," I shout over to Cole, standing at the water's edge, leaning down to examine a shell. "This makes me feel young. I don't know why I never come here."

"You're not exactly old." Cole walks over, putting the shell in my hand. I can barely see it in the dim moonlight, but I run my thumb over the ridges and place it safely in my pocket.

"I used to come here all the time," Cole says, settling down on the rock. I join him, pulling my knees up and wrapping my arms round them. "Usually when you live somewhere you never take advantage of all it has to offer. I had a girlfriend once who was from London. She had lived in London for thirty years and she had never been to the Tower of London, or seen the changing of the guard at Buckingham Palace. She'd never been to the Houses of Parliament or Westminster Abbey. I was horrified. She'd taken them all for granted, saw them as tourist attractions for visiting Americans."

"Were you her visiting American?" I am curious, forgetting I had wondered, albeit briefly, whether he might be gay.

"I was," he says, and laughs. "I dragged her to every tourist attraction I could think of, including the Edinburgh Festival, and she loved it. She kept saying she couldn't believe there were so many amazing things right on her doorstep."

"Edinburgh's not exactly on her doorstep."

"No, but you get the point."

"So what happened?"

"At Edinburgh?"

"No!" I push him playfully. "To the girlfriend."

"Same as with all of the others," he says simply. "I wasn't able to stay in one place for any length of time. I had a penchant for choosing women who wanted the very opposite of what I wanted. I think that perhaps they saw me as a challenge, thought that they could change me, that I would fall so deeply in love with them I would give it all up to become a husband."

"Did you not love any of them enough?"

"I loved Imogen very much." He turns to me then, just a sliver of his face visible in the moonlight. "She was the London girl. But the timing wasn't right. I knew that if I had stayed in London, as she wanted, and married her, a part of me would have died, and I would always regret it. And at some point I would doubtless end up blaming her, and she would wake up one morning and find a note on her pillow and a missing backpack, and that wouldn't be fair to anyone."

"You loved her enough to leave her," I murmur.

"I suppose I did. However, the story does have a happy ending. Imogen is married to Stephen, who is a barrister, and they have three beautiful girls. I am godfather to the eldest, and get on with Stephen like a house on fire. The only travelling he is interested in involves luxury hotels with staff that wait on you hand and foot, and a children's club."

"Was it a lucky escape?"

"I would never have been able to offer her stability. Not back then, for sure. Or, let's face it, a Georgian house in Islington." He smiles as he says this. "But I do sometimes think about what might have been."

"So what is it with the travelling?" I press. "Aren't you a little old to still be chasing the dream?"

"I'll remind you that I'm the same age as you." He laughs. "And yes, I am a little old to be doing what I have done for so long."

"Which is what, exactly?"

"Painting, mostly," he says.

"Houses?"

Cole smiles at me. "No. Portraits. Some landscapes."

"On beaches in Thailand?"

"That's one of the perks that come with the job. Sometimes I arrive someplace new with a show already set up, and sometimes I just show up, set up an easel, and by the end of the day I invariably have new friends, a commission or two, and often a show. You'd be amazed how fascinated people are. When I show them my portfolio, you can see the flicker in their eyes. They'd love to be painted, or have their children painted, or a family portrait, but art is beyond their means, or so they've always thought. I keep my prices incredibly low. The pleasure I get from knowing they're being given something that they will enjoy for ever is worth every penny."

"How low is low?"

"It varies. I've even been known to do it for free. Not the paintings, though, that's too time-consuming, but the sketches."

"How can you do it for free?" I ask, knowing how every penny counts in life. Particularly mine. Particularly now. "How can you possibly afford to do that?"

Cole shrugs. "Look at my life. There's so little I actually need. I have no mortgage, no children to support, no bills to pay. I rent apartments short-term, or find rooms in people's homes, and stay for however long feels right. It has been as little as a couple of days, and as long as a year. When I get a show, I can ask far more for the paintings, which supplements the other work I do."

"Where did you go that you stayed a year?"

"Siena. It was the least lucrative year of my life, but I loved living there."

"Yet you didn't want to stay?"

"I did. Until I didn't. And then it was time to go."

"And you've never thought of settling down? Of finding one place to call home and, what's the expression, laying your hat? Isn't it tiring, taking off all the time?"

"This is home —" Cole gestures all round us — "Old Lyme. My school was home. Middlesex. And Yale."

"Yale." I raise an eyebrow, impressed.

"It's not as impressive as it sounds," he says. "I only got in because every member of my father's family has gone there since the year dot. There is a Wellesley Hall and a Wellesley Library. It was all rather embarrassing. But these places are home for me, although I never felt myself bound to them until . . . well, more recently I've found myself beginning to change. It's not a longing, exactly, but I have found myself thinking more and more about this place, and, of course, my parents. And then today, being surrounded by everything familiar, and good, made me wonder if it might be time to come back." He sighs. "But then I read an article about Costa Rica, and all I want to do is grab my stuff and go."

"You could," I say. "Why not? Being here doesn't necessarily have to tie you down. It might be lovely to spend proper time with your parents, and you could leave whenever you got the urge, just don't stay away as long. They miss you enormously, and you don't need me to tell you they're not getting any young—" I stop suddenly, embarrassed. "Oh God! I'm so sorry. I'm telling you what you should be doing. I'm controlling again. I am so sorry. It's none of my business. Ignore me."

"What?" Cole frowns at me. "What do you mean, controlling again? You're not controlling, you're just giving me your opinion, and I'm grateful for it. I've been thinking the same thing myself. My parents are, as you have discovered, wonderful. I want to spend time with them. Please don't worry. You haven't said anything wrong. Come on," he adds, jumping off the rock. "Let's keep going."

"My parents were right," Cole says when we're home again and we've got out of the car. I have said goodnight, and thank you, and I am about to walk up the path to my cottage, but I turn back.

"They said you were nothing like the media portrayal of you. They said you were lovely, and warm, and real. And a great mother." There is a smile in his voice. "All of which you are."

I'm glad we are now in pitch darkness and he can't see the flush of pleasure that spreads across my face.

"Night night," I call, knowing my voice doesn't hide the smile that is currently stretching from ear to ear.

"Sleep tight," he calls back.

"Mind the bed bugs don't bite," we both say at the same time, and the last thing I hear as I let myself into my house is his laugh.

CHAPTER
FIFTY-SIX

Buck

At 11.29 I hear Mom come in, and my decision is made. I've spent the last two hours trying to figure out the right thing to do, even though I know Grace is going to kill me. I figured if Mom came home before 11.35, I'd tell her. If she came home after that, I'd still have to work something out.

Most of the time I feel way older than seventeen, except when I have to make an adult decision. My mom may be the last person I should be turning to, but I also know that she has a huge heart; she will help; she will know what to do.

She's already collapsed on the sofa with her feet up, a smile on her face, as I walk down the stairs, and she turns to me with a dreamy expression.

"You can't even begin to imagine how beautif— What is it?" She frowns, knowing in the way that mothers always know that something's wrong. "What's the matter? Who is it?" Her voice catches as she inhales sharply. "Is it Grace? It's Grace, isn't it?"

"No." Although I think, yes. It is. Not in the way she thinks, but this involves Grace too.

"It's a friend of Grace's, but it's more complicated."

"Is she . . . pregnant?" Mom gives a shrewd look.

"No. Mom, I was on Facebook with Grace this evening, and a friend of hers has turned up and is staying with her, and the friend is ill. Like, really ill. Grace doesn't know what to do."

"Can't they go to a doctor? Or hospital? What's the matter with the friend?"

"Grace says she's anorexic. She's been in and out of treatment, but Grace says she hasn't eaten anything since she got there, and she's just had some kind of fit. Grace is freaking out."

"What do you mean, some kind of fit?" Mom asks slowly.

"I don't know. Grace said she had some kind of seizure the other day, and Grace was freaking out then, but afterwards the girl said it was fine and not to worry. But the friend's just had another one and now she's practically comatose in bed, and Grace says her breathing is weird and she can't wake her up."

"She has to call an ambulance. Now! You have to get hold of Grace at once. Or I'll do it. I'll call them."

Now it's my turn to freak out. "Mom, you can't. It's . . . this girl has run away. Her . . . mom . . . doesn't know where she is. She doesn't want anyone to know where she is, and she made Grace swear not to call her mom or the authorities. She said she'd be fine, but it doesn't sound like it."

My mom starts shaking her head very quickly. "Oh no," she says. "No, no, no. I don't care what the situation is, her parents have to know. Jesus," she says under her breath. "Grace needs to call her mother

393

immediately. If this girl is sick enough for Grace to be freaking out, this girl is sick enough that her parents need to get involved right now. You need to get hold of Grace at once, Buck, and tell her how urgent it is. This sounds about as serious as it can be, and anorexia kills. She has to get an ambulance and call the parents."

I don't know how to tell her this. I just don't know how to find the words. All I can say is, "She can't."

"I'll do it, then." Mom is already heading to the computer to look up Grace's address. "I'll call an ambulance now. Do we know the girl's name? Do we know anything about the family? How to get hold of them?"

I take a deep breath. There's no way out.

"It's Eve," I say quietly. "Eve Haydn. Sylvie Hathaway's daughter." I watch my mom's eyes open wide as she freezes in her tracks.

"What? I don't understand. What do you mean, Sylvie Hathaway's daughter? She's staying with Grace? They're friends? How . . . when . . ."

I shrug, because the truth is I didn't even know they were friends before tonight, and it's only relevant because someone has to help, and they have to help quickly.

When Mom said she'd call the girl's mother, I knew, instantly, that was the right thing to do, but the girl's mother isn't just anyone.

It's the one woman Mom can't bear to help.

My mom doesn't say anything for a while. She sits down suddenly and leans forward, her elbows on her knees, rubbing her eyes, before letting out a big groan.

"I have to do this, don't I?" She looks up at me and I can't say anything. I just nod, before sitting next to her and taking her hand. "Jesus," she whispers. "I can't believe I have to do this but if it were the other way round . . . if it were Grace . . ." She shudders at the thought. "This girl is ill, and we have to help her. It's what mothers do," she murmurs, not to me particularly, but I think to herself, to help her understand why she needs to do this. "We look after each other's daughters. It doesn't matter who they belong to. It's the responsibility we take on when we become mothers. Buck?" She looks at me again. "Do you think you can get her mom's home number for me?"

I nod. Eve's mother has a job. I can Google her, find out where she works, and take it from there.

"Okay." Mom takes a deep breath. "Okay. I'll call an ambulance while you get the number. Do it quickly. We haven't got any time to lose."

CHAPTER
FIFTY-SEVEN

Maggie

"Hello?"

"Hello? Is that Sylvie?"

There is a gut-wrenching silence during which I imagine I can hear Sylvie's heart plummeting in disappointment. I know she was praying it would be her daughter.

"Yes."

"Sylvie, this is Maggie Hathaway. I'm phoning about your daughter."

"What?" she barks down the phone. "Eve? What about her? What do you know?"

"She's with Grace. In New York. I didn't know myself until just now. She swore Grace not to tell anyone she was there, but Grace is worried sick about her. It sounds like Eve's had a seizure, and Grace is having trouble rousing her. Eve had made her swear not to call for help, but I've just called an ambulance and it's on its way."

"Oh God!" Sylvie lets out a cry. "Where is she? What's the address?"

I give her the address, my heart tearing at the sound of Sylvie sobbing. I feel like I know everything about this woman, a woman I have made it my business to scorn, a woman who destroyed my life and ended up with everything.

"Sylvie —" I wait for her to finish, and I haven't even thought about what I'm going to say, can't believe the words that start to come out of my mouth — "I can get there quicker than you. I'm leaving now. I'll find out which hospital she'll be taken to and I'll let you know. I'll meet you there."

"What if it's too late?" Sylvie's voice rises to a panicked shriek. "What if it's too late?"

"The ambulance will be there any minute and I'll be there in two to three hours," I say. "I'll stay with her until you get there."

Sylvie's sobbing subsides and she takes a deep, hiccuping breath. "You'd do that? You'd drive in the middle of the night to see if she's okay?"

"Wouldn't you do the same for my daughter? For anyone's daughter who was in trouble?"

"Yes," Sylvie says. "I wouldn't think twice."

CHAPTER
FIFTY-EIGHT

Grace

Just wake up, I keep thinking. Please, please wake up. I know she will, at some point, because she did the other day, and when she recovered she said it was fine, she'd be fine, she just sometimes goes into this state, but it's nothing to worry about and, whatever I do, I must not let anyone know.

I was freaked out then, but I thought maybe it was just a one-off. She seemed okay afterwards, just really tired. But it's weird that this is the same girl who came with me to our house three years ago, the same girl who Chris thought was totally hot, who was skinny, but normal.

When she showed up here a week ago I actually gasped. I couldn't help it. She looks like she's about to die, and she's like a shadow of who she was. Each time she's woken up in the morning, I've breathed a sigh of relief that somehow she's still alive.

I've tried to talk to her about it, but every time I go there she just clams up, so I've stuck with the usual bullshit about school, people in my dorm, boys.

She hasn't wanted to go anywhere. I'm not surprised. I don't know how she has the energy to do anything; in fact it seems she doesn't have the energy to do much at all other than sleep.

We've had this amazing online friendship for ages now. It didn't happen immediately — after that weekend when we all found out about Dad, I didn't want anything to do with her — but after the court case she Facebooked me, and we started chatting a ton. She was the only one who could truly understand what had gone down with Dad. We had that in common. We would always have that in common.

I've been up the last two nights reading about anorexia, and I know that seizures happen in late-stage anorexia. When it happened the other day she said it definitely wasn't a seizure, and she would know, given that she was the one having it. Or not.

It was easier to believe her, even though I'm pretty sure she's having seizures. Today it was so much worse. I rolled her over onto her side so she wouldn't swallow her tongue, and the thing is, I could feel her body underneath all the sweats she wears, and there's nothing.

Nothing.

When she was twitching, her eyes rolled back and her sweats rode up with the jerking of her body, and she's a skeleton. It's disgusting. It's devastating. I stared at her bones, and then I just burst into tears.

I don't know what to do. This isn't something I feel able to cope with. She's sleeping now, but it's not like normal sleeping. Her breathing seems . . . hard, like she has to fight for every other breath. I've just been sitting in the corner of my room, on the floor, crying, because I don't know what to do. I think she may be dying.

I have to call an ambulance, even though she'll hate me. Unless she wakes up soon. Maybe she'll wake up and it will be okay. But I should call an ambulance. Even if she never talks to me again — what else can I do?

Buck sent a message on Facebook and I told him. I know I shouldn't have, but I had to tell someone. I need someone's help, without getting the authorities involved.

He looked totally freaked out too, and he said he'd get hold of Chris. Chris will know what to do. I just hope he gets here soon, because I'm seriously worried about what will happen. I keep picking up the phone and starting to dial 911, but then I stop, because she'll kill me.

I hear noises coming down the corridor. Loud voices. Radios. A banging on my door makes me jump, and I run over to find three EMTs there.

"What the . . .?"

"We're here for Eve Haydn," one says. "This is very serious. Please move out of the way." I step aside, relief mingling with fear as more tears come.

They rapidly assess her; equipment appears; IV drips are plugged in. A crowd gathers in the hallway outside, everyone peering in as Eve is lifted onto a stretcher. Even the EMTs gasp at how tiny she is, how light, talking to each other in hushed, urgent voices.

She does not move. Does not wake. I am filled with remorse, and shame, that I did not call them immediately. That I did not call the other day. That I let Eve, who was so clearly, so obviously, desperately ill, talk me into abiding by her rules.

They check her breathing, murmur to each other with concern, and suddenly the one leaning over her with his stethoscope shouts out, "She's going into cardiac arrest."

I am pushed out of the way as they race for more equipment, immediately performing CPR while I stand, backed into a corner, shaking with fear, unable to believe this is happening.

She is surrounded, paddles are put on her chest and her tiny body jerks off the stretcher, neither of us breathing until the fourth time, when she starts to breathe.

They are so focused on Eve, on making sure she is alive, they do not notice me running behind them to the ambulance. I'm about to climb in, when they try to close the doors on me.

"I'm coming with her," I say as one of the EMTs turns to study me. I am waiting to see judgement in his eyes — how could I have waited so long, how could I not have called them myself? — but I don't. I see sympathy.

And fear.

"Are you a relation?" he asks gently.

I don't even have to pause. "Yes," I say. "I'm her sister."

CHAPTER
FIFTY-NINE

Maggie

There is a long line of people waiting to give their names at the hospital, and it is moving slowly. Everything feels nail-bitingly slow. I reached New York in record time — there is no traffic on the highways at night — but now I feel as if nothing is moving quickly enough, and I am scared.

Eventually I'm at the front. I lie, saying I'm Eve's aunt, and with no expression in her voice the receptionist directs me to a bank of elevators.

They take me to the Cardiac Unit.

I am terrified of what I will find. The whole way down here I imagined finding Eve in hospital, but in a room, awake; ill but grateful someone is here, relieved to hear her mother is on her way.

Cardiac Unit. What does that mean? How does a twenty-year-old girl end up in the Cardiac Unit? I steel myself as I walk down the corridor. Remember who you used to be, Maggie. The committee chair. The organizer. The woman who held all the power. This is the time to draw on the old Maggie, not the quiet, invisible Maggie I've become.

My eyes glance into a room as I pass, barely registering what I've seen until I am past. I pull to a halt, turn and go back to the room. There is a girl curled up on a chair, her sweatshirt balled up to make a pillow, her neck at an awkward angle as she sleeps.

Grace's cheeks are tear-stained, her face puffy. She looks just as she did when she was a little girl, and I can't move, I can't do anything but stand there and look at her as my heart threatens to break.

Grace. Gracie. My beloved daughter. I want to sweep her into my arms and hold her close, squeeze her and cover her with kisses, make up for all the lost time, all the years I wasn't present for her, wasn't able to be the mother I can be today.

She stirs. I catch my breath. Her eyes open and she looks straight at me, not really seeing, until she focuses and I see a frown, a look of shock, as she uncurls, sits up and rubs her eyes, looking again at me.

"Hi, Gracie," I whisper. Without thinking, I am moving slowly towards her, and suddenly her face crumples, and she is in my arms, my beautiful, beautiful baby girl, sobbing as if she will never stop. I squeeze her hard, feeling her body that is, immediately, almost as familiar as my own, as the tears trickle slowly down my cheeks.

The doctor explains that Eve went into cardiac arrest again in the ambulance on the way over here. Her heart stopped for twelve seconds.

She is alive. Just. But there are problems. She has bradycardia — dangerously slow rhythms — and a

403

severe electrolyte imbalance. She is on an IV drip to replace nutrients and minerals, but it has to be slow to stop her body, her heart, going into shock again.

"You mean she could have another heart attack?" I am still struggling to understand how a twenty-year-old can be this ill. How anyone allowed a twenty-year-old to get this bad.

"Her heart and her kidneys are our biggest concern right now. She has a significant amount of oedema in her hands and feet due to the build-up of fluid in her body because of the damage to her renal system. We're trying to stabilize her. There isn't much else we can do other than wait."

"Is she going to die?" Grace asks, her eyes wide with fear.

He hesitates. "If she can make it through the next twenty-four hours, we'll be in a better position to know where we stand. Are her parents on their way?"

"Her mother is flying in from California," I say. "Her father isn't . . ." I tail off.

He nods, then lays a hand on my arm and gives it a light squeeze just before he walks off, and it is this that sends a shudder of fear running through my body.

He wouldn't have done that if he thought she was going to be okay. Grace sees it too, but neither of us mentions it as we turn to go in and see Eve.

Oh God. Oh no. Sweet Lord. I take one look and have to walk straight out, straight to the bathroom where I lean against the door and try to swallow my tears, the lump in my throat. I splash my face with cold water as

I try to compose myself before walking back to join Grace, pretending to be the grown-up, pretending I am in control.

Asleep, tubes surrounding her, Eve is skeletal, her cheeks and eye sockets so sunken, her skin and hair so colourless, it is like looking at an old black and white photograph of a corpse.

This is a child. Sylvie's child. It might just as well be mine. She is as close to death as I have ever seen anyone, and it takes a few minutes before I can look at her face without feeling a sob rise.

I place her tiny birdlike hand in mine, stroking the bones, looking down at her brittle, pale, jagged nails, as my tears drip down.

"It's bad, isn't it?" Grace whispers as she cries too, holding Eve's right hand in hers on the other side of the bed.

"I don't know," I say, wiping my tears with my sleeve, like a child, "but it doesn't look good."

How could anyone have let her get like this, I think again, until I remember Grace going off the rails after we first discovered Mark's betrayal.

And then I realize.

How could anyone have stopped her?

We sit for hours, Grace and I. We both stroke Eve's hands, until I send Grace downstairs with my credit card to buy moisturizing cream in the hospital store. She comes back up with the softest, fleeciest pink blanket, which we carefully tuck round Eve, before gently massaging the cream into her poor skin, which is as dry and brittle as that of someone four times her age.

We quietly sing the songs of Grace's childhood to her: "Itsy Bitsy Spider", "Hot Cross Buns", "Ring Around the Rosie", "Mary Had a Little Lamb".

We sit, Grace and I, telling Eve the stories of Grace's youth. The funny ones, the sweet ones. We tell her that when she wakes up Grace will demonstrate the dance she did for her ballet recital when she was five, including the tremendous trip that had the entire audience holding their breath, until she stood up and announced loudly, "I'm okay, I'm okay!", before giving a huge grin and bowing, while the audience cheered.

We laugh softly at the memories, all the while glancing up at the heart monitor, making sure the line doesn't go flat, ready to leap up in an instant for help if it does.

I tell Grace she can take a break, but she won't leave. In the early hours of the morning a nurse brings me yet another coffee, while Grace, still holding Eve's hand, sinks her head onto the bed and falls asleep.

I hear Sylvie before I see her. Or rather, I hear the doctor I spoke to earlier leading her in.

I stand up and move quietly away from the bed so she can take my place, be with her daughter, and I watch for a while as she strokes Eve's hair, murmurs into her ear, kisses her forehead.

Grace wakes up and looks at Sylvie, startled, then finds me, in the doorway. I gesture for her to come with me, to leave Sylvie on her own with Eve, and she does,

Sylvie seemingly not even noticing that Grace is there: all her attention is on her own daughter.

We walk down the corridor, Grace still in the half fog of sleep, and I catch my breath as she leans her head on my shoulder, slipping her hand into mine.

Grace is fast asleep — borrowed pillows and blankets turning the sectional into a makeshift bed — when Sylvie appears in the doorway of the visitors' room.

This woman I have hated, blamed for the demise of a marriage I now know was flawed and wrong from the outset, stands a few feet away from me, broken.

I look at her and feel nothing but concern, care. Even love. I stand up awkwardly, about to ask if there is news, but instead we move towards each other, propelled by an unknown force.

Sylvie and I stand in the centre of this tiny room, and I lock my arms tightly round her, trying to absorb her pain, trying to let her know she is loved, as she leans against me, her body wracked with sobs.

PART FIVE

Family

CHAPTER
SIXTY

Sylvie

Sometimes Sylvie will find herself thinking that this is just like the old days, but it is never like the old days. The old days can be broken into three parts in her mind: years ago, with Jonathan, when life was simple and happy; marriage to Mark, when life seemed simple and happy but was in fact a lie; and after Mark, when Eve fell apart.

Sylvie will say this is like the old days because when Eve visits from New York, where she is now at NYU, she will perch on a stool at the kitchen counter, with a wooden cheese board in front of her and a glass of wine, while Sylvie flits round the kitchen, cooking. The doors will be flung open to catch the persimmon glow of the fading sunset, and Angie and Simon will pop in, joking and laughing as they all prepare dinner together.

When Sylvie thinks it is like the old days, she means the days post-Jonathan, pre-Mark. The days when it was just her and Eve, and both were happy.

There are, of course, differences today. Sylvie does not miss the subtle changes. Eve may be out of the woods, but she will never be the same; it will always be one day at a time. Watching her now, cutting a paper-thin sliver of cheese, Sylvie breathes a sigh of relief that these days Eve is eating anything at all.

For years Sylvie could not watch her eat without the familiar mix of fear and panic curdling inside her, a mix that was impossible to hold in, sometimes coming out in a bark of anger.

Now, as she watches Eve reach for just one grape, she merely takes a deep breath and repeats to herself, as a mantra: I am powerless over people, places and things.

And she is powerless over Eve. However much she wanted her daughter to get better, she was powerless until Eve decided to change. It took two cardiac arrests before Eve made that decision.

The turning point came in the Cardiac Unit after Eve was hospitalized. When she regained conscious-ness, the first things she saw were her mother's eyes, filled with fear, and love. She knew immediately that she couldn't continue doing this, not only to herself, but to her mother. She vowed to Sylvie she would change.

This time she meant it.

Since then kidney disease and osteoporosis are just two of the serious problems Eve has had to deal with, the mountains she has had to climb.

Eve was transferred to the Center for Eating Disorders at New York-Presbyterian, and remained there for months. Sylvie temporarily moved her headquarters to New York, never thinking about what the future might hold, trying to keep her mind firmly on each day as it came.

Two years later, Eve is back. Changed, but smiling again. Laughing. Still thinner than most, she has a regimen she follows: three meals a day, two snacks in between. And she does not, will not, waver from the regimen.

"What's this?" Eve takes more grapes, piling them next to the cheese for her afternoon snack, before turning the small ball jar around and examining the label. "Fig Jam? A new line?" She tosses her hair back over a shoulder, hair that is now glossy and shining again, a sure sign she is getting the nutrients she needs.

"It's a sample. We've been trying some out. That's the one with orange. It's my favourite." The old Sylvie would have implored Eve to eat it. Try some. Just a little. And then been upset when she said no. This time Sylvie says nothing, just turns away. It's up to Eve.

She turns back to see Eve tasting a spoonful. "This is good, Mom," she says. "Really good." Instead of laying down the spoon, she reaches in again. Not a huge spoonful, not one that foretells an upcoming binge, but a normal one.

"Told you," Sylvie says, her face lighting up with a smile of pleasure.

"How come you're in such a good mood?" Eve peers at her mother thoughtfully. "Do you have . . . a man?"

Sylvie breaks into a peal of laughter as she shakes her head. She is happy, perhaps happier, without love. She has had enough of love.

Jonathan was her true love. She never wanted, never thought she deserved another, but Mark was so persuasive, so smitten, and being taken care of was so seductive, she allowed herself to be looked after; she allowed herself to be drawn into something she would have been far better off without.

Other things have filled the space once filled by a husband. Success, creativity, gratitude for a life she hadn't expected, and joy at her daughter finally being healthy.

Sylvie gazes at her daughter, noticing how Eve suddenly has a dreamy smile on her face as she nibbles on the cheese.

"Wait a minute," Sylvie says. "Do I have a man? This isn't about me. This is about you. Look at you, all glowing and happy! You can't fool your mother, you evil girl!" She pulls up a stool next to her daughter, whose smile now stretches from ear to ear, and settles in for the evening. "You're not allowed to move a muscle until you've told me everything."

CHAPTER
SIXTY-ONE

Maggie

Barb gasps as she unwraps the small box and prises open the lid to reveal a gold orb necklace studded with citrines, her favourite stone.

"Oh my . . . this is too . . . oh . . ." Her eyes are filled with tears and her hands are shaking, as my own eyes fill with tears.

"It's not too anything. I know you love citrines and I know you admired the orb I was wearing a couple of weeks ago so I bought one for you."

"But this is too much!"

"Oh stop!" Patty shushes her, lifting up the necklace. "When someone gives you jewellery, you just smile prettily and say 'thank you'."

"Thank you," Barb says. "It's not enough, but thank you. Thank you, thank you, thank you!" She flings her arms round me in a big hug.

"You know it's my birthday tomorrow," Patty says suddenly. "And I think I have another one the day after that."

I laugh, just as Patty's face turns serious. "I know things are changing for you," she says, "what with Buck away and everything, but you can't leave us, you know.

You, me and Barb are a team. Neither of us has the time or the patience to start training some new girl to work here."

I can't deny it, the thought has crossed my mind, but I couldn't afford to leave my waitressing job, not yet, not for a long time; but I have wondered whether I will ever reach a point where I could stop.

"I have no plans to leave. Not unless I have a long-lost aunt who suddenly dies and leaves me her millions. Which, given my family background, is not very likely." I laugh.

Barb squints at me. "What about if you get married?"

"Barb!" I yelp with a giggle. "I'm never getting married again. But even if I did, I'd still work here."

"See?" Patty looks at Barb, shaking her head. "Hear that? She's getting married again."

I won't get married again. I thought, all those years ago, that marriage was the ultimate cherry on the icing of the cake; that marrying the right sort of man, a man who could give me the lifestyle I had always dreamed of, would make me happy.

Look where I ended up.

I don't believe in marriage any more, even though I have Mr and Mrs W as an example of how it can work. I believe it can work for other people, but not for me; it's not what I choose. And yes, I know I felt the same way about happiness until I was proved wrong, but this is different. This is my choice.

Which is not to say I don't believe in love. Oh, how I believe in love, now that I know what it is. How I believe in trust, and kindness, and peace.

I believe in lust, in being reduced to a glazed, gasping wreck at the mere memory of how he pulled the strap of my nightgown down to expose my breast, slipping his fingers inside me as I moaned.

I believe in certainty. That my man is where he says he is; that he does not disappear to work, leaving me with no way to get hold of him; that when he is with me, he is with me. One hundred per cent.

I believe all these things because of Cole. A man I never dared dream I deserved; a man who has restored my faith in all things good, and pleasurable, and right.

A man I love.

This is a relationship that feeds my soul, that doesn't need a piece of paper to explain to the world how committed we are.

"Hello?" My arms are filled with grocery bags as I push open the door with my hip, but I see no one in the house. "Anyone home?" I call upstairs. Silence.

I dump the bags on the table, checking my watch. A few hours to go before everyone arrives. I'm still not entirely sure how we'll fit, but Cole assures me Thanksgiving will be more fun if we're all squashed together. There's no doubt we'll be squashed.

Buck, Grace, Chris and Eve. Together.

Chris and Eve have been inseparable for the past year, each helping the other to become the person they are supposed to be. Sylvie and I have our fingers crossed it will last. How can it not, when Chris is more of a man in the warmth and security of her love — and Eve? Eve has blossomed into a beautiful woman, fully inhabiting her grace, her skin. It is impossible to relate the Eve who almost died with the radiant girl who lights up every room she enters. They are glorious with, and for, each other. We all feel it.

So my family are all coming, joined, naturally, by Mr and Mrs W and Cole.

And Sylvie.

My dearest friend.

I wash my hands and tie an apron round my waist to start prepping the food, turning the music on so Jason Mraz can keep me company. Onions are sliced and placed in a stainless-steel bowl, butternut squash is peeled and diced, spices are measured out and toasted, crushed in a pestle and mortar.

The turkey is brining, the stuffing almost finished, as the door opens and Buck runs in, his cheeks flushed with cold.

"Boots off!" I yell from the kitchen, knowing he will forget, hearing him mutter as he stomps back to the door. "And before you say anything about rules, it's not about rules," I say. "It's about not tracking mud everywhere." I turn to look at him. "Where've you been?"

"Cutting down trees. We took down all the dead wood by the cattle gate. We're never going to have to buy wood again," he says with a chuckle, his eyes bright. "Tomorrow we're going to split the wood."

"Not tonight, okay?" I warn. "I need you to help get the table ready."

Buck rolls his eyes and backs out of the room, as the door opens again.

"Boots!" I shout again, and Cole stops and kicks off his boots before walking over to the stove and peering over my shoulder, wrapping his lovely big arms round my waist as he nuzzles my neck.

"Something smells great," he says, and I laugh, leaning back against him for a few seconds, loving how solid he is, how he smells of wood, and sweat, and . . . work.

He is the most unexpected of joys. Mostly here now, with me, sharing my bed, sharing my cottage, he occasionally takes off on his trips. Sometimes, if I can get the time off work, I will go with him. When he's away, I am perfectly happy on my own, and I'm truly on my own this time, not filling my time with committees, and PTAs, constantly having to keep running from myself.

I travel to see the kids, Buck now at SUNY Purchase, Grace working in New Haven, Chris and Eve in New York; I work; I have girls' nights out with Patty and Barb, and every day I talk to Sylvie.

That day I held her, sobbing, in my arms when Eve was in the hospital, everything changed. Whatever each of us may have thought of the other, whatever anger, blame, resentment I had held, it was gone.

In that moment, she became my sister.

Whether it's the midday report, the afternoon report, or the evening report, there is not a day that goes by

419

without us checking in with each other. We have been on vacation together, giggling over too many strawberry daiquiris and unwanted advances from terrible men. We have shared our fears, our doubts, our deepest darkest secrets.

And we have shared the stories of our marriage to the same man.

I have no doubt that Sylvie was the love of Mark's life, or, at least, the woman he truly loved. I was . . . a convenience, the right thing, a woman who fitted the picture he had in his mind, just as he fitted the picture in mine.

Sylvie and I shared many of the same experiences within our marriage — the disappearances, the lies — but in all of hers it is clear that Mark loved her. He truly loved her. In much the same way that Cole loves me.

On my first "date" with Cole, which was several months after we started sleeping together, I thought that maybe I ought to dress up, make an effort, make him like me more. I pulled out a leftover New Salem outfit, painted my face, curled my hair.

When he saw me come down the stairs, Cole did a double take. I thought it was pleasure, but later, much later, he said it was dismay.

"You are at your most beautiful when you are entirely natural," he said, and I now believe him.

The children adore him. Everyone adores him. He has become a father figure to Buck in a way his father was never able to be.

Poor Mark. He missed out on so much. His letters to me have stopped. I hear he's out of prison on early parole for good behaviour. Well, of course. No one can be more charming, nor behave better, than Mark.

A year ago I wrote to him. I thanked him: if it weren't for him, for what he did, I might still be living that false life, pretending to be someone I'm not, desperately unhappy but with no idea that there was any other kind of life to live.

I was careful with my wording. I gave him no openings and was not particularly warm, but I was polite. I asked him not to respond, told him it was unnecessary, that this was about my closure; but he did respond.

I didn't understand his response. He asked for forgiveness. He seemed to think my reaching out was some kind of an invitation, a glimpse of a way back. He filled his letter — pages and pages long — with memories of times we had shared, and talked of a future that could be ours.

I read it to Sylvie, both of us unable to believe what he had written. I would never have shared it with Sylvie had I thought it would cause her pain, but I knew it wouldn't; I knew she would see, as I saw, the sadness, the desperation.

I knew Sylvie would find the letter hard only because she has a need to help people.

A week later, she received exactly the same letter, the memories adjusted slightly to pertain to her marriage, but otherwise it was a replica.

She didn't feel the need to help him after that.

We both hope he finds peace. I hope he finds contentment. I hope he finds his place in the world, one that is founded on truth, one that gives him the same sense of joy Sylvie and I have now.

But if he doesn't, we're both very okay with that.

Epilogue

Sylvie rests her chin on her hand and smiles as she watches her daughter fold into Chris. When she thinks of what Eve has been through, she can't believe that this glowing girl sitting in front of her is Eve.

She is back to the child Sylvie knew: funny, confident, kind. The girl who was utterly confident in her skin.

While Eve started on the road to her own recovery by herself, there is no doubt that Chris made the biggest difference. Initially Sylvie couldn't help her nerves about the two of them dating. His physical resemblance to Mark was so unsettling, Sylvie presumed this was the basis of Eve's attraction to him, but their relationship is built on a far stronger foundation, and he is as solid and reliable as his father is not.

Sylvie lifts her wine glass and sips, finding herself locking eyes with Maggie, at the other end of the table. Maggie raises her glass in a silent toast, then glances at the kitchen with an almost imperceptible tilt of her head before pushing back her chair and standing up.

The others look questioningly as both women head for the kitchen, but Maggie tells them to stay at the table, that she and Sylvie are just going to check on dessert.

Sylvie watches Maggie pull an apple pie out of the oven. "Have I ever told you how much I like your mother-in-law? Her gardening knowledge is amazing. I could talk to her for hours."

Maggie smiles. "She's not my mother-in-law."

"Not yet," Sylvie teases.

"I won't get married again."

"How can you be sure? None of us know what the future holds."

Maggie stops and raises an eyebrow. "Will you get married again?"

"Ah. I see what you mean." Sylvie nods, instantly understanding. "Still. He is a lovely man. And he feels like an honest one."

Maggie lets out a bark of laughter. "You and I are hardly the best judges of character, are we? All those years of marriage and neither of us knew." She shakes her head.

"And yet," Sylvie says, shrugging, "as you yourself acknowledged when you wrote to him, we have so much to thank him for. We're unrecognizable from the women we were. Look how happy you are, how you glow. And if not for Mark I wouldn't have re-found my creativity, built a business —"

"Do you mean empire?" Maggie grins.

"Empire, then," Sylvie acknowledges with a smile. "The point being that I am happy and fulfilled in a way I never was before. And, most importantly, we found each other." She walks up to Maggie and lays her head on her shoulder, and Maggie reaches out to put her arms round her friend.

"We'll never be able to thank him enough, you know," Maggie says, planting a kiss on the top of Sylvie's head.

"I know." Sylvie laughs. "Who would have thought?"

"Thank GOD!" Chris shouts dramatically when the two women walk back into the dining room. "We thought there'd been a murder-suicide in the kitchen. What were you doing? Growing your own apples?"

"You've been gone for ages," Grace says. "We were worried about you."

"What are you all? Our mothers?" Maggie chides, and the children sheepishly shrug.

"Believe it or not," Sylvie says, "we were catching up."

"See!" Cole is triumphant. "What did I tell you? They were gossiping. But it's perfect timing for a picture. Come on, everyone, let's do this thing."

"No!" Grace moans. "My hair's awful."

"It's beautiful," Maggie says. "It's always beautiful. Who's taking the picture?"

"Already set up," Cole says with a grin. "It's on self-timer." He gestures to his camera, balancing on a pile of books on a shelf. "Everyone over on this side," he announces, and there is much mock-grumbling and laughter as those on one side of the table push their chairs back and squeeze round to the other.

Cole waits until they are all in position before adjusting the camera, pressing a button, and quickly running back to the table as everyone cheers him on.

He reaches it just in time for the camera to go off.

It captures the children of both families, their heads thrown back in laughter, Eve and Chris, as always, entwined, Chris in mid-tease at Cole's lack of speed.

Mr and Mrs W, the unofficial patriarch and matriarch, are at one side, Mrs W leaning her chin on the palm of her hand and Mr W laying a gentle arm round her shoulder.

Behind everyone, Cole, just in time, is giving the thumbs up to the camera, and in the middle, luminous with gratitude and love, are Maggie and Sylvie: two women who were supposed to want nothing to do with each other, who beat the odds to become best friends . . . to become sisters.

"A toast!" Cole says, as the group disperses, shuffling round the table to find their seats. "To family!" he says, solemn now, a shimmer of tears in his eyes as he looks round the room.

"To family," they echo, Maggie and Sylvie both wiping a tear from their own eyes as, one by one, they all raise their glasses to their lips.